ABOUT THIS BOOK

Three novellas (books 26-28) in the young adult paranormal fantasy series Havenwood Falls High, Home of the Dragons – and vampires, wolves, fae, and much more.

Predestined by Valia Lind

When Niccola's mother disappears, she needs to find her long lost father. Shortly after arriving in Havenwood Falls, she learns that her family's history is much more complicated than she ever knew. She's no stranger to keeping secrets, but even she's not prepared for what she finds. While she tries to unravel her past, she meets a gorgeous deputy in training who could be her future. She's spent her whole life protecting her secret, yet Warren sees past the labels and straight into her heart. Together, they must do whatever it takes to find the truth and save her mother—or lose it all forever.

Rediscovered by Morgan Wylie

Brice Blackstone is a black sheep, the only male ever marked as a witch hunter in Havenwood Falls. He knows others exist, but he fears becoming like them: rogues, assassins not only after witches but all supernatural kind. Sunny is also an anomaly and a valued member of the rogue hunter crew. When she shows up in Havenwood Falls, Brice's family goes on full alert. She knows things nobody else does—like how Brice can control the witch hunter within before it takes control of him. And in a town full of witches, he must master himself or lose everything he knows and loves.

Ashes of Fate by Apryl Baker

Cora Hartwood lost everything in a single heartbeat, and she's left with crushing guilt and dark thoughts that drive her to consider even darker ideas. She and her grandmother came to Havenwood Falls for a new start, to get away from the memories of the tragedy that took her family. Or so she thought. When her grandmother reveals that what happened to her family wasn't an accident, the secrets of her family's past are revealed, leaving Cora to question everything. And she's not as safe as she thinks. It will take the magic of Havenwood Falls to save her.

HAVENWOOD FALLS HIGH BOOKS

Predestined by Valia Lind

Rediscovered by Morgan Wylie

Ashes of Fate by Apryl Baker

Stay up to date at www.HavenwoodFalls.com

HAVENWOOD FALLS HIGH
VOLUME NINE

A HAVENWOOD FALLS HIGH COLLECTION

VALIA LIND   MORGAN WYLIE   APRYL BAKER

PREDESTINED

VALIA LIND

HAVENWOOD FAILS HIGH

Predestined

USA Today Bestselling Author

VALIA LIND

~ A Havenwood Falls Young Adult Novella ~

BOOKS BY VALIA LIND

Hawthorne Chronicles

Guardian Witch (Hawthorne Chronicles, #1)

Witch's Fire (Hawthorne Chronicles, #2)

Witch's Heart (Hawthorne Chronicles, #3)

Tempest Witch (Hawthorne Chronicles, #4)

The Skazka Chronicles

Remembering Majyk (The Skazka Chronicles, #1)

Majyk Reborn (The Skazka Chronicles, #2)

The Faithful Soldier (The Skazka Chronicles, #2.5)

Majyk Reclaimed (The Skazka Chronicles, #3)

The Titanium Trilogy

Pieces of Revenge (Titanium, #1)

Scarred by Vengeance (Titanium, #2)

Ruined in Retribution (Titanium, #3)

Falling Duology

Falling by Design

Edge of Falling

For Mom, my greatest inspiration for the kind of a person I strive to be

CHAPTER 1

F *ind your father.*

For the hundredth time, I stare at the piece of paper with my mother's handwriting and the three simple words that shatter every notion I've ever had. I thought my mother hated him. I've hated him my whole life. Now I have to find him?

My mother's magic is all over the paper, but I can't tell if it's meant to help me or just residual from whatever happened here. We were supposed to go to dinner together. I ran out to pick up mail from our PO box and came back to my whole life ruined.

Looking up, I glance around the disarray that is our living room. The apartment is small, but we've lived here long enough to collect all kinds of keepsakes. Which are now thrown all over the area.

The panic I felt when I first walked through the open door hasn't really subsided. But Mom has taught me how to control it—and my magic—enough that I can keep a clear mind.

Whatever happened here, she's in trouble, and I have no choice but to follow the clues she left. Which is why I don't call the police or the coven. Instead, I walk over to her room, picking up a few discarded items, then I settle myself in front of our coffee table. After I flip it over back on its feet.

Next I light a candle, then I place my phone facing up in front of me. It's the closest thing I have to a black mirror, and I need it to scry. I pull my necklace over my head, the small quartz crystal dangling on the bottom. It's all I've got.

Holding the crystal in my hand, I close my eyes and set an intention. When I open my eyes, I place a tip of my finger against the phone, and ask for my mother's location. My body buzzes with magic, heating the crystal I'm holding. Leaning in, I look closely, studying the fuzzy image appearing on the surface of the phone.

But it's gone before I can make out too much of it.

"Come on," I whisper under my breath, as I try to force myself to stay calm and focused. The crystal heats up again, a town's name coming into focus before it's gone again.

"Denver?" I mumble, incredibly confused and a bit frustrated. This isn't giving me much information. When I try the third time, I end up with nothing but some mountains in the distance.

"This is useless!" I snap, sending some of my unchecked magic at the candle and throwing it against the opposite wall. Thankfully, the flame goes out, or I would be in so much trouble.

But that brings me to the problem at hand. I can't be in trouble, because my mother is not here to declare I'm in trouble. My chest grows heavy, and I try to keep my breathing centered.

"Think, Nic. You got this," I say out loud, just to hear a voice. Reaching for my phone, I open a browser and type in Denver, followed by mountains.

"Denver, Colorado? What the heck is in Colorado?" As far as I know, my mother has never been to Colorado. Or anywhere near it. I spent my whole life between California and Nevada. But if there is one thing she has taught me, it's to trust my magic. So that's what I'm going to do.

I walk over to my room, pulling out my backpack and stuffing three changes of clothes into it. After grabbing a toothbrush and paste, I search for my favorite lotion but can't find it anywhere. My body moves on autopilot, reaching for what I need, but my mind is completely on my mother.

What did she get herself into?

She's been acting weird for weeks now, but she wouldn't exactly share what was going on. Maybe I should've pushed harder and tried to figure it out. But I'm only seventeen. It's not like she was going to trust me with a huge problem, no matter how close we are. She's still my mother, and she will do anything to protect me. Of that, I have no doubt.

But she's gone now. And it's my turn to do the protecting.

Determination fuels my every move as I do another sweep of the apartment. Satisfied that I have everything I'll need for the trip, I swing the backpack over my shoulder and walk out of my room.

One last long look at the mess of our apartment, and I'm out the door. It's no time to be sentimental, or to let the feelings creep in. If I break down, there's no going back. I have enough problems as it is. Like figuring out how I'm going to survive a plane ride, since I hate flying.

∼

It doesn't take me long to land in Colorado, but it's way longer than I'm comfortable with. Surprisingly, I got a flight out in just a few hours. Even though I tried, I couldn't sleep on the plane. My body is in constant hyperawareness; every person I meet is a possible threat.

With my backpack slung over my shoulder, I step outside the airport doors, trying to think of my next move. My eyes are instantly drawn to a pair of vans parked at the curb. They're nothing special, standard-issue passenger vans, except for the gorgeous images wrapped all around the body of the vehicle. Before I realize what I'm doing, I've taken a few steps toward the vans.

I freeze in my tracks, confused by this sudden pull toward the vans and the town painted on the doors. It's not like I'm sentimental about outdoorsy places, or unknown towns in a state

I've never been in, so the only explanation must be magic. My mom taught me to trust my instincts, and my instincts are telling me to get in the van.

"Looking for something?" The deep raspy voice reaches me before the man walks around the front of the van. Dressed in a flannel shirt, jeans, and a leather coat that is much warmer than my own, he looks like what I would imagine my grandfather would look like. If I had one.

"A ride?" I don't sound sure of myself, so I clear my throat and try again. "A ride please. To . . ." I wave my hand toward the van's décor, and the man smiles.

"It would be my pleasure."

For someone who doesn't trust people, I find myself completely okay getting in the van with this stranger. I'm not the only one. A few people get in after me. I can tell they're human right away, dressed to go skiing, so I move to the back, keeping my eyes on them and the driver.

My hand reaches into my pocket to make sure my mom's note is still in there. I find instant comfort the moment I touch it. It's like a part of her is with me. For just a second, I let myself feel. The worry, anger, and emotions all rush in at once, and I have to keep myself from audibly gasping. Tears well up in my eyes, but I'm done feeling sorry for my situation, so I push them back. Along with the feelings. The only thing that's left is determination.

Maybe I should be more scared. Maybe I should be a crying mess on the floor. But my mom raised me to take care of myself, and a part of me thinks she's been preparing me for this exact moment. I may only be seventeen, but I'm no weakling. I will do whatever it takes to find my mother. Even if that means finding the man who abandoned us before I was even born.

CHAPTER 2

I blink my eyes a few times, completely lost in my thoughts, when I see a sign flash by as we drive. I'm so out of it, the six-hour drive just flew by.

Welcome to Havenwood Falls.

Can't say I've ever heard of the town, but then again, I don't know everything there is to know about Colorado. The people in front of me are chatting away, but all I can do is stare at the passing trees. I don't even know what I'm doing here. Once I get to town, I'll need to do another spell to try to get myself out of this mess.

A few miles down the road, the town opens up below us. It looks like something out of a movie. I think that even more once we pull up at the inn. Everyone piles out, so I have no choice but to follow. The crisp late autumn air and the altitude hit me at once, and I pull my jacket tighter around me. I'll probably need to invest in something warmer if I'm to stay any length of time.

"I hope you find what you are looking for," the old man says as I reach to give him cash for the ride. "This one is on me." He smiles warmly, and for some reason, I think he knows more than he's saying. But before I have a chance to ask, he's talking to someone else, and I'm on my own once again.

I study the building in front of me, Whisper Falls Inn. The name is a bit strange, considering. Shouldn't that say Havenwood Falls Inn? Shrugging, I study the three story Victorian-style manor. It's gorgeous. Like something out of a gothic novel. A Christmas garland, red bows, and lights adorn the exterior. From where I'm standing, I can see a large tree in the front window. If I had my camera with me, I'd probably walk around the property and take some pictures. But that's not why I'm here.

Instead of going inside, I turn my back to the door. Right in front of me is what I can only call the town square. It's like this town stepped right off the front of a postcard. I shake my head as I start walking. The decorations are everywhere. Even the lampposts are sporting garlands and bows. My eyes are drawn to the large gazebo off to the side, with its lights and Christmas decor. When I look closer, I notice a few sun symbols and decorations, which makes me think someone here celebrates Yule. Snow blankets the area around me, completing that magical small-town look.

School must be out for break, because even though it's early afternoon, there are kids and teenagers everywhere. Thankfully, that means I don't stand out. As I walk, I can't help but feel like I belong here. I'm not what my coven calls a reader witch, so I'm not as in tune with emotions, but I do have a few reader talents.

With my own magic, I can decipher humans from supes pretty easily, and I can tell this town is full of both. But I don't know how many of them are friendlies. I have to tread carefully. Glancing up, I see that I'm on Main Street. This seems like a perfect place to start, so I decide to head away from the inn.

The town square is surrounded by businesses on every side, each decorated for the holidays. From what I can see, there's everything from a music store to a pawn shop to a coffee shop. My stomach growls the moment my eyes land on Coffee Haven, and I realize it's been a while since I've had anything to eat.

When I step inside the cafe, the smell of coffee is instantly welcoming. But there's also an undercurrent of something otherworldly here. My eyes scan the area, landing on a few strategically placed crystals, pine cones, and candles. I smile to myself. Someone here definitely loves Yule. I bet norms eat this atmosphere up. But I'd be lying if I said I didn't enjoy it myself. It's nice to know there is someone like me here. Even though I'm not about to broadcast it.

"Hi. What can I get you?" The woman behind the counter is a few years older than me, with silvery hair and the most beautiful bluish eyes I've ever seen. Her voice is soft, and she seems friendly enough. I can absolutely see her as the one who placed all the crystals around the place.

"Hi. Could I get a caramel coffee and one of those blueberry scones, please?" I glance down at her name tag: Willow. She gives me a smile before ringing up my order, and I hand over the cash. The exchange makes me a bit apprehensive, since I have a very limited supply of money at the moment. Getting that flight to Denver took more of my savings than I would've liked. With that worry, all the others rush in. The only reason I would be drawn to this town had to be because somehow it would help. But I have no idea where to start, and the panic starts to set in.

Willow's demeanor changes just enough that I know she must've seen something in my eyes. Even though her customer-friendly smile hasn't left her face, she's studying me carefully. With a quick thanks, I grab my order and move to one of the tables. But I can still feel her eyes on me. Clearly, I need to be even more careful about keeping my demeanor neutral. Maybe they just don't trust outsiders. If there's a magical community here, I can understand that all too well.

It takes me five minutes to eat my snack, and then I'm up and out. A part of me wants to march back in there and demand answers. But I doubt Willow knows about my father or what happened to my mom. She might have her own reasons to be suspicious. I shake my head again, trying to keep the panic at bay. I need to shut it all down. I can't afford emotions right now.

When I leave the cafe, I just walk, looking for some kind of a clue as to why I was led here. I probably should've seen if there was a room at the inn before I decided to explore, but it's too late now.

When I stop in front of the old red three-story building, all thoughts of cold and homelessness are forgotten. There's something curious about the building, and when I look over at the sign, I read it out loud.

"Havenwood Falls High."

Of course a small town would have one of these movie-esque high schools, and something inside of me twinges at the idea of attending one. But this isn't why I'm here, and once the fascination subsides, the frustration sets in.

After taking a deep breath, I pull out my necklace and Mom's note, closing my eyes in concentration. My magic sparks as I try to see past what's here. I don't even know why I'm doing this, except that it seems like a locator spell would be a good idea. But after a few tries, there's nothing.

"Now what?" I ask out loud, wishing my mother were here to help.

"Now I think you should answer some questions."

I spin around at the voice, coming face to face with a gorgeous dark-haired guy. He seems to be a few years older, and definitely a few inches taller, than me. His dark blue eyes are narrowed as he studies me in turn. He's wearing jeans and a dark-colored shirt with no jacket.

"Excuse me?" I finally seem to find my voice. "Did you need something?"

Maybe I'm being a little rude, but the way he's watching me is making me uncomfortable. I've never had to use my battle magic as of yet, but my mom has taught me, just in case. There's something about him that's putting me on edge.

"As I stated previously, you need to answer some questions."

"And what questions might those be?" I ask, but for some unbelievable reason, I calm my magic.

"What brings you to Havenwood Falls?"

"Are you the Havenwood Falls police? Am I not allowed to be here?" He may be gorgeous, but he sounds like he's lost his mind. I reach out with my intuitive magic, and I can tell he's a supe too. I just can't pinpoint which kind. Not a witch, that much I can tell.

"I am the police." His voice shocks me back to present. "And you're allowed to be here, but you've set off some alarms that need to be discussed."

"I'm going to need you to explain yourself, because you're not making any sense."

Now I am being a bit rude, but I don't have time for this. I should've guessed he was police though. He carries himself with some authority.

"State your business, please."

That's how we're going to play this? I'm getting more irritated by the minute. Since some part of me has decided he poses no physical threat to me, my magic has gone dormant. But the other side of me—the attitude side, as my mother likes to call it—is all fired up.

"How about you state your business, Mr. Officer? I don't seem to be breaking any laws." I wave my hands around myself. His eyes narrow once more, and I wonder if that's just his regular state of being. The smell of burgers drifts over to me as a couple opens a door to a restaurant on the other side of the street.

"You came to town on a mission."

"Maybe I just like small towns during the holidays." I shrug as he narrows his eyes once more. As I study him, my magic flares up, and I have no idea if it's because of how tired I am or if it's because of the guy standing in front of me. I'm annoyed at him, but there's something that I can almost call a pull to him, and I don't get it. Knowing I'm not going to be liked for this, I ask anyway, "What are you?"

"What?" His whole body goes rigid in a split second, and it seems like he's grown a few inches. The growl that emanates from somewhere deep gives me an answer I'm looking for.

"A shifter, then," I say, smiling a little, because that explains a lot.

"How do you . . ."

"I'm not exactly human myself," I say, rolling my eyes. His own dart around the area, as if he's making sure no one heard us. I was right to assume they have a tight-knit magical community, and by the way he's acting, the humans know nothing about it. He hasn't relaxed with my proclamation, which means I'm really not handling this well.

"Look, my mom has gone missing. I think something or someone took her. The only clue I found was her telling me to find my father. When I did a scrying spell, it led me to Colorado. I have no idea what possessed me to get on the shuttle, but here I am. Explain that."

I hand the piece of paper to him like a peace offering, and after a moment's hesitation, he takes it. After reading over it, he meets my eyes once more.

"I'm sorry to hear that." He sounds like he means it.

I look away toward the shopping center and the people milling around. The last few days seem to be catching up with me, and this shifter's scrutiny is not helping.

"This is how the town works," he continues, and this time his voice is a little softer. Maybe he's picking up on my mood, and I really need to reel it in, before I become a blabbering mess.

"Okay, cool. I'd love to hear all about it, but I'm tired, and I probably should find a place to sleep tonight."

"I should really take you to meet the sheriff first. He'll go over the rules with you and . . ."

"Listen, I'm not stupid. I'm not going to walk around using my powers."

That stops him. "You have . . ."

"Powers. Yes." I shake my head at the shifter, wondering if everyone is this cagey and suspicious around here. "I've had them since I was five. I know how to keep a secret."

"That's young."

"Yes, thank you for that, shifter."

He growls again, his eyes once more on the people in our vicinity. I almost laugh out loud, but I know not to push shifters too far. I also know how close you have to be to overhear something, and none of the humans are that close. I've spent my whole life in their society. I know how to blend in.

"Some of us are a little more powerful than others."

He doesn't miss the dig at his species, and I grin a little broader. He pauses for a moment, as if to collect himself.

"There are rules in Havenwood Falls."

"Which I'm sure you'll be more than happy to share with me." Resigned to my fate, I pull my jacket a little closer to my body. "Fine. Is there an adult who wants to talk to me?"

He doesn't like how I phrased that question, and I know it. But if he's going to talk down to me, I'm going to fight fire with fire. I could actually use some real fire at the moment, because Colorado is freaking cold.

"Sheriff Kasun wants to speak with you," the shifter finally says, as if coming to some conclusion. "Also, if you're planning on sticking around, you'll need to register and get your temporary tattoo."

"Why?"

"Think of it as a visitor's pass."

I roll my eyes but don't argue any further. No matter how much I may not like it, I need his help. And this town's. Once I figure out why that is, maybe I'll feel better.

"Fine. Then lead the way, Mr. Officer."

"It's Warren."

I pause, glancing up to meet his eyes. He puts out his hand, waiting for me to take it.

"I'm Warren."

After only a moment's hesitation, I take his offered hand.

"I'm Niccola."

When our skin touches, my whole body warms from the inside out. There's a moment when I think the space around us has lit up like a Christmas tree, and then I drop his hand, and I'm back in front of the high school once more. That is definitely not a response I've ever had to anybody. This town is just full of surprises.

CHAPTER 3

*H*e leads me to a dark blue Toyota 4Runner, and I'm thankful the moment I'm inside and in the warmth of the car. Warren gets in without a word, turning the heater on right away.

"Is this a standard-issue police vehicle?" I ask, because I need to fix whatever this sudden weirdness is between us. What I felt when I touched him isn't normal for me, and it's making me off kilter.

"It's a trusty little thing."

The quick smile he flashes my way changes his whole demeanor. I wouldn't call him cuddly, but he's way more approachable. And if I thought he was gorgeous before, he's a bit breathtaking with that curve of his lips. Which are more than kissable, if I'm being honest.

Snatching my gaze away, I focus on the town outside the window. Shifters can pick up on a lot, so I need to be a little more controlled with my emotions. I don't need him sniffing out anything I don't want him to know. I'm also a bit shocked at myself. I don't remember the last time I was attracted to anyone like this. Actually, I'm going with never. My one barely-there boyfriend definitely doesn't count.

We pull up at the town square in no time at all. The police station is across the park from Coffee Haven. Maybe Willow alerted them to my presence, which just brings up another question as to why she would. But right now, I need to play nice and talk the sheriff into letting me stay, because like it or not, I feel like I need to stay.

Warren opens my door, taking me by surprise. At first, I'm taken by the gesture. No one has ever done that for me before, but then I realize he's probably just trying to get me out of the car. I've been sitting here for longer than I thought.

However, when we come to the police station door, he reaches in front of me to open that as well.

"Thanks," I mumble, not sure how to take the chivalrous move.

"You're welcome." And he sounds like he means it.

When we step inside, I'm not sure what I expect, but it's not the tan-colored walls. The place looks a little sad, but then, it is a police station. What immediately catches my eye are the two people standing in the front.

One is a man around my mother's age, taller than anyone I've ever met, with dark hair that is graying at the temples. He's dressed much like the rest of the town, in a flannel shirt and jeans. Even though he's not in uniform, I can tell he's the sheriff.

The other is a girl who appears to be a few years older than me, dressed in ripped jeans and a dark hoodie, with a pentagram on the front. She radiates confidence and authority, even with a nose ring. I like her instantly.

"Ric, this is Niccola." Warren makes the introductions, then steps to the side.

"Hi, sorry to cause such a stir in the cosmos." I try on a smile, but neither of the people in front of me relaxes. I think about putting out a hand, but I'm not sure if either of them would take it. Instead, I pull my jacket tighter, which has apparently become a nervous tic.

"I'm Sheriff Kasun," the man says, and surprisingly I find his voice soothing. "This is Adelaide."

"Addie," the girl speaks up, taking a step toward me. She does a quick scan with her eyes, and I wonder what she sees. I didn't even stop to look in a mirror when I stepped out of the airplane. After all the travel, I probably look the worse for wear.

"What brings you to Havenwood Falls, Niccola?" the girl asks, her full attention still on me.

"Honestly, I'm not sure." I decide to be up front about everything. "My mom—she's missing. All she left was this." I take out the note once more, as it has become my most precious commodity. Addie takes it, looking it over before passing it to the sheriff.

"I'm sorry that happened to you," Addie says, taking another step toward me. "What brought you here specifically?"

"I used a scrying spell for my mother, and that led me to Colorado. I'm not sure what possessed me to get into one of the vans, but I had no direction when I stepped off the airplane. This seemed like the right thing to do."

I pause briefly, then take a deep breath, deciding to put everything on the line. I glance at him, asking him with my eyes if I can talk to these people. I can tell they're supes, too. Addie's energy is similar to mine, so she must be a witch, as well as something else. Although witch is the dominant trait I'm picking up. The sheriff reads similar to Warren, so he's a shifter. But I need Warren's reassurance that I can trust them. He gives me a small nod, and I take that affirmation for what it is.

"Look, I'm not trying to cause any trouble. My mother and I are witches, and I can only imagine it was some kind of magic that led me here. I've had magic since I was five years old, and I know how to control it. I'll be eighteen in two months, and until then, I don't have any way of accessing my mother's records. Coven rules. I don't know my father. I don't know anything about this town. But if you would be willing to help me get some answers, I'll be out of your hair as fast as I can. Please. I don't . . . I don't have anyone else."

That last part is difficult to admit, but I know it's the right thing to say. It's that little bit of vulnerability that finally gets to them. I can see it in their faces. They exchange a look, then come to a decision.

"You may stay," the sheriff speaks up, before glancing over at Warren. "But you are to be accompanied by Warren at all times."

I open my mouth to protest, but Ric waves me off.

"This isn't open for discussion, I'm afraid. We'll have to discuss your stay with the Court of the Sun and the Moon, our governing body, so to speak. We have resources, and we can see if we can help. Warren knows this town. He'll be able to help you ask the right questions. Also, while you are here, please limit your magic use. We have strict rules about it."

I glance over at the shifter as he nods at the sheriff. In truth, I can't say that I'm surprised. I'd be suspicious too.

"Thank you," I say, turning my attention back to the sheriff. "I really appreciate it."

"We'll need to get you tattooed," Addie speaks up. "You look exhausted. I can do that in the morning. Do you have a place to stay?"

"Not yet."

"Warren can take you to the inn."

And that's that. Everything has been decided for me, and a part of me is glad. For the last two days, all I've done is keep myself afloat. I can't say that I trust these people completely, but I don't sense any wrongdoing from them. They're genuinely concerned for their town, and I can understand why I would make a few waves with my appearance. Especially since they know I have magic.

"Thank you," I say again, as Warren motions for me to follow him out.

The sun has set, and the temperature has dropped. I'm colder than I've been in my whole life, but I feel just a tad lighter.

Because now I have a place to start and a plan. Somehow, I'm one step closer to finding my mom.

∼

"We'll get you checked in at the inn. Where is the rest of your luggage?" Warren asks, as he opens the passenger door for me. Once again, I'm taken by surprise at his gesture, and it takes me a moment to reply.

"This is all I brought." I lift my shoulder, pointing to the backpack. He doesn't question it, just shuts the door and gets in at the driver's side.

"Hey," I begin, as he turns the warm air full blast, "I appreciate your help."

"Just doing my job," he replies, but it doesn't sound mean. That elusive smile graces his face for a moment, and I have to remind myself to breathe.

"You know, we could've just walked here," I say when we pull up to the inn.

"Yes, but you looked like you needed defrosting first."

He doesn't wait for my reply as he jumps out of the car. I get my own door this time, before he can get there.

"Don't fancy yourself a knight in shining armor." I raise my eyebrows at him. "You'd need a horse for that."

"Who says I don't have one?"

I can't help it. I chuckle. My outburst brings a full-blown smile to his face, and I stop in my tracks. My whole body warms up with that otherworldly fire once more, and it feels like we're the only two people in this town. It lasts only a moment, but I feel it everywhere.

"Come on," Warren says, and for some reason, I think he felt it too. There's a softness in those two words that wasn't there before. I don't reply, but follow him up to the inn. He opens the door for me, and I step into the warmth.

"Hey, Aurelia," Warren greets the girl behind the front desk.

She's around my age and dressed like she's ready to walk down a catwalk at a fashion show.

"Hi, Warren. What brings you in?" She's all flirty smiles as she leans forward on one arm, her eyes on the deputy. She doesn't even spare me a glance, completely focused on the gorgeous guy beside me.

"Niccola here is visiting and needs a room, if you've got anything available." The girl swings her large brown eyes to me, giving me a once-over. I have no idea what she sees, but she's not impressed. She gives Warren another flirty smirk, then puts on her practiced customer smile for me.

"Sure, we have a room. Could you fill some information out for me, please?" She hands me a sheet of paper before turning back to Warren. She seems like she has to work at the whole being nice thing, but mostly her eyes are on Warren. I mean, whose wouldn't be? I fill out my information quickly as they chat, then hand it over.

"There's a dining room here, but if you'd like, I can come pick you up at eight, and we can grab breakfast before we meet up with Addie," Warren says, as Aurelia types my information into the computer. She's not very chatty with me. A few more clicks and she's handing me a key.

"Your room is upstairs. Enjoy your stay." That customer smile is back in place, though she glances over at Warren. He doesn't seem to notice, still waiting for my answer.

"Yes, that would work," I reply quickly, but I don't move. I'm not sure why I'm feeling so awkward, but here we are.

"Let's see that room." Warren takes the key from my hands and heads toward the stairs. A second later, my brain kicks into action, and I hurry after him. Okay, I really need to reel in my teenage hormones. I'm becoming a complete mess.

Warren doesn't seem to have any reservations, though. He marches right to my room, unlocking it and letting me go in first. I step inside and study my surroundings quickly. The bed looks the most inviting, and I can't wait to lie down.

"You've got one of the private bathroom rooms," Warren comments, stopping in front of the second door.

"I didn't know that was an option."

Warren chuckles, taking a few steps toward me.

"Get some rest, Niccola. You'll be safe here." He places the key into my hand, his fingers lingering on my skin for a second longer than necessary. I glance up, once again fascinated by the dark blue of his eyes.

"Nic."

"What?"

"My friends call me Nic."

He smiles, disarming me completely. Then he steps back, walking over to the door and swinging it open.

"Good night, Nic." And just like that, he's gone.

CHAPTER 4

I take a long, hot shower, washing away the last two days. My hair has become a tangled mess, and there are smudges of mascara under my eyes. What a great first impression I've made on this town.

When I'm in my pajamas, I climb into the bed, reaching for my phone. There are no messages, no phone calls. The coven won't wonder where I am until sometime tomorrow. Then someone will probably reach out. But Mom and I keep to ourselves most of the time. I'm not exactly popular with our people.

I have a secret.

The only thing my father has ever given me is a shifter gene.

That's right. I'm half witch, half shifter. Not winning any popularity contests with that one. I'll have to tell the sheriff this, and maybe that tattoo chick. But I don't want to tell Warren.

Witches and shifters aren't exactly known to play nice. And we are definitely not supposed to break out of our own circles to fall in love. My mind instantly drifts to Warren and the undeniable pull I feel toward him. Is it my shifter side calling to him? Or something else?

I lie back down, wondering if I'll sleep at all, and when I close my eyes, the tears I've been holding at bay for days spill out. Clutching a pillow to my chest, I let it all out.

The pain.

The fear.

The loneliness.

For just this moment, I'm a kid once again. I want my mom, and that is as simply as I can put it.

It's with tears in my eyes that I finally fall asleep.

When I wake up next, I'm surprised to see that it's morning. I expected nightmares to keep me awake once again, but I slept right through. Stretching my hands over my head, I consider just staying in bed all day and forgetting about the horror that's become my life. I'm all on my own, with no one to turn to.

I grab my phone, seeing that I have about forty minutes before Warren arrives. Maybe I'm not so alone after all. There's something about him that keeps me intrigued in a way I'm not used to. Also, he's hot, and I'm not blind.

After a quick shower, I pull on my trusty T-shirt and jeans combo, then braid my hair down my back. Because I'm still a teenage girl who's about to hang out with a very hot guy, I swipe some eyeliner and mascara onto my eyes. They're bleaker than I'm used to, but that's what happens when your whole life falls apart. When I reach for my red lipstick, there's a knock on the door. With a few quick swipes, I have my battle armor on, so I head to the door.

Pulling it open, I'm greeted by a spine-tingling sight. Once again in jeans, this time Warren is sporting a dark blue pullover sweater that makes his eyes look even deeper. A coat is draped over one arm, and his other hand is in his pocket. He stares at me as if he's never seen me before.

"Good morning?" I make it a question because I'm completely unsure of myself for the first time in a very long time. But the way he's looking at me is making all of my insides melt, and I don't know how to handle that.

"Good morning." He finally seems to come back to himself. "Here." He thrusts his coat at me, as if it's on fire.

"What?"

"You'll need it."

"I have a jacket." I wave my hand in the direction of my room, where my very thin jacket is visible on the bed.

"That won't be enough."

A part of me wants to continue arguing, since I don't really have people controlling me on the regular. But I quickly realize that's not what he's doing. He's concerned, and after last night, I can see why. I was basically a popsicle when I got to my room.

"Thanks," I mumble, unused to this kind of chivalry. He's got a lot of that in his blood. I pull the material over my shoulders, instantly swallowed up inside the warmth. Warren watches me a moment longer, then clears his throat.

"Shall we?"

I nod and step back inside long enough to grab my room key, phone, and credit card. Warren leads the way down the stairs, and the moment we're outside, I am beyond thankful for the coat. This weather is not something I'm used to. I might've thought that a time or two already.

"What kind of breakfast would you like?"

"Quick one. And one that involves a big cup of coffee," I reply instantly. Warren chuckles, and I'm warmer than I was a second ago.

"Coffee Haven it is."

When we walk into the cafe, I feel that calming presence washing over me once more. This time, however, I'm not sure if it's the place or the company. Warren greets the same woman I ordered from yesterday before turning to me.

"We weren't properly introduced yesterday," she says, giving me a small smile. "I'm Willow."

"Nic," I reply, looking from her to Warren. "Were you . . ."

"The one to call the sheriff? Yes. I won't apologize for that."

"I don't expect you to."

That earns me another smile, before Warren orders his coffee and I order mine, with a scone once again. There's no one in front of us, so we get our breakfast and take a seat at one of the tables. I want to say something, anything, but I have no idea where to start.

"I know I said this yesterday," Warren beats me to it, then pauses to take a sip of coffee. "But I'm sorry about your mom. It must be tough."

I shrug, which is my typical response for any conversation about emotion, but Warren doesn't buy it. He watches me carefully, but there's no pity in his gaze. Just quiet understanding. Maybe that's what prompts me to say what I do next.

"It's just me and her. My whole life. I feel a bit lost without her."

"That's understandable," he says, and I think he means it. "But I won't let you wander away."

His words make the world disappear for one split second so that all I see is him. The pull I've felt toward him since the moment we met wraps around me like a heavy blanket, then he's the one to break the eye contact.

"Where would you like to start today?" he asks, clearing his throat.

"Besides going to meet the tattoo chick?" I ask with a smile. He returns it, with a quick nod. "I was thinking of maybe trying another locator spell? Now that I'm in Colorado, maybe I can try reaching out toward my mom's energy."

"I don't know if it'll work within the town's limits. You're protected while you're here, and no one can find you," Warren says carefully, and I nod.

"Of course, duh. Maybe you can drive me to the outskirts?"

It's the best I got, but it makes sense. And Warren seems to agree. When I'm finished with my scone, we take our coffee to go, and he leads the way toward the police station. There's no one inside, which seems strange, but it's not like I know anything about small-town business. I turn to Warren, but before I can ask a question, the doors open, and Addie walks in.

"Let's do this," she says by way of greeting. I look at Warren, and he motions for me to follow Addie.

"Okay, girl. The tattoo can be visible or invisible. It'll disappear either way when you leave town. I spoke to the Court, and they're letting you stay until you find what you need about your mother. But listen carefully. If you display any kind of magic, or break any rules, you're out. Number one rule: don't harm the humans. Number two: protect our secret."

"Understood," I reply immediately, and that seems to pacify her. I don't think any of these people will trust me any time soon, but I will do whatever it takes to let them know I will play by their rules. I have no other choice.

"I can sketch out whatever you'd like," Addie continues. "Visible or invisible?"

I don't even have to think about it.

"Visible." I lift my left arm, pointing to a spot below my thumb on my wrist. "Right here."

"A girl who knows what she wants." Addie smiles, her pencil ready to go.

"A jasmine flower, on a branch."

"We're heading outside the wards for a locator spell," he tells Addie, and she nods before getting to work.

It takes her less than a minute to sketch the perfect delicate tattoo and about twice that long to have it on my wrist. When she stands, she gives me one long look before turning to Warren.

"I added a bit of extra magic. The tattoo and her memory will keep. But don't stay long." They exchange a look I don't understand, then she leaves.

My eyes are drawn back to the tattoo now residing on my wrist, and I wish it wasn't temporary. It's small and beautiful, and it reminds me of the first time I felt in control of my magic.

"What does it mean?" Warren's soft voice breaks through my thoughts. At first, I don't want to tell him. But when I meet his eyes, it's like I don't have a choice anymore.

"I was eight when I finally found my center," I almost whisper, unable to look away from him. "My magic had been out of control for two years, and I made a mess of things in the park. I had to hide in a jasmine bush, and when my mother finally found me, I found my control."

I glance down at the flower on my wrist, overwhelmed with emotion. I push it all back, shutting it away for later examination, then tug the jacket over my shoulders again, covering up the memories.

"Shall we?" I ask, echoing his earlier words. He grins and leads the way.

~

When we make our way to his truck, the town is fully awake. Without using my magic, I can't discern whether the people passing us on the street are supernaturals or not, but either way, I'm amazed at this community.

I'm also fascinated with the boy walking beside me. There are so many questions running around in my mind. He's a shifter, but how old is he really? And what kind of a shifter is he? And does he feel the weird pull between us or is this just my response to him?

That last one is the question that's bugging me the most, because I am not the type of girl who swoons over guys, but that is the only thing I want to do when I'm around Warren. This is definitely not the time or place, but here we are.

"You might as well ask." Warren's words break through my thoughts, snapping me back to reality. At first, I'm terrified he can read my thoughts, but then he continues. "I can see that you have a lot of questions about this place. Most people do. You can ask, and I'll try to answer."

"Because I won't remember any of this anyway?"

Not sure why, but that question makes me ridiculously sad for a second, and I have to school my features into a neutral expression before I give it away. I'm also not the kind of girl who's open with her emotions, but it's all I can do to keep it all bottled up right now. Which is understandable, considering my mother is missing, but it's not constructive, so I need to reel that in. And fast.

"The memory wards are necessary," Warren says, and it sounds like even he's a little sad about that fact. We study each other in silence for a moment, before I'm the one to look away.

"Tell me about yourself," I ask, if only to keep him talking. I like the sound of his voice.

"Well, you guessed it right. I am . . . what you said I was." I smile at that as a few people push past us. "The sheriff and his mate found me when I was barely even a pup and adopted me for the first few years. Then there was some unrest within the pack about letting me stay, and I was sent away to live with another . . . family."

My heart squeezes at his words, and I can see why he understands my search so well. He knows what it feels like to be alone. Suddenly, the desire to reach out and hold his hand almost overpowers me, so instead, I stuff my hands into his jacket and stay silent as he talks.

"Jefferson took me in and raised me as one of his own. Hawthorne is a town run by the Hawthorne coven, and their community lives and works closely with shifters. When it was time for me to leave, I ended up here. Angry and lost, because . . ."

He pauses for moment, as if trying to find the words, and I can see the pain in his eyes as clear as day. This time, I don't hesitate. I reach for his hand, taking it in my own. His gaze narrows on the spot our skin touches, and I swear my whole body is on fire.

"Gabriele, Ric's love, she died giving birth to the twins. She was the only mother I knew, and I didn't even remember her. Not until it all came crashing back."

"Do you wish the memory wards kept you from remembering?"

I'm not sure what prompts me to ask such a personal question. Maybe it's the way Warren's thumb keeps making circles on my skin. Maybe it's his proximity. But when he meets my eyes, it's like he's been waiting for this exact question.

"Yes and no. I'm glad I have those memories of her back. But they brought a lot of pain with them. Something I've had to deal with."

"I can understand that," I say, because it's how I feel about my father. "I think I would like to know who my dad was, but also wouldn't. It's a strange place to be."

"It is."

And just like that, I think we've reached a point in our new acquaintance where we're no longer strangers. He understands the cracked parts of me, because he's got plenty of his own. Even though it's an unsteady foundation, it feels surer than anything in my seventeen years of life.

When Warren starts walking again, he doesn't let go of my hand, and I hold on just as tightly.

CHAPTER 5

*W*hen we drive past the town's limits, a part of me
grows sad. One day soon, I'll be doing that for real,
without a chance to ever come back. I'm not sure how a place can
get under my skin in less than two days, but I feel it.

"We should move fast," Warren says, as we get out of the car
some time later. I nod, understanding the urgency. Without much
hesitation, I plop myself on a fallen tree, reaching for my phone
and crystal.

"Do you need anything else?" Warren asks, and I understand
the confusion. Most witches scry with much more than a phone
and a crystal. But my intuitive magic helps amp up my spell
without anything extra.

"I'm good," I say, before I place the phone on the log beside
me and close my eyes. The crystal warms up once more, this time
more intensely than before. Instead of keeping it inside my palm, I
uncurl my fingers from around it.

"Nic!" Warren's voice snaps my attention to him, and I open
my eyes to glance at him. But he's watching me. I look over and
find the crystal hovering over my hand.

"What?" I ask, but then quickly push the questions aside. The
crystal is still buzzing with the spell, so I focus my intention on it,

34

keeping my focus strong. What happens next takes me completely by surprise, and it's a moment before I'm on my feet. The crystal zooms away, as if being pulled in a particular direction.

"Come on!" Warren reaches for me, and I barely have time to grab my phone. Hand in hand, we take off after the crystal. After almost ten minutes, we're barely keeping up with it. Suddenly, with a whoosh, it imbeds itself into a tree, making the forest around it echo from the impact.

Warren and I stop, then approach it carefully. There seems to be a small opening in the trunk, but I'm not sure if I should reach for it.

"Has that ever happened to you before?" Warren asks, and I shake my head.

"Can't say that it has," I reply, still not taking my eyes off the tree. "But I was doing a locator spell for my mom. I doubt she's in the tree." And I'm not picking anything up from the area. It's like my magic has gone completely dormant.

"Let me try something," Warren says, and then I feel the air around me move. Glancing over, I come face to face with a gorgeous dark colored wolf. My mouth drops open, and I quickly close it. There are no articles of clothes, so he must be charmed to keep them within his shift. I've heard of it before, but have never seen it myself. The magic fascinates me, and maybe I'll be brave enough to ask him about it one day.

I swear Warren grins at me before he walks over to the tree. I know shifters have heightened senses, even more so in their animal form. So when he begins to sniff the area, I don't interrupt. After a few moments, he turns back to me, as if giving me the go-ahead.

Carefully, I make my way to the tree and reach for my crystal. I work at the opening, prying it apart, until a piece of paper falls out. I feel Warren move toward me, and realize he's shifted back. For some reason, I can't bring myself to reach for the paper, so he stoops down and grabs it.

"It's a diploma," he says, bringing my attention to him.

"What?"

"From Havenwood Falls High. It's made out to Matilda Nile."

I jerk at the name, stepping closer to look at it myself. Warren sees the change in me, the rigid way I hold myself, sensing my mood before I can even pinpoint what I'm feeling.

"What is it?"

"That's my grandmother," I whisper.

We hike back over to the truck in silence. Warren is giving me the time I need to process what we've found, but I can't wrap my mind around it.

"My grandmother died when I was three years old" was all I said before he led me away from the tree. I've only ever known her from my mother's stories. She was a powerful reader witch, which is where my mother gets her powers from. But she died suddenly, as far as I know, and that's when Mom settled us in California.

"I don't understand this, Warren," I speak up, as we cross back into the town's limits. He glances over at me, then looks back to the road.

"Mom must've lived here, when she was a teenager," I continue. "But she never mentioned it. She never told me where my grandmother was from, just that she was gone."

"Nic, she couldn't have, remember?" Warren says, keeping his voice soft. "The town's memory wards would've wiped your grandmother's and mother's memories when they left."

"But she left a clue anyway."

"Are you sure it was your grandma who did that?"

"What do you mean?" I ask, as Warren pulls up in front of the inn and parks.

"It could've been your mother, which is why the spell found it when you were searching for her. Maybe she was here too."

I mull that over, staring out the windshield, as a few tourists walk by. The more answers I find, the more questions pour in. Was

I actually led to this town by accident, or did something call me here? I don't understand any of this, and I just want my mom.

"Hey." Warren is the one to reach out this time, taking my hand into his. "We'll figure this out. This is a good place to find answers. And you've got pretty great help."

I chuckle as he grins at me, surprisingly feeling better. It seems that I don't know much of anything anymore, but I do know that I'm not alone. Somehow, I was led to this town and to Warren. Of that, I have no doubt. Whatever comes next, I can handle it.

Taking a calming breath, I look up at Warren and give him a small smile.

"I think we should go to the school."

CHAPTER 6

$\mathscr{T}$he school looks just as intimidating as it did yesterday.
Warren leads me inside, and the empty halls instantly
get to me. I've never gone to an actual high school. Even though
I'm supposed to be graduating this year, I'm at least a semester
behind. It would be so interesting to go to this school, to be part
of the regular hustle and bustle of a teenage lifestyle. Something I
don't have much of.

"Do you have any idea what we're looking for?" Warren asks,
stopping right inside the front doors.

"No," I reply honestly, and try not to feel frustrated by that
fact. After all, that's why we're here. To see if we can figure this
out. "Maybe we can walk around and see if anything jumps out
at me?"

"Sounds good."

We fall into silence as we begin wandering the halls. Some of
the lights are on, and I briefly wonder if a teacher is here working
on some lesson plans. I think teaching would be an interesting
career and something I've thought about pursuing more than
once. But since I can't even graduate from high school, I'm not
sure how well received that'll be.

We stop in the main hallway, in front of the trophy display case. I look over the awards and the silver-and-blue paraphernalia everywhere. The case goes from floor to ceiling, with dark wooden trim and four shelves in each section. Two jerseys hang against the wall; they look like football and basketball to me. There are quite a few medals and certificates, as well as a few large trophies.

"The mascot is a dragon? Of course," I comment.

Warren chuckles beside me and turns to go when my eyes zero in on a photograph. I glance down at the plaque that reads *Basketball – Conference Champions, 1990*. Next to it is a picture of the team and a few other guys. It looks like they were on some camping retreat. My eyes roam over each person, unsure of what exactly made me pause when I saw it. Warren must notice the way my body tenses, because he's back at my side.

"What is it?"

"I'm not sure," I reply, then pull out my phone. Opening the photo app, I scroll through, my heart beating so hard I think it's going to jump out of my chest. Warren moves closer, as if offering his support, because I'm sure he can sense my anxiety even without his supernatural hearing.

When I stop scrolling, my eyes don't believe what they see. It's almost like I've lost all ability to breathe, and I force myself to inhale.

"Nic?"

"It's . . . him," I whisper, looking up and studying the picture in the display once more.

"Who?"

"My father."

Warren turns immediately, eyes zeroed in on the photo, before I show him the phone. The picture I have is taken maybe ten years later, the one piece of him that my mother kept in her album. When I was little, I used to open it up to see if I was going to look like him. When I got this phone, I took a picture of the photo, just in case.

"He went here?" I mumble, my mind racing. How is this possible? What does it mean?

Warren takes my hand, pulling me around to face him.

"Hey, breathe, okay?"

I don't even realize I'm shaking until Warren is pulling me into his arms. I cling to him as if my life depends on it, as the emotions bombard me on every side. After all this time, every notion I had about my father is closer to realization than ever before. This is where he went to high school. Maybe even grew up. This makes him more real than he's ever been to me, and I don't know what to do with that information. So I do the only thing I can and hold Warren close, hoping that I can hold myself together a little longer.

I sit across from Warren at Burger Bar, staring at the cup of water in front of me as if it holds the answers to the universe. Honestly, I don't even remember walking across the street or into the restaurant.

"Do you want something to eat?" Warren asks, breaking my concentration. I glance up at him, finding concern there, and my heart squeezes at the sight. We're way past acquaintances now, and I'm a bit embarrassed at how clingy I was with him.

"Maybe just some soda?"

He nods and goes to order, giving me a moment to myself. I have so many questions, but no idea what to do next. For years, I thought mom made him up, telling me romantic stories of a witch and a shifter who fell in love. It was very Romeo and Juliet, until it came to the same tragic end. Now I have definite proof of not only his existence, but of his history. And of my grandmother's, apparently. I've only ever known of my grandmother outside of this place, but what if my mother was here too? There are just too many variables. When Warren sits down in front of me, he pushes a cup of soda my way with a smile.

"The fizzy water always helps me too." He shrugs, and he looks younger than before, with that boyish grin on his lips. My heart flips, but for completely different reasons this time, and I take a sip just to do something. I'm probably blushing like crazy.

"You really had no idea?" he asks as I swallow, and my eyes fly back to his. I shake my head.

"I didn't even think he was real half the time. But now I find out he lived here? In the same town as my grandmother. That's crazy to me. I don't even know what to do!"

"I have an idea."

I put the next fry down, leaning over the table. "I'm all ears."

Warren chuckles at my enthusiasm, then leans back and stretches.

"Seriously?" I roll my eyes, and this time he laughs outright. I let the sound wash over me and instantly feel better. I know what he's doing, and I appreciate it oh so much.

"I think," he says, leaning toward me across the table, "that we should talk to some of the people in that photograph."

"Wait, I didn't even think of that!"

"I mean, I am training to be a full-fledged police officer." He leans back, spreading his arms out in front of him. "I'm pretty good at this."

I grin, and my heart feels lighter already. In this moment, I am so thankful Warren is here to help, because I'm so caught up in my emotions, I couldn't even see the next plausible step.

"Okay, so we should get the names and start there?"

Warren pulls out his phone, putting it on the table between us. I didn't even see him take the picture, but there it is. Grainy but recognizable. He points to the person to the right of my father.

"You've already met this person."

I stare at it for a second and then sit back in my chair. "The sheriff?"

"The sheriff," Warren agrees, taking his phone back. "We should talk to Rusty as well. He's been around long enough that he would've met your father."

"Paul."

"What?"

"His name is Paul. That's all I really know about him. I don't even know his last name. I've always just been Niccola Steven." The sadness is so heavy on my chest, I wonder if I look down, I'll see it as a physical weight. I feel a whisper of a touch on my hand and glance over just in time to see Warren place his hand over my own on the table.

"We'll figure it out, Nic," he says, looking deeply into my eyes. "You are not alone in this."

We watch each other quietly, the noise of Burger Bar fading into the background. Warren and I started on such a rocky ground, and now I can't imagine doing this without him. I never understood how my mom could've been so madly in love at such a young age. But now, here I am going through the exact same experience I've always found so doubtful.

I pull my hand back, giving him a small smile. But I can't let myself feel anything for him. I mean, once I have my answers, I'll be leaving. And forgetting all about him and this place. I realize I don't want to forget him, and that's a dangerous place to be.

I need to be more careful about my thoughts and my emotions in this town. Who knows if there's someone here who reads thoughts? And I know shifters can pick up on more than what's visible to the human eye. I'm already plenty embarrassed. I don't need to make a bigger fool of myself.

When we get up to go, the question I've been sitting on bursts out of me.

"How old are you?"

Warren stops for a moment, then his eyes flash, and he smiles. "I'm twenty-one."

"Actual twenty-one?"

"Yes." He chuckles. "Actual twenty-one."

I nod, but don't comment further. This is all the confirmation I need. Guys like him don't fall for teenagers like me. He's just a genuinely kind shifter, and I can't allow myself to mistake his concern for something it's not. I'm becoming the cliché I hate. I'm the girl with the unrequited infatuation with an older guy. Just what I needed.

CHAPTER 7

"The sheriff will meet us at the library," Warren says as we walk out of Burger Bar. The temperature has dropped another few degrees, and I wonder where my shifter gene is because I am cold. Unlike Warren, who barely has a sweater on.

"Why the library?" I ask, as I burrow deeper into Warren's jacket. I don't think I'm ever giving it back at this point. I catch the quick smile he throws my way and think I'm never getting my heart back either. Is that a fair trade? His jacket for my heart?

"It'll be easier to talk in there. It's pretty quiet at this time of the day and year."

I don't argue, and in no time at all, we're standing in front of a beautiful gothic Victorian-style house straight out of some novel. There is a definite charm to this town. And it has nothing to do with the guy standing beside me.

When we walk inside, I am greeted by a vast foyer and the smell of books. Since I've always wanted to be a teacher, books are kind of my best companions. This place is more beautiful than I can put into words.

Sheriff Kasun is already there, with another man who looks to be in his late twenties. He's dressed much like the sheriff, in flannel and jeans, and I briefly wonder if this is just a pack uniform at this point. I almost chuckle at my stupid thoughts, but decide against it. I need to work on making better first impressions.

"Hello, Niccola. Warren." The sheriff greets us as we walk up to the two of them. The other man turns, his brown eyes serious and calculating. I can't imagine him smiling easily, but man, do they make them sexy in this town. He looks like he could be featured in a magazine article entitled "Sexy Mountain Men."

And now I'm fidgeting under Warren's jacket, because I'm pretty sure they can smell my hormones at this point. What is wrong with me?

"This is Rusty. He may be able to help you."

I nod, not trusting my voice as I follow the men up the stairs and to the second floor, which I find out is called the Ravenal Wing. My fingers itch to pick up and study each of the beautiful books I see on the shelves, but I resist. Maybe after it's all said and done, I can come back here and explore. Shaking my head, I try to focus. Warren looks at me, waiting for me to speak up.

"We found a picture at the school," I begin, and Warren pulls his phone out to show the others. "The man next to you is my father."

Ric glances up and meets my eyes. I can't read him, but I let him study me for a few tense minutes. But then it's Rusty who speaks up.

"I can see it in your eyes." We all turn to look at him, as he takes a step closer. "I remember him. He was only here for four years. He left a year after graduating."

"Do you know his last name? Or where he might've gone?" The excitement and anxiety rise up as one, and I try to keep myself from bombarding Rusty with more questions.

"He didn't tell anyone he was leaving. One day, he was just gone. Left his family and girlfriend behind. You look a little like her too."

"My mom? You knew my mom?" So she was here; it wasn't just my grandmother. For some reason, I thought they met outside of this place, but now I see I can't assume anything.

"Lissa. Yes. She was a sweet girl. For a witch."

His words take me aback, but then I realize he's making a joke. His eyes sparkle for just a moment, and I relax, as Warren and Ric chuckle. I like this man.

"All I have is this picture of him," I say, pulling up the photo on my phone. The men in front of me study it, then share a look.

"That wasn't taken anywhere here," Rusty comments. "Not that I know of, at least. It could've been sometime after he left. Lissa left a year after him and never came back. As far as I know, Steve hasn't crossed the boundary since the day he left."

I freeze, whatever question I had dying on my lips. Warren moves toward me, a comforting presence at my back.

"What did you just say?" I whisper, my blood running cold. "What did you call him?"

"Steve. Steven. That was his name."

"And his last name?" Warren asks, realizing at the same moment what I'm trying to get at. Ric and Rusty exchange another look before Rusty answers.

"Knight. Steven Knight."

"Do you . . ." I'm almost afraid to ask. "Do you know my mother's last name?"

"Summers. Lissa Summers."

My world shifts for what seems like the tenth time in so many days. I step away from the men, my head spinning. My vision tunnels, and my magic races to the surface, as I struggle to breathe. I can hear voices all around me, but they sound so far away. Nothing is how it's supposed to be. I can't get air into my lungs.

Suddenly, there are arms around me, pulling me around, and then Warren's face comes into focus.

"Breathe, Nic. Breathe."

His voice pushes through the panic, and as I focus on him, I come back to myself. We're on the floor, and he's holding me on his lap, cradling me as if he can protect me from everything in this world. I bury my face into his shoulder, trying to pull myself together.

"I don't know what happened," I mumble.

"You had a panic attack," Warren says, and I can feel his reply against my cheek. I've never felt safer than I do in this moment, and that realization makes me push against him. I can't let myself become this person, but it's already too late.

"Can you explain your reaction?" the sheriff asks, as I pull away from Warren and stand. I forgot they were here for a second. After I straighten my clothes, I turn to the two men.

"Apparently, my mother has lied to me my whole life." I shrug, trying not to let the panic back in. "She told me my name was Niccola Steven. I carried my dad's name with me this whole time, and I didn't even know it. I don't know anything. I don't have anybody. No one I can trust."

Tears stream down my face as suddenly as the panic attack hit. I can't meet anyone's eyes, so I push past them and run down the stairs and out the door. I don't know where I'm going. I just know I need to get away. I wish I could run from my problems as easily as I ran out of the library. But that's not how things work.

All I feel is betrayed and scared, and I no longer just want my mom. I want the truth.

I end up at the town square once again. My whole body feels numb, and it's not just the cold. I keep expecting someone to come after me, but they don't. Maybe they understand I need a minute to process.

A sign on a building catches my eye: *Havenwood Falls Music and More*. The "and" is a musical clef symbol, and it makes me smile. I push the doors open, walking into the store. It smells clean and fresh, and it's calming somehow. I've stopped crying, but I'm on the verge of starting again.

I've never been a musically inclined person, but I've always loved music. As I study the instruments hanging on the wall, I wonder if my dad knows how to play any. The thought instantly brings tears to my eyes.

"Hello there," a quiet voice sounds from behind me, and I turn to see a petite blonde offering me a comforting smile. She studies me, and it feels as if she can see right into me. The silver cross around her neck sparkles as she almost glides toward me, and for some reason, I lose it all over again. I'm crying before I know it.

"Oh, sweetheart," she says, stepping closer to me and placing a comforting hand on my upper arm. "Can I help?"

"I don't think anyone can help," I hiccup, embarrassed at my display of emotion.

"I can listen."

And apparently, that's all the invitation I need before I'm telling her everything. Minus the magic parts. As I talk to her, I can feel the anxiety leaving my body. She doesn't interrupt or ask questions. Just lets me get it all out.

"I'm sorry," I finally say, wiping at my eyes. "I don't know what came over me."

"You miss your mom, even though you feel like she betrayed you. It's perfectly normal. No matter what she's done, she's still your mother. I'm Cece, by the way."

"Thank you, Cece. I'm Nic," I say, because even talking it all out made me feel so much better. She seems like she carries all the wisdom in the world, and I want to ask her opinion on so many things. Warren included.

The doors open, bringing cold air with them, and at first, I think it's going to be him. But it's a woman, and my eyes are instantly drawn to her dark hair and red highlights. I've wanted to do that to my hair for ages, but Mom always says no.

"Are you ready to go?" The question dies on her lips as she sees me.

"Sherry, this is Nic. She's going through a rough time right now. What do you say we take her to lunch with us?"

"Oh, no. I wouldn't want to intrude." If my mother has done

something right, it's that she raised me with manners. The two women exchange a look like they're on the same wavelength.

"Nonsense, Nic," Sherry says, giving me a comforting smile. "We would love to take you with us."

Looking from one woman to the other, I feel like this is exactly what I need.

"If you really think it's okay," I say, with a tentative smile. Sherry doesn't hesitate to return it, sliding her arm through the crook of my own and leading me toward the door. Cece is right behind us, and in no time at all, we're back at Coffee Haven.

Cece and I find a table, while Sherry goes to order. Even being in their presence is lifting my spirits already. They're not my mother, but they're the older, wiser guidance I need right now. I've never felt more like a kid than I do today.

"It's my treat," Sherry says, placing a cup of coffee and a scone in front of me. "It's blueberry and my favorite." She doesn't wait for a response, just turns and walks back to grab her coffee and Cece's.

"Thank you," I say when Sherry takes a seat. "I . . . thank you for being nice to me." I think I might start crying again, and I don't understand where all this emotion is coming from. It's taking all I have not to make a scene.

"You can talk to us, Nic," Sherry says, reaching over and placing her hand on my arm. I glance up, because even though I just spilled a lot of my worries on Cece, I'm still not done. Without hesitation, I give Sherry the same rundown I gave Cece. Both of the women listen carefully and fully, making me feel like I'm the most important person in their lives at this moment.

"People have a tendency to disappoint us," Sherry says, her voice soft and comforting. "Even our parents are not immune to that. I'm not trying to excuse what your mother did, but maybe she had a good reason."

"But it's not like I can ask her!" I snap, instantly ashamed at my outburst. "I'm sorry, I just . . . I don't have anyone but her.

What if I don't find her? I'm seventeen. I need my mom. I need a home. I don't even have that anymore."

What I said is true. I don't think that apartment will ever feel like home again. I feel more so here, in this town, than I ever did in Palmdale.

I wonder if the two women in front of me are supernatural. With my emotions such a mess, unless I call on my magic, I can't quite discern it, but I don't want to push my luck and get kicked out for my curiosity. Warren will probably know. The moment I think of him, my body heats up.

"Home isn't always a place, Nic," Cece says, her voice that same comforting tone it was in her store. "Don't lose hope that you will be able to find that again."

And I'm thinking about Warren again. Maybe this isn't the best place and time, but I need to talk to someone about him. Even after this small acquaintance, I feel like I can trust these women. Which is very unusual for me.

"Do you believe in fate?" I blurt, before I chicken out. I glance up at Cece, and there's a quiet sadness in her eyes that makes me pause. She smiles, but even with my untrained eye, I know there's a story there.

"I do," Sherry replies, bringing my attention back to her. There's a dreamy look about her, and it makes me curious.

"So you think people are meant to be together?"

"Absolutely. Some people just connect, like two pieces of a puzzle. It's almost like magic."

The word makes me pause, but I don't question it. Because I understand. It's how I feel when I'm around Warren. It's like we're in our own world, and I feel safe with him.

"Do you . . . do you think you have to be a certain age to experience something like that?"

Sherry and Cece exchange a look, then Cece asks, "Is there someone specific you have in mind?"

My first instinct is to deny it, but then I realize I'll never get the answers I'm searching for if I keep hiding from my own feelings. So I lower my voice, leaning towards them, before I reply.

"There's a guy . . ."

"I knew it," Cece whispers, moving forward as if she doesn't want to miss a single word.

"Cece loves a good love story." Sherry chuckles, glancing at her friend. "And so do I."

"I wouldn't call it a love story," I reply, instantly embarrassed. "Maybe I shouldn't have said anything."

"You don't have to share anything you don't want to, but if it helps?"

I grin at Sherry and Cece and their eagerness. Maybe they need this as much as I do. Throwing caution to the wind, I decide I have nothing to lose and everything to gain.

"I just never met anyone like him before." I begin, keeping my voice low. I don't need any supernaturals overhearing my confession. "I've had one boyfriend, last year, if you could really call him that. But I always thought destiny was just something grownups used as a way to justify their decisions. I mean, if destiny was real, wouldn't my parents still be together?"

"Sometimes people love each other deeply, but their paths separate at some point, never to intersect again," Cece says, and a part of me thinks she's speaking from experience. "It doesn't mean that their destiny wasn't to fall in love. It just means that that point in their lives made them who they needed to be."

I mull over those words, understanding them in a way I wouldn't have two weeks ago. My mom has always loved me, and done what is best for me. She must've loved my dad very much to give him up, if that's what happened.

"You don't think seventeen is too young to find that kind of a connection?" I'm almost terrified of the answer, but I have to know.

"I think only you could really know the answer to that," Sherry replies. "But in my personal opinion, love doesn't have an age to it."

I think that over, and I feel the seed of hope within me soaking it up. Yet, I still can't let it become a full-blown plant. There are so many obstacles in front of me. The biggest one being that this is all one-sided.

"What if it's just you, feeling it, I mean."

"As in unrequited?" Cece asks, as I take a sip of my coffee. It's grown lukewarm since I've been sitting here, spilling my guts to two strangers. If only Mom could see me now. She'd be as surprised as I feel.

"Yeah. I'm not exactly his type. Or his age."

And there it is, boiled down to the simplest terms. He's clearly out of high school; I can't even graduate. I don't even know how many credits I would need at this point. Plus, I'm a complete stranger, passing through town. My love for books has made me a romantic.

"Age is a tricky business, but we can't really give you more unless we know more," Sherry says carefully. I know she doesn't want to intrude, but I'm sure she knows Warren, and it would be weird if I said something.

Right?

Maybe.

I'm so confused.

Before I can make a decision, the doors open and in walks the guy of the moment. His eyes instantly find mine, and I can see the relief in them at seeing me. The sheriff and Rusty are right behind him.

"Hey, you!" Sherry exclaims, jumping to her feet and launching herself at Rusty. They share a kiss that makes me even more wishful than I already am. "What brings you here?"

"We've been looking for Nic," he says, glancing over at me, and I feel guilty for making them worry. The others greet Cece as well, but Warren hasn't taken his eyes off me.

"Are you okay?" he asks, stopping on the other side of the table. I nod, not trusting my own voice, and that's when I feel Sherry's and Cece's eyes on me. They glance from me to Warren, settling back on me. Without a doubt in my mind, I know they know it's him I've been talking about. I duck my head, unable to meet their eyes. Why did I open my big mouth in the first place?

"If you're up to it, we can go see if we can find more information at the library?" Warren continues, but I suddenly come to a decision.

"Actually, I was hoping to go back to the inn. I think . . . I think I need to lie down."

"That's a great idea," Sherry comments, smiling down at me.

"Okay, I'll walk you there," Warren says, but Sherry is already shaking her head.

"We'll take her," she says as Cece stands up as well. Warren glances between the two women, a bit confused, then turns to me. I don't think I can handle being in his presence right now, so I stand as well, moving to Cece's side.

"I'll see you later, okay?" I say, moving past him to the door. With a quick goodbye to the sheriff and Rusty, I leave them behind. It doesn't take long for Cece and Sherry to catch up to me.

"So, that's him?" Cece asks, keeping her voice gentle, and all I can do is nod.

"Four years isn't that much of an age gap. Not in our world."

I glance at her sharply, wondering what exactly she means by that. Because she can't really mean that she knows. Can it? I think Sherry might, considering she's in a relationship with a shifter, but I don't feel any magic in her. Not without sensing further.

"Don't look so scared." Sherry chuckles. "We know all about Havenwood Falls."

"I'm not sure what you mean," I say, trying to keep myself from giving up too much.

"You don't think I know Rusty is a shifter?" Sherry asks, grinning at me.

"And you are?"

"Human."

"But it works?"

I think of my own heritage—a witch and a shifter. It's been

taboo for so long, I've never met anyone who was comfortable with such a drastic difference in species.

"He's the love of my life," Sherry replies, and I believe her.

"What about you? Are you human too?"

"Far from it. I'm an angel," Cece replies. At first, I don't think I hear her right. But she's completely serious, and that literally stops me in my tracks. Cece and Sherry pivot to face me, waiting for me to digest that information.

"Wow, I mean, wow. I've never met one before. That's . . ."

"Wow?" Cece smiles, and now I can see why her presence is so comforting to me. She's actually a being of light. Instantly, I feel embarrassed by my petty problems.

"Hey," she says, taking a step toward me. "I am here to help, no matter what problems arise."

"Can you read my mind?"

"No, but I can read you. You carry a lot of weight on your shoulders for someone so young. It's not an easy position to be in, but you are strong. Even stronger than you give yourself credit for. Of that, I have no doubt."

Tears pool in my eyes, and then I do another very uncharacteristic thing for me. I take a step toward her, and Cece opens up her arms as I fall into them. She hugs me close, and I can feel her comforting touch even through the layers of my clothes and Warren's jacket. It's a brief hug, but one I needed very much.

"I'm sorry about that," I hiccup, wiping at my face.

"You needed it more than you needed words." Cece smiles, patting my arm. And just like that, I feel better.

"Would you like me to bring you some clothes?" Sherry asks, when we arrive at the inn. "Or a jacket?"

I glance down at myself, pulling Warren's coat closer to me. It's true that I'm not really great at accepting help, but this is something else. I don't want to give up this piece of Warren that I have.

"I'm okay, but thank you."

"Don't hesitate to come by if you need anything," Cece says,

Sherry nodding in agreement. I watch the two women, amazed by their differences and their friendship. They belong in this town. I wonder what it would feel like to belong.

"Thank you so much for your help today. I know I came out of nowhere and—"

"You are welcome," Sherry interrupts before I start apologizing. She hugs me quickly and tightly to her body, then steps back. "We're here for you, Nic. You are not alone."

"Warren told me the same thing," I find myself saying.

"You should listen to him," Cece comments, smiling warmly.

"And you should let him in a little," Sherry adds, pulling my collar a little tighter. "I think you both can use it."

They don't stick around any longer, waving as they head back toward Cece's store. I get myself inside the inn and up the stairs without meeting anyone's eye. A big part of me was running from Warren back there, but the moment I'm inside the room, I realize just how tired I really am. Without shedding the jacket, I lie on top of the covers and close my eyes. For the first time in days, I fall asleep instantly, with fresh tears still on my cheeks.

CHAPTER 8

a knocking pulls me out of my dreamless sleep, and I sit up, rubbing my eyes gently. The knock comes again, and I realize someone is at my door. The light outside the window is gone, and I wonder how long I've been asleep. Padding over to the door, I swing it open to find Warren on the other side.

"Hi." He looks a little unsure of his welcome, which is understandable. I've been acting very irrationally where he's concerned. "Did I wake you?"

"What time is it?" I run my hand over my hair, wondering if I look as unbalanced as I feel.

"A little after seven. I thought you'd be hungry."

I slept for a few hours, but I guess my body needed it. The moment Warren mentions food, my stomach growls. He chuckles, and I roll my eyes. Of course this would happen to me.

"I guess that answers that." He smiles, catching me by surprise. Just like every other time. There's just something about him when his lips curl up that sends my world spinning. "Would you like to go to dinner with me?"

I stare at him for way too long, finally nodding my head. Motioning for him to come inside, I shed his jacket and hurry into the bathroom. Checking myself in the mirror, I see that my eyeliner is all gone, leaving some black streaks on my eyelids. But at least my mascara is mostly in place, since it's waterproof. My hair is a squished mess, having been in a braid all day and then slept on.

As quickly as I can, I fix my makeup, donning my trusty red lipstick, then take another look at my hair. Pulling the elastic out, I unbraid it and run my fingers through it, letting it fall around me in loose waves. Re-braiding it will take too long, so I leave it down and step into the room.

"I'm ready."

Warren has been staring out the window, but he turns at the sound of my voice. He freezes at the sight of me, as if seeing me for the first time. I want to say something, anything, but I've lost all control of my motor functions. A lock of hair falls forward over my shoulder, and it's like that small movement spurs him into action.

"Here, I brought you this," he says, coming to stand in front of me as he pulls something out of his back pocket. "It's colder out now since it's dark. I thought you could use it."

I look down and find him holding what looks like a dark beanie. Glancing up, I go back to staring instead of taking the offered gift. Warren watches me for a moment longer, then closes the rest of the distance between us and pulls the beanie over my head. His fingers graze my face, sending a shiver up my spine. We're standing way too close, and as I look up at him, I realize I would stay here forever.

"Thank you," I say, barely above whisper.

"You're welcome," he replies, his breath warm on my cheek. It wouldn't take much for me to reach over and pull him down to my level. To wrap my arms around his neck and find out if his lips feel as soft as they look. But no matter how brave I may be, in this moment, I'm terrified.

Of these feelings.

Of myself.

"We should get going," Warren says, taking a step back with a small smile. I'm not sure if it was him or me who moved away first, but he must've seen it in my eyes. I reach for his coat, and when I pull it over my shoulders, I turn and find him watching me. He smiles quickly before he gestures toward the door.

The moment we're outside the inn, I'm thankful for the hat. The wind has picked up a bit, and I burrow myself deeper into the jacket. Warren stays close beside me, and my hand itches to reach for his. I really need to get a hold of my stupid hormones.

"What sounds good?" Warren asks, pulling me back to the here and now.

"Pizza," I answer immediately, and he chuckles.

"Perfect. Because Napoli's is just across the square."

We begin our walk, taking our time. It's like neither one of us is in a hurry. I look for something to say, but the silence isn't uncomfortable, which is also new for me.

"Are you doing okay? With all of this, I mean?" Warren asks after a moment.

"You mean the part where everything I've ever known about my family or myself is a lie? And I'm homeless and motherless? Sure, I'm doing great. So great."

My sarcasm isn't wasted as Warren laughs, and the sound warms me even more than the coat does.

"It's a lot. I can't even imagine," he says. "But you're handling it better than I could."

"Oh, I don't know about that."

"I do."

His tone is serious, and I sneak a peek at him. He looks like he really believes what he's saying, and that makes me feel better.

"Hey, Warren!"

A girl's voice sounds before I can say anything else, and we turn as one to see a beautiful blonde heading our way. She's holding hands with a guy, who's a little less blond, but just as cute. They look to be about my age, but I really should stop guessing ages. In this place, nothing is sure.

"Hey, Celeste. Jonathan."

The boy nods his head in greeting, but doesn't speak up. He looks like a bad boy in his black leather jacket, while she looks fashionable enough that I would like to be friends with her.

"Where are you headed to?" the girl, Celeste, asks, as her eyes swing briefly to me.

"Napoli's. Celeste, this is Nic. Nic, this is Celeste and her boyfriend Jonathan. I volunteer at their high school from time to time."

"It's nice to meet you both," I say, offering a smile, which is easily returned by the two. Of course Warren volunteers. I've noticed firsthand his kindheartedness.

"We're headed to Napoli's too!" Celeste says, beaming. "Can we join you?"

Warren and I exchange a look. Even though a big part of me wants him all to myself, I know that's it's probably better if we have company.

"Of course," I'm the one to reply, and we turn as one toward the restaurant. It's not far, and once inside, Celeste and I find a booth, while Jonathan and Warren go to say hi to a group of guys at a table.

"So what brings you to Havenwood Falls?" she asks, not beating around the bush.

"I'm actually looking for my mom. And dad," I add as an afterthought, thinking I probably should've come up with a cover story. But it's too late now. A lot of people already know why I'm here. If these two aren't aware of the supernatural aspect, it's a bit of an unbelievable story, but it's what I have to work with, so there's no turning back now. I pull the hat off my head, patting my hair down.

"What happened to your parents?"

"Well, I've never met my dad. I just know he's from here. Mom sent me this way to see if I can find him, I guess?" That seems legit enough.

Celeste studies me with a puzzled expression on her face.

"I know, it sounds crazy to me too." I shrug.

"So you don't know your dad at all?" she asks, as the boys return, taking a seat. Warren's body slides into the booth beside mine, and I can feel the heat off him instantly. It takes some serious self-control not to lean into him.

"No. I mean, I know what he looks like. And I now know that he went to Havenwood Falls High."

"That's where we go!" Celeste exclaims, leaning a little against Jonathan. He really doesn't seem like the talkative type, but he seems nice at the same time. Go figure.

"I'm a senior this year. I'm pretty excited. We both are. Are you in school?"

Just then a waitress comes over, and we order some drinks and a pepperoni pizza.

"I'm supposed to be," I reply honestly, as soon as she's gone. "But I've never been to an actual high school."

I can feel Warren's eyes on me as I talk, but I don't want to look at him. If I look at him, I'm afraid I'll spill all my insecurities in front of him.

"How is that possible? How old are you?"

"I'm almost eighteen. But I've mostly been homeschooled. And taught in a small classroom setting by our . . . friend," I almost say coven leader. I need to be more careful.

"Jonathan was homeschooled too!" Celeste says, turning to her boyfriend.

"I was," he agrees, speaking up for the first time. It's fascinating to see their dynamic. Celeste doesn't seem like someone who is used to being in the background. It's like she expects people to listen to her. But Jonathan is completely content being almost invisible.

"How do you like Havenwood Falls High, then? Is it really different?" I find myself asking, because apparently I want to torture myself with the knowledge. Up until coming to this town, I didn't realize how badly I was missing out on the whole high school experience.

"It's not bad. I'm pretty new to it myself, but it's got some perks," he replies, giving his girlfriend a look that makes me smile. They're adorable. It's the best word I can find for them. Our pizza arrives then, and we dig in as if we haven't eaten in days. That's definitely what I feel like, even though it's only been a few hours.

"Is that all you know about your dad?" Celeste asks, once I've polished off a piece of pizza.

"Well, today we found out that he played basketball. He was on the team that won a championship in the nineties."

"Wait." Celeste sits up taller, her full attention on me. "What year did he graduate?"

"1990, we think?"

"Oh my goodness, my dad played basketball in high school!"

"Seriously?"

I turn to Warren. "Let her see the picture."

He pulls out his phone, and I make a mental note to get the picture from him, when Celeste looks up at me.

"That's my dad!" She points to a man two over on the left of my father.

"That's mine," I say, pointing to him. "Do you think your dad remembers him?"

"I would think so. My dad has a pretty good memory. He's an accountant, so he kind of has to."

"That's amazing," I breathe out, my heart once again anxious and excited at the same time.

"You can totally come over and talk to him. We can go tonight," Celeste announces, taking a bite of pizza. I meet her eyes as she grins at me, and I answer in kind.

"Thank you so much," I say, turning to Warren. He looks just as excited as I feel. That need to reach out fills me once more, but he beats me to it. His hand covers my own on my lap, squeezing it briefly, and that small touch makes my heart soar.

∼

We finish up our food fast, because I can barely sit still from excitement. Talking to the sheriff and Rusty has provided us with some information, and I'm nervous to see what else this town can tell me about my family.

It doesn't take us long to get to Celeste's house, and she's shouting for her dad the moment we're inside. Warren takes my jacket and hat, placing it by the door in the foyer. Before we take two steps, a man in his late forties rounds the corner. He looks approachable, which makes me feel better instantly.

"What's all the shouting about?"

"Hi, Dad. Meet Nic. She's got some questions for you about her dad," Celeste says, before she takes Jonathan's hand and drags him behind her and into what I'm assuming is the living room.

"Hello, Nic," Celeste's dad says. "I'm Brian. How can I help you?" He nods at Warren in greeting, but his attention is completely on me.

"I'm not sure if you remember him," I begin, a little shaky. Warren's hand wraps around mine tightly, and I hold on with all my might as I turn the phone toward Brian. "The man two to your right. He's my father. I don't know much about him. Just his name . . ."

"Steven," Brian says softly, studying the photograph before looking up at me. "You look like him."

His words bring tears to my eyes, but I hold them back. Now is definitely not the time. Brian motions for us to follow him. We end up in the living room, where Celeste and Jonathan are already on the couch. Warren and I take a seat, not breaking contact, and I'm thankful he's here. Brian walks over to a shelf, pulling out a book. He walks back over as he leafs through it, then hands it to me.

It's a photo album. There in the middle of a plastic sleeve is my dad, his arm around Brian, both of them holding basketballs over their heads. They're grinning, and my heart squeezes at the sight of him.

"He was one of the best players on our team," Brian says, a

faraway look in his eyes. "We were close. Our whole team was pretty close. I sometimes felt like he was holding back, though, when we played. He was funny too. Always kept us laughing."

Brian takes off his glasses, running his hands over his face before replacing them. I wonder if my dad would have a bit of gray in his hair, or if his shifter gene keeps that from happening. I can't even begin to guess how old he really is.

"Do you know what happened to him?" I ask.

"No. One day he was just gone. Lissa was heartbroken. He didn't tell her he was leaving. They'd made a lot of plans for the future. They had this journal, where they would write everything down. Lissa carried it with her religiously."

"My mom," I say, and Brian meets my eyes once more.

"You're Lissa's girl? So she found him."

"Found him?"

"She swore she would, after he left. It took her almost a year, but then she left too and never returned. Her mother left a few years after. I always hoped they found each other. Seeing you, that means they did."

"I guess," I say, not sure how to respond to that. "He didn't stick around."

"That doesn't sound like him."

"What do you mean?"

"He was fearlessly loyal. And he loved your mom more than anything. If he left, there had to be a life or death situation in play. I didn't think anything could keep those two apart. It's like they were destined to be together."

I glance at Warren, and he's already looking at me. Maybe he feels it too, that intense reaction to the whole destiny thing. Because when he's near, I absolutely believe in fate.

"I'm sorry I don't have more information for you," Brian says, and I shake my head.

"No, you gave me a glimpse into who he was. That's not something I had before." Which is true. Rusty and Ric mentioned my mom, but this was different. Brian and my father must've been close.

"Thank you," I say to Brian, then glance over at Celeste. "Thank you for bringing me here."

"Of course," she replies with a smile.

When Warren and I leave, I don't know what to say or do. I definitely don't know what to feel. But I know that every single person I've met in this town has somehow given me a gift. They've given me clues to help find not only my parents, but myself. Warren included.

I look over at him now as he waits me out, letting me come to terms with what we found out. After all that, I have one huge question that I want to ask him, but I don't know if I should. The fact that I keep second guessing my every move is frustrating and very unlike me. But I guess that's what happens when you're no longer standing on solid ground. I can't seem to find my footing.

Annoyed with myself and my lack of courage, I stop walking. Warren turns, inclining his head at my sudden stop.

"Do you believe in fate?"

This seems to be the question I need the answer to most lately. Maybe it's because of my parents. Maybe it's because of him. But I need to know what he thinks about it. It's become an actual need deep inside me.

He doesn't answer right away, and I'm afraid I've shown too much with my question. After what seems like an eternity, he walks back over to me, standing close enough that I can feel his body heat.

"I do," he finally answers, and I let that wash over me. I don't know what I'm expecting or what I'm looking for.

"You think people are meant to find each other? That there's some cosmic balance that's fulfilled when they do?" My chest feels heavy, and I think I'm on the verge of another panic attack. I've never had one, not until that moment in the library, when I found out my mother lied to me. But now, I feel the pressure for a whole lot of different reasons. Mainly because I know when I leave, all of this will cease to exist for me. And I don't know how I will ever survive that kind of loss. I think I'll feel it even if I don't remember it.

"I think some people are destined to cross paths, in a way that changes their lives forever. Ric and Gaby were my first evidence of that. They found me, they saved me, and I think that was meant to be. Sending me to live with Jefferson wouldn't have happened if it wasn't for the Kasuns."

Of course he thinks I'm talking about family. I shake my head, glancing down at my feet. His priorities are where mine should be, but I'm over here swooning because of a pretty face.

"Thanks for your help today," I say, changing the subject abruptly. He watches me curiously, but doesn't comment, waiting me out. He does that a lot. It's like he understands that I need to stay in some sort of control over my life. If only in this one aspect.

"We can start early tomorrow."

I glance up at that, meeting his eyes. "You're going to keep helping?"

"Of course." He flashes that smile I'm becoming ridiculously attached to. "We'll figure this out, Nic. I know it."

"Thanks, Mr. Officer."

"You're welcome."

CHAPTER 9

The next morning, I'm up even earlier. Warren and I spend the whole day in the library, looking up old records, but find nearly nothing new. There are yearbooks from the years my dad was in school here, but outside of a few pictures, there's not much information. I do find a picture of my mom and dad together, her smiling up at him, as he looks at the camera. They're inside the gym—I can see the bleachers in the background —and they look happier than I've ever seen.

Warren and I keep up a steady conversation throughout the day, and the more he talks, the more I like him. When I go to sleep that night, I dream of him and wake up sadder than I should be. I'm not sure what I dreamt, only that it led to heartbreak. So basically, kind of like my life right now.

The next two days go by in the same manner. Nothing new, just more time spent with Warren and the inevitable truth that I will eventually be leaving, just like my parents did. And never returning. It's the fourth day that finally brings some results.

"Look at this," I say, pulling up a photograph I found at the back of a yearbook. This one is a year after my parents graduated, so I didn't look at it until now. But there is my mom, standing beside my dad, in Town Square Park. She's holding a book tightly against her stomach, as he leans over her shoulder toward the camera.

"I've seen this book before."

I grab my phone and pull up the picture I took of the yearbook photo earlier. There they are, in the gym, the same book pressed against her side.

"Do you remember Brian mentioning a book they shared? With all their plans?" Warren asks, looking up at me.

"Yes. This must be it, right? I mean, these photos were taken a year apart, and she still has it."

"You've never seen it before?"

"No. I guess it would be too much to hope that she kept it, but I've never seen it. It must've been too painful, you know. To keep it."

"But she wouldn't have remembered," Warren reminds me gently, and there they are, those frustrating memory wards.

"There has to be a way that she did. How else would she have met up with my father outside this place?"

"Maybe they didn't remember each other, but their love still guided them to the same place, at the same time."

I glance up sharply, my gaze colliding with Warren's. He sounds almost wishful, and the intensity in his eyes makes my head spin. He doesn't take his eyes off me as he speaks.

"Maybe they felt so strongly about one another that no matter what magic came between them, they were still led to each other."

"Do you think that's possible?" I whisper, afraid of the answer and looking for it all the same.

"I do. I think love is the strongest magic there is."

"Have you ever been in love?" I'm surprised by my own words, but I don't regret them. I need to know. Because what I feel for him, it's more than I ever thought possible. It doesn't matter that I'm only seventeen. I can't deny myself these emotions.

"No, never before."

And I don't know why that makes me feel lightheaded. Why it turns my world upside down once more. He's not telling me he loves me. It's too soon for both of us. But . . . I still hope; I still yearn for that to be true. And so I'm the first to break eye contact. It's the way things have to be.

I stare at the picture of my parents, and I want to ask them so many questions. One of which is whether I can trust what I'm feeling for Warren. My whole life I was taught that teenagers don't know the meaning of true love, but this thing between us, it's bigger than anything I've ever imagined. Regardless of how he feels, it has shaped me forever.

"Do you have any idea where such a book might be kept?" I finally ask, focusing on the task at hand. Warren is silent for a moment, so I'm forced to face him. He's watching me steadily, and only when our eyes meet does he reply.

"I don't."

"Would the library have it in storage?"

"Not this library, unfortunately. There was a fire. This place only opened up a few years ago."

I almost groan out loud, but it really isn't Warren's, or the library's, fault. Getting up, I begin to pace, walking from shelf to shelf.

"The only thing I can come up with," Warren says, bringing my attention back to him, "is going back to the school. Maybe we missed something."

I nod, because it sounds like our best move. But not tonight. Tonight, I just want to rest and not think about anything.

"We can do that in the morning, right?" I ask, and receive one of Warren's smiles. He's begun to understand my moods, almost better than I do myself. Standing up, he reaches for his jacket, holding it out for me. I step into its warmth, pulling it close around me. I wonder if I can take it with me when the time comes to leave.

Just like that, I'm back here again, in this sad and lonely place. I want to find my mother. I want to know more about my dad. But I also want to stay in Havenwood Falls. And that's a new one for me.

~

Warren parks at the inn, then comes around the front and opens the door for me. He's been trying to keep me as warm as possible. I give him a small thanks, and we begin to walk toward the front doors when we're stopped.

"Warren!" a guy's voice calls from behind us, and we turn to see a cute blond boy and a pretty petite girl heading our way. There's something in the way they're holding hands that makes me take notice. It's like they're afraid one of them will disappear.

"Joe! You're back."

The two hug in that manly, pat on the back kind of way, beaming at each other. The girl stays quiet, grinning at the two of them, until Warren turns to her.

"If it isn't Infiniti." He gives the girl a quick hug as she says hello.

"Nichols," the blond guy says, "you finally talked them into giving you a badge."

Warren laughs, turning my attention back to him. He's comfortable with these two, in a way I haven't seen before. There's a deep-rooted friendship here, mostly with the guy, and it raises plenty of questions. I guess I'll just add them to my always growing list.

"They let you guys out of prison for the holidays?"

"It's college, not prison." Joe chuckles, pulling Infiniti closer to him once more. It's like he has to keep his hands on her at all times, and from what I can see, she's soaking it up. My heart thuds in awareness, but I push the jealousy aside. It's only wishful thinking on my part, and I keep my eyes on the couple instead of Warren, just to prove to myself that I can.

"This is Nic," Warren says, bringing me into the conversation. Both Joe and Infiniti turn to me as one, assessing me quickly. Infiniti seems like a free spirit, but she's cautious. Joe is territorial, and I wonder if he's from Warren's pack. That would explain their familiarity.

"Welcome to Havenwood Falls," Joe says, and I focus back on him.

"How do you know I'm new around here?"

"I've been here my whole life." He smiles at me, and I feel better. He's not trying to pry, but when you live in a small town, visitors must stand out.

"How do you like it?" Joe asks, and I shrug a little in response.

"It has its perks, I guess."

That makes the group laugh, and for a moment, I feel like I belong here. With them. In this town.

"Fin is pretty new to it herself, but she tells me she wouldn't want to be anywhere else," Joe says, and the pretty girl snuggles closer. They look so in love, it's blinding.

They share a look that's only meant for the two of them, and this time I can't help it; I glance over at Warren. His eyes are already on me, and it's like the intensity Joe and Infiniti have is being passed on to the two of us. I need someone to teach me how to not make a fool out of myself anytime I'm around Warren. It's becoming a problem.

Warren and Joe seem like they have something to discuss, so I step to the side, turning to face Town Square Park. A moment later, Joe steps up beside me, and I glance over to see Infiniti on the phone and Warren talking to an elderly gentleman.

"Whatever brought you here, Warren is a good guy to have on your side."

I glance at him sharply, wondering how much he knows.

"He's helping me find my mom. And dad, I guess."

"It sounds like there's a story there."

"There is. It's one I've been telling a lot lately." The sadness comes fast, like an arrow slicing through my shoulder. Even though a part of me is still mad, at this moment, I miss my mom something fierce.

"We all have stories." Joe breaks through my thoughts, and I look over to find him watching Infiniti. "This place is good for that. I think you are all led here for a purpose. It'll be interesting to see yours, Nic."

Joe can't be a year or two older than me, but there's depth in his eyes of someone who has been through a trial or two. Infiniti comes up then, and they reach for each other at the same time. Whatever they may have gone through, it brought them together, and that's something that gives me hope.

"It was nice to meet you, Nic," Joe says, then with a small wave, he and Infiniti walk off. Warren comes up to stand beside me, but doesn't say anything at first.

"What was that all about?" I finally ask, shifting from foot to foot. It's getting colder by the minute.

"Joe was just giving me some friendly advice," Warren replies, turning to head back to the inn. I don't pry further than that, even though I want to. We walk in silence until Warren speaks up. "He told me not to get myself in trouble."

"What does that mean?"

"It means he knows from firsthand experience what it feels like when someone leaves this town and the memory wards kick in. He knows what it's like to live with losing someone."

"You mean Infiniti?"

"They've had quite an ordeal, that's for sure." Warren's expression turns serious for a moment, and my curiosity is piqued. We reach the inn, and he follows me inside. The warmth makes me feel better instantly, and when I turn to say goodbye, he shakes his head. "I'll see you to your room."

I don't argue, for once, because after today, we both need this time together. Soon, I'll be leaving. And when I do, I'll be forgetting everything about this place. I want to scream in frustration, at the top of my lungs, because what I found here is something I've never had. Home. Friends. A place where I belong. A place where I don't have to hide.

"Warren, there's something I have to tell you," I say, unlocking my door. He stops just on the other side of the doorway, and after a moment, I motion him inside. Shedding his jacket, I go to the window, too restless to sit.

"Maybe I should've told you this earlier, but it's something I haven't shared with many. It may change the way you look at me. Maybe. I'm not sure. I'm afraid it might."

Without turning around, I know he's moved to stand behind me. I can feel his heat reaching out toward me, as if coaxing me to speak up. Still not looking at him, I push the words past my lips.

"I'm not just a witch, Warren. I'm half shifter. My dad was a shifter. That's the only thing I truly know about him."

I say it all in one breath, my body shaking at the thought of what this could mean. Warren might walk out of this room and never return. But I know I had to tell him. It was no longer a secret I could keep.

He doesn't say anything, and I'm too afraid to turn around. But then I feel his hands on my arms as he gently turns me to face him.

"I guess we do have something in common after all," he says softly, and the tears I've been fighting spill over onto my cheeks. I laugh and cry at the same time, as I work at getting a hold of myself.

"You're not . . . disgusted?" I finally manage through all the emotion.

"This just makes you more of who you are."

I launch myself at him, all reservations forgotten, and he catches me easily in his arms. We stand like that, body to body, and he holds me just as tightly as I cling to him. With all of my heart and soul, I beg the universe that I never forget this moment or how it feels, for as long as I live.

CHAPTER 10

J'm sleeping worse every night. The impending doom of me leaving brings with it nightmares. My constant worry for my mom doesn't help either. We have to find out something before I run out of time.

My dreams are keeping me restless. I know I'm dreaming, but I can't seem to pull myself out of the nightmare. There's my mom, bloodied and bruised, lying in the middle of Town Square Park.

"Why did you let this happen?" she whispers, looking up at me as I reach down to help. The accusing tone makes me pause, and then there are more of them.

Warren. My dad. Ric. Sherry. They're all around me, all bleeding and watching me like it's all my fault.

"I didn't mean for this to happen," I shout, trying to convince them, as well as myself. But I stand accused, and when they begin to close in on me, all I can do is scream.

I sit up in my bed with a jerk, sweat dripping down my back. The light pours in through the half-closed curtain, drawing my attention to it as I orient myself. My phone buzzes, and it's a text from Warren saying he'll be a few minutes late. Pushing all thoughts of the dream out of my mind, I jump out of bed and get ready.

When Warren shows up at my door, there are two cups of coffee in his hands. And a blueberry scone in his pocket.

"You're a lifesaver." I thank him, accepting the cup eagerly. A part of me thinks that I will need a refill a few times today. I'm bundled up in Warren's coat and hat, with jeans and boots on, and I'm still chilly when we step outside.

"Let's take the truck." Warren motions me forward, and I could hug him. It takes us much less time to get to the school this way. I'm lost in my own thoughts, and Warren doesn't try to make small talk, for which I am very thankful. Just being in his company is comforting, and I need all the comfort I can get right now.

The school is still on break, so there's almost no one there. Especially this early. We wander the halls, visiting some of the classrooms. Once again, I wonder how it would feel to go to a school such as this. I can feel the history of this place, but also the way it fits in the here and now. That's a special kind of teenage magic I've never known.

When we step inside the gym, my breath catches. Slowly, deliberately, I walk toward the place my parents stood all those years ago when that picture was taken. My head spins with memories and emotions, and I can't tell which are mine and which are just remnants in this place.

"They must've been in love, right?" I find myself asking out loud. Warren walks up to stand in front of me, watching me carefully.

"I believe they were."

"Then something horrible must've happened to keep them apart."

"Sometimes . . ." I thought he would agree with me, but there's something else here. I glance at him sharply, catching his eye. "Sometimes, it's not a life or death situation. Sometimes it's just a decision that's best for both parties."

The way he watches me . . . for the first time, I think he feels it too. The invisible pull we have toward each other, despite the age difference and the present circumstances. He gets me, in ways I don't fully understand myself. My heart doesn't want to hope, and it doesn't want to let go of what's standing so close within reach.

We move as one, as if being tugged together. Warren reaches for my hand, holding it tightly in his, as I place my other hand over his heart. I can't look away, even if I tried. The intensity of his gaze roots me to the spot, and when he leans down, I know this is the moment I will remember for the rest of my life.

But when I close my eyes, I'm somewhere else. The magic—actual magic—pulls me in, and without a second thought, I answer in kind. The bright light behind my eyelids becomes unbearable, and I squeeze them tighter. Images and voices begin to assault me on every side. I scream, stumbling, but I can't get away. Or get out.

Warren's voice sounds somewhere far away, but I'm still lost in the brightness. Magic washes over me, and then a door opens with an audible click. I pinpoint the sound, pulling myself toward it, and then I'm hurtling through.

Then everything goes black.

~

Voices sound all around me, and I try to sort them out. Warren's is the first one I understand.

"Is there anything you can do to wake her?" he asks, his voice laced with concern. I want to open my eyes and tell him I'm awake, but I can't seem to muster up enough energy. Panic sets in, making it hard to breathe. Or was it already hard to breathe? I can't tell. It feels like I'm spinning out of control.

I feel my body dip to the right, as if someone has sat down next to me, and then Warren's voice is much closer.

"It's okay, Niccola," he whispers, before I feel his touch on my forehead. "I'm here. Everything will be okay." His voice soothes me, and after a few feeble attempts to open my eyes, I decide to save my strength and listen.

"Whatever has her under, it's not our magic," a vaguely

familiar voice speaks. "From what I can tell, it's as if she stepped through a spell specifically attuned to her."

"Like blood magic?"

"Yes." The room grows quiet for a moment before the voice speaks up again. "She has to pull herself out of it. All we can do is make her comfortable."

There's a commotion, and I think more people are in the room, if that's where I am. It feels like I'm lying on a bed, so we must've migrated from the gym. Which is the last thing I remember.

The brightness.

The rush of power.

And then nothing.

Before I can do anything else, I'm fading.

The next time I wake up, the room is dark. I manage to open my eyes, just barely, and I find that I'm back in my room at the inn. A chair has been pulled up to the bed, and a very tired Warren is sitting in it, lost in thought.

I must move before I can think too much about it, because Warren's eyes snap over to mine and he's instantly moving toward me.

"Nic, hey," he whispers, as I turn my face to the side. I feel clammy all over, my body alternating between hot and cold.

"What happened?" I barely manage, trying to force more air into my lungs.

"You're sick," he replies, reaching for something on the table before bringing it in front of my face. It's a glass of water and a straw. He lifts me, just a bit, and I drink my fill. After I'm finished, he sets it back on the table, then props me up further. For a second I think I'm going to fade again, but somehow I hold on.

"How long have I been out?"

"Two days."

"What?" I glance at him sharply, making my head spin with the jerky movement.

"Hey, take it easy. You've been in and out. Addie tried to see if they can break through the spell, but nothing worked. I was . . . terrified."

Warren's voice is but a whisper at that last word, and it squeezes at my heart. I've come to see him as this strong capable figure, but here he is, a bit vulnerable at my bedside.

"I'm okay," I say, reaching out and placing my hand over his where it rests on the bed. His eyes zero in on the contact, and I can see his shoulders relax. It's as if he's been waiting for this specific moment.

"There's one more thing," he says, looking up at me once more.

"What is it?"

"Your hair . . ."

I reach for my locks immediately, but they're still there. Confusion shadows my vision, but then Warren reaches over and brings a lock in front of my face. I look down to find my hair no longer brown, but silver.

"What happened?" I want to jump up and go look at myself in the mirror, because if there is one thing I love about myself, it is my hair. When I turned eighteen I was going to experiment with different colors and styles, as a rite of passage, since it's always grown so fast anyway.

"It started changing when you passed out. We don't know what it means. Or if it'll last."

"I need to see," I say softly, holding tears at bay. I never thought of myself as a vain girl, but my hair was something that was mine. Suddenly, Warren's arms are around me, and he's lifting me up.

"What are you doing?" I would've squealed if I had that much energy. He holds me close to his body, and I entwine my hand around his neck.

"Helping you see."

He carries me over to the bathroom, placing me carefully on the countertop. We're almost eye to eye, and at first, he's all I can look at. My stomach is filled with nervous butterflies as I watch his own eyes darken in awareness. I lick my lips, and his gaze flickers there before it's back on mine. I think this is the moment I've dreamed about my whole life, as he leans closer. But before our lips can touch, the door to my room opens, and Ric walks in, followed by Cece.

"How are you feeling?" the angel asks, giving me a quick study.

"Awake," I reply, glancing in the mirror. My hair is completely silver, matted and dirty from sweat, but still very shiny.

"Glad to see you up." Cece directs my attention back to her. "We were worried." She glances at Warren, then gives me a warm smile. I'm sure I'm blushing.

"I don't know what happened," I say, shrugging my shoulders. "Something clicked in that gym. I remember my head spinning and being blinded by a light and then everything going dark."

"Nothing else?"

"No, I . . ." My mouth stops working as my head spins once more. Warren catches me in his arms before I can topple off the counter, cradling me to his chest. I cling to him as if my life depends on it, pushing the dizziness away.

"Get her back to bed," I hear Ric say, before I'm being carried once again. Warren places me gently on top of the covers, and before I can form a coherent thought, I'm gone.

The next time I'm fully awake, I'm so thirsty I can't even swallow. I know I've been in and out, but at this moment, I'm finally feeling a bit like me. Raising myself onto my elbows, I look around and find Warren sleeping. He's still in the chair, but his head is on the bed next to my legs. He looks so young with his eyes closed. I think it's because I can't see the intensity behind them, the history he carries with him. The desire to run my fingers through his hair is uncontrollable. It's soft to the touch, as delicate as a feather.

He opens his eyes, but doesn't move, and for some reason, I don't stop. I continue my exploration, growing bolder to the point where I move my fingers lightly over his cheek and chin. His lids fall for a second, then he's looking at me once more. There's that intensity I've come to admire. I pull my hand back as he sits up.

"You look better," he says, studying me as if his life depends on it.

"I feel less . . ." I try to say, but my throat is dry. Warren reaches over and hands me a cup of water, and I drain it completely. "I feel less . . . unbalanced," I reply honestly, not sure what I mean by that but knowing it's true.

"You've been out for a while."

"How long is a while?"

"Three days."

I gasp, shocked at losing so much time. Five days in total that I've been completely out of commission. It feels like I've been hit with a very bad flu. My whole body feels sticky, and I'm pretty sure I smell.

"Tell me what happened."

"You had a fever for two straight days. Then your body temperature went the opposite direction, moving to cold then hot again, and we couldn't elicit any kind of responses. There was magic at work, unlike anything this place has seen."

I don't remember anything, so it's not like I can give him any answers. Instead, I ask him another question.

"Did you stay with me the whole time?" I whisper.

"I did," he replies, not breaking eye contact. I'm not sure what this thing inside me is, but right here and now it grows into something huge. And I know without a shadow of a doubt that Warren is it for me. Maybe it's crazy to know that at a young age, but I don't think I will ever meet another person, human or supernatural, who's going to fit into the crook of my heart like Warren does.

"Can you stay a while longer?" I ask.

"I'm not going anywhere."

And it feels like a promise that goes much further than staying with me today.

"I'd like to take a shower," I say, scooting down the bed. Warren doesn't hesitate. He stands, pulling me carefully with him and leading me to the bathroom.

"I'll be here."

I take that promise and tuck it into my heart. Forever.

CHAPTER 11

The water feels heavenly against my skin. I wash my now silver hair, still amazed at the change. I'll have to figure out if there is a reason for this, just like there must've been for the spell. I focus on trying to remember anything from when I was out. There's something nagging at the back of my mind that I can't quite pinpoint. There were colors and numbers and emotions, but nothing I can hold on to for long. A knocking on the door makes me jump.

"Are you okay?" Warren's voice comes through muffled.

"Almost done," I reply. As quickly as I can, I dry off and put on my pajamas. Carefully, with calculated moves, I make it out of the bathroom in one piece. Warren is standing by the window and turns when I walk out.

"I called Ric, letting him know you're much better. He's relieved. He'll let the others know."

I nod, but don't comment, making my way slowly to the bed. I'm sure I'll be interrogated a few times, but I have nothing new to tell them. This is the time when I would ask my mom for help.

"Hey." Warren is suddenly kneeling in front of me, his eyes full of concern. "It's going to be okay."

He reaches over, catching a stray tear, and that's when I realize I'm crying. Everything in my life feels so unmanageable. I've been spinning out of control since I found our apartment in disarray. The only time I've felt grounded is with Warren near. That is scary all on its own.

I look up at him, trying to find the words for what I want to say, but he must not need them. He takes a seat beside me and pulls me into his arms. I cling to him as the tears fall, letting all my sadness and frustration out. I've never cried this much in my life, but here we are again.

"You keep saying that," I mumble against his chest, "but I don't know if I'll ever be okay."

"I know you will, Niccola," Warren replies, and there's no doubt in his voice. "You are the strongest person I've met, and I've met plenty of people. Both young and old. Your spirit will see you through. I have no doubts."

"Well, that makes one of us."

"You're stronger than you give yourself credit for," he says, and I shake my head against his chest.

"You only say that because you like me," I joke, but I can feel his body tense instantly.

"I do like you, Niccola," he whispers, and I know he means it with every part of his soul. I can feel it too. I want to tell him just how much he means to me. I want to accept that I'm never going to be the same. Not without him. But what can we do? Exchange phone numbers and emails when I leave? Because I am leaving. I . . .

"Phone number."

"What?"

I sit up, pushing back from Warren as he looks down at me. There's that nagging thought in my mind again, trying to push through my confusion. He doesn't say anything else, waiting me out as I try to sort myself out.

"Phone number. I remember numbers, and I think it's a phone number."

Warren reaches over and hands me my phone. Carefully, I push all the numbers I can remember into the screen, and when I'm done, it does make up a phone number.

"What is this from?"

"I have no idea. But while I was out, I know I dreamt. Or something. And I remember these numbers. Like they're important."

"Then let's dial."

I glance at him before pushing the button. The phone rings and rings, and after a while, the answering machine picks up.

"Well, at least we know it's a real phone number," Warren says as I disconnect. I stare at the phone, unable to push away the nagging. It feels like I'm missing something. Something big.

"Hey, let's worry about this in the morning." Warren takes the phone out of my hands, and I realize it's two in the morning. I do feel tired, even though I've slept for days. When I move back against the headboard, Warren settles into his chair.

"Could you . . ." I begin, and his eyes fly up to meet mine. That one look gives me the boldness I need to ask the question I want. "Could you stay with me?"

"I am."

"Here." I point to the side of the bed, embarrassment heating up my cheeks. It's so quiet in the room, I feel inclined to hold my breath. But then Warren moves, and the spell is broken. Carefully, he takes a step toward the bed, as I slide down to my back. After another moment, he lies down beside me, a few inches between us. This is the first time I've ever invited a guy into my bed, but I've never felt like I wanted to until this exact moment.

With him beside me, I don't hesitate to relax and let dreamland take me.

Two days go by before I'm feeling better. It's like whatever the sickness was, it drained all my energy. I'm still feeling the effects, but at least I'm back to being outside. Even though this weather is kicking my butt.

Warren sets a cup of coffee in front of me, bringing me out of my thoughts. I've been spending a lot of time at Coffee Haven. Since I ventured outside, all the people I've met have come by to check on me. It's heartwarming to know how close-knit this community is. The thought also brings sadness, because I know I'll be leaving it soon. As soon as I figure out where to go.

"Hey, what are you thinking about?" Warren asks, gently running his fingers over the top of my hand. Since my sickness, he's been staying close and sleeping beside me every night. We don't touch, and we haven't talked about us in so many words, but I know I scared him.

"I'm thinking that I don't know where to go from here," I reply honestly. I don't want to hide my feelings from him, or from myself. A part of me from before would've put on a brave face. But the part of me from right now just wants someone to share everything with.

"We'll figure this out."

"You keep saying that, but there's nothing more to figure out," I say, but there's no venom in my voice. Just sadness. "It's time for me to move on, to search somewhere else, but I've got nothing. No family to go back to. I'm not sure what waits for me at home."

"You could always stay."

I glance at him sharply, but he's not looking at me. His eyes are on where his hand continues to dance over my skin. There's nothing more I would want than to stay here. But we both know it's just wishful thinking.

I'm not even old enough to be on my own. My savings are running dry. I'll have nowhere to live soon enough. If I'm hoping to find my mother, I'll need to go sooner rather than later. So instead of pouring my heart out to Warren, I turn my hand over and latch on to his.

"Maybe in another life," I whisper, and he looks at me then.

There's so much emotion there, it makes my chest hurt. In that moment, the pull I've felt toward him intensifies a hundred times over, and it's all I can do to stay seated. His hand trembles under mine for a moment, and I think he feels it too. We cling to each other as if we're making a promise, but it's a promise neither one of us will be able to keep.

~

"What do you think you'll do next?" Warren asks, as we walk out of Coffee Haven. There are a lot more people on the street now, tourists coming in for the winter break. It feels unreal to think that there's a whole other world underneath this regular one.

"I think going back to our coven would be the best," I reply reluctantly. It's the last thing I want to do. When I called and checked in with them a week ago, they hadn't even noticed we'd been gone. I guess that's what happens when the rules of close-knit, thirteen-member covens go out the window. Although, maybe it's just the coven back in Palmdale. The one in Havenwood Falls seems to be doing just fine.

"When I spoke to them, they did say I will have a place to stay. And they'll help any way they can."

They're not a bad coven, but they don't feel like mine anymore. Nothing from before Havenwood Falls does.

Warren stays quiet as we walk, and I wonder what he's thinking. We don't seem to have a destination in mind. It's like we both need this time together, as much of it as we can get, while we can.

Suddenly, Warren stops in his tracks, and I turn to face him. He runs his hand over his hair, looking a little awkward all of a sudden.

"Warren?"

"Would you like to go to dinner with me?" he blurts out a little too loud. A few people glance over, with big smiles on their faces, as Warren continues to fidget. Considering we've had almost every meal together for a week, it's strange for him to be nervous. But then I realize he's asking me on a date.

"Yes," I reply without hesitation. His grin blinds me for a second, then he steps closer and tentatively reaches for my hand, as if giving me a choice to pull away. Instead, I meet him halfway, twining our hands together. Sure, we've held hands before, but this feels different. It feels like a beginning.

His phone rings then, and he shrugs apologetically before reaching for it. I take a step away from him to give him some privacy, but he tugs me to stay close. Smiling internally, I tuck myself into his side and wait for him to finish up.

"I can be there in ten minutes," Warren says into the phone, glancing down at me. I nod to let him know it's okay, and we turn to head back to the inn.

After Warren leaves, I sit on the bed, trying to figure out what I'm going to wear. I didn't exactly pack formalwear or anything special. But for Warren, I wanted to dress special. Heading to the bathroom, I stare at myself in the mirror. I don't even recognize myself anymore. It's not just the fact that my hair is silver now, or the fact that I look a little paler than usual. There's a sort of maturity around my eyes that wasn't there before.

I wonder what my mom would think if she saw me now. Would I still look like her little girl or am I a grown woman now? Is there really an age on that or just experience?

As I run my hands over my long locks, a sudden urge almost overtakes me. Marching back into the room, I grab a pair of scissors before walking back over to the mirror. Before I can think too much of it, I take a handful of my hair and cut it right below my collarbone. The weight falls off, and it's like I've been waiting for this. I've wanted to cut my hair this short for years, but Mom always said I'd regret it if it doesn't grow back. Even though my hair grows fast. Now, I'm making this decision for me, and it feels amazing.

I finish cutting my hair in no time at all, and I have to say,

I'm a huge fan. I style it the best I can, without any heating tools. I'd love to see it straightened, but that'll have to wait. I go for a more dramatic look with my eye makeup, drawing a thicker and longer cat eye. After a few quick swipes with my mascara, I'm satisfied. I still have nothing to wear, but I decide my black T-shirt and black jeans will look good against the silver hair.

The only thing that's missing now is lipstick. The bright red is my armor, my wall of protection. And right now, it makes me look badass.

I look like the version of myself that I've always seen inside my head. I guess it's true what they say—experiences mold us, in a way nothing else can. I definitely don't feel seventeen anymore. And maybe that's okay.

When the knock on the door comes, I'm ready. I swing the door open to find Warren on the other side, dressed in a dark blue shirt and dark slacks. As cliché as it may be, he takes my breath away. I don't know if anyone else ever will, the way he does. This feels like a magic all on its own.

"You look amazing," he finally says, his eyes roaming over me. "Love the haircut."

I beam at him, every reservation forgotten. The anticipation of tonight has my whole body buzzing. Sure, I've been on dates. But nothing has had me this excited before.

"You ready to go?" Warren asks, and I nod. Walking back into the room, I reach for his jacket, pulling it over my shoulders. It messes with the whole look, since it's so much bigger than I am, but I wouldn't trade it for anything. I turn to see him already grinning at me. If I was a mind reader, I'd guess he likes that I'm still wearing it.

"Let's go," I say.

But before I can take two steps, my phone buzzes, surprising me. I haven't received a phone call in a while. Glancing down, I find the number I called earlier staring back at me. With FaceTime attached to it.

"What is it?" Warren asks, instantly by my side. Turning the phone, I show him the screen.

"Answer it."

I nod and slide the button over. A face comes into the frame, and it makes my head spin.

"Mom."

CHAPTER 12

"Niccola." Her voice sounds exactly how I remember it, but there's a hint of exhaustion on her face that I'm not used to.

"Mom, are you okay? Where are you?"

"What did you do to your hair?"

We talk over each other, then burst out laughing. Seeing her frees me in a whole new way, and I reach for Warren's hand, gripping it tightly. He's still beside me, just out of frame, as I take a seat on the bed.

"I'm so sorry, Nic," my mom says, tears pooling in her eyes. "I never meant for any of this to happen."

"What happened?"

"My past caught up with me."

"I'm going to need more than that, Mom," I say, not pulling any punches. My tone makes her pause, and then she smiles.

"You are so grown up, Nic. I'm sorry for that. I know I pushed you when I disappeared. But it was the only way to keep you safe."

"From what?"

"Some very bad people."

"That's not enough, Mom. This hair? It wasn't by choice. I was sick. A spell did this. I've been worried. I've been left alone with no one to turn to. I need answers, and I need them now."

Warren squeezes my hand in solidarity, and I glance at him for just a moment. But it's enough. Mom sees it.

"Who's there with you?" The alarm in her voice is evident, so I have no choice. I tug Warren into frame.

"This is Warren. He's a deputy. He's been helping me."

"So you've found it."

Warren and I startle at that, sharing another look. She's not making much sense, and I tell her as much.

"Do you remember your grandmother?" Mom asks, instead of answering my question.

"Yeah, she was . . ." But I stop before I get any further, because new images assault me. I'm seven years old, my grandmother and mom are in front of me, arguing about binding my powers. Binding my shifter side. Then they fight, with their magic, to a point where grandmother is banished from our house forever.

"You kicked her out?" I ask, incredulous. Warren glances over at me, but I can't take my eyes off my mother.

"There was a lot you saw as a child that you should've never seen, Nic," Mom replies, regret filling her eyes. "The only good thing your grandmother did was to suppress your memories."

"So, what? I activated a spell that brought them back?"

"You did. It's blood magic, Nic. Wherever you are, something triggered the spell to dissipate it. It's tied heavily to our emotions."

"How did I know to call this number?"

"I made you memorize it when you were little."

My mom exhales visibly, her eyes on mine. Even through the phone screen, I can feel her regret. Her worries over her decisions.

"I'm sorry I left you, Nic," she apologizes once more. "I'm sorry there was no other way. I had to do what I had to do. For both of us."

"What did you do, Mom?"

At first, she doesn't answer. Then she glances to her left, and I realize someone else is there with her. Warren's hand tightens on mine, as if he's making sure I know he's there. And then, *he* steps into the frame.

"Dad?"

"Hello, Nic," my father says, leaning over my mom's shoulder. He looks much like his high school basketball photo, with just a few more years of wear on him. "It's nice to finally talk to you."

"You're . . . what do you mean?" I stumble over my words, trying to find meaning in what I'm seeing and hearing. This is not how I expected the day to go.

"The last time I saw you, you were barely a few years old," my dad says, a small smile on his face that looks much like my own. "I'm sorry I've been gone for so long."

"Please stop apologizing, both of you," I snap, fed up with all of this. Warren trades his hand in mine, putting his right one behind me and rubbing my back a little. I sink into the feeling of him beside me.

"Was Dad one of the things I was meant to forget?" It's taking everything in me not to scream. "I need answers, and I'm done listening to excuses. Why did you both abandon me?"

There are tears in my eyes that I'm not fighting. They've hurt me, in a way a child shouldn't be hurt. I've ignored that this whole time because I wanted to find them. But now that they're in front of me, I won't hide my feelings.

"Oh, Nic," Mom says, reaching towards the screen. "I'm so . . ."

"No. I don't want to hear it."

"We can't tell you everything right now. We're . . ."

The connection freezes for a second, cutting off whatever Mom was going to say.

"Mom?"

The spinning wheel of doom shows up, and I squeeze the phone tighter in my hand.

"We'll explain everything," Mom says, coming back online. "Soon."

Then she reaches over and shuts the call off. Tears spill free as I stare at the black screen, until Warren pulls me into his arms and holds me while I cry all of my frustration out.

~

We stay like that for a while, with Warren holding me tightly, as if with just his arms, he can protect me from the world. But I know I can't stay like this forever, so with great difficulty, I push myself away.

"What now?" I ask, wiping my tears away. I'm sure I look like a mess, most of my makeup smeared down my face. But I can't bring myself to get up, to move away from him. He's holding my hands in his, and it's the only thing keeping me from spiraling.

"I wish I could tell you, Nic," he replies, his voice coated with emotion. "But this is a decision you need to make for yourself."

"I know."

In that moment, I wish for my magic. I can feel it in my blood, in every breath, but I wish I could just let it all out. Send the wind spinning, just so I know I can do something right.

"I'll be leaving in the morning," I announce, coming to a decision right then and there. There's no point in prolonging this, and now that I know my parents are alive, maybe our coven can help me track them down. The longer I stay, the more I don't want to go, so I need to rip off the Band-Aid.

Warren doesn't say anything at first, but I can feel the tension radiating off his body. I'm not sure if there's really anything to say. He knows this is what must be done.

"You know, I'm glad I met you, Niccola Knight-Summers," he whispers, and I grin through the tears.

"I kind of like the sound of that."

"It has a nice ring to it."

We sit in silence, both of us trying to figure out what to do or say next. But all I can think of is how much I wish my life was different.

"Some date this turned out to be," I comment, wiping more

tears off my cheeks. Warren reaches over, his own hand following suit, as he studies my face carefully.

"I wouldn't trade it for anything," he replies.

I smile, even though my heart is breaking. There's one thing I do want before I leave, and I think that we both owe ourselves this one moment.

"Can I ask you for something?"

"Anything."

"Can you let me see your wolf?"

He stares at me for a long moment, then nods. I've seen his wolf before, but this feels more personal. Something between just the two of us. Two people meeting on the same playing field.

I close my eyes as I let his magic wash over me and then I feel a small pressure on my hand. Looking up, I find his gorgeous wolf in front of me. He's so big, he comes up to my chest. Even in the dim light, his dark fur glows, and his eyes pierce right through me.

I reach over, plunging my hand into the fur, and I swear he sighs the same moment I do. Without hesitation, I let my hands explore over him, memorizing this form, if only for a small time.

"My magic doesn't allow me to shift," I whisper, as if telling him a secret, "but I can light up the sky."

I let it pool in my palm, the energy from within me, and then I throw it up in the air. The whole room brightens with twinkling lights, dancing around the two of us like stars. Warren shifts while I'm still looking at the ceiling, and I feel his hand take mine.

"You are pretty incredible," he says softly, and I meet his eye, my magic twirling over our skin.

"Right back at ya," I reply, and before I lose my nerve, I ask, "How do you keep your clothes within the shift?"

"It was a gift." I can hear the smile in his voice before I even glance at him. "The Hawthornes enchanted the shift before I left as a way to help me. I was lost back then, missing a part of myself. I'm not so lost anymore."

Every nerve in my body is reaching out to him, but I don't know if I will be able to leave if I give in to it now. Warren doesn't push, but I see the desire mirrored in his own eyes. He's leaving it in my hands once again, and I do the only thing I can. I save us both when I let go and move away.

"I'll come by tomorrow morning," Warren says, moving away as my magic disappears. Just like that, we're back to being polite acquaintances. I want to ask him to stay and sleep beside me one last time, but that feels like too much.

So I walk him to the door, and I lock it behind him. I go back to the bed and lie down on it, clutching his coat to my chest, as tears fall down my cheeks.

CHAPTER 13

"*A*re you sure this is what you want to do?" Sherry asks, as we stand in the lobby of Whisper Falls Inn. The place has become like a home to me, and I'm sad to be leaving it. Warren must've called them, because both Sherry and Cece meet me downstairs in the morning. The sheriff came by earlier to check on me as well.

"Now that I know she's out there—they're both out there," I say, "there's nothing for me here."

"Are you certain of that?" Cece asks, just as Warren walks through the doors. My eyes catch on his, and no, I'm not certain. But it is what I must do. It doesn't matter how I feel, or what I want. I turn to the angel, tears pooling in my eyes.

"Thank you for your kindness," I say, and Cece pulls me into her arms. Her warmth envelops me, and I cling to her for a moment longer. Then Sherry is there, pulling me into a hug, and I feel like my heart is shattering right here, in front of them.

"I wouldn't have survived without you two," I say, because even though our friendship is brief, I feel like they're the older sisters I've always wished I had. But also the motherly encouragement I needed. I wish I could say I would never forget them, and a part of me thinks I won't. I'll carry their kindness in my heart forever, even if my memories are gone.

"If the winds ever carry you this way, I hope you find us," Cece comments softly, before she and Sherry leave. Each of them give Warren a look, and then they're gone.

"Well, deputy in training," I begin, my whole body buzzing with heartbreak. "I say you've nailed this assignment. Will that earn you your merit badge?"

"I think I might have a chance of adding one to my sash." He smiles, but it doesn't reach his eyes. We both know we're just prolonging the inevitable. But I still can't make myself move. I want to hold onto this moment for as long as I can, even though I won't remember it soon.

"What will you do when you find them?"

I'm grateful he says *when* and not *if.* I need all the confidence I can get right now.

"Demand answers. Maybe yell at them a little and be a typical angsty teenager."

Warren chuckles, and once again, I grab that sound and tuck it into my heart. Maybe I'm being an angsty teenager right now. Maybe I'm being melodramatic. But this right here, it's all I ever wanted, and I want to be selfish and stay.

Taking a deep breath, I walk toward him, knowing that if I don't do this now, I won't be able to do it later. Warren accepts it, and for a second, I wish he didn't. The romantic side of me that I try so hard to repress wants him to fight for me. Wants that epic movie moment where the guy won't let the girl go. But the mature side of me knows that what he's doing, supporting me in this quest of mine, is more important. We're both acting in the best interest of the other, and what is more romantic than that?

The shuttle for the airport sits outside, and the same kind man who drove me here is standing by the open passenger door. Warren and I take our time walking over, not touching, but staying close enough to each other that I can feel his body heat. I'm still wearing his coat, and when we finally stop by the van, I go to shrug it off. His hand lands on my upper arm, halting the process.

"Keep it," he whispers, looking me straight in the eye for the first time this morning. "It'll keep you warm."

And just like that, I'm a puddle of mush, and I reach for him, just as he reaches for me. His arms pull me close, and I tuck myself into him as if I've been custom made for this exact spot. We stand like that, the only two people in the world. A witch and a shifter. Holding on to each other as if our lives depend on it.

"I wish . . ." Warren begins, but I shake my head into his chest. I can't allow him to give me the words, because when I forget them, he won't. This whole time, he hasn't just been protecting me. I've been protecting him. It's why, no matter how much I want to, I can't let myself be selfish and kiss him. I can't let him carry that within his memory, when I won't.

"You're a great deputy, Warren Nichols. You will serve this town well."

"And you, Niccola Knight-Summers, are the most amazing person I have ever met, and you will have a wonderful life."

Tears stain his sweater, but I don't try to hide them. Or how much my heart is breaking. Before either of us can say anything else, I'm pulling away and rushing to the van. Without a look at Warren, I tuck myself in between the seats, my body shaking with silent tears. The driver doesn't question me. But I can feel his eyes in the mirror as he gets behind the wheel. I keep my eyes downcast, until I can't any more. As we pull away, I twist in my seat, my gaze finding Warren. My heart pounds with an intensity that makes my chest hurt as I watch the first guy I've ever loved grow smaller and smaller in the rearview window.

When we pull up to the airport terminal entrance, I feel like I'm coming out of a fog. Tugging my backpack over my shoulder, I pull the coat close to my body as I get out of the van. The movement makes me pause, and I glance down at said coat with confusion. My memory is fuzzy, and I can't quite remember where I got it, but it seems important. My phone dings with a reminder, and I glance down at my ticket.

Something happened, something monumental, but I can't seem to place my finger on it. I glance around, but nothing seems to stand out. Shrugging, I head into the airport. Clearly, Colorado was a bust.

When it's time for my flight, I'm asleep as soon as I sit down in my seat. Exhaustion coats my bones and weighs down my mind. I feel different somehow, but without recalling what happened to me, I can't begin to guess.

The flight doesn't take long, and when I wake up, it's like I haven't rested at all. There was something in my dream, though—a jasmine branch—and I reach for my wrist, almost expecting to see it tattooed there. But there's nothing.

It's like I'm walking through water, just moving from point A to point B, with no coherent plan. I know I bought a ticket, and when I get off the plane, I'm back in my hometown. I know I found out something about my mother, but I can't remember what. I've never felt so lost in my life. By the time I reach our apartment, my face is stained with silent tears and my head is full of pain.

I don't hesitate to lock the door behind me and go straight to my room and my bed, ignoring the mess that still clutters the floor. Lying down, I pull the coat closer to my body, soaking up the comfort it offers, and close my eyes. The tears continue to fall, and for the first time for as long as I can remember, I don't hide from my emotions. I let myself feel it all.

Sometime later, a noise wakes me. I'm not sure how long I've been in this weird semiconscious state, but something pulls me out of it. Carefully, I get off the bed, my battle magic at the ready. It feels good to have it rush through my body, as if I'd been holding myself back before. When I creep over to the partially shut door, I see the shape of a large body in the moonlight. Without hesitation, I step into the living room with a shout.

"Hey!"

The person turns, and my battle magic flies out as a shield around him. But before I can completely disarm him, my mother is there, waving her arms.

"Nic, it's us!"

I drop my hand, relief washing over me like a big wave.

"Mom!"

We rush to each other, and she hugs me close, holding me up in the process because it feels like every ounce of energy I had has gone out of my body. I shudder against her, and more tears leak through my tightly shut lids.

"I'm so sorry, Nic," Mom mumbles against my hair, rubbing my back gently. "I'm so sorry I left you to deal with all this. I'm sorry I kept things from you. I'm so sorry."

"It's okay," I say, pulling back. "You're here now. And you're not alone?"

I haven't forgotten about the man standing at my mom's back. Glancing at him now, I realize he looks a little familiar. He's watching me carefully, as if afraid I'll get spooked again.

"Oh, Nic. This man . . . this is your father."

Shock chills me to the bone as I stare at the person I've never met before, the one I've fantasized about for most of my life. What would it be like to meet him? What would I feel if he suddenly showed up? I thought all I'd feel is joy. But right now, I'm full of questions and caution. Whatever happened changed me. Made me more grown up than my teenage years. And I hold on to that now.

"I think . . ." I glance between my mom and this stranger. "You'd better explain yourselves."

And that's what they do.

CHAPTER 14

"When your father and I met, we were both running from something. Your grandmother forbade the two of us to be together, and I never understood that, because she wouldn't explain. "

"But you got together anyway."

"Love is the most powerful of magics, Nic," the man who is my father speaks up, his eyes intensely on mine. "It breaks through our own spells and rules. I loved your mother the moment I saw her in that parking lot."

"I don't believe in love at first sight," I say, and for some reason, it doesn't taste as true as it used to.

"Do you believe in soul mates?"

The question makes me pause, because a few weeks ago my answer would've been a complete no. But now, something stops me, and I don't understand it.

"That's what I thought," my father says with a knowing smile. "When two people, magic or otherwise, are meant to be together, the rules fly out the window. It's what brought us together," he continues, glancing at my mom. "It's what kept us going all these years."

"But why send me to find my father?" I exclaim, throwing my hands up in the air, "if you knew where he was?"

"I never knew where he was. He left to keep us safe. I had to lead the danger away from our doorstep, and I knew that if anything happened to me, he would be the only person to help you."

"Safe from what?" I stand up, needing to pace, to dispel some of this nervous energy rushing through me.

"From the reason why I had to leave in the first place."

I turn to my father then, picking up on the regret he's feeling, but I'm still not ready to forgive him.

"Explain."

"I come from a very prominent pack," he begins, his gaze on me unwavering. "My father, the alpha, did something that caused a huge fallout, way before I was in the picture. It's too complicated to get into now, and even I don't know the whole story. All I know is that blood must be spilled as repayment—my blood. He thought we would be safe, but we weren't. He sent me away when I was younger, to train, to keep me safe. But as I grew older, the past caught up to me. I'd been on the run for years, and then I met your mother. I thought we could be safe together. But after you were born, you were taken."

"What?" I freeze in my tracks.

"Those who wanted to harm my pack found us and took you, until I promised to return with them. It wasn't a hard choice, Niccola. I gave you up—I gave you both up—to keep you safe. And I would do it all over again."

I didn't think I could feel anything more for this man, but he's shattering my every expectation. I glance at my mother and find her crying silently. It must've broken her, but she pulled herself together and she raised me on her own. All of her lessons, all of her instructions now made sense. She was training me to take care of myself.

"They didn't know then what a powerful witch you would become," my father continues, bringing my attention back to him.

"Half witch, half shifter. Both sides from powerful clans. You're the one they want now."

"They're after me?"

"It's why we sent you to Colorado. We've been working on hunting these supes down, but it'll take time. And you needed to be as far away from us as possible."

With that, I turn away, walking over to the window. Everything they're saying makes sense, but it still doesn't bring back my memories. All I remember is a small pretty town. And some skiing tourists. But I can't bring up anything else. I feel like I'm missing a vital part of myself, and I have no idea why. Taking a deep breath, I turn back to my parents.

"So what now?"

"Now"—my mother stands, walking over to stand in front of me, as she takes both of my hands in hers—"now you go back."

"What? What do you mean?"

"Wherever you were, you were safe. We couldn't even find you. That means you'll be safe there. We're close, Nic. We're close to figuring this out. You need a home. A place you can finish growing up, in safety I can no longer provide you."

"Mom, you can't be serious. Let me help you!"

"This is our fight," Mom says, running her hand over my face. "Yours will come sooner than you think. But I need you to be a kid for a little longer and let us handle this."

"I don't want to. Not when I just got you back." I've never sounded so young, even to my own ears.

"We're never too far away, honey," my mom says, pulling me into her arms once more. After a moment, we both turn to my father, and he stands in one fluid motion before he hugs us both.

I hold on to my parents, hold on to the truths they told me. The sacrifices they made. And I vow to myself that I will always be the best person I can be. I will make them proud.

~

Five days later, my mother and I are standing on the side of the road next to a rental car in Colorado. I spent three glorious days with my parents, getting to know my dad and both of them as a couple. But then real life set in, and he took off to give Mom a chance to bring me back to Colorado. We took quite a few precautions, flying to places nowhere near here, and cloaking ourselves in half a dozen spells. Now we're in a truck stop in Durango. Without knowing where we're going or what we're looking for, Mom and I decided to drive around to see if we can find whatever we need.

Just as Mom heads back to the car, a van pulls up that looks vaguely familiar. It's the same type of van I got out of at the airport.

"Mom!" I exclaim, feeling a pull toward the pictures on the vehicle.

"What is it?"

"I think—I think we should follow that bus."

She watches me for a tense moment, then glances at the van and the people piling in. Without hesitation, she nods, and we get into the rental.

The drive is twisty, but Mom keeps up with the van well enough. The closer we are to the shuttle, the more determined I feel that this is a sign. That we need to be here. When we pass the *Welcome* sign, it flashes in my memory, but I still can't place where I've seen it before.

Main Street spreads out in front of us, and we pull up a few spaces away from where the van parks. For a moment, I can't seem to move. Everything about this place calls to me, and I don't understand it.

My mom gasps, and I turn to her instantly. I find her eyes are full of tears, and I reach for her, alarmed.

"Mom?"

"Oh my, I remember this place."

"I don't understand." I wait for her to explain, but she just watches the street through the windshield, tears running down her face.

"It's okay, honey," she says, patting my hand. "You will."

She gets out of the car, reaching for her phone. I have no idea who she's calling, but she walks off far enough that I can't hear what's being said. I stand on the side of the street, watching the town, fascinated by all the holiday decorations and snow. I don't think I've ever seen so much snow in my life. Again, something prickles the back of my mind, but I can't quite place it.

"We're all set," Mom says, coming up to stand beside me. She takes my hand, gripping it tightly, and I want to ask her what's going on.

But then a dark blue Toyota 4Runner pulls to the side of the road, and a door opens. Mom and I turn, hand in hand, as a body steps out.

"Hello, Ms. Summers," the man speaks, still covered by the light of the headlights. "I've been sent to retrieve Nic . . . Niccola."

I don't miss the way his voice catches or the familiarity with which he speaks my name. My mom greets him in return as he steps around the vehicle. Gorgeous, like the break of dawn, the guy can't be but a few years older than me. His dark blue eyes meet mine, and in that moment, my whole world rights itself.

It becomes hard to breathe as images assault me, one after the other.

His smile.

His touch.

His reassuring presence.

My mom calls out to me, but it's like I have tunnel vision, and he's the light at the end. I feel a buzzing start in my chest and spread out across my body. I'm hot and elated and completely enthralled by the sight of him.

"Warren," I breathe out finally.

His eyes flash with surprise, quickly overshadowed by desire. We move at the same time; I throw myself at him and he catches me and holds me close. He feels like coming home, and I hope I never have to know what losing him feels like. It's as if all of my limbs are finally properly working again, as if the darkness has lifted.

He sets me down on my feet, gazing down at me in wonder. And something else.

"You remember everything?" he asks, not taking his eyes off me, and I nod.

"You're bonded."

Warren and I turn to my mother, standing just a few feet away with a soft smile on her face.

"Bonded?" I ask, as I reach for Warren's hand and entwine our fingers together. Mom doesn't miss the gesture, nodding her head carefully.

"Remember how your father said there is a magic stronger than ours?"

"Love," I say, blushing as I glance at Warren. "He said love is more powerful."

"And even more so, the soul mate bond."

"But we're not—" I begin, but can't finish. Because Mom's words make sense. The pull I've felt toward him since the moment I met him, the feeling of belonging. The pain of my heart breaking when I drove away. The memories of him returning the moment I set my eyes on him. It happened so fast, but it's the only thing in my life that makes sense like no other.

"We are," Warren says, looking deeply into my eyes.

I want to pull him close and finally find out what he tastes like, but I'm not about to do that in front of my mother. When I turn to her, she steps toward me, opening up her arms.

"Now I can rest easy, knowing you will be not only safe, but loved."

I hold onto her, realizing she must remember this town. Her memory came back faster than mine did.

"You remember?" I ask.

"I do. And I wish I could carry that memory with me. I wish I could share it with your father."

"Maybe one day, you can come back here and you will."

I cling to her, realizing that she'll be leaving and forgetting all about where I am. And I will have no way of reaching her. Dad has made arrangements for finances for me, so I know I'll be taken care of on that front.

"You are a strong, smart, beautiful girl," Mom says, pulling back to look me in the eyes. "You are going to do amazingly well in school, and you will have a good life. Just be brave, Nic. Stay brave."

CHAPTER 15

The next week goes by in a blur. Mom and Dad are gone who knows where, and they have no idea where I am. The Luna Coven's magic is strong, and my mom no longer remembers where she dropped me off. Or the fact that she knew my dad when they were younger. It'll be up to me to find them when the time is right.

My jasmine tattoo is now a permanent addition to my wrist, and I had Addie add a moon behind it. I don't want to forget that I come from two worlds. My witch and my shifter side are each a part of me, and now I accept them both.

Sherry and Cece have helped me get my apartment in order. I'm now a resident of Havenwood Village, and as weird as it seems to be living on my own, I'm not opposed to it. It feels like the natural next step in my life. And I won't be a child for much longer. My birthday is a little over a month away.

It's funny how things work out sometimes. A month ago I didn't know what I would do with my life. But here I am, getting ready to finish high school at an actual school. Looking for a part time job so I can buy some decorations for my apartment. And going on a first date with a guy I'm completely crazy about.

I look at myself in the mirror, running my hand over my

silvery locks. I've come to appreciate my new color. Mom said the spell must've activated my shifter gene. Silver is the color of Dad's wolf. It's kind of cool that I get to carry that part of him with me everywhere I go.

My dress is black and simple. I've got black leggings on underneath, with tall black boots. Getting used to this weather is going to take a while. For some reason, I definitely didn't inherit my dad's shifter temperature regulator. The knock comes as I'm applying my signature red lipstick.

"You look incredible," Warren says the moment I open the door. He's wearing dark slacks and a dark sweater, and he makes my knees buckle. I smile and reach for the coat.

"Didn't you get a warmer coat?" he asks, as I shrug on the coat he gave me. I grin at him, stepping close and twining my hand through his.

"But this one is my favorite."

He grins, leading me out of the apartment and to his truck.

"Where are we going?" I ask, as he opens the door for me. Warren walks around the truck before replying.

"What have you been craving for days?"

"Umm, Chinese food?"

"You got it."

I clap my hands as he turns the car on and chuckles over my enthusiasm. Since this whole ordeal, I have grown a lot as a person. I have learned how to appreciate the smallest things in life. Getting Chinese food when I've been craving it is one of those.

"Sakura Buffet," I read the sign, while Warren parks. "You know, we could've walked."

"And have you become a frozen popsicle? No, thank you."

I laugh as he opens the door for me and takes my hand once more.

"I'm not that bad."

"Maybe. Maybe not," Warren replies, before leaning down and whispering right in my ear. "But I was not taking any chances. This date was not getting cancelled."

Tiny goosebumps race up my spine as his breath washes over my skin. My body heats up to a point where I probably don't need this coat anymore. I match his intensity completely. Between getting myself situated in town and dealing with my parents being gone, we haven't spent any proper time together. But the need in his eyes matches my own, so I tug on his arm before we can walk inside the restaurant.

"Then let's get this date started properly," I say, right before I pull him down to me. His lips crash into mine, and it's as if the whole world has exploded around us.

He tastes like adventure and comfort.

Like desire and friendship.

Like I belong to no one else but him.

I am his, and he is mine.

I have staked my claim, and he has answered in kind.

"Now that's a way to start off a date." Warren grins when we finally come up for air.

"Can't wait to see what comes next," I reply.

Whatever it is, I'm thankful I have found my way to Havenwood Falls.

ABOUT THE AUTHOR

USA Today bestselling author. Photographer. Artist. Born and raised in St. Petersburg, Russia, Valia Lind has always had a love for the written word. She wrote her first published book on the bathroom floor of her dormitory while procrastinating studying for her college classes. Since graduation, she has moved her writing to more respectable places, and has found her voice in Young Adult fiction. Her YA thriller *Pieces of Revenge* is the recipient of the 2015 Moonbeam Children's Book Award.

REDISCOVERED

MORGAN WYLIE

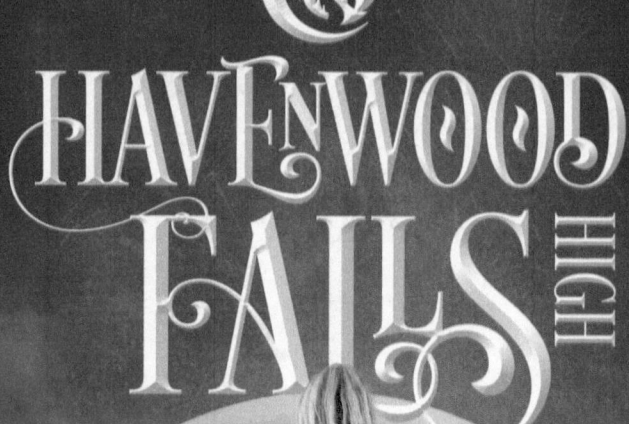

HAVENWOOD FALLS HIGH

Rediscovered

USA TODAY BESTSELLING AUTHOR

MORGAN WYLIE

~ A Havenwood Falls Young Adult Novella ~

BOOKS BY MORGAN WYLIE

YA FANTASY:

Silent Orchids (Book 1)

Veiled Shadows (Book 2)

Daegan (Novella 2.5)

Fractured Darkness (Book 3)

Fading Light (Book 4)

The Sol-Lumieth (Forthcoming)

The Rise of the Paladin (An Alandria Short Story Prequel ~ Free with Newsletter subscription)

YA PARANORMAL/SUPERNATURAL:: HAILEY: THE NECROMANCER (A SHADOW REALM NOVELLA 1)

JAX: The Doppelgänger (A Shadow Realm Novella 2)

WILLOW (A Shadow Realm Novella 3) (Forthcoming)

SOLANGE: (A Shadow Realm Novella 4) (Forthcoming)

NA/ADULT PARANORMAL ROMANCE:: RYLEN (THE TANGLED WEB BOOK 1)

MATHER (The Tangled Web Book 2)

JET (A Tangled Web Novella)

ENOCK (Forthcoming)

LUCIUS (Forthcoming)

ADDITIONAL COLLECTIONS:

Reawakened (A Havenwood Falls High Novella)

Dawn of the Witch Hunters (A Legends of Havenwood Falls Novella)

Rise of the Witch Hunters (A Legends of Havenwood Falls Novella)

Redefined (A Havenwood Falls Novella)

Rediscovered (A Havenwood Falls High Novella)

To all the loyal HF readers, I hope you enjoy this next story in the saga of the Havenwood Falls Blackstone witch hunters.

CHAPTER 1

"Come on, Brice, don't be a baby!" a guy from school taunted from the other side of the fence enclosing the skate park located in Danzan Park. Chadwick Linton was a basketball jock, a witch, and a jerk. Brice ignored him, but a tingling sensation he had never felt before started in the palms of his hands, then moved into his wrists and up his forearms. Brice instinctively flexed his hands and swallowed a gasp. The sensation in his forearms was the telltale sign a witch hunter felt when in a witch's presence.

Could he be transitioning right here, right now? He was almost eighteen, after all, and that was the golden age when the witch hunters from his family tended to come into their own. He knew some of what might happen from his sister Macy's experience when the witch hunter reawakened within her, but he was different. Or so he'd been told all his life. Brice didn't know *all* of what to expect, so he couldn't be sure his transition had begun. He shook his hands out, trying to make the tingles go away, but Chadwick was too close to him.

Head in the game. The only way out of there was to skate his way out. Otherwise, he wouldn't outlive the jokes and comments from the other guys. The skateboard world could be tough, even in

Havenwood Falls. Either you were a skateboarder or you were a poser. Brice wasn't a poser.

"You've done harder tricks than that. Don't get psyched out!" another guy shouted from the sidelines. Brice recognized all the kids there. Most were classmates he'd known the majority of his life, either from attending Havenwood Falls High School or more recently from the private school, Sun and Moon Academy. Out of the corner of his eye, he noted Jordan Woods hanging out in his football jersey, surrounded by Zoey Mills, Emma Cardin, and Celeste Long, along with the newer guy, Jonathan Burns.

Brice had gone to Havenwood Falls High—the public school —since he was a freshman, but the family, concerned for what might happen when he did transition, pulled Brice out of Havenwood Falls High his senior year and enrolled him in the private school. They gave explicit instructions to the headmaster to not put Brice in any classes with witches. As the witch-to-anything-else ratio at the Academy was higher than at the public school, Brice ended up with a lot of independent study time for his senior year.

His older brother, Brock, who now runs Soothing Sips tasting room in the town square, also attended the public school, so Brice was bummed to be the only one in his family who wouldn't be a Havenwood Falls High graduate. He hated leaving some of his friends, but the truth was he liked the change of pace at the Academy. He had more freedom and independence. Some thought the private school was for troubled kids who couldn't control their magic—and maybe that was the case—but others attended whose parents wanted to keep their kids more exclusive to the supernatural sector.

Brice's friend Samuel Milton, who didn't ride a skateboard, stood behind him with a few others, including Cade Peters, a hellhound a couple years younger from his new school. Dalton Underwood, a Havenwood Falls High sophomore, stood nearby with his board, waiting his turn. They had set up a bit of a practice competition and invited a bunch of people to come out and watch. For the middle of October, it was an unusually pleasant afternoon, and all the kids wanted to be outside after school.

Samuel playfully punched the back of Brice's bicep.

"Don't listen to 'em, Brice. Don't do it if you don't feel it," he encouraged with whispered vigor. Samuel Milton still attended HFH, and Brice had missed hanging out with him every day. Samuel was a lynx shifter and also Macy's best friend Ruby Jean's little brother, so they had practically grown up together. But Samuel didn't understand the skateboarding culture, nor the pressure to perform in a way to prove legitimacy.

Brice cringed inside, knowing the other guys would make fun of him if they heard Samuel attempting to help him back out. The last thing Brice wanted was to back out. He knew he could make the run; it was a standard drop into the bowl, maneuver some tricks, then make his way through the half pipe and finally complete the course with tricks on the rails. But something inside him held him back.

And that made him mad.

Brice wasn't a chicken. He was a good skateboarder, one of the best in Havenwood Falls, in fact. Quickly he glanced all around him to ensure nothing littered the ramps. While doing so, he noticed the Blaekthorn twins—wolf shifters, Weston and Drake—standing nearby, as well as other kids, including Gianna Augustine and Aurelia Petran. Another girl named Ellie Lewis stood by, which made him smile. She'd had a rough past couple years losing her brother, and he hadn't seen her much.

Halloween was quickly approaching, and in Havenwood Falls, even the playground got decorated. He chuckled internally, then got back to business. If he didn't make the drop soon, his spot would be taken by another rider, and he'd be out of the competition, forever seen as a coward.

"I'm going!" he announced, swiping the floppy dark hair from his forehead and taking a deep breath. *Piece of cake.*

Brice jumped on his custom-designed skateboard, dropped into the bowl just deep and wide enough to gain momentum before attempting to stall at the top edge rail, then back down into the depths of the bowl for another round. Once out of the bowl, he did a kick turn and flew down the ramp, dropping into the lower half-pipe, gaining speed as he went. From there he'd complete the course with kick turns and tricks from grinding the axle of his board on the rails to grabbing his board in the air for a 180 turn. He had visualized this moment over and over again. It was a no-brainer in his mind.

His mom would freak if she knew he didn't wear his helmet, but he never did and neither did the other "real" skateboarders. It was one less thing they could make fun of him for. It wasn't like he really cared what they thought, but he didn't want to be *that* guy —the one who always obeyed the rules, the one who always listened to his mommy, the one who still answered to his parents. He wasn't a rebel by a long shot, but he still had moments where he felt like he wanted to be one.

His mom rode his ass like no one else in his family. She was overbearing and treated him like a baby. Lilith Blackstone might sit on the Court of the Sun and the Moon, but she didn't need to dictate his life. After all, he was going to be eighteen soon, and then he could move out and live his own life just like Macy had wanted to, except this time he was prepared for his hunter awakening—at least as much as he could be, being the only male witch hunter in Havenwood Falls.

After Macy had left Havenwood Falls a few years ago, afraid of what her hunter side would become, she made sure her family told Brice everything he needed to know. Brice appreciated that she cared so much, but he didn't understand what the big deal was anyhow or why they made it an event to awaken the hunter. From Macy's stories, he knew the rogue Blackstone witch hunters had other males, and their gifts weren't suppressed early on. They grew up knowing all about themselves and their talents and what they could do. Brice didn't want to be a witch hunter in the sense the rogues were, but he didn't understand why his family made it such a big deal in Havenwood Falls.

Brice made several smaller jumps and did some tricks along the way as he gained speed and confidence leading up to the big jumps at the end. He heard a group cheering off to the side. He turned his head and gave the ladies on the sideline a tip of his head. He should focus but wanted to be the cocky jock type just for a moment. But when he looked, he caught only one set of eyes in the crowd. Bright blue ones surrounded by light golden-blond hair.

He knew those eyes—witch hunter eyes—though he didn't know who they belonged to. His vision tunneled as his eyes locked onto hers. Electrical shocks sizzled across the back of his neck. Definitely a hunter, one he didn't know.

Brice flew through the air. The ground went out from underneath him. The girl made him feel weightless like he could fly. Or perhaps he was flying.

Her blue eyes went wide, and her face paled more than it already was.

"BRICE!" several voices screamed from somewhere in the distance. Brice couldn't understand what was happening. He felt like everything moved in slow motion. Life had suddenly become crystal clear. He wanted to be free to be all he could be. All the bottled up potential he felt brewing inside him was ready. This was his time. His body tickled with energy surging through from his head down to his toes. Tingles shot up and down his arms. Witches were near. He had never fully felt them before. Maybe he would finally discover the kind of hunter he would become. Maybe this was his awakening.

Instant pain replaced euphoric energy.

"Dude! You flew!" said a voice Brice recognized but couldn't put a name to.

"Are you messed up, bro?" a rather hesitant male voice asked. "What were you doing?"

"Brice, can you hear me?" an unfamiliar female voice called as if she pushed her way through to him with those bright blue eyes.

"Brice, are you all right?" a separate male voice said, filled with panic.

"Keep him still. I called the clinic." That had to be Ellie Lewis. Her stepfather was a doctor at the clinic.

"And I called his mom," a voice—Samuel—offered. Of course Samuel called his mom. He was going to be in so much shit, but until the pain subsided, he wasn't sure he really cared.

Then darkness replaced the pain, and he felt no more.

CHAPTER 2

*B*rice heard heavy breathing and the occasional snore. Keeping his eyes closed, he took a moment to listen for the beeping sound of machines. Not hearing anything, he figured he wasn't at the medical clinic. Peeking between his lids, he spied his older brother Brock sprawled out in the corner chair, dead asleep. Brice breathed deeply and filled his chest with relief until the truth of his situation dawned on him—he was in his own room at his house, meaning his mom knew what had happened.

What had happened? Brice tried to remember what went down at the skate park. All he could remember were bright blue eyes hypnotizing him—that must have caused him to fall!

He tried to sit up, but quickly lay back down. His head swam and pain shot up his arm. He couldn't help the groan that escaped his throat.

"Hey, slugger," his brother said, his eyes shooting open. He stretched like a feline. "You broke your wrist."

"I can feel that," Brice said dryly, his head lolling in his brother's direction.

"The doc gave you some pain meds, and Mom has a salve from the Luna Coven that will help your wrist heal quickly, but she wants to talk to you before she gives it to you."

Brice groaned with a different kind of pain, and his head fell back against his pillow.

"You messed up, little brother. I know you don't wear a helmet when you're with the guys, but Mom's gonna kill you for it. You're lucky you didn't do more damage. In fact, we aren't sure how you got out with only a broken wrist, unless perhaps there was some magical assistance in cushioning your fall."

"I felt magic. And I felt the presence of a witch."

"Like more than usual? Your hunter gifts starting to reawaken?" His brother sat forward, concerned anticipation etched on his face.

"Maybe? I'm not sure. That thought ran through my head when I fell, but now I'm not sure."

"What do you remember?" Brock prodded.

"Blue eyes," Brice let slip, and the blush invading his face revealed it to his brother, too.

"Blue eyes, huh? Well, that's an interesting detail to remember. They belong to anyone in particular?"

Brice slowly shook his head. "I don't know. I just saw her on the sidelines while I was riding."

"Ah. So she was the distraction. I knew you were better than to fall on that jump." Brock shook his head in denial but then let out a laugh. "I can't believe my little brother got sidelined by blue eyes. I never thought I'd see the day. I thought for sure you'd end up single, sitting in the basement playing video games the rest of your miserable life."

"Shut up, Brock. Why are you here anyway?" Brice threw a pillow at his brother. The truth was, he much preferred having his brother than his mom sitting there when he woke up. At least this way, he could gauge her response before he had to take her on.

"Mom had to run to the vineyard to help cover NamaStays Inn for Grandma while she had a meeting regarding the new school year." Brock huffed. "I still can't believe Grandma is going to try teaching at the new Sun & Moon Academy College. I can't wait to hear from Macy and Gallad how she does at it."

"I know, right?" Brice laughed, then winced, wishing he hadn't, as he gripped his left wrist to keep from moving it wrong. Brice found the image of her teaching weapons to be comical—not that she couldn't do it justice but because she looked like a pretentious woman of wealth who wouldn't be caught dead holding anything as barbaric as a sword, especially one worn and bloodied from battle. "I can't wait to see that myself."

"You'll be lucky if Mom lets you live long enough to even graduate," Brock goaded.

"You gonna let her kill me, Brock?"

"He might not have a choice in the matter," his mom's voice came from the open doorway, down the hall.

Brice closed his eyes and groaned again.

"Didn't know you were coming back so soon, Mom," Brock sheepishly acknowledged as his eyes widened like a kid caught in the act.

"Macy came to take over at the inn, so I came back to see if Brice had woken up." Lilith came fully into the doorway. Her eyes quickly took in her son lying on the bed, and though her face held little concern or emotion at all, the fear behind her eyes subsided once she saw him. Lilith Blackstone was a tall, thin, authoritative woman. She loved her family fiercely, but everything about her screamed fierce. To Brice's knowledge, there had never been a soft edge on his mom. She loved them and took care of them, but if it weren't for the softer, caring side of his father, Reggie, they might have been more messed up as children. As it was, they had their issues, but overall he thought his family was pretty cool.

"Are you in pain, Brice?" she asked with some concern.

"Some. But I can feel the meds helping too," he quietly answered her.

"Good." She was back to business. "What the hell were you thinking out there?" She didn't yell, but sometimes he wished she would. It always felt like the perfect storm brewing with her, ready to burst open at any moment and drown them all in it.

"That I could do it."

"Without your helmet?"

Brice looked away, knowing he was wrong, but still had to try like the high school boy he was. "The other guys don't wear theirs —you're not considered a *real* skater if you wear one, and I knew I could do it."

"But you didn't."

"I would have been able to, if I hadn't been distracted," Brice said with a frustrated huff.

"By a pair of pretty blue eyes, no less," Brock offered as only a big brother could—with a dramatic teasing flare.

"Whose blue eyes?" Lilith asked, not missing a beat.

Brice locked his face down with a tight frown, glaring at Brock. Then he shifted his gaze to his mom's and sighed, knowing she wouldn't let him off that easy.

"I don't know. I haven't seen her before, but she had hunter eyes, and I could feel her presence. I haven't been able to do that yet, but I did. Does that mean my hunter gene is kicking in?" Brice hoped offering a different subject would get him off the hook about the girl, but no such luck.

"A witch hunter girl? Here in Havenwood Falls? One you don't know?" Lilith interrogated, suddenly on high alert.

Brice shrugged. "Yes, I didn't know her. She was off to the side of the skate area. I didn't talk to her or anything."

"But you felt her?"

Brice nodded.

"Well, perhaps it is your time, Brice. Keep me informed as you experience different changes in your body so we can gauge if your transformation is any different than any of ours." Lilith stood to leave. She expected full participation.

"This is almost worse than puberty." Brice fell back against his pillow. "You're going to hound me, aren't you?"

Every witch hunter in Havenwood Falls was born with a natural mark indicating they would have hunter abilities. However, at a young age, they were given a second temporary mark to subdue the hunter tendencies. Being surrounded by witches was hard enough as an adult witch hunter in control, but a young one having to encounter witches daily would have a hard time controlling their urges. So for the greater good of the community and for the young hunter, they were marked with a ward to prevent possible issues. Around their eighteenth year, the hunter began to emerge as the ward wore off. They learned to control the strong sensations and urges to attack every witch they encountered. Then the hunter had the choice to stay and receive their permanent marking as a resident of the town, also taking the edge off their urges, or they could choose to leave.

"It's not hounding, son. It's making sure you enter into your powers as a witch hunter with all the grace I know you are capable of, even without a crash helmet on." She gave him a sarcastic smile, ruffled his hair, then turned to leave the room.

He knew she wasn't going to let go of him not wearing his helmet. At least she didn't make a bigger deal about the girl. He still wondered who she was and if he'd get to see her again. Something about her drew him in, and he wanted to know what she was doing in Havenwood Falls.

CHAPTER 3

*B*rice woke up drenched from a cold sweat to find himself still in his room, but the view outside the window revealed night had finally come. He hadn't meant to fall asleep, but the meds he'd been given made him deliriously sleepy . . . so much so, his dream could be explained away. Brice steadied his heartbeat.

"It was just a dream, a crazy messed up dream, but only a dream," he said to himself as he shook the rest of his sleep away. Stiff and sore, Brice slowly stretched what limbs he could and made his way off his bed and into the attached bathroom. His stomach growled, and he was grateful to feel a little more himself.

On his way downstairs to the kitchen to find the rest of the family and some food, he realized that his mom forgot to give him the healing salve for his wrist. He was just about to yell out to see where his family members were when he heard hushed voices coming from the downstairs den: his mom, Macy, and another female voice growing in familiarity—Hollis Blackstone.

Hollis had only come to Havenwood Falls in the last six months from the rogue witch hunter group headed by Dante Blackstone, her father. She was sent in as a spy but defected and chose to change her ways as a hunter, fell in love with Ryne Calloway—a half witch, half phoenix—and chose to remain in Havenwood Falls with no further attachments to her dad or the *other* Blackstones. He knew many still were skeptical about her, but he liked her. She brought a fresh perspective to their home and added another level of attitude to stand up to his mom when called for.

"Brice saw her at the skate park," Lilith stated.

Brice wondered who and why they were talking about him and some girl at all. Did they mean the girl he saw with the bright blue eyes? The girl who caused his wreck?

"Who?" Macy innocently asked. He would thank Macy when he saw her.

"She's here?" Hollis returned.

"Who's here?" Macy again, with a little more frustration.

"Did you know she was coming?" His mom.

Brice wondered about the girl even more now. Where was she from? Since Hollis was brought in on the discussion, he was curious if the girl was from the rogue Blackstones. But Dante's group had no way of knowing where Havenwood Falls was located or how to find it, unless someone told them, but no one there would tell anyone—under penalty of possible death. The supernatural residents of Havenwood Falls took their secrecy and privacy extremely seriously.

"No. I had no idea. Does the Court think I did?" Hollis asked with added panic. Brice knew if she broke her agreement with the Court, she would be kicked out of Havenwood Falls for good with no memory of ever being there.

"Not yet, but they will wonder how she found us," Lilith concluded.

"I mean, I know I've been busy becoming a guardian at the college and all, but will someone tell me what's going on?" Macy said with exasperation.

"Sunny is in town," Hollis finally answered.

"Sunny? Seriously?" Macy's voice rose with surprise. "I liked Sunny. She helped me when I was with them."

Brice couldn't take it any longer. He entered the room without the girls noticing. "Who is Sunny and why are you making such a fuss about her?"

His mom's lips were pursed in frustration, probably because he had heard them.

"She is one of the rogue witch hunters who used to live with Dante," his mom said matter-of-factly, as if that should explain it all. Since Hollis had encountered her father back in May, Brice had heard rumors of Dante's disappearance: that he had not returned to the other Blackstones. If anyone in Havenwood Falls knew the truth, they weren't sharing it with him.

"How did she find us?" he asked.

"We don't know. She shouldn't have been able to," Hollis said, throwing her long dark hair back over her right shoulder. Brice looked at her eyes. They were the same blue eyes he saw in Sunny, his mom, his sister, his grandma, and any who bore the mark of the witch hunter. He saw those same eyes in the mirror every day.

"Well, has anyone just asked her?" Brice said with a tone that held a hint of the obvious.

The room went silent.

"I haven't seen her, or I'd have asked her," Macy said with a shrug, causing her blond hair tied high on her head to bounce.

"Actually, no one has seen her except you, son," Lilith said with a strange tone, "and also one of the boys who told me about the 'strange girl who approached you after you fell to see if you were all right.'" He hated when his mom used air quotes.

Brice looked at her and cocked his head. "You got Sunny from that information?"

Lilith shifted her feet, slightly uncomfortable. "No. I received a warning from Mathilde Augustine last week. She said we would have a visitor, and she described her to me. You know how Mathilde sometimes has moments of premonition. Well, I didn't think much of it, as I didn't think it was possible for her to find us." She paused and gazed out the window. "But then you mentioned seeing someone who fit her description, and I put them together."

"Detective Mom," Macy said with a giggle, then glanced at Brice with a wink. Lilith responded with an expression akin to an eye roll, without actually stooping to that level.

"Anyway, we'd been on the lookout for her but somehow she still got in unnoticed until recently, and for some reason she sought you out first . . . I wonder why?" Lilith took on an inquisitive look with her hands placed upon her hips.

"Maybe she didn't seek me out, but stumbled upon the skate park and happened to arrive in time to see me," Brice offered, but his words lacked conviction.

Hollis shrugged but shook her head. "No, Sunny is anything but random. She can be quirky and strange and seem haphazard, but everything she does is with purpose. I have lived with Sunny her entire life, and I still don't understand her. There is something unique about her. For example, Dante never treated her the same as everyone else. She's always been special. I thought at one point, there might be something mentally unpredictable about her, but it seems she just moves to the beat of her own drum . . . and Dante always let her."

"Interesting," Lilith mumbled under her breath.

"When I was there, she was so sweet to me and made a point to help me understand that I did not, in fact, kill a witch they tried to convince me I had killed in order to break me. She didn't have to do that," Macy added.

"I'll let the Court know," Lilith said. She pulled her phone out from her jacket pocket, texted something short, then put her phone back.

Brice grew more intrigued the more they spoke of Sunny. He couldn't wait to meet her and see what kind of drama a cute, petite teenage girl could stir up.

"Hey, Mom, I was looking for you to see if I could get the healing salve for my arm so it heals faster," Brice changed the subject, pointing at his injured and wrapped wrist.

Lilith slowly moved her vision to hold only Brice—the effect was unnerving as only a mom could do. He had a bad feeling.

"Your father and I talked about it. Since you heal relatively quick, we decided to let the natural consequences of what you did sink in, so you will make a smarter decision next time regarding your helmet."

"What? You're not going to give it to me? I just have to let it heal like a human . . . all slow and natural?" Brice guffawed.

Macy giggled under her breath but apparently couldn't help but let it slip out a bit. Brice glared at her.

"You know what I mean. Why wouldn't we use the healing gift when it's been offered?" he whined.

"You have medication from the doctor for your pain. It will not hurt you more than you can handle to wait a few days."

Brice dropped his head to his chest in utter despair and defeat as only a teenager could.

"You can get through this, little brother!" Macy annoyingly cheerfully patted him on his good shoulder, then headed out the door toward the kitchen. "Come on, I'll make you some food."

"Macy, why aren't you at college anyway?" Brice asked suddenly, realizing she probably shouldn't be home. Macy moved into the dorm when she got accepted into SMA for the year and hadn't been around much with her full schedule.

"That school is insane. A lot of dark energy with some weird stuff happening. I just needed a break, get out of the mountain, you know. Plus I had to come check on my little brother to make sure he wasn't brain damaged, but I think it was already too late for that," she said and laughed from down the hall.

After Macy left, Brice turned back to his mom. He wanted to say something to his mother, but when he looked at her, he knew there was no argument, and he sighed with resignation. He wished his dad had been there. He might have been able to persuade his dad to see his side: the side who'd have to go to school and face the others with his screw up . . . again. He just wanted to fit in, and somehow he figured this would do the exact opposite of that. So instead, he went to drown out his frustrations with whatever food his sister would make him.

CHAPTER 4

*T*he next day, his mom kept Brice home from school to ensure he was fully recovered—except for his wrist, which was going to take much longer since he wasn't allowed to use the magical ointment. He grumbled all morning and knew he was surly to his parents, probably contributing to their speedy exit to Stone Falls Winery to check on "things," but he was miserable, and he wanted them to know it. In the end, the only person it was truly annoying was himself, since everyone had left.

Looking out the window, he saw dark clouds rolling in. Up that high in the mountains, the snows usually came early, and he was ready to hit the half pipe up on the mountain. Snowboarding wasn't much different from skateboarding, and he loved them both. It was a sport he actually felt competent at. The skate park was still open this time of year due to "in-ground heating," also known as a little magic from the covens to keep the ground from freezing. Skating had been a lifeline for him. Life for him in Havenwood Falls was everything he loved. His brother Brock had gone away to college for a short term but ended up coming back because he, too, loved the town. Macy had always wanted to leave, but when she did, it was to escape her fear of becoming a witch hunter because their mom hadn't prepared her for what was to come. But Brice loved everything about where they lived and all he could experience. He only wished he understood more about himself and who he was meant to be.

Brice was the *great mystery* among their family. With dark hair, he defied all the Blackstones who had hailed from Havenwood Falls. And until Macy had visited the rogue hunters a couple years ago, they thought Brice was some kind of anomaly, being the first male they knew marked as a hunter, and on top of that, one with dark hair. He didn't think it was a big deal, but everything seemed to be a big deal in his family. Brice didn't even care if he became a witch hunter. His brother Brock and his dad weren't. He was content to just play video games, skateboard, and have a good time. The revelation that he had to grow up swiftly approached as he was now a senior in high school, but he had been putting it off as long as he could. Plus, he figured, the plan for his life was all laid out for him by his mom anyway: graduate from high school, then go to work on the family vineyard. Now, with the Sun & Moon Academy College of Supernatural Guardians open for young adults after high school, he had another option to at least prolong starting work at the vineyard. Not that he didn't want to join the family business. He thought their businesses rocked. And since Brock had been experimenting with microbrews, he hoped to join his brother in that endeavor and maybe even open their own side business. Of course, he hadn't talked to Brock or his parents about his venture idea, but in his mind *The Blackstone Brothers Brewery* had a nice ring to it.

But more than anything, he wanted to not be the odd man out. He didn't feel any real sense of purpose or drive to anything special. Even throughout high school, he had been labeled "the loner" or "the skate dork" by those other than his friends. He had dated some, but none of the girls at school really caught his eye.

Until those blue eyes at the skate park.

Brice relocated from the interior great room of his house and stepped outside onto their large covered deck with an amazing view of the town square. The town was decked out with decorations for fall, but especially for the upcoming celebration for Halloween. Havenwood Falls loved Halloween and went all out for it. All the lampposts were tied up with bows in oranges and purples to match the bunting draped across the buildings and signs for each business around the square. It really was a magical time of year for their town, especially the supernaturals. From his vantage point, he could also see people going about their day, and he wondered, if Sunny was in town, what she was doing.

With nothing else to do for the day—unable to play video games or do much of anything with his broken wrist—he settled himself on the comfortable exterior couch, took his pain meds, and laid his head back for a nap.

"Brice," a voice whispered through the dark cavern of his mind. Though it was hard to decipher the gender of the voice, it grew in strength and clarity. *"Brice, I know what you want. I know what you need to be free, to be truly all you were meant to be."*

Brice, lost in a sea of darkness and confusion in his mind, called out into the void. "Who are you? Where are you?"

"It doesn't matter who I am, but know that I'm close, closer than you think. And I have the answers you've been seeking, the answers to why . . ." The voice trailed off as if the connection had been severed.

Brice sat up in a rush, frantically looking around him, only to find he was still on the couch outside on the deck of his own house. He had fallen asleep.

He groaned and flopped back onto the cushion, wiping the sweat off his head with his free arm. "Only a dream. What is in those pain meds?"

Brice gathered himself, then got up to get a glass of water from the kitchen, only to find the front door inside his house opening.

His mom, Aunt Letti, and Hollis walked in like a gaggle of geese one after the other. Internally, he rolled his eyes. He did not want to have to converse with them at the moment. He loved them all, but before his dream, he'd been enjoying the solitude of his home. After Hollis walked in, however, another shock of blond hair came around the corner into the great room from the hall. She observed the home with such focused attention, she didn't even see him until their eyes met.

Bright blue eyes. Her eyes. Sunny.

And she was definitely that. Everything about her appearance and disposition was bright and electric. Somehow even her mid-length blond hair appeared shinier than the others.

Brice inhaled sharply; an electric shock ran through his body. *What the F was that?* he wondered internally. He'd never had anything like that happen before.

Oblivious to what he had felt, his mom began introductions.

"Brice, this is Sunny. Sunny, this is my youngest, Brice."

Sunny smiled and rocked onto her toes. "Hello again, Brice. You could have been hurt the other day, but I'm glad you weren't, or things would be much different."

Brice cocked his head, confused, and when he tried to say something in return, he couldn't find the words. He tried to raise his hand in a wave, but he raised the wrong one and pain shot through his arm, and he cried out.

CHAPTER 5

*A*unt Letti clucked her tongue as she moved toward him and held out her hand for the arm he now clutched. "Lilith, why aren't you giving the boy the witch's salve? It would speed up this process so much faster for him."

Brice breathed a sigh of relief. Finally someone was on his side. "Thank you, Aunt Letti, but she won't give it to me."

Lilith scowled at the two of them. "He is being reminded why he should wear a helmet when skating—that could have been your head fractured like that, Brice! Your grandmother is on her way over. Wait until she adds her two cents in."

Brice groaned. He loved his grandma, Eva, but she could be a real tough woman. She had expectations and thought everyone should fall into line accordingly. Brice had heard his mom and dad talking once, and she had explained that Grandma and Aunt Letti were cousins. Eva had wanted to be the family matriarch and sit on the Court, but Letitia was older and got the seat instead. They loved each other, as they'd had over a hundred years to do so, but they had their moments of discord due to very different personality types and ideals.

Brice cleared his throat as he moved to finally get that glass of water he desperately needed. "What brings you all home at this hour of the day?"

"We found Sunny aimlessly wandering around town," Aunt Letti started in.

"Oh, I wasn't aimless, Letti. I was waiting for you to find me," Sunny interjected with a smile, gazing around the room in an almost wistful manner.

"As I said, Sunny never does anything without a reason," Hollis added. "She's very purposeful."

Sunny gave her a deep nod of approval and turned back to the mantel and the family photos she now studied.

"Of course, dear. Well, we found Sunny and decided to bring her back here to have a bit of a chat and get to know her more," Aunt Letti finished.

Brice knew she meant they needed to know why Sunny was in town before they informed the Court of her arrival, so they could determine what should be done. If she was to stay for a bit, they needed to register her as a guest so they could keep tabs on her.

"Sunny?" Hollis walked over to her. Brice knew from Hollis that Sunny had been one of the few she truly cared about. "Sunny, I'm glad to see you, but why are you here? Last time I saw you, you didn't want to come to Havenwood Falls with Ryne and me last summer. Did someone send you?"

"Nope. I told you it wasn't my time before, but now it is. So here I am," she said innocently enough, as if it should be that simple.

Brice leaned over to Aunt Letti, and with his eyes asked the question, *Is she okay?*

Aunt Letti gave him a sharp nod of affirmation.

"How did you get here, dear?" Aunt Letti jumped in before Lilith had the chance.

"Oh!" Sunny smiled and faced them all, her eyes beaming with innocent excitement. "I found a bus with a sign on it. I asked the driver if it would bring me here to you, and he said yes, so I got on."

Lilith cocked her head and stared at Sunny with her eyebrows pinched. "Yes, but how did you find the bus?"

Sunny frowned. "I knew I was supposed to, so I did. Was that wrong?"

Hollis reached over and looped her arm through Sunny's, which made her smile again. "You're fine. Just most people can't find this place. Remember Dante was trying to find it for so long, but couldn't? So they're just curious how you were able to."

"He did have a hard time finding it, didn't he, Holly? I had a map in my head, but I wasn't supposed to tell him, so I didn't. But that's how I found the bus. I followed the map." She tapped her head.

"Good girl, Sunny." Hollis looked to Lilith and then Aunt Letti and shrugged as if asking *what else can you say to that?* It sounded pretty simple. Brice was curious what went on in Sunny's head. She was obviously special, but not in a mentally challenged sort of way. More in a someone-was-telling-her-things-inside-her-head kind of way. He was suddenly struck with a reminder of the dream he had earlier, when someone was talking in his head. So he didn't have much room to speak. Plus, with all the supernaturals they knew, hearing voices or having dreams of premonition were hardly rare—perhaps still uncommon, but the impossible seemed possible in Havenwood Falls. He'd mention that to his mom when Sunny wasn't around.

"Where will you stay while you're here, Sunny?" Brice asked her, once his voice had found its way back.

She smiled at him, and his heart melted. "Holly said I could stay with her!"

Brice looked at Hollis with a sly grin. "Holly, huh?"

"Only to her." She glared at him as if to say, *Don't even try it.* She then turned back to Sunny. "Where are the others? Grace, Nala . . . everybody."

Sunny frowned. "They all argued a lot after Dante didn't come home. Nala thinks she's in charge, but some of the families have disbanded and gone their own way. It's how it's supposed to be for now. It gives them time to try to focus on other matters now instead of hunting witches."

"Where is Dante, if he didn't come home?" Brice genuinely asked. After Hollis was granted permission to stay and got settled, there hadn't been any discussion of Dante or plans to defend the town against him and his rogues. He had forgotten until now to ask about him. But apparently now was the wrong time to ask, as the room went dead silent. His mom and Aunt Letti exchanged a brief glance, and Hollis chewed her bottom lip, which was very unlike her and very telling at the same time. *Oops.* They probably didn't want to let Sunny and thus the other rogues know if they did something to him.

"We don't exactly know what happened to him," Sunny jumped in, saving them all from having to answer the question. "Some think he's dead. He followed them back to their camp after he chatted with Hollis and Ryne—who I can't wait to see again, by the way." She clapped her hands in sudden excitement when she realized she had yet to see him. "But then he was gone the next day. I know where he is, but I haven't told anyone, don't worry." She looked to Lilith and gave her a strong nod as if they had discussed it previously.

"Thank you, Sunny. We appreciate that," Lilith responded. Brice was unsure if his mom really thought Sunny knew or if she was just playing along. Either way, he would ask his mom the truth of the matter later. Apparently, that was one more thing they didn't feel the need to discuss with him.

"Now what should we do?" Sunny asked, looking around the home again. She wandered into the kitchen area, trailing her hand along the backs of the chairs at the dining table.

"Since you are new to town, Sunny, we will have you meet with a group of people who are the leadership in town and get you registered as a guest," Lilith instructed.

"Speaking of registering, do you know how long you will be staying? And do the people you live with know where you are?"

Aunt Letti asked in a nice way that sounded like regular conversation.

"I plan on living here! I want to go to school here. Macy told me about her school before she started to forget it, and it sounded fun. No one knows where I am. I just left. I come and go as I please usually. I did leave Grace a note that I was leaving and wouldn't be returning. I imagine she'll worry, but I think she knew the time was coming soon anyway." Sunny frowned. Brice wondered if talking about Grace or leaving upset her.

"Maybe you could send her a letter letting her know you're okay and with friends," Brice suggested, then amended at the scowl of her mother, "without telling them where you are, of course."

"That's a brilliant idea. Thank you, Brice. We're going to be good friends, you and I. I'm excited to go to school with you."

Brice blushed. He knew he did. He couldn't have stopped it if he had tried. "We'll have to get permission for you to attend for the remainder of the year."

He didn't think it was likely, but thought he'd shoot for the moon. It would be nice to have her at school. She was fun and pretty and it might be nice to have the fellas think he had a girlfriend for once. Not that she would be, of course.

"It will be fine. They let me go," she said as if it had already happened, which caught everyone off guard again.

"Sunny, how old are you?" Brice followed up to break the silence and to appease his own curiosity, "You know, so we can request to get you in the right grade."

"I'm sixteen." She paused and thought for a moment. "Well, I might be seventeen."

"They didn't know her exact birthdate when she came to live with us. So we guessed," Hollis answered before anyone asked.

"Ok, so probably a junior then," Brice offered as a safe bet.

Lilith sighed with exhaustion. "Well, let's start preparing for tacos, then we'll meet everyone at Court. The sooner we get this out in the open, the sooner we can figure out what comes next."

"It's not Tuesday, Mom," Brice stated. The Blackstones always had a family dinner for Taco Tuesday each week.

She stopped and stared out the window thoughtfully. "Tonight it's Tuesday. We're having tacos. Call your father and Brock. Hollis, Ryne is also invited. Aunt Letti, would you like to stay and invite Uncle Tranner too, please? Eva is on her way, so we'll make it a family gathering." Since Macy hadn't been able to make many of the family dinners, his mom had taken to inviting more of the extended family.

Brice shot Aunt Letti a look. His mom seemed a little off. They hadn't seen her like that in a long time. Brice gave Macy a look then a nod. He was concerned about his mom. Something in her facial expressions looked haunted.

"I'll call Dad," Brice offered, then shot out of the room to use the landline in the office. Cell coverage was spotty in the mountains unless you had a magically altered phone, which was reserved for the members of the Court and perhaps a select few others. But not Brice.

CHAPTER 6

The next day, Brice went back to school. The Academy started early, and he usually rode his skateboard if the weather allowed, as it wasn't that far from their house in Havenwood Heights, but Brice still felt drained from his restless nights, so he asked his dad if he'd drop him off. He'd struggled getting dressed with a sling over his arm. Thankfully, the doctor didn't deem it necessary for him to sport a full cast since he could heal faster with the witch's salve.

"Are you all right, son? You look a little pale," his father, Reggie, noted as they turned out of their aged but prestigious neighborhood of old money, passing through the iron gates and onto Blackstone Road—named after his ancestors who first arrived by wagon train in the 1850s with the other settlers of the town.

Brice appreciated his dad's concern. He turned himself sideways in the passenger seat to face his father. Reggie—Reginald to no one—was human, but his superpower was putting up with Brice's mom, at least in Brice's opinion. His dad was taller than him still and more muscular—but hopefully not for too much longer—and his hair was dark like his, but his eyes were a warm brown. To many others looking in from the outside, his dad was soft and let his mom walk all over him. But those who knew him knew that wasn't true. Reggie was strong and more than capable to handle a bunch of different situations including marrying into a family of witch hunters. He had climbed his way up the family business, and Brice's grandfather wouldn't have given Reggie all the responsibility he had just because he was in the family. Reggie had earned his place there, and he could handle Lilith Blackstone as well. His father just had a natural ability and temperament to come at things with a big-picture perspective that allowed him to come across as more relaxed. No one worked harder than his dad did—at least in Brice's opinion.

Brice considered his dad's question and decided to offer up some honesty. "I'm in pain from my wrist and not happy about having to wait out the healing without the witch's salve, but I understand why you and mom are holding it back. But I've been having strange dreams too, I think from the pain meds, so I haven't been sleeping much."

"She may not show it, Brice, but you scared your mother something fierce when she heard you had an accident and how bad it could've been. But I'll talk to her and see if we can get you that salve soon. As far as the dreams go, we can alter the prescription dosage if they're too strong, but what kind of dreams are you talking about?"

"Strange voices, someone talking to me, some electrical shows, and sometimes I think I can even feel little shocks from them . . . that kind of stuff." Brice shrugged, uncomfortable mentioning his private dreams.

"Interesting," his father started. "Keep me in the loop on that one and let me know if it keeps happening or changes, all right? And I'll talk to Dr. Underwood about lowering the dosage."

"Thanks, Dad." Brice gathered his backpack as his father turned right on First Street, then up to the guarded gates. Reggie rolled down his window and gave the morning guard a friendly salute as they passed through the tall gates. From there, it was a drive up a long stone road lined with trees on either side until the old stone mansion of a building loomed before them. The school was located on acres of pristine manicured lawns and stone pathways surrounded by stone walls to protect and guard it from humans. Multiple smaller buildings were set around the larger one. The entire school held more of a college-campus vibe than a high school. More traffic came and went than in years past; the portal to the Halvard Campus for the SMA college was located near the Falls Campus and students and faculty both used it. They came upon the school's main entrance, and the drive circled in front of the school for easy drop-off access. When there was an extra car to drive, Brice would park in the lot off to the left side.

"Have a good day, son," Reggie offered as Brice got out of the car.

"You, too, Dad. Hey, did you hear how the Court hearing with Sunny went last night? I wasn't allowed to go, and I couldn't stay awake to hear from Mom." He glanced to the side of the car and watched as another car pulled up behind them and let out some students who waved to Brice as they proceeded into school.

Reggie smiled. "I heard they are going to let her stay on a trial basis, truly in order to see why she might really be here. Elsmed Fairchild tested her, and she passed everything. But they are all there to be skeptical and protect the town, so they think she might have ulterior motives or at least be sent by someone, similar to the way Hollis arrived."

"She doesn't. Have other motives, I mean. I can just tell. There is an innocence to her that is disarming, don't you think?"

Reggie watched his son, then nodded. "She does indeed. Oh, also they are going to let her come to school, also on a trial basis. She should be here today as a junior, I think." Reggie knowingly smiled and waved his son off. "I have to get to work. See you afterward!"

Brice backed up and let his dad drive away as he waved.

"She might be here today?" he said quietly under his breath. Brice's heart rate sped up, and his feet felt like lead. He straightened his tie and shifted his blue blazer with the school crest on it to its proper place on his shoulders. Slowly he moved through the large arched entryway into the interior courtyard, the heart of the Academy. Brice didn't know if he should wait for her or not, but if he did wait much longer he'd miss first period. Since he didn't have classes with her anyway, he assumed Hollis would be bringing her and would help her get settled, so he went ahead to homeroom so he wouldn't be late.

His morning classes passed in a blur; he could barely remember what was assigned for homework. Too much was on his mind. At lunch he sat with some of the guys he'd skated with and gave a wave to Cade Peters at another table. He also saw one of the twins, Remy MacKinnon—but Remy didn't want to be there, if his expression said anything about it. Maybe he just didn't want to be there without his twin, Roxy, who was allowed to skip senior year and go to the college of guardians a year early. The dining hall, as well as administrative offices and old original classrooms, were located in the Founder's Hall, one of three wings of the Academy. But Brice's favorite room, contrary to what many would suspect, was the Havenwood House Book and Manuscript Library. The Academy was old but well maintained, beautiful, and held a magic all its own. Brice loved it.

Without warning, he felt a buzzing, more like a low-level itch at the back of his neck. He scratched at it, but nothing was there. He scratched a second time until he realized the tingles at the base of his neck meant another witch hunter was nearby; only he had never felt it before. His head shot from one side to the other, scanning each end of the lunchroom for the source of his discomfort, until he saw her.

Sunny had made it to school.

CHAPTER 7

The interior of the dining hall was large and medieval looking, constructed of large gray stones with vaulted ceilings. Long, wooden tables a century old stretched in multiple rows from one end of the room to the other. Brice knew a kitchen existed, but he had yet to see the proof. The room, and entire hall, essentially looked like the interior of a Gothic castle but with modern updates to accommodate the school. The electrical system had been updated, but still the sconces appeared as if they had fire burning in them, complete with flickers of light playing with shadow against the stones for effect. Other parts of the school were more modern, especially Memorial Hall, but Brice liked the old-world feel of the older parts of the Academy.

Sunny made a beeline straight for Brice without even needing the time to look for him. He had to admit she looked pretty cute in her navy blue blazer, crisp white shirt, and blue skirt with knee-high dress socks and shoes. With the dining hall filled with people and their chaotic noises like it was, he was surprised she found him so quickly. Though if he could feel her just barely with his hunter gifts awakening, she could probably pin him down like a needle in a haystack since she had grown up with her abilities and learned how to use them long ago. He understood and even agreed with why the town and his family placed restrictions on them until they were older, but it sure would be nice to already have full access to whatever he was going to be able to do.

His heart sped up as she moved closer, though she took her time absorbing the surroundings of the room. He realized she was much more observant than she let on. Brice didn't know if she put on an act with the whimsical, almost oblivious, way she seemed to move through life or if she somehow processed life a little differently than most. Her blond hair, fair complexion, and overall shininess was a pure juxtaposition to the doom and gloom of the architecture.

And he wasn't the only one to notice. A hush fell over the room, and many stared. Brice suddenly felt uncomfortable with how they stared at her, knowing she was on her way toward him. He had enough trouble with standing out. He hadn't thought through what her presence might actually mean for him. He had hoped for the benefits of her arrival, but now considered there might be drawbacks as well. A catcall and a few whistles reverberated from the back of the hall. Sunny didn't seem to notice or care, but Brice was shocked at the instantaneous surge of jealousy and anger that rushed through his body. She wasn't his. She didn't belong to him. He barely even knew her, but something inside him said otherwise. He stood from his seat and shot a glare at the offender who, of course, happened to be Chadwick Linton. So surprised at his sudden action, he didn't notice the tiny sparks that shot from his fingertips when he did so.

Sunny came right up alongside him and placed her small, delicate hand around his elbow.

"Hello, Brice! See, I get to come to school with you." She went on as if she hadn't noticed anything about the altercation about to happen right in front of her eyes. Perhaps she didn't, or perhaps she knew just what to do to quickly defuse the situation.

Brice deflated and looked at her. Something in her eyes brought peace to his soul, and he gave her a quick nod, inhaling through his nose to calm his adrenaline-filled body.

"Great . . . really, that's great news, Sunny." Brice brought his train of thought on track to where she had directed. "Hey, do you want to see some of the campus before our next classes?"

Sunny's face beamed, and she nodded with excitement. "Please!"

Brice showed her around the Founder's Hall they were already in, then moved to the other two wings.

"This wing we are entering is Memorial Hall. It has more of the newer and more modern classrooms in it. Which is pretty cool, if you like that sort of style." He glanced over at Sunny to find her eyes wide, soaking in all the details.

"Show me more, Brice! There is so much to see," Sunny said with a huge smile.

"Okay, this next wing is the Falls Campus. You'll find classes for supernatural training at Castor Center in this wing, as well as sports fields and access points to areas around the falls."

They walked in silence for several more minutes as they circled their way back to Founder's Hall, ending at his favorite room: the library.

"This is the best room in the entire Academy—at least that's what I think," Brice said as he opened the door and smiled. "This is the Havenwood House Book and Manuscript Library."

Sunny gasped and practically squealed as she did. Bouncing on the balls of her feet, she innocently asked, "Are we allowed to go in?"

"Of course," Brice said and ushered her in.

"I love libraries. Dante always chose my books for me, but I love to read." She twirled as she stepped completely inside. "This is like a world I want to live in."

Brice smiled and simply watched her enjoy one of his favorite spaces. Even when he was a student at Havenwood Falls High, he enjoyed coming to this library for evening classes or whenever he could. The afternoon light flooded the room with a warm glow through the wall of stained glass windows, overlaying the colors along the wood beams bracing the room for the incredible dome at its center. The dome was a work of art depicting supernatural creatures of all kinds throughout the ages and lent to the sacred feel of the library. The room was spacious in the middle, but lined with two stories of mahogany shelves filled with books from ancient leather-bound tomes to modern works of fiction and nonfiction alike. Brice followed Sunny as she moved as if guided by the wind through the mahogany tables carved with beautiful detail.

"Can you feel it?" Sunny asked with a reverent whisper.

"Feel what?"

"The presence. The history. The weight of knowledge. The magic. It's all in this room." She held out her arms, taking it all in.

Brice thoughtfully considered what she said and extended his senses, trying to feel what she felt.

"I'm not sure I feel it, but maybe I do, and that's why I love this room." He shrugged, uncertain what else to say.

"You'll feel it all in time," she said with a smile and pranced over to one of the shelves. With a featherlight touch, she brushed her fingers along several of the spines as she read them.

"You talk as if you know things already."

She stopped and turned to look at him. Her eyes shone, and her face reflected some of the reds and oranges from the stained glass. She smiled then and said, "I do. But don't tell anyone else."

Sunny winked at him and returned to her perusal of the shelf.

Brice paused. "Why do you think you know what's going to happen?"

"Because the voices tell me. Well, sometimes they show me pictures," she told him, as if what she said was everyday conversation.

Brice was surprised to hear she had voices in her head. Maybe she was on meds, too. Or maybe if his voices didn't go away, she could help him figure out what to do about it. He hoped that wasn't the case, though.

"Sunny? Can I ask you about your voices?"

"Yes, but you need to know they are a part of me. I know

them. They've been with me all my life, unlike yours. Your voice is new. Your voice is hiding. Be careful, Brice. Your voice is giving me a headache," she said suddenly with a groan, as her hand went to hold the top of her head.

Brice rushed over to her and put his hand under her elbow, guiding her to one of the bench seats under a window pane. "Sunny, are you okay? Should I get someone?"

He looked around. They were the only ones in the library, as it was still lunch time. He started to get up, but she pulled him down to sit next to her.

"No. Not yet. It's magic, and it's blocking me for some reason. Just give me a second. It will pass," Sunny said quietly as she focused on her breathing.

Brice realized he had never felt so helpless to do anything for someone. He realized he cared. After a moment, Sunny inhaled slowly and opened her eyes, releasing her head.

"It's over." She stood up and pulled Brice up with her, his hand in hers. "Thank you for sitting with me. No one has done that for me before. It's nice." Without any other words, she let go of his hand and made her way all around the room, studying everything. Brice stayed where he was, unsure what had just happened.

"Sunny, are you sure you're okay?" he asked, concerned. Nervously, he put one hand in a pocket, and the other kept swiping at the shock of hair continuing to fall into his eyes.

Sunny skipped over to him. "I am sure. It will stop soon enough, just a little longer."

"Are you a fortune teller?" Brice skeptically asked.

She cocked her head in confusion at him, but then added a small smile. "What do you think?"

"Um, no?" he ventured uncertainly.

"You will just have to wait until after school, because I need to get to my next class. Bye, Brice!" she said with a friendly wave and swiftly blew out of the room as if ushered by the same wind that guided her in.

Brice shook his head. "That was weird. She is . . . I don't know what she is. She's something special for sure and maybe something more."

Remembering how he felt in the dining hall when the other boys had jeered at Sunny, he wanted to see if he could find any information regarding witch hunters or strange occurrences during awakenings. In fact, he could have asked Sunny, and maybe he should have. He would have to remember to ask her after school. She had to have seen the sparks and known it was part of the reawakening, or she chose to ignore it. He had some study time before his last class, and he would spend it there, researching anything he could find. Being a senior, he had a little more free time, plus the campus functioned more like a college, allowing the students to study independently when not in class. He just hoped he could find something to help him or he'd have to ask his mom. That was a conversation he didn't want to have yet.

CHAPTER 8

*B*rice searched for what felt like hours and countless tomes with no luck of any information that would help him find answers. Out of frustration, he laid his head down on the table.

"*Brice? Can you hear me?*" The same voice from his dreams spoke to him, but this time he could tell it was male. Brice's head shot off the table, and he looked around frantically for the source.

"Who's there? Where are you?" he answered out loud.

"*Brice, I can sense you are beginning to allow your hunter to reawaken.*"

"You can? How can you know that? Are you spying on me?" He quietly tiptoed around the room, grateful he didn't find anyone, but at the same time unnerved because someone was speaking into his mind.

"*Let's just say I have my ways and leave it at that.*"

"What do you want? Why are you bothering me?" Brice asked, starting to get frustrated.

"*I do not intend to bother you. I intend to help you. Your family does not have time to fully help you through your transition. They haven't been completely honest with you.*"

"What do you mean?" Brice had a sinking feeling, most likely because he'd had that thought before, and having it confirmed by a bodiless stranger hurt.

"I think you know. Ask your mother about the family journal and the dagger."

And just like that, the voice was silent. Brice's heart raced. He tried to calm himself down. The voice said it intended to help him. He didn't trust a random voice, but maybe it was his guardian angel. He knew people who actually had those. Might be cool if he had his own too. Once he was calm, he thought the advice might be sound. It might be wise for him to dig more into his family history. He knew the rogue Blackstones had several male witch hunters. There had to be a record of why somewhere.

Brice looked at the clock on his phone and realized he had to hurry.

It felt like forever, but in reality he had only used up his study period, and he had one more class before the end of the day to get to. Still slightly shaken, he put away the books he had pulled down to a table and cleaned up the space he used. He rolled his neck and stretched his arms. The tingles shot through his forearms again, and his skin felt like it was crawling. He had to get ahold of himself and shake off the agitation; he felt like he needed to run laps or something.

The door opened and in walked Ronya Augustine, Gallad's mom and Macy's future mother-in-law. Gallad and Macy had gotten engaged earlier in the year but decided to make it an extended engagement so they could both attend SMA.

"Hello, Brice. Catching up on some studying?" Ronya said with a cheerful smile as she carted a box into the room. Brice felt a low-level zing up his arms as she entered. He flexed his fingers and shook out his hands, not used to the sensation, hopefully before she saw him.

"Oh, just a little research . . . hold on, let me help you with that." Brice ran over to her just in time. He grabbed the box awkwardly with a broken wrist right before she dropped it.

"Oh, my hero. Thank you, Brice. I thought I could get it all in one trip, but apparently I should have made two." She placed her purse and another bag onto one of the tables and directed him to set the box there too. Brice realized the box was lighter than when he first grabbed it and felt a zing of power under his wrist. Ronya was using magic to help him help her. He would have been embarrassed except it really helped and he thought it was pretty cool. She winked at him and held her finger to her lips. "Shh, don't tell."

"I know nothing." He smiled, then gestured to the box. "Is this for your class tonight?"

Brice knew Ronya—or Mrs. Augustine—taught the Awakening Lab for supernaturals learning their powers after hours. Her son, Gallad, also assisted with supernatural histories class in the evenings, but since he enrolled with SMA Gallad's involvement was limited.

"Yes, I'm a little early, aren't I?" she said with a wink. He liked Ronya. She had a sunny personality. That thought instantly sent his thoughts toward Sunny herself.

He hoped Sunny was enjoying her classes and wished he could be there to watch her. Her fascination with all things was oddly refreshing.

Oblivious to the wandering of Brice's mind, Ronya continued talking. "I am grabbing some books, then meeting Gallad here after his classes. And I'll have him help me get this box over to the Falls Campus for class tonight."

"How is Gallad liking SMA? Macy is pretty cryptic about it all," Brice said to be conversational.

Ronya stopped and looked at him conspiratorially. "Gallad is the same way. He says it's hard, but deep down I think he loves it. He has always liked a good academic challenge, no matter what kind of image he was trying to portray. That's one thing I love about your sister—she understands that about him, and she likes to learn, too, which I admire." She smiled. "But you don't need to know that, do you? He also said he's having a blast with all the new people the school has enrolled . . . supernaturals from all over. But we probably won't see too much of them in Havenwood Falls, considering they are there in secret, right?" She giggled to herself as she pulled item after item out of the box.

"True. I hope to check it out when they have hopefuls apply for next year. Seems like a cool thing to do."

Ronya looked up at him and then she looked around him as if sensing something amiss. "Brice? Are you alone here?"

She slowly scanned the room.

"Yes, I've been reading for the last hour. Why?"

She pursed her lips, then shook her head as if lost in thought. "No reason, I guess. There's just a negative energy residue, like something was here but then not really. It makes no sense. Never mind."

Brice was shocked at her keen sense of the supernatural. He didn't know if his voice was negative or not yet, but perhaps Ronya would be someone he could talk to.

"Mrs. Augustine, I don't have much time before my next class, but could I ask you questions sometime about awakenings?"

"Of course you can, Brice." She walked over next to him and placed her hand on his shoulder. She joined him as he moved toward the door. "However, I think your family would be best suited for witch hunter awakenings, if you think that's what's going on."

"No, it's actually for a friend. He isn't from a witch family but has been experiencing some strange things, and he doesn't know who to ask or what's going on with him. I told him I'd ask around."

Ronya glanced at Brice, but to him, it felt like she peered into the depths of his soul, reading everything about him he didn't want anyone to know. Of course, she wasn't, but still.

"You tell your friend I'd be happy to help anyway I can. He could come to one of the Awakening Lab classes, too. That might help. Or you could come with him or for him, if he didn't want to be outed just yet, and take notes," she offered with such grace and ease, he almost agreed right then. "The class takes place in Castor Center."

"Thanks, Mrs. Augustine. I'll let him know. And maybe I will try to get him to come to the class tonight. Gotta go. Talk to you later!"

"See you at class, Brice." Ronya waved to him with a knowing but friendly smile.

CHAPTER 9

$\mathcal{A}$fter school, Brice waited outside in the courtyard for Sunny. His brother, Brock, had pulled into the parking lot in their grandfather's old pickup truck, meaning he was working at the vineyard, and waved to him out his rolled-down window. Brice held up his finger signaling for Brock to wait a minute. Brock saluted then turned up his music and leaned his head back against the seat.

After another minute, Sunny came bounding out from the courtyard through the large archway with a smile on her face and her hair bouncing along with her.

"Hey, Brice! I've had the best day. School is amazing."

"Hey, Sunny, was everyone nice to you? Did you find your classes okay?" Brice asked, concerned.

"I don't worry about other people so much, but the ones I talked with were friendly. Did you know there are all kinds of supernaturals that go here?" She lowered her voice as if it were a secret.

"I did know. They go to the public school, Havenwood Falls High, too. Here they can be more open about who they are and what they can do. But they can't at the public school because there are unknowing humans that go there, too."

"So the humans can't go here. That would explain why I didn't see any," she said absently.

Brice cleared his throat. "Sunny, do you have plans for today? I was wondering if you would like to visit the great falls, then my family's vineyard—well, I have to check in there anyway after school, but we could take a detour."

Sunny smiled and clapped her hands together. "Yes, I would love to see the waterfall. Hollis told me to go home with you however you got there after school. So that's what we shall do, then."

"My brother, Brock, is right over there to drive us."

"I haven't met him yet." She followed him to the truck and Brock got out.

"Hey, Brice. And you must be Sunny. I'm Brock—the big brother." He stuck out his chest proudly. "Hollis told me to be on the lookout for you," Brock said.

Without warning, Sunny grabbed Brock around the middle in a big hug, catching both guys off guard. Brock awkwardly shrugged at Brice who felt like he had been punched in the gut. She hadn't welcomed him like that. "I've always wanted a big brother. The boys at my other home were . . . not who I wanted for a brother."

"But this guy will work?" Brice questioned, then laughed when Brock lightly socked him in the stomach.

"Yes, he is perfect." Sunny stepped back. "Brice mentioned you might able to take us to the great waterfall. I'd really love to see it."

"How can a brother say no to that face?" Brock said and ushered her around to the passenger side of the truck, gallantly opening the door for her to slide in. He looked at Brice, who was at a loss and simply laughed.

"To the falls, good man." Brice joined in the fun.

The falls weren't that far from the Academy, but they had to go back out to Blackstone Road and turn up a couple blocks later on Alverson Road.

"It is really special you have a road named after you," Sunny noted as they turned off it.

"Well, in truth, it's named after our ancestors who came with the first settlers to establish this town over one hundred fifty years ago," Brock explained, as he drove up the road that would lead to the trails into the falls.

"Having history is important. I admire that you have that." Sunny seemed to drift into a daze, then looked at Brice with a vacant expression. "You should understand Judson more."

Brice and Brock exchanged a quick look. Brice was confused. "How do you know about Judson?"

She came back to her bright self and lowered her head as if to tell him a secret and tapped her head. "The voices, remember?"

"Do you mean Judson Blackstone? He was the husband of Marie Blackstone. They were the ancestors I just mentioned," Brock said with fascination. He found the timing wild, as he had just been in the library looking for information on his family history.

"Yes, that sounds right," she said.

The rest of the ride remained quiet until Brock pulled them into an area at the trailhead. "This is your stop, m'lady."

Brice opened the door and helped her out. "Will you tell Dad, or whoever is at the vineyard today, I'll be late but we'll be there after I show Sunny the falls?"

Brock nodded.

"Thank you, kind sir, for safe passage," Sunny said in her most formal tone and did an elaborate curtsy for Brock.

He howled and blew her a kiss. "I like this one!"

Brice rolled his eyes. Then Brock drove away. He knew his brother was harmless and most likely why he didn't feel the same surge of jealousy he had at school when the others paid attention to Sunny. With his brother, they were safe.

"I like him, too!" Sunny joyfully declared. "Yes, he will make the perfect brother."

"Yeah, he's pretty cool," Brice agreed. "Follow me. I'll show you something else pretty cool."

They walked up one of the trails, and as they got closer, Sunny gasped before they even saw the water. "I can feel it. It's magical."

She took a deep breath and let the mist rolling through the forest wash over her.

Brice watched her with awe. He had never met anyone like her before. She was so open and free—he longed for that feeling. "What's it feel like?"

She smiled with her eyes closed. "It's refreshing and reenergizing. The magic tingles along my skin. That's the hunter in me, that I can sense it so strong. I can also feel there are witch wards around it—many of them, for different reasons."

Brice was shocked. "I've never heard of a hunter who could decipher magical wards—sense them maybe, but not that strong."

"I'm not like all hunters, Brice. In case you haven't noticed."

"You know you're not like the others?" Brice was hesitant to ask, but since she opened the door he was curious.

"Yes, I know. I've always known. Dante tried to make me like the others but soon realized I couldn't be, because I'm not."

They continued to walk in a little farther. He really wanted to see her reaction when she actually saw the water. Rushing water splashed as it hit the pool at the base of the falls. Brice helped her over some rough terrain as they emerged from the trees into a small clearing made only for the falls. The water at the base was shimmering at the reflection of the sun and surrounded by large boulders and an explosion of foliage.

"Wow," Sunny breathed with awe. She appeared speechless as she fully took the sight in. "This sight alone is magic. Can I live here?"

Brice chuckled. "I don't think so."

"How tall is the waterfall?"

"From my history book . . . I think about three hundred feet high."

"And the water is magical?" she said more as a statement than a question, but since no one was supposed to know that, he took it as a question.

"Well, most don't know that, but yes, it has magical properties," he explained. "But you can't tell anyone that, okay?" he added, suddenly wondering if he was supposed to be showing her secrets of the town.

"I don't plan on going anywhere, Brice," she stated honestly. "Your Court will end up liking me, and I'll get to stay."

"Sunny? Is Dante your father?" Brice ripped off the Band-Aid and just asked what was on his mind.

CHAPTER 10

*S*unny giggled, then quickly sobered. "No. Many think that. He made many people think that, but no, he is not. I think he took me from them."

Brice frowned. "Took you from who?"

"My parents. I don't remember them. I was young, but I have flashes of them in my dreams."

Brice was in way over his head. Should he hug her? Hold her hand? "Even if he didn't, I'm sorry you didn't have them in your life. What do you think happened to them?"

"I miss who they could've been. He told me they died in a fire when I was about three or four. I think he killed them."

Brice reared his head back. She spoke so casually of the situation, but for her, he reminded himself, it was so long ago, and she didn't remember them.

"Why would he do that, Sunny? I mean, I know he didn't care for witches and killed a lot of them, but why would he do that to his own people?" Brice asked, genuinely confused.

"From what little I've learned, my mother was a powerful witch hunter, but my father was a Seer—and that, to Dante, was too close to a witch. He hated him, but Dante let them stick around after having me. He was curious what I would become. There had never been a witch hunter with seer abilities before."

"Does that mean you can tell the future?"

"No. Well, kinda. I *see* things. They don't always make sense, and I told you I hear voices—the voices are my family, the seers who have gone before me. They help me to decipher and understand things I see."

Brice was surprised at her honesty and seriousness.

"Dante thought he could use me to find you all, and predict how well his witch hunting raids would go. My gift doesn't work on demand, though. He tried to find ways to make it work for him, but he ultimately found if he just let me be, I'd cooperate." She snickered a little, then whispered as if Dante was within earshot, "I only gave him some information. And I never told him where your family was."

"So you gave him little nuggets and he left you alone?" Brice asked.

"Yep." She smiled again like she held the secrets of the world in her hand and she controlled how much got out, which he guessed she kind of did.

"And that's how you found your way here, to Havenwood Falls?"

She nodded. "I saw where the bus would be, and the driver did the rest!"

"Handy," Brice acknowledged.

"I saw you, too," she said with a smile.

"You did? Doing what?" Brice was a little concerned with what she might have seen. He didn't know what kinds of things her ancestors showed her, but he hoped he was portrayed in a good light.

"I saw you skateboarding just like you did the other day. So I knew where to find you."

He breathed a sigh of relief. He at least thought he looked cool when he rode his board.

"I also saw us at school . . . and then later together dancing. I don't know how to dance, though, so I thought that one was iffy." She shrugged as if it was no big deal she just told him they might be on a date together. "Sometimes the visions don't always work out how I see them, but mostly they do."

Brice's mouth went dry. He didn't know what kind of dancing they might do. They'd already missed homecoming at Havenwood Falls High by only a couple weeks. The Cold Moon Ball was still coming up in December, or maybe it was further away in the future. His heart raced, and his palms grew sweaty.

"Brice, don't worry about it. You have time—I think. I don't know exactly when the dance is, but it will be great when it's time." She smiled and moved toward the water's edge. She knelt down and dipped her fingers into the cool sparkling water and laughed.

He ran up next to her and kneeled on the ground.

"What is it?" He couldn't see anything out of the ordinary.

"The water tickles my skin. It's inviting me to play. Try it!" She playfully fluttered her fingers in a tickling motion within the water.

Brice awkwardly pushed his good hand into the water, but he didn't feel anything but cold, wet water. "I don't feel anything."

"You're trying too hard. Here, let me show you." She grabbed his hand in the water and pried open his tight fist, extending each of his fingers. She placed her hand against his, palm to palm and finger to finger. She slid each of her fingers loosely between his then moved his hand back and forth in the water.

Brice tried to remember how to breathe. He thought his heart was going to thump right out of his chest. He had never held hands with a girl—aside from the occasional assist to a girl by steadying her hand or you know, his family—not like that. She was so innocent, he was sure she meant nothing by it other than to help him, but in that moment, he wanted her to mean it. He wanted her to want him. He felt close to her, like he belonged, like he was seen for who he was and not just what he would be like when his hunter gifts reawakened.

"Can you feel it, Brice? Close your eyes and simply feel the water. Feel the magic in the water as it touches your skin." Her voice was calm and sweet and without any pressure.

Brice closed his eyes and slowly inhaled through his nose, working on steadying his breathing and racing heart as he did. He concentrated on the water, how it felt viscous and cool against his hand. He thought of the magic that flowed through the waters, providing the town and witches with a steady source of natural magical energy. Brice pictured that magic touching his skin and the water seeping into his pores, then crawling up his hand to his wrist, then encapsulating his forearm.

Sunny gasped with glee. "You did it!"

Brice opened his eyes to see water actually surrounding his arm —the water somehow did what he pictured and climbed his arm.

"How . . . how . . . I don't understand. How did the water do that?" Brice couldn't take his eyes off the water, then realized he was still holding Sunny's hand and quickly let go, breaking the spell, and the water splashed back into the pond.

"I did not see that. Brice, you have magic. Maybe that was why you always looked like you had mini fireworks around you when I saw you in visions." Sunny trailed off in thought, oblivious to Brice's near meltdown.

"Magic . . . I don't have magic," Brice mumbled as he stepped away from the falls. "How could I have magic? I'm a witch hunter —at least, I'm supposed to be." He looked at his hands. Tiny electrical arcs moved around the surface of his hands while simultaneously shocks formed at the base of his wrists and shot up his forearms all the way to his shoulders. He flexed his fingers, then shook his hands.

Shook his hands. Brice looked down at both hands and then solely at the right one. He could move his wrist without pain. "I can move my wrist! My wrist is healed." He rotated it again with more awe than he had the first time. "How is this possible?"

Sunny scrunched her face up, then her eyes widened.

"Well, if you have magic, you're a witch. You healed yourself with your witch magic," she concluded, as if it was completely obvious.

"Except I'm not a witch. How would I be a witch? Everyone in my family is witch hunter, human, or something else other than a witch. Gallad's the only witch who will be in our family, but he's not blood, and they don't have children yet. I wonder what will happen when they have kids?" Brice rambled as he continued to back away from the falls in a bit of a confused stupor. "I can't be a witch. I just thought I might be having a different kind of awakening."

"You are!" Sunny jumped in with excitement. "You're awakening both a witch and a hunter." She instantly frowned. "Well, that's why your body is so confused. You must be fighting against yourself. Interesting."

Brice shook out his hands, alleviating the electrical charges. "We need to go. My parents will wonder what's taking so long." He paused and looked at Sunny. "Hey, will you not tell my parents or anyone about all this yet? I want some time to process whatever this is that's happening." He looked to see his hands once more to ensure they were free of any evidence of magic and that his wrist was still healed. "Maybe I should put my brace back on, too, until I know why it happened."

"Okay. You'll be okay, Brice. I can't wait to see the vineyard," she said, as if none of the previous events bothered her in the slightest. They simply were the way they were meant to be.

Brice wished he could accept whatever it was that easily, but he felt sick to his stomach. Maybe he would go to Ronya's class after all.

CHAPTER 11

*A*t their visit to the vineyard, Brice introduced Sunny to several workers and to his Uncle Tranner, who happened to be there picking up Aunt Letti for the evening. He showed her around the vines, where they made the wine, the bar area, and NamaStays Inn with all its small cabins they rented out to visitors. She seemed particularly interested in the Yoga in the Vines classes and wondered if she could attend one. She and Aunt Letti made plans for her to come back with Hollis to take a class one morning before school the next week. Sunny loved everything about the vineyard and made everyone she encountered smile. Brice envied the ease and simplicity with which she saw life, even though what she truly saw had to have been anything but simple. He thought on that while he and his dad prepared the barbecue and food for dinner that night at the vineyard. Hollis and Sunny had left, saying they had plans for dinner to meet Ryne and his mom, Jessica Calloway.

Macy was still at school and not coming home, so it was just Brock, his mom and dad, and his grandma Eva who stayed for dinner. His mom and grandma set the table on the patio in front of the bar area. The winery was still open, but it was a slow night, so the few people who lingered sat on bar stools inside, chatting it up with Brock while he wiped down the counters. Brice moved over to where Brock was working when he finished helping his dad and looked out the windows of the modern garage doors, now closed as the evening air grew chillier and chillier. The patio area was filled with small table sets surrounding one big wooden table with bench seats and interwoven with barrels for personal fires. Over their heads was a fun canopy of strung Edison lights.

"Need any help in here, Brock?" Brice asked his brother just as he finished the last table.

"Nope, I think I'm done. You timed it just right." Brock snapped the dish towel he had at the back of Brice's legs, causing him to jump out of the way before he remembered to clutch his arm as if it had caused him pain. "Oh shoot, Brice, I'm sorry. Forgot about your arm."

"It's okay. It's not as bad as it was." Brice absently rubbed his wrist, thinking of what had happened at the falls earlier.

"You all right, man? You seem kind of out of it tonight," Brock intuitively observed.

"Yeah, I'm okay." Brice picked up a couple random glasses Brock had gathered onto one table and started to take them into the kitchen area. "How are your micros?" Brice asked, referring to the microbrews Brock had been testing out in the cellar until his operation got too big and had to move into the out building where they made the wine.

Brock gave Brice a big cocky smile. "I think they are doing awesome! You gotta try some of 'em out, little brother. I just need you to get a little older."

"Dude, we own a winery. I've tasted the wine we sell."

"There's that." Brock nodded his concession.

"I was thinking, maybe in the future it would be cool to work together with the micros—I love making 'em with you already. It could be fun!"

Brock really looked at Brice like he had never thought of that idea before. He seemed to be considering the idea then suddenly smiled. "I like it! Finish school, then we'll talk, but I'll keep it in my mind. Mom and Dad need to take on a few more employees here anyway since Macy went back to school. Maybe they could look for a couple more to give me a little more time, so we can plan for it.

"It could be a division of the winery or Soothing Sips. We could call it *Blackstone Brothers* or *The Blackstone Brothers Brewery*. The name has a nice ring to it, don't you think?" Brice asked, suddenly self-conscious about his idea and name until Brock smiled again. This time his smile touched the edges of his eyes, and he knew he had him.

"It's perfect. I'll start working on a logo. I was trying to think of how to brand the micros. You just solved it. Good job, little brother." Brock reached over and shook Brice's hand. "Future partners?"

Brice smiled and shook his hand in return. "Partners."

"All right, boys, food is ready. Come and eat!" their grandma called through the door from outside. She was a tall and regal woman with her hair cut into a short, sharp bob and a fierce attitude not unlike the one she must have passed on to her daughter.

They all gathered around one end of the large wood table now filled with plates of steak, hamburgers, and chicken. There were also bowls of various salads, both green and pasta, as well as platters of fruit. They entertained small talk while they ate and even visited with the last of the customers as they came to say their goodbyes. The fall nights were quite chilly up in the mountain, but the barrels of fire kept heat radiating close enough to keep them warm. At the end of their meal they sat and sipped on coffee or wine as twilight replaced daylight after the sun had descended behind Miles Mountain.

"Brice, your mother and I have decided to give you the witch's salve to speed up the rest of your recovery," his father said, passing him a small box filled with what he knew was a healing balm for his already healed wrist. They didn't know that, however, so he took the box.

"Thank you," Brice said.

"How did Sunny do at her first day of school?" Lilith asked dryly.

Brice could tell his mom was not thrilled to have Sunny in town. He didn't know if she didn't trust the girl's intentions even though she passed Elsmed's test or if she didn't like that others from the rogue group were infringing upon her self-importance in the little town, and bringing with them possible new ways of being a witch hunter—still without doing the hunting part.

"I think she did okay," Brice answered. "She was talking with some girls when I saw her outside one of her classes. I gave her a short tour of Founder's Hall, then she had to go to her own classes. I spoke with Ronya a little too. She was setting up for her class tonight, and she invited me to come check it out as my hunter abilities will be showing up soon."

"That was thoughtful of her, son, but she knows very little about the witch hunters, being a witch herself," his mother said absently as if lost in another thought, not fully engaged with the conversation she began herself. She then looked up at him. "But you aren't experiencing any more symptoms yet, are you," she said as more of a statement, though that bothered Brice because she didn't even truly ask or maybe she didn't even want to know. So he wouldn't tell her.

"Hey, Grandma? Can you tell me more about Marie and Judson Blackstone? I was looking in the library for any mention of them since they were some of the town founders. I wanted to learn more of our history, but couldn't find much."

She pursed her lips at first then nodded to Lilith, who turned her head away and looked up at the mountain.

"Is it a secret or something?" Brice asked hesitantly.

"No, no, boy, it was just a very long time ago. Their history is mostly passed down through stories, and I suppose it's time to share them with you. It would be convenient if your sister were here, as well. She learned some of it at her orientation for her reawakening, just as you will. But tonight is as good a time as any."

Brice was interested to learn more of his history. He didn't understand why they made it such a big deal to share it when they were approaching their reawakening, but maybe he'd finally find out.

"Their history takes place in the mid-1800s on the East Coast in Virginia. The Blackstones were an affluent family of tobacco farmers who ventured into grape cultivating for the wine business. The matriarch of the home was Cessily Blackstone, who was also an ambassador and friend to the neighboring village of witches called the Stronghold Coven. Marie, the youngest, wanted to follow in her mother's path after she died, but Dante, her brother, wanted the power of being the witch hunter he felt they had the right to be. Marie's best friend was the daughter of the coven leader, and her secret husband, Judson, who was human, was raised by the witches. Dante didn't like it, and he rallied the other siblings and relatives who had the hunter gene to rise up and take the birthright he felt they were owed. He hated that Marie was—as he called it—blinded to the truth of who they were and that she associated with the witches even after their mother had gone. He burned down the Stronghold Coven's village, killing many of the witches, including the leader. Marie, their father, and several others, including a handful of the coven, fled Virginia and headed west on a wagon train that ultimately met up with the other founders such as the early—and some current—Beaumonts, Bishops, Augustines, Fairchilds, Mills, Stuarts, and our Marie and Judson." His grandma paused and took a drink of her wine and a much needed break from speaking.

"So Dante has been pursuing Marie and her descendants this whole time?" Brice asked with dumbfounded awe. "Why?"

"He believed if he could find Marie and take away all her outlets for her dream to find a new life and way of living as a witch hunter, she would see the error of her ways and come back to him, the family, and their way of life. He felt it was his job to make sure they were all where they were *supposed to be*," his father added with air quotes.

"That's absurd, it doesn't even make that much sense."

"To him it did," Lilith quietly said. "He was very persuasive."

Brice watched his mom. "Did you know him?"

Her gaze found his, and the flatness he saw there told him she had and wished she hadn't.

"It was quite some time ago." Her tone suggested she wouldn't say more on the issue.

"Does anyone know where he is now?" Brice asked, his eyes darting from each member of his family. It was quiet for an awkward moment.

"He's in the Infernum, Brice," his mom finally answered.

CHAPTER 12

"He's in the Infernum, and nobody said anything?" Brice stood from his seat. The Infernum was a part of Hell reserved for supernaturals. "That's kind of a big deal, don't you think? He's been searching for us for years. Does Macy know?"

His mother looked down for a fraction of a second.

"She knows," Brice guessed. "Does everyone know but me?"

"No, it's been kept quiet around the town. We detained him last May after he confronted Hollis. Her truth hit him more than he would let on, and he made a mistake, allowing us to follow him. We were ready, and with the help of Uncle Tranner, Roman Bishop, and Saundra Beaumont, we were able to capture him. He's now and forever secured in the Infernum."

"It's good he's out of the picture, but why not tell me?" He sat back down in a slump.

"Because there was no reason to," his mom answered, then added, "and the less information you have about him, the better."

Brice reared back as if she had slapped him. "Why?"

No one said anything, but eyes drifted toward Lilith. Finally she answered, "Because I don't want you to have anything to do with him."

She slowly stood and went into the bar area to grab another bottle of wine.

"Fine," grumbled Brice. "I'll let it go for now. But I'm sick of being in the dark all the time." He inhaled a deep breath and sipped on his coffee, then looked to his grandma while his dad and Brock cleared the table. "Can you tell me anything else about Judson?"

His grandma cocked her head and stared at him. "Why the sudden interest in him?"

Brice shrugged. "I heard his named mentioned, and I realized I should know more about my great-great-grandfather."

"Sunny," his mom breathed with frustration as she sat back down at the table. "This is Sunny's doing, isn't it?"

Brice didn't say anything. He didn't want to bring Sunny into their discussion.

"I'm just curious," he said with more conviction.

"Well, I know some, but without knowing what you're looking for, I'm not sure what to tell you about him. I got my information handed down from my mother," his grandma said. She bit the inside of her lip and shot a glance at Lilith.

"There may be a way to find out more . . ." his grandma hesitated.

"Mother," Lilith said with a warning in her tone, "it hasn't been found in generations."

"The kids have a right to know about it. Plus, he might be able to find it," she shot back in their secret code speak.

"He's not ready yet."

Eva looked Brice over from top to bottom and nodded. "I think he's ready."

Brice's head bobbed back and forth between the two as if watching a tennis match. "Ready for what?"

"Marie had a journal from her ancestors that is rumored to hold all the knowledge of the witch hunters from our past. It was supposedly hidden, and no one has found it," his grandmother explained. "We searched all the places we could think of, but at some point, we stopped searching."

"A journal? What else could it hold that we—*you*—don't already know?" Brice asked, slightly disappointed in the big secret.

"According to my mother, it worked magically in conjunction with the family dagger, which we have."

"I know that part of the dagger is magic, and our family keeps that part a secret." Brice paused. "The stone holds magic and allows us to infuse a bit of the aether from the falls into each weapon we make for the town, right?"

His grandma nodded along with his father, who returned to his seat. "That's right, son. The aether gives us the ability to continue to reproduce weapons even almost two hundred years later. Passed down from Judson—a blacksmith—was the secret to do so. Somehow, and we don't understand it completely—maybe it would tell us in that journal, if we ever found it—the magic infusing the weapons will adapt to each race, giving them a tailored weapon for them to use with their specific talents. It's brilliant during an actual fight."

Brice smiled, imagining a weapon that could be used by a witch and then by a fae, working differently for each. "That's pretty cool. I didn't know that part."

"When you turn eighteen, that is part of your orientation into being a hunter and an official part of the businesses of the family. Brock got the background just the same so he understood everything the family went through, even though he isn't a hunter. He also helps with the weapons, which you know. He oversees and protects the underground armory at Soothing Sips since he's there every day."

"Could the journal be hidden there?" Brice thoughtfully asked.

His father shook his head. "No, because that was built after Marie and Judson's time. We've also looked in the secret area in the basement of the house as well. But so far, no luck."

Brice's excitement rose with the idea of a hunt. He found

himself wanting to look for the journal. He wasn't sure whether it would be helpful, but the idea of finding it for his family was appealing. An idea suddenly came to him. He remembered what the voice had told him to ask about the dagger and now found himself quite curious. His mom hadn't participated in much of the conversation, he thought because she didn't think he should be a part of it. Not for the first time, he wondered if his mom was ashamed of him because he was different and disrupted the so-far pristine record of all female witch hunters in the family.

"Mom? What do you think of the dagger? Have you ever got to use it, like in a battle?"

Lilith, who had been quiet and appeared to be lost in thought looking at the mountains, swung her head in Brice's direction. The haunted look in her eyes pierced his soul. All the color drained out of her, and she stood abruptly to her feet, throwing her wine glass to the ground, the glass shattering.

"I told you he wasn't ready," Lilith fumed, looking to her mother and then to Reggie.

"Lilith," Reggie said, his tone low and steady.

In the past, something would trigger Brice's mom, and she would become so disconnected from the family, she would stay in her room, sometimes for days at a time. No one—at least none of the kids—knew why. Even now, Brice couldn't figure out what he said that could have triggered such an outburst.

"I blame Sunny."

"This has nothing to do with Sunny," Brice said, heat flooding his words.

His mother's eyes widened at his tone. "She shows up, and all hell suddenly breaks loose. You're going to sit there and tell me she has nothing to do with this?"

"She doesn't! She wasn't the one who told me to ask about it," Brice said, then instantly regretted it. He could feel the surge of energy shoot through his body, but just before it hit his hands he breathed in, trying to stop it. He couldn't lose control here. He just couldn't. Not yet. And he couldn't reveal he had a voice in his head—at least not until he knew who it was or why it was happening.

Lilith and Eva both swung their heads back to Brice in confusion.

"Brice, who told you to ask about it?" Eva asked.

Brice stared at Lilith, his eyes hard and set. He wasn't going to answer if she didn't have to. He folded his arms across his chest in protest.

"Who told you?" Lilith asked barely above a whisper, her teeth clenched together.

"No one."

"Sunny brings trouble. She needs to leave."

"Keep Sunny out of it, Mom." They had a momentary stare-down. Brice turned away first and inhaled sharply through his nose. "Why is it so hard to answer the question about the dagger?" Brice asked. Lilith's eyes flashed.

"Brice," his father's single word held a warning.

"No, this is ridiculous, Dad. It's a simple question."

Lilith simply turned and left, leaving everyone staring after her.

"Some things are as far from simple as they can get, son," Reggie said as he stood. He tipped his glass back and downed his beer, then gently placed the pilsner now empty of Brock's latest brew on the table. "I'll go after her."

"Sorry, Dad. Brock and I will finish any cleaning up," Brice said reluctantly.

His father nodded, then paused. "There are things you will learn soon enough, I'm afraid, then much of this will make sense."

Brice sighed and slumped back in his chair. He snuck a look at his grandma, who still sat in her seat, her back straight and her head held high, sipping on the last of her wine as she gazed up at the mountain.

"Doesn't her behavior bother you, Grandma?"

Eva turned her head to the side, offering Brice a rare sympathetic smile. "Yes, but I also understand it."

She gracefully rose from her seat and patted him on his head as she walked by.

"I wish I understood."

CHAPTER 13

"*Y*ou want a ride home, little brother?" Brock asked as they closed up the winery after cleaning the mess from dinner.

"Nah. Thanks, though. Plus it's out of your way."

"Not like it's that far." Brock chuckled as they walked to the parking lot.

"True." Brice paused. "What time is it?"

"Almost eight, why?"

"Actually, if you don't mind dropping me at school, I think I might check in on the Awakening Lab tonight. Ronya said I could go. Maybe something might be helpful to me as I'm approaching such a delicate stage in my development," Brice said sarcastically.

"Nice. Well, it couldn't hurt. Even if it's about other types of awakenings and supernatural gifts, you'll need all the help you can get." Brock shrugged, then punched Brice in the arm. They both laughed and got in the truck. Brice knew his brother didn't really get it, but Brock also wouldn't look down on him for it.

"Thanks, man."

After arriving at the Academy, Brock dropped Brice off right in front. At night, the Gothic mansion took on a spookier vibe than it did during the day. Old original light fixtures glowed with an otherworldly light, ushering him into the interior courtyard. As other students walked to the evening class, their shadows played games with his mind as they grew and shrunk, depending on the way the lights flickered. He saw Ava Tate—who honestly scared him a bit after rumors of her run-in with police—as she headed in alone. He quickly made his way back to the Castor Center, where Ronya Augustine had told him to go earlier that day. He could hear her calling for everyone to take their seats just as he snuck in through the door. She spotted him and gave him a quick nod, and he found a place to sit near the back.

"Welcome, everyone, to tonight's Awakening Lab," Ronya announced as she opened the class. "If everyone one is here, let's begin."

For the next hour, Ronya used physical examples she had brought with her and even demonstrated some simple magic for the new witches in the room. Brice could feel the magic simmer beneath the skin of his forearms as she did so, but the sensation was still pretty mild in his opinion. His wrist ached, and he tried to flex it without moving it too much. Most of Ronya's teaching was geared toward the new witch or anyone dealing with magic. But she had several general topics and ideals and rules for the newly awakened supernaturals coming into their powers. He was impressed with Ronya's ability to teach and share with many different types of supes and still have it be relevant to them all. After class, he tried to duck out first, but she caught him at the door.

"Brice, I'm so glad you came tonight. Do you feel like you learned something you can help your friend with?" Ronya's eyes were bright with understanding, but also lit with a backdrop of concern. She was worried about him. He was touched.

Brice nodded. "I do. Thank you, Mrs. Augustine. It was most enlightening."

She smiled. "Good. Please come back next week if you want to."

He waved and said goodbye to her and others he saw, then

quickly moved back toward the entrance of the school. As much as he didn't want to face his mom, it was time for him to go home. Not having a ride, he walked to the back of the school to find a shortcut rather than go back out front to the road. The way home through the forest and trails near the falls was a darker way to go, but it would be shorter for him to get home. He wasn't scared, but there had been plenty of stories about things happening in the forests at dark around Havenwood Falls.

"Don't think about that, Brice. Keep your mind focused and stay alert," he coached himself audibly as he walked, soon leaving the lights of the school behind.

However, he didn't get far before he stumbled upon a group of guys he knew from school—both the Academy and Havenwood Falls High. Unfortunately, they weren't friendly guys. And according to the tingles now shooting up his arms, he recognized some of them as witches. In fact, he was pretty sure one or two of them were from Chadwick Linton's group who made catcalls at Sunny in the lunchroom. Chadwick a.k.a. "Chad" was an entitled, rich jock who happened to be a witch. He was also at the skate park the day his troubles began.

"Great," he mumbled to himself. If he stopped, they would know he didn't want to face them or worse, they might think he was scared of them. He wasn't scared, but he didn't want to deal with them either. Instead, he widened his path and pretended not to see them. Maybe if he was quiet, they wouldn't . . .

"Well look who's here, boys. It's Brice Blackstone," one of them called out.

"Where's your new girlfriend, Brice?" another yelled with kissy sounds, which the others joined in chorus.

Brice kept walking, kept ignoring, kept clenching his fists so he wouldn't react.

"She's probably locked up in the loony bin for the night," another jeered while others laughed. "Maybe they only let her out during the day for good behavior."

Keep control. Don't listen to them. Brice ran mantras in his head and kept walking.

"Brice, I know you can hear me. I sense you're alarmed. Are you all right?" The voice was back.

"How do you know?"

"It doesn't matter. What's wrong?"

"Nothing I can't handle. Just bullies saying dumb stuff about a friend of mine." Brice spoke under his breath so the group wouldn't hear him and accuse him of anything.

"Does she treat you right, Brice?" one of the guys taunted with rude gestures, and the others laughed.

Brice stopped. He couldn't make his feet go any farther. Even as he tried to talk himself down, he felt the energy surging within him, building up enough to break through the dam.

"Brice, the only way to take care of bullies is to stand up to them. Don't let them make a fool of you," the voice pushed through the fog in his mind.

"I'm afraid I won't be able to control it. My hunter abilities are just now surfacing. They're witches."

"Forget trying to control it. Let it out. If they deserve it, then let them have it. It's the only way to stop them."

"What's the matter, Brice?" another from the group yelled, but then stopped and spoke to his buddies. "Hey, Chad! Maybe the problem is she won't treat him right. Is that the problem, Brice— she won't put out? She looks like she might be a tease . . . or a tramp!" They laughed.

"She's a tramp, and she won't put out to poor Brice because his power is lame!" another taunted.

Brice roared and took steps in their direction. "She is NOT a tramp. Sunny is the purest and most amazing girl, and you'll never meet anyone like her," he shouted.

"Sunny? Sunny is there?" The voice took on a new tone Brice couldn't decipher in the haze of his fury, nor did he care to.

"Oh, so she's a prude. I bet I could get her to give it up to me," the leader of the group said with a dark sneer. He tossed around a ball of light between his hands, the gesture oddly threatening.

"NO!" the voice in his head shouted at the same time Brice yelled and surged forward, releasing whatever was within him he had held back.

"Wait! Not yet," the voice spoke with an authoritative calm, enough to interrupt his blind rage.

He shot his arms out, and a bolt of light was thrown from one of his hands. The group cried out as they jumped to the sides, split down the middle.

"Whoa! Did you see that? Did he do magic?" different voices said with shock.

The leader stood tall, glaring at Brice. "Nice trick, hunter. A witch give you some fire powder?"

Brice looked down at his hands with both surprise and disgust. How could he have done that? He intended to hurt that boy but at the last second pulled back. He was so angry, but the voice stopped him. Grateful, confused, and flat-out in trouble, Brice turned and ran all the way home.

He didn't stop when he heard the group laughing at him again.

He didn't stop when he ran through a freaky part of the forest.

He didn't stop when he heard the small voice of a tree nymph utter a cry as he broke a tree branch that got in his way.

He didn't stop until he landed in his bedroom, heaving for breath while at the same time wishing for death.

CHAPTER 14

*B*rice slept fitfully that night. His dreams were a mix of him destroying Chad with magic or conversely stealing his magic, leaving him with nothing left. He tossed and turned until the early morning light pierced through his blinds and woke him up at an ungodly hour. However, because of the night he had, Brice was more than ready to wake up. He lay there, dreading going to school after what happened the night before. Finally, his alarm went off, and he got ready for school, putting on his uniform of corduroy pants, dress shirt and tie, and blue blazer. He missed being able to wear skinny black jeans, Vans, T-shirts, and hats with various skater brands on them.

Brice trudged downstairs to the kitchen for breakfast, but as soon as he heard his mom in the kitchen, he veered toward the office in hopes of escaping an encounter with her. But it was too late. She had heard him.

"Brice? Is that you? Come in here, please," she called from behind the wall.

Brice's heart fell to the floor. He had such mixed emotions regarding his mom. He didn't know what mood she would be in.

"Coming," he called anyway as he grabbed his backpack off the floor and brought it with him.

He paused in the entry to the great room and took a deep breath as he moved toward the bar-height counter where his mom read the *Sun & Moon Tribune* while drinking her coffee. She looked up, and their eyes locked on each other, neither one choosing to be the first to speak. He figured she was the parent, so he shouldn't have to.

"Brice . . ." She cleared her throat and tried again, apparently choosing a different tactic. "Your father tells me you confided in him you were experiencing some more sensations of a hunter. Is this correct?"

Brice relaxed his shoulders in relief. Even though they definitely needed to clear the air, he wasn't ready to yet. "A little bit. Maybe. I've been sensing when a witch is near and also a witch hunter."

"Do you feel me right now?" she asked, studying him as he spoke.

He paused and reflected inwardly, gauging his senses, then bit his lip. "Hmm, I guess not. Maybe it's coming and going?"

She nodded as if she figured that was the case. "It is beginning, but it seems you might have a little ways to go yet. You're not quite ready yet. However, I'd like to get your orientation started officially so we can go over any questions you might have. I know Macy made us tell you things earlier on, but I believe there might be more to discuss. Could we make an appointment for next week?" she said, opening her calendar app on her phone.

Brice frowned. "Couldn't we just talk about it at home whenever something comes up?"

Lilith frowned in return. "Don't be difficult, Brice. This is the way it's always been in our family, and it's one of our traditions. We will abide by them so we don't lose them or get off track."

Brice sighed but gave in for now. "Okay, I'll look at my school schedule. I know I have art club with Mr. Weaver at Havenwood Falls High on Tuesday after school and I'd like to go to Awakening Lab again on Thursday night. Other than my work schedule, which you know, that's all I have."

"I'll look and offer a couple options for you. I'll need to double check with the other hunters as well. They all join in on the first part of orientation." She raised her eyes over the rim of her coffee cup just before she took a sip, but he knew she was waiting for a reaction. Macy would have given her one, but Brice remained steady and simply nodded—though inside he was groaning at the rigidity of it all.

He didn't know any other supe in town who had such a rigid awakening as the witch hunters did. He supposed it stemmed from always having to prove themselves to the townspeople they weren't there to hunt the witches. He'd thought after so much time had passed they would be able to relax about it, but apparently not yet. He mentally sighed. Someday. Maybe when Dante and his rogues were gone or out of the picture for good and they didn't have to worry about them. Even with Dante in the Infernum, there seemed to be a feeling of unfinished business, like he was hanging over their shoulders. As far as Brice was aware, it was near impossible to get out of the Infernum once one was held within it; however it had happened a time or two where someone escaped the supernatural part of Hell. Brice had no idea how someone like Dante without any magic could get out, so that gave him peace.

"I'm glad you were able to use the witch's salve on your wrist. Is it healed already enough you don't need a brace?" Lilith asked, eyeing Brice's wrist with a bit of surprise.

Brice rotated his wrist more slowly than he actually could and flexed his finger. "Oh yeah, it's healing up nice."

Brice smiled, grabbed his bag and his board, and headed out the front door.

He skateboarded quite a ways down Blackstone Road before he heard a car pull up behind him. He waved the driver to go around him without looking back to see who it was. After a minute of the car creeping behind him, he turned around with frustration.

Hollis was driving Ryne's truck with Sunny sticking her head and arms out the passenger window, waving. He laughed and smiled at them as he jumped off his board. Hollis pulled up alongside him.

"Morning!" Brice said as he smiled at Sunny.

"Want a ride?" she asked with too much cheer for the early morning. He nodded, and Sunny scooted over to the middle to give him room.

When Brice got settled, he noted the tingles at the base of his neck, recognizing Sunny and Hollis as fellow hunters. The sensations had returned and felt stronger than they had the last time he saw them the night before at the vineyard. He wondered if it was because they were confined in the cab of the truck—or perhaps that had nothing to do with it.

Hollis drove down the long drive to the Academy and circled in front of the building. Both Brice and Sunny got out of the truck.

"Thanks for the ride, Hollis," Brice said with a wave, heading toward the arched entry.

"Wow, Brice, look at all the Halloween decorations!" Sunny said with great admiration as she took in the scene before them. Overnight Halloween had made an additional pass over the school and barfed décor all over. After a few more steps, both Brice and Sunny paused and slowed their movements. She looked at him with a raised eyebrow.

"Do you sense them?"

Brice nodded. "I do. The feelings have been getting stronger. They're nearby."

"Good. There are several together. So we will go around them," she said with a smile, but it seemed she had lost some of the extra enthusiasm she normally carried. Brice gave her an odd look and wondered if she *knew* something. Still learning, he would take his cues from her. They stepped to the other side of the courtyard and carried on as if nothing was out of the ordinary. "It's about trusting your instincts and listening to your heart," she added as she reached down and held Brice's hand.

He almost froze but didn't. He almost passed out from holding his breath, but thankfully he didn't. He kept his cool until the group of witches from last night—Chad's gang, as he thought of them—fanned out from their huddle in the corner and blocked the path, crossing their arms and opening their stance. There was a no-fighting policy at the Academy, and Brice didn't want to get kicked out. He would remain calm and talk his way through the group of six guys.

"Good morning, gentlemen," Sunny said with a smile.

Chadwick leered at Sunny, his eyes roving from top to bottom. Brice stepped in front of her, pulling her behind him.

"Stay away from her," Brice warned in a calm tone.

"What are you going to do about if I don't want to?" he came back. Brice remained quiet. "That's what I thought." Chadwick scoffed with a sarcastic laugh.

"We need to get to class," Brice said loud enough the other students passing by could hear. Many stopped to see what was going on. "This isn't the time or place, Chad." He gripped Sunny's hand and tried to get by the outside of the group.

"I think it's the perfect place to shut your dumb skater face up," Chadwick said.

CHAPTER 15

Several things happened at once. One of the goons reached for Sunny's arm. She squealed. A surge of energy shot through Brice like second nature. He pushed Sunny toward the wall and flung a magical energy shield in front of her to protect her, then threw a punch in the face of the guy who'd tried to pull her. Another guy—he couldn't tell which one—jumped on his back and put him in a chokehold. Brice grappled for a grip, sucking in air so he didn't pass out. Adrenaline soared through Brice, and he held the guy's wrist, then violently bent himself forward, throwing the guy over his head to land on his back. Chad came at Brice and punched him in the eye, then whispered words under his breath. A spell. He enacted a spell against Brice while he was down, clutching his eye.

Hell no. Brice shot out a hand and slammed Chad in the gut with a burst of energy that pushed him against the stone wall. He followed up by putting his other hand right in front of Chad's neck. He didn't physically touch him, but he felt the magic go to the guy's throat. He didn't squeeze. He just kept his pressure there as a threat. He didn't want to hurt the guy, no matter how angry he was at him.

"You need to leave us alone, Chad," Brice said through gritted teeth, barely holding on to control. Something else inside him felt like it was fighting, clawing its way out of his chest. His head turned fuzzy. He tried to focus on the face in front of him. Brice was so tired of being picked on, left out, and thought less of. "I deserve respect," he added.

"Yes, Brice. Yes, you do." The voice was back, whispering in Brice's head.

Nice timing, Brice mentally shot back.

The kid was stupid enough to laugh through the magical pressure Brice put on his throat. Blood trickled out of his nose from a punch.

"You deserve nothing," Chad spat in Brice's face with a sneer.

"Borrow the witch's magic. That'll make him respect you."

How? What's happening to me? Brice asked, feeling his new and limited powers fading as he grew weaker.

"Your hunter is awakening in the presence of a witch. It's the greatest feeling, isn't it? Soak in the power, Brice."

I can't hold him much longer. He's stronger than I am.

"Your mother won't tell you this, but you can have access to your full power right now. All you have to do is pull the boy's energy out and absorb it into yourself. Your hunter will lock on. You just have to let it."

Won't that kill him? Brice asked with a rush. He could feel his metaphysical grip on Chad's neck slipping. Then he'd really be the laughingstock of the school. He'd never live that down, and Chad would never leave them alone. He'd have to homeschool or leave Havenwood Falls.

"He should be fine. Might hurt a bit, but you'll have the upper hand. He'll never bother you again. And everyone watching will respect and revere Brice Blackstone!" the male voice shouted and reveled gleefully in Brice's mind.

A crowd had gathered. Several tried to intervene and stop the fight, but the other witches from the group put up a force field that kept everyone else out. All they could do was watch. Sunny stood outside the barrier now with Hollis, who must have heard the altercation before she left the school. Brice could focus on the bully in front of him, knowing Sunny was safe.

Brice closed his eyes and let his hunter rise to the surface and take over. Within an instant, and almost too easily, he felt the magical energy siphon away from Chad. Brice didn't feel like he had control of himself; his body was on autopilot. He didn't know that would happen. The boy screamed in agony. Brice couldn't stop. He had to keep going.

He needed the energy. He needed the magic. He needed the power!

"Brice, stop!" He heard Hollis shout, but she sounded so far away. "Don't listen to him!"

Brice paused. He wasn't sure he heard Hollis right. Listen to who?

Chad struggled under his invisible hand. Brice had to focus on pulling the energy out and absorbing it into himself. The guy gasped for breath and clawed at anything he could try to grab ahold of, but Brice was just out of his reach.

"You don't want to kill him, Brice." Sunny. Her voice—her simple, non-judging voice—penetrated the fog of his mind. He gasped as he let go of the power his hunter used to suck the magic out of Chad's soul, and he flew back as the magic in his system seemed to backdraft when he completely let go of all control.

Magic? You wielded magic? the voice asked with complete and utter disgust. *How could this be?*

Brice was too exhausted to reply. Chad fell to the ground with a thud and lay limp. His goons released the shield around them and ran to his aid. Brice let Hollis pull him back and away from everyone.

"Is he . . . Did I . . . ," Brice stuttered. He tried to get up and make his way back to Chad. "I need to see . . ."

"He's all right, Brice. You didn't pull his magic out far enough. He'll be fine after a while," Hollis explained with more sensitivity than he had heard used before. Brice nodded and let her pull him back against the wall. She whispered near his ear,

"This isn't good, Brice. The faculty is here. We can't make this go away."

"Everyone get to class now," Mr. Hale demanded without raising his voice. A supernatural mist rose throughout the courtyard, obscuring everyone's sight lines to Brice and Chad. He had a presence about him; people were intimidated by him and students feared him.

"Members of the Court of the Sun and the Moon are on their way." His gaze—though his eyes couldn't be seen well behind his ever-present sunglasses—bored into Chad. "Chadwick Linton, your parents are also on their way," he said, though Chad lay on the ground, still unconscious. He then swiveled his head toward Brice. "Brice Blackstone, you will accompany the members of the Court into town, where your parents will find you."

Brice nodded. He knew better than to say anything at this point. Mr. Damien Hale hadn't been in Havenwood Falls too long. He had transferred under mysterious circumstances from another school where he taught. Brice didn't know much about him other than he was a hellhound and he was a single guy who kept to himself. Mr. Hale turned and went back into the school, fully expecting his orders to be followed.

Brice leaned his head back against the cool gray stone and sighed. He was in so much trouble, but more than that, he had no idea what it was he had even done to Chad. He opened one eye and could see the rise and fall of Chad's chest. One of his buddies stayed with him as well as the secretary, who must have been told to watch them until those responsible for each of them had come.

"It will be okay, Brice. You'll see," Sunny said, then added, "Remember we're on your side."

"I'll try," Brice croaked out when he saw a shiny black sedan pull up right in front of the school. Saundra Beaumont, Michaela Petran, and Addie Beaumont got out of the car. Another vehicle pulled up behind them, and Sheriff Kasun got out.

"The sheriff is here, too?" Brice groaned.

The group walked over to where they were. Saundra knelt

down in front of Chad and felt his head, then his chest. She rose to her feet and faced Brice with a grim expression.

"Brice Blackstone, did you do this?" Saundra gestured down at Chad.

Brice slowly stood. "I did."

The buzzing sensations in his arms became more agitated with their added presence. Saundra was not only in a high position within the Court, but she was also one of the leaders of the Luna Coven and a very powerful witch at that.

"How? Chadwick was attacked with magic, and it seems his magical energy is stressed," Addie provided her own assessment.

"Looks like history finally came back around," Saundra said under her breath.

Brice gave her an odd look, trying to understand what she meant, when he realized she knew Marie and Judson. Saundra would have been young, but she would remember them. He couldn't believe he didn't think to talk to her or others who were still around from that time period.

"Well, let's get this over with." She held out her hand, palm up, in front of Brice.

"What do you propose we do?" Michaela asked. She looked from Addie, one of her best friends, to Saundra.

"Brice, please hold out your hands," Saundra instructed.

Brice did so and watched as she said a spell and a magical cuff encircled his wrists, binding them together. His eyes widened, and he hoped none of the kids from his class could see him. He glanced over to Sunny, but she seemed unfazed by what was happening and gave him an encouraging nod accompanied by a quick smile.

"Handcuffs, Grandma? Is that really necessary? He's not going anywhere," Addie questioned. She pushed her sunglasses to the top of her nose and put her hands on her waist. Addie was a witch and in the last year had found out she was also part hellhound. Brice noted she caught Mr. Hale's attention through the window and gave him a curt nod.

"It is standard procedure, Adelaide," she said.

"It's okay," Brice quietly said. He deserved it. He hurt someone, and so he deserved to be handcuffed. He watched Saundra do something interesting with her hands and then whisper some words before she placed her hands on Chad's chest.

"Brice Blackstone, you are under arrest for the attack on Chadwick Linton. You will come with me, and your parents will meet you at the prison, as you are still underage," Sheriff Kasun explained.

Brice gave Sunny and Hollis one last look of defeat, then he simply went to the truck and waited for the sheriff to let him in. He spared a quick glance at Chad, relieved to see him coming to and being helped to sit up by Saundra.

Brice got shut into the cab of the truck. "Take me to jail, Sheriff."

CHAPTER 16

*B*rice sat on the hard bench up against a cool stone wall in his prison cell. He never thought he would see the inside of a cell in his lifetime, especially not while still underage. Sheriff Kasun had told him he was just being held until his parents came to collect him. He also mentioned that the Court would be involved but he didn't know to what extent—if he would have to have a trial or not. The police station was to the east of City Hall and was small, with only two cells for humans and other special cells for supernaturals.

Leaning his head against the stone, he had time to think. It all had happened so fast, Brice wasn't even sure exactly all that did happen. How had he used magic? Did he really use magic or was it a fluke with his hunter awakening? He could try to explain it away as much as he wanted, but deep down Brice knew he accessed magic. He just couldn't comprehend how. The voice that had been in the back of his mind the last several days was mysteriously quiet. During his encounter with Chad, it felt like the voice was right there with him, even enforcing its will through Brice. He was pretty sure he wasn't possessed. Wouldn't someone know if they were? And if he claimed "the voice made him do it," he was pretty sure that wouldn't go over well with anyone—except maybe Sunny, since she had her own voices.

Brice thought of Sunny and hoped she was all right. He tried to protect her the best he could in that moment, but he didn't have much time to check on her and see. It was strange, now he had time to think on it, how the voice seemed to know Sunny. And Hollis had made reference to not "listening to him," when Brice hadn't told her—or Sunny, for that matter—anything about his voice. Irritation crept up through his chest. How could the voice just leave him hanging like that?

"Hey! Are you there?" Brice said out loud, forgetting where he was.

"I'm here, Brice. What do you need?" Sheriff Kasun responded from down the hall.

Brice backpedaled, unsure what to say. "Uh . . . do you know how much longer my parents are going to be?" That should work.

"Your dad just called and said they would be here in ten minutes. Hang in there, son. You won't have to stay too much longer."

"Thanks, Sheriff."

Brice tried again, but this time he closed his eyes and thought of the voice. He thought of the cadence in the way he spoke, and the timbre of his tone. He directed his energy toward wherever that voice had come to him from. Without truly understanding it, Brice accessed the energy he had felt move through him before, and then it suddenly stopped, as if hitting a brick wall. Brice wasn't sure what to do now, so he guessed.

Hello? Are you there?

"*Brice? How did you contact me?*" the voice said with a hint of alarmed surprise, or even a hint of anger—Brice couldn't tell for certain through the connection.

I backtracked the way it feels when you speak to me. Brice mentally shrugged like it wasn't that hard to figure out. *What happened earlier? What did you have me do?* Brice felt himself getting worked up and slowly inhaled, calming his racing heart.

"I simply helped you access the power you have within you as a witch hunter. You shouldn't have to suppress it and be treated like a caged animal until their appointed time. You and I are destined to work together, to be an unstoppable team. Be free and be who you are meant to be! I helped you become powerful!"

Brice had a moment of confusion, torn between liking the feeling of being powerful and afraid of what it could do to him. The uncertainty of the voice's identity weighed on him. Though he was afraid to admit it, he had an idea of who the speaker was.

"Is he speaking to you, Brice?" a woman's voice interrupted his connection.

Brice startled and opened his eyes to find Hollis standing on the other side of the bars, watching him intently.

"What are you talking about?" Brice played dumb and looked away from her eyes.

"My father. He recently tried to talk to me, but because of the new wards around me, he had a hard time getting through. But because you're in a transition period with fluctuating energy, the wards aren't quite as strong until you turn eighteen and reinforce your commitment to the town," Hollis explained, as if she were an old veteran of Havenwood Falls protocol.

"Your father?" Brice stood. The color drained from his face, and he felt light-headed. He didn't want to acknowledge it, but hearing her say it out loud confirmed his own suspicions.

Hollis watched him and nodded knowingly.

"How could he even do that? He's in the Infernum, and he doesn't have that ability, does he?"

Hollis shrugged. "There are ways. Maybe he has a witch working for him even in there. I chose to ignore him, and he went away, frustrated to not get through to me."

"Anyway, he's not speaking to me. I don't know what you mean."

Hollis gave him a small smile and shrugged her shoulders. "Well, that's good then. I just wanted to make sure and get a moment with you before your mom gets here."

Brice sat back down. "Thanks, Hollis. I appreciate you checking on me."

Hollis turned and left down the hall, leaving him to his thoughts once more. Her father? No, he didn't think that was possible.

Are you still there? Brice went back into his mind. He needed to find out for himself.

"*I'm here. I'll always be here for you. Seems I might be the only one that gets you. You need the power, unlike the others, don't you? You can handle it better than they could. That's why they make everyone wait for it, because they can't handle it. But you can.*"

Brice rubbed his eyes then pinched his nose. Some of the words hit him as truth. He once more felt confused by all the rules they had to abide by in Havenwood Falls. If everyone would simply trust him with information and include him without all the secrecy, they wouldn't be in this mess. This was their fault. He knew deep down that wasn't true, but he was angry, alone, and wanted someone to blame.

You're right.

"*Of course I am. Now, what is this nonsense of you using magic? You don't need filthy magic unless it advances your needs. You and I are the same in that way.*"

I . . . I don't know exactly. I think I have magic, my own magic.

"*Impossible!*" the voice roared.

Well, is it? If a witch and a witch hunter had children, isn't it possible one might have magic? Brice asked, suddenly thinking of Marie and Judson. But as far as anyone knew, Judson didn't have magic.

"*That is an abomination! Our kind does not mix with their* kind. *That's what your sister couldn't seem to let go of. That is her failure.*"

Brice scrunched his face. The pieces to his puzzle were beginning to create a pretty strong case regarding who he spoke with. And he didn't like his sister being involved in whatever this was. He started to feel wary of the voice. His strong feelings about mixing of the types of supernaturals was a bit harsh considering he didn't know any of them personally—again adding to the clues stacking up.

"I know more than you might think, being where I am."

Where are you? Brice asked suspiciously.

"In a cage, similar to yours. Time to go. Stay away from the magic, Brice, or I won't help you."

What? How can you say that? What if I need help? Hello? Brice asked over and over, but there was a mental block. How did he do that?

"Brice?" his father's voice penetrated his mental preoccupation.

"Dad!" He rushed up to the bars. "Is Mom here too?"

Reggie nodded. "She's talking to the sheriff, then will be right here. Go easy on her, Brice. This is harder on her than she's letting on."

"Hard on *her*?" Brice said with an outraged whisper. "What about me? I don't know what the hell is going on with me!"

"That's what I want to know," Lilith sternly said as she walked into the cell area.

"Mom," Brice acknowledged, but sat back down.

"I thought you might like to know Chadwick Linton will recover just fine. The Court has agreed to not arraign you based on your age, but is requiring that you undergo not only your orientation into being a witch hunter, but also community service."

"Community service?" Brice complained. "He started it."

"And you could have killed him!" his mom shot back. "Be grateful his parents aren't pressing charges. It was all Saundra and I could do to keep them from coming down here themselves. And I wouldn't blame them. What the hell happened out there, Brice? How could you lose control like that?" Lilith's voice rose and something akin to shock filled her expression. Her voice lowered and tightened as if the words choked her throat, and she gripped the bars. "How could you not know what you were doing to that boy? How could you do this to me again?"

She gasped and folded in on herself. Brice watched something transpire in his mom he hoped he would never see. She was broken. Her control slipped, and she instantly seemed a shell of the woman she normally was.

"Mom?" Brice asked, then looked to his dad, who placed his hand on her lower back with tears in his eyes.

"Brice, this is my fault. This is all my fault." She appeared to be having a revelation. So as long as she wasn't blaming him, Brice remained quiet and let her continue.

Lilith turned haunted eyes on her husband who, with understanding, nodded encouragement to her. "Go ahead, Lilith. It's time you let this go. To help your son, you need to deal."

"Eighteen years ago, I killed a boy . . . a witch."

"What?" Brice practically shouted. How did they not know about that?

"I was having a hard time conforming to all my mother's rules and the traditions of the town. I wasn't sure if their way was how I truly wanted to live. Even though I already had your brother and sister, I felt I was missing out on something. I left town and found Dante and his rogue witch hunters. I lived with them for a season. I trained with them and worked with them and one day, I killed with them. I had a reality check when I realized I was pregnant with you, and I knew I didn't want to live like those Blackstones lived. I missed my family and determined that from that day on, we would live by the traditions and rules of our town and our Blackstone hunters even more than before. Not long after I had you, I took Aunt Letti's seat on the Court. Then when Macy ran away a couple years ago and found Dante, I realized my actions had more of an effect on my children than I thought. In my efforts to protect you all and myself, I ended up pushing you all away. And I . . . I'm sorry, Brice."

Brice's mouth hung wide open. He looked back and forth between his father and his mother. A bomb had dropped, and he didn't know what to do . . . what to say.

"I . . . uh . . .wow, what to say after that . . . Thank you for being honest, Mom. Wow. We always knew you carried around something big, but we had no idea what it could be."

Brice sat back down and stared at his parents through the bars. "Now what?"

CHAPTER 17

Sheriff Kasun entered right at that moment and unlocked Brice's cell. "You can use the conference room if you would like some privacy, or you can stay here. Whatever suits your needs."

"Thanks, Ric. I think we'll just take a few more minutes and sit here with Brice," Reggie said. They entered the cell and sat on either side of him on the bench.

"Now, Brice, tell us what happened, please," Lilith said with a softer tone.

"Chad and his goons—who happen to be witches—had been giving me a hard time at school. Since Sunny arrived, they added her into the mix. We tried to enter the school, and they blocked us. One of them tried to pull Sunny, and I lost it. I hit him."

"Like physically?" his dad asked.

Brice nodded. "I punched him in the nose."

"He deserved that," Lilith said, to both their surprise. "What? They manhandled a girl against her will. Continue."

"Then the fighting started. I somehow threw out a magical shield and pushed Sunny out of the way. One got on my back, and I threw him over my shoulders, then Chad was working up a spell. He was going to use magic against me. I defended myself, and instinctively, I threw out a lightning bolt type energy that pushed him against the wall. It held him there. He said nasty things. I got closer to him. I was so angry." He paused, reliving the moment and taking a breath. "Then I felt my hunter side take over, and I pulled at his magical energy." He stopped and looked at his parents. They hadn't said anything. "That's it. That's what happened."

"First, you defended yourself and your friend. I would expect nothing less," his dad interjected, and his mom agreed.

"Secondly, I didn't pay attention to the signs, or give you the opportunity to share with me that you were having symptoms of your hunter reawakening," his mom added. So far Brice was liking the direction this talk was headed. "But Brice, we don't understand how you think you used magic. Witch hunters don't have active magic. You know this."

"Could one of the witches be playing a prank on you? Or would one of your friends make it look like you did magic?" his dad asked.

Instantly deflated, Brice lost hope in their conversation. "No. No one would do that. I did magic. And I have nothing further to say if you don't believe that." He moved his wrist back and forth. "How do you explain my wrist all healed?"

"I gave you the witch's salve, Brice. Although, that does seem awfully fast even for that assistance." His mom examined his wrist and cocked her head with a frown.

"Why don't we take this home and continue to talk about it? Brice, we're not saying we don't believe you. We just don't understand yet," his dad tried to explain as they all got up and walked out of the cell.

With goodbyes to Sheriff Kasun and release papers signed, they left to head home. Brice felt lost again. He thought something amazing had just happened with his parents, and it had, but it only lasted but a moment. Once again, he didn't know why he was the outcast in his family. He stared out the window of the backseat of the car, watching the town pass by in a blur. His mind fogged over, and he heard the voice loud and clearer than it had been before.

"Brice. I was harsh before. I didn't think it possible for you to wield magic, but I believe you. I still believe we are destined to be a team."

Can you help me understand how to use my hunter? I think the magic is fighting with it inside me. But it feels strong and wants to be dominant.

"I will help you. I know a witch in town who will help you, too, if you tell her I sent you."

Brice thought over the proposition for a second. This was it. Final confirmation. *I need to know who you are.*

"First, I'll tell you your friend Sunny had a vision long ago where we of the same name were together. Then I disappeared, and you took my place. It meant you are to be my successor, and I am to be your mentor."

Brice didn't like the sound of that. He also didn't like that Sunny would have had a vision about him that important and not told him about it. Perhaps he shouldn't have trusted her so fast. But that thought broke his heart.

Are you telling me your name is Brice? Brice couldn't help himself.

He heard a haughty chuckle in his mind. *"No, I'm saying there are two Dantes."*

Silence. Hollis was right. Somehow Dante was communicating with him from the Infernum.

Shit. His forehead broke out in a cold sweat, his hands grew clammy, and his breathing escalated. He thought he might pass out. And yet he had also wanted Dante's help. Brice felt sick.

"Dad, pull over. I'm going to be sick," he said through a hand covering his mouth. Reggie pulled the car over right next to the cemetery on their way home after having to run a quick errand at Miller's Plaza. Brice threw open the door and jumped out, falling to all fours on the grass to the side of the road.

"Brice, are you okay?" his dad said, coming up next to him.

His mom stood nearby, looking uncertain of her role for the first time. She had never been very maternal before. He didn't think she needed to start now.

Brice nodded. "I think so."

"Brice, we are meant to be a team. I will help you in a way that no one else can. I have experience and connections that could all be yours if you let me pass them on to you."

No, this isn't the way it's supposed to be. Sunny was wrong.

"Sunny is never wrong!" the voice shouted in his mind. The fog grew to where Brice could barely think for himself. He had flashes of things in his mind's eye he didn't even know about. He saw Sunny. He saw Chad holding Sunny with a knife. He felt his feet begin to move, to run so fast he almost couldn't keep up with them.

"Brice! Brice!" He barely heard his parents' voices as they grew distant.

Sunny. Sunny was all Brice could think about. Something bad was going to happen to Sunny if he didn't get there soon.

Brice absently realized he ran through the cemetery proper for the humans. The lawns were meticulously cared for and the headstones were neatly kept. He was compelled. He couldn't stop if he wanted to. In the back of his mind he wondered if Dante was somehow controlling his movements, but the other part of him that cared for Sunny beyond anything he had ever felt before didn't care. He had to get to her.

Swiftly, he followed the path to the stone-pillared arch leading to the tunnel that went under Blackstone Road. He came out in the other side of the cemetery—the supernatural side. This section was far less neat and tidy, but he could feel the sacredness, even as fast as he ran. Vaguely, he noted he ran toward the section of mausoleums near the back. His arms crawled with the tingly sensation indicating the presence of magic; the wards in this part were extremely strong and very old.

He came to an abrupt stop in front of one of the oldest structures. The gray stone was intact, but chips and pieces of it had crumbled with time and weather. But what he couldn't stop staring at was the sight of Sunny standing before him.

And the sight of Chadwick Linton standing behind her with one arm around her neck in a head lock and the other holding a knife poised at her throat.

"Sunny."

CHAPTER 18

$\mathcal{B}$rice quickly caught his breath. He was afraid to move. He didn't know what to do. Chad had an evil sneer across his face as he proceeded to slowly poke the tip of the knife into Sunny's perfect, smooth, porcelain neck. His eyes found hers. She was calm, and her eyes held a deep well of emotion. She smiled at him. He couldn't believe it. He guessed when someone knew what was going to happen, they could be prepared for it.

"I was waiting for you. I knew you would come," Sunny said. Brice smiled at her.

"Of course I did. I will always come for you, Sunny." And in that moment, Brice realized it was true. Sunny had found a way into his heart.

"I know." She smiled again at him.

"Shut up. Both of you!" Chad said, wiggling the knife back and forth to remind them he still held it.

"Chad, don't do this," Brice said with an even tone, not wanting to scare him into to doing something even more stupid.

"Chad's not here at the moment, Brice," the voice he had heard in his mind said out loud through Chad's mouth.

Dante.

"How are you doing this? Why are you doing this?" Brice questioned.

Chad's eyes were vacant. The only thing Brice could think of was one of his zombie video games. Chad was Dante's puppet.

"Because, Brice, I need you. I already told you we are meant to be a team. And now that you have magic, I realized it can lend to my agenda."

"Which is what?" Brice asked, feeling like he wasn't getting something important.

"With enough magic, I can escape this hellish place," he spat out.

"Is it even possible for you to escape the Infernum?" Brice asked.

"He figured out how to use a very powerful witch also in the Infernum to communicate out," Lilith explained, coming up behind Brice with his father. "Apparently, he also is using her to manipulate bodies as well." She gestured toward Chad and Sunny. Brice was sure he was also being manipulated physically both just now and earlier at the school.

At that moment, Sunny cried out in pain. Chad had pierced her skin with the knife.

"I expect you to pay attention to me," Dante said, using Chad's voice. "Hello, Lilith. It's good to see you again. I've been instructing your boy. You've been neglecting him in such a time of transition. Someone had to step in."

"Dante. I'll take it from here," she said with complete control, not giving him the fight he sought after. She stood tall and strong, fierce as she always did in a battle, but something new— confidence in herself perhaps—came through as she spoke. Brice admired his mom for maybe the first time, understanding more of what she had been through. He supposed that was part of growing up: seeing your parents' faults and realizing they were fallible and doing the best they could too, making mistakes and everything. Just like he had.

"Dante, you came for me. Let Sunny go and deal with me,"

Brice said. His mom gave him a look that said she wasn't happy with his tactic. He shrugged. This was his mess. He intended to see it through, whatever the outcome.

"I like this boy, Lilith. That is why you named him after me, isn't it? Because you knew we were ultimately destined to be together, for me to take him under my wing and train him as my own."

Dante was demented, but apparently he believed it.

Lilith was about to say something, but Brice held up his hand to stop his mother. Brice moved slowly closer toward the mausoleum.

"Let her go, Dante. You don't need her. You need me," Brice coaxed.

"You're right. I don't need her," Dante spat, then took the knife and stabbed her in the side as he shoved her away.

"No!" Brice shouted, about to run after her, but Dante quickly changed tactics and put the knife to himself—or to Chad.

Sunny stumbled into Lilith's arms. Reggie typed something into his phone, then helped lay Sunny on the ground. Sunny waved at Brice, letting him know she would be okay.

"That wasn't necessary, Dante," Brice scolded, his voice taking on a strange new authority.

"I needed assurance." The sight was strange. It looked as if Chad was about to take his own life, holding a knife to his own neck at an odd angle.

"What do you need from me?"

"Take his magic. Absorb the energy of his soul into your being as soon as I say," Dante instructed with vehemence.

Brice didn't know enough about how that part of him worked, so he agreed.

"No, Brice. You don't understand what that will do to you," his mom pleaded from behind him.

He turned his head and looked into his mom's eyes. Yeah, he had an idea what it might do to him. Then his gaze found Sunny's.

The confidence she held in her eyes for him made all the difference.

Brice stepped forward, closer to Chad. Being that close when he wasn't fighting him felt awkward and anticlimactic, but he positioned himself to be within range.

"Okay, Dante. I'm ready. Let's be a team."

Chad let out a maniacal laugh. The sight would haunt Brice the rest of his life, if he lived much longer. Unexpectedly, Dante shoved Chad's own hand with the knife into his chest. A gurgled scream pierced the air.

At the same time, Brice felt a hand at his back.

"Take this," his mom whispered into his ear while he felt a sharp sting in the palm of his hand. He flinched but didn't lash out like he wanted to. Then she gripped his hand around the hilt of a sword. He was familiar with that feeling, working with the weapons in their basement. He nodded but kept it behind his back. Did his mom want him to finish Chad off?

Just as Chad's body slumped to the ground, he heard Dante's voice back in his mind. *"It's time, Brice. Do it now!"*

Brice knelt on the ground over Chad's body and placed a hand on his chest. He barely felt Chad's life force. His breathing was low and shallow.

No. This is not how this was supposed to happen. Brice leaned forward, closed his eyes, and let his hunter come to the surface. He inhaled deep and slow, imagining himself taking the energy from Chad, while hoping to keep him alive.

"The dagger, Brice. Use it," Lilith said.

He pulled what he thought was a sword from behind his back and looked at it. It was the family dagger they used with the creation of weapons. He frowned when he saw red smeared over the hilt. His blood. It covered the now glowing stone set in the middle.

Glowing. The dagger glowed!

Brice's hunter pulled at Chad's witch energy against his will. But then Brice felt the other energy within him. He felt magic surging forward in his body. The magic collided with his hunter. He could feel the tug-of-war within his chest. He struggled to focus. The dagger grew brighter and brighter. He didn't stab Chad with it but instead laid it against his chest and made his intentions clear.

His hunter pulled and pulled, then combined with the magic and with a great burst, pushed it back into Chad instead. Chad's body lit up like a star in the sky. Brice pushed the magic further and further, sending it along the mental channel he felt connected with Dante until he heard a bloodcurdling scream in his mind.

Brice blacked out.

CHAPTER 19

*W*hen Brice came to, he was once more in his bedroom. Maybe the entire thing was a dream. He rolled over and closed his hand, but pain shot through it. He looked and saw a bandage around the center of his hand where his mom had sliced him.

Nope. Not a dream. A nightmare. Had Dante killed Chad while Brice stood by and watched? He almost didn't want to know what had happened. He got up and went to his window. The sun was making its way down for the evening. All he wanted to do was go back to bed, but he needed to face the music.

Downstairs he heard voices in the kitchen. A lot of voices.

"Brice! Hey, Brice is awake," Macy shouted as she ran and threw her arms around him, practically choking him with her hug.

"Hi, Mace, what's going on?"

"Macy, let him breathe," his mom scolded as she came over to look at him. Instead of keeping her distance, though, Lilith looked at him, then brought him in for an awkward hug.

"I'm so glad you're okay, Brice. You scared us like you'll never know," she said.

"What's going on here?" Brice asked and rubbed the sleep out of his eyes.

"We're beginning your orientation and having family dinner, too," Macy said. "Mom and Dad are springing for Napoli's pizza!"

Brice looked around the room and saw almost everyone: Macy went to stand with Gallad, who helped get out paper plates. Grandma Eva stood near the window and smiled at him. Aunt Letti and her husband, Uncle Tranner, the dragon shifter, were outside on the patio with his father and Brock, and as he scanned the room, he realized the only people not there were Hollis, Ryne, and Sunny. He frowned.

"They are on their way, don't worry," Aunt Letti said as she entered the house.

"Is Sunny okay, Mom? Shouldn't she be in the hospital?" Brice couldn't help but remember how Chad who was Dante had stabbed her in the side. His throat bobbed.

"She is just fine. Luckily, Sunny had told the Luna Coven and Dr. Underwood to be at the cemetery at that precise moment. They were able to heal her immediately," Lilith explained.

Brice's shoulders relaxed. "Good. That's good." He looked back to his mom. "What about . . ." He dreaded the possible answer.

"Chad?" Eva impatiently supplied for him. Brice nodded gratefully.

"Chad's going to be fine," Gallad said from the other side of the room. When Brice swiveled his head in Gallad's direction, he continued. "I checked in on him this morning at the clinic, since he's part of the coven."

Brice nodded, then paused. "Wait, this morning?"

"Brice, it's Sunday. You've been asleep for two days," Macy said, her face holding concern for him.

"I slept for two days? Whoa." Brice shoved his flopping hair out of his eyes and inhaled. "That's kinda cool!" He smiled, then laughed with so much relief that he didn't kill Chad or Sunny. He might not have been holding the knife, but it was because of him they were both involved.

"What else did I miss?" he asked.

Macy moved back in a little closer to him. "Mom told us

everything she told you while you were in jail. Makes so much more sense, doesn't it?"

Brice nodded. "Yeah, crazy, right?"

"She's been acting different since you've been asleep. Like . . ." She chewed the inside of her cheek while she thought of a word to describe their mom. "Like . . . nicer!"

"I heard that, Macy Marie Blackstone," Lilith said from the kitchen.

Macy punched Brice in the shoulder. "I still can't believe my little brother was in jail."

Brice huffed. "That's the part you're focusing on?" He shook his head. "Go for it. Makes things easier for me."

"We want to know, but we're waiting for the rest of the family to get here," Macy added. Brice understood and nodded. They wanted to know the rest of the story from his perspective, but they would wait for everyone.

At that same moment, the front door opened.

"We're here. Can we come in?" Hollis shouted.

"Of course, dears, come in," Aunt Letti yelled back. And into the great room walked Ryne holding several Napoli's pizza boxes and a big smile on his face. Behind him Hollis also carried several of the same boxes.

"We have the pizza!" Sunny said with a playful shout as she skipped in behind them. She instantly spotted Brice and went straight for him. "Brice!" she said and threw her arms around his neck and hugged him tight. He wrapped his arms around her waist and hugged her back. He even added in a twirl, lifting her off the ground. She giggled, and he put her down.

"How is it you are all here when I woke up?" he asked, curious.

"Sunny," they all said in unison, to which she smiled and shrugged.

He gave Sunny a secret look and whispered, "Do they know about your gift?"

She nodded with enthusiasm. "I had to explain why I told them all to be at specific places at specific times."

It seemed the Blackstones were ready to tell all—at least to each other.

They all grabbed their pizza and went outside to sit on the patio and enjoy the last of the daylight before the sun set.

Brice took a few bites, then asked, "So what happened after I blacked out at the cemetery?"

Reggie stood from his seat. "Not much, actually. The Luna Coven arrived just as the light exploded from the dagger and had Sunny and Chad taken to the medical center. They checked you out as well, but as you had simply passed out from exhaustion and spent magic, we took you home."

"And what about . . ." Brice hesitated, especially as his gaze landed on Hollis's, then figured he'd just out with it. "What about Dante?"

Lilith pursed her lips. "I don't know how you did it, but according to the hellhounds that guard the Infernum, there was a burst of light inside the prison and a shower of ash. You . . . extinguished Dante." She also glanced quickly at Hollis. He was a bad man, but he was still her father—or had been.

"Hollis . . ." Brice started, but he really didn't know what to say.

"Don't be sorry, Brice. I've had a couple days to process it, but in truth I had to process him and all he had done and him going to the Infernum months ago. You did what you had to do to protect people and your town." Hollis offered him a small smile.

"I'm sorry I lied to you when you came to me while I was in jail. I'd been hearing your father, but I didn't know for sure it was him until then. There may have been some part of me that thought it might have been, but I didn't want to believe I would have been so naive and desperate to listen to him."

"I've been there, Brice. I get it. And I knew you were, but wanted you to come to it on your own." She gave him a nod, acknowledging that he did come to it.

"So the big question on everyone's mind is: how does Brice have magic?" Macy bluntly asked.

"I had the opportunity to speak with Saundra Beaumont while Brice was asleep," Letti began as she put her food on the table. "She was there when Marie and Judson were alive. She was young then, but she said she remembered them and what happened. She and the others who also were around during that time took an oath not to reveal their secret until it was time to be revealed."

"What does that even mean, Letti? Get on with it," Eva prodded.

"I'm getting there, Eva. Hold your horses. What she said was that sometime after Marie and Judson had arrived in Havenwood Falls, Judson discovered, with the help of the aether in the water from the falls, that he actually was a witch." There was a collective gasp. "He had been spelled to hide his magic for his protection apparently from a feuding coven, but he never knew it. The Luna Coven unbound his magic, and he became a practicing witch. Then, after their children were born with both witch hunter tendencies and magic, things went wrong. They didn't know how to guide the children, and their counterparts were at war within themselves. After some trouble, they all—including the children— decided to spell the children's magic side, allowing only the hunter side to come out. For the sake of the children and ease of the bloodline, they didn't pass down that information and locked it away with the Blackstone journal."

Everyone remained quiet for a moment.

"Wow, that's a lot," Macy said. "So why don't any of the rest of us have magic, as well?"

"Because the spell was broken when I broke my oath as a witch hunter," Lilith said with some revelation.

"Do I have to have that part suppressed, too, then?" Brice asked with disappointment.

"I don't know, Brice," Lilith answered. "Do you think you can manage both sides?"

Brice thought for a moment and honestly replied. He also

thought of the future for Macy and Gallad; they would be in a similar situation to Marie and Judson's. He wanted to try for their sake as well. "I think so. I would like to try."

Lilith nodded. "I'll appeal to the Court, then. As long as you can learn to control it and we don't have any issues, I don't see why you would have to."

Brice smiled. For the first time, he felt his mom heard him and respected him as a person and as a member of their family.

CHAPTER 20

$\mathcal{B}$rice performed community service as his punishment required by the Court of the Sun and the Moon. Hollis and Sunny had just picked him up in Ryne's truck from the police station. Brice got in the car and instantly reached for Sunny. She smiled and gave her hand to him. Since things had calmed down, Brice and Sunny had gone out on several dates. She had told him they would be together, and in his mind, it was forever.

They were turning onto Blackstone Road to take them up to the Blackstone house for family Taco Night when Sunny gasped with glee and gripped Brice's hand hard.

"Sunny, what is it?" he asked, while Hollis slammed her foot on the brakes, abruptly stopping the truck.

"I know where it is!"

"Where what is?" Hollis asked, and glanced at Brice, who shrugged.

"The journal. I know where it is! Well, kind of," she said, then frowned.

Brice turned toward her in the small cab of the truck. "The Blackstone journal?" Sunny nodded profusely. "Where, Sunny?"

She closed her eyes and said, "At the vineyard. I see grapes. I see bookshelves. I see a stone room with a box."

Brice frowned. "That's a little vague, but let's head to the vineyard!"

Once there, they searched in all the outbuildings and even recruited Aunt Letti, who was working there at the time. Taking a break, they went inside the main lobby for NamaStays Inn and sat in the couches. Frustrated, Brice looked around and noted how the decor in that building was as rustic modern as the winery and the tasting bar, Soothing Sips.

"Aunt Letti, this building was here first, right? I mean, our house was not the first place Marie and Judson lived, right?"

"Correct. They lived here first while they built the vineyard and then as it succeeded, they built the bigger house—your house —sometime later. Why?" she questioned.

Brice stood and slowly moved around the room, examining it. "Well, we renovated it when we updated the other buildings for the winery. So I'm imagining what it might have been like as their home."

"Well, the rooms upstairs would have been bedrooms, similar to what they are now. The kitchen would be the same. We opened up a wall over there to create a bigger sitting area." She pointed to the area just before the hall.

Brice's eyes widened as he spotted a row of bookshelves. "Sunny! Didn't you see bookshelves? Do these look familiar?"

Sunny ran over and studied them. She smiled, then nodded. "Yep, those are them!"

"Brice, I hate to burst your bubble, but we've examined all the books in those shelves and the secret basement behind it. The Court knew all about it, as this was the original weapon cache. It was close to Judson's forge and had easy access to store them. We had the very thought that you do: that perhaps the ancestors would have left information or anything pertinent to the family, such as a journal. But over the years we found nothing."

Brice frowned. "I'm going to do my own search, if that's okay."

"Go for it."

"Brice, I didn't see the book in the shelf. I saw a box in a stone room," Sunny reminded him.

"Right. Let's just look to make sure we aren't missing something."

Brice, Sunny, and Hollis spent the next several minutes looking at all the spines and examining different books. But came up with nothing. "Hey, Aunt Letti, can you tell me how to open the bookcase?"

Aunt Letti shook her head in denial. "No way. This is your adventure. You can figure it out."

She gave him a wink and a sneaky smile.

Disappointed, Brice put his hand on one of the books—he didn't even look which one—and pulled it out. Something clicked and a mechanism whirled. Brice jumped back and watched in awe as the bookshelf moved to the side.

"Whoa!" Reggie and Hollis said simultaneously, as Reggie entered the room.

"Looks like you found it," Aunt Letti said with a smile, straightening up a pile of papers on the front desk counter.

"Call the family, please, Letti," Reggie said, watching the bookshelf move seemingly on its own as it opened up into a doorway with stairs leading down.

Reggie stuck his head into the hole next to Brice's. "What do you think, Dad?"

"Well, it's been searched multiple times, but there's nothing wrong with a fresh pair of eyes." Reggie peered down into darkness.

"We're going to need some flashlights." But just as Brice took one step down, light illuminated the stairwell. "Or it could be made with a spell that defies time itself," Brice said with awe.

"That is awesome," Hollis said, watching from behind with Sunny, her face an expression of pure joy.

"Go ahead. I'll let Lilith know where you are when she gets here," Letti said, shooing them to go explore.

Brice, Reggie, Hollis, and Sunny all made their way down the stairs into a decent-sized stone room. It didn't make up the entire footprint of the house, but it was at least the size of the living room area upstairs. Floor-to-ceiling gray stone surrounded them on all four sides. A few weapons still hung on the walls, ready and waiting to be used. A large, long metal slab upon wooden triangles for legs created a type of worktable. The room was covered in dust, and cobwebs graced every corner and edge.

"Anybody see anything resembling a journal?" Hollis doubtfully asked, running a finger down the table, leaving a trail in the dust behind her. Each of them looked around the room, but there weren't too many places anything could hide.

"I saw a box," Sunny said. "It had pretty details on it, but I don't see it here."

Reggie silently studied the room, calculating something under his breath.

"What is it, Dad?"

"Something is off about the stonework in this area." He walked over to one wall and pointed out a section with his finger, drawing the outline of a shape for the others to see. "I've never noticed it before."

"I see it!" Brice said with excitement. He ran his hands over the area. "It feels different too."

The others each took a turn, wanting to feel what had Brice and his dad in a quandary.

"This is it!" Sunny clapped her hands.

"What's it?" Hollis asked.

"The journal, it's in there," she said, with an expression saying it was obvious. "It's Brice's turn!"

Reggie looked at Brice with a question in his eyes. "Well, how do we get it?"

Brice chewed his bottom lip in concentration. "Maybe magic?"

"Can't hurt to try it," Hollis stated. She and Reggie stepped back in case something backfired, but Sunny stayed right up beside Brice, expectation on her face.

Brice closed his eyes and concentrated. He focused on the

magic within him. Different witches including Jessica Calloway, Ryne's mom, and Mathilde Augustine had been working with him little by little. He had been getting familiar with it in his free time and had been able to find it easier. He called on his magic and focused it on the wall. Brice focused on his intention to have the journal and placed his hand on the wall. Something depressurized underneath his hand and part of the wall separated and flung out toward him.

"You did it!" Sunny clapped, and the others rushed forward next to him. "Pull it out."

Brice's eyes were wide. He did it, he really did. He didn't see anything at first. "What if there's a trap or something, and it takes my hand off?"

Sunny laughed. Brice gave her a funny look, but he realized she still simply waited for him to do what he had come there to do. So he reached in and felt around. Sure enough, his hand touched something book-sized. He gently gripped it and pulled it out.

"The journal," he said with awe. The journal was a very old leather-bound book with a strip of red suede connected as a bookmark. On the cover of it was detailed metalwork that looked to be an opening for something to fit inside it. Brice gently ran his fingers over the cover.

He looked up and smiled at everyone there. "We did it."

He passed the journal to Sunny, but she bit her lip and shook her head. He handed it to his father, who examined the book for a moment and flipped open to the first few pages. "We need to be very gentle; this is extremely old."

"They're here," Aunt Letti shouted down the stairs.

"We're coming up," Reggie announced. "We should show it to everyone." He handed the book back to Brice, who cradled it protectively in his arms as they went back upstairs.

At the top, those who could get there on short notice had gathered in the lobby area. Brice took the time to take the journal around to his grandmother, his mother, his sister, his aunt, and his brother.

"What should we do with it?" Macy asked.

"Study it," Brice said. "Everything Marie and Judson knew has to be in here." He thumbed through to the end of the book. "Look, there's personal entries in here from Marie and from Judson too!"

"You study it, little brother, and let me know what's in there. With all my new classes at SMA, I'm not going to have the extra time to study that, too," Macy said, a bit disappointed.

"Is that all right with everyone, if I read it first?" Brice asked. His family all agreed, and he couldn't wait to get started. "One question I have that I don't think I need the journal for, because Mom has evaded it for many years . . ."

"What is that, son?" Lilith asked with hesitation.

"Why is my hair dark and I'm marked a hunter?"

"And Hollis's hair, too?" Macy threw in.

"From the little I've gleaned, when you kill a witch then proceed to have offspring marked as a hunter, their hair can turn dark as a part of the curse or evidence of your actions. It doesn't mean the same if you have human children, however," she said, giving a nod in Brock's direction.

"Interesting. I did not see that being the reason at all," Macy said, half disappointed.

"I have a question," Sunny spoke up. "Why did you give Brice and Macy the middle names of Marie and Dante?"

"Yeah, considering you already knew he was a bad guy when you had me?" Brice added. "I'm not sure why I never thought to ask about it. I just thought it was a family tradition type thing."

"Before both Brice and Macy were born, actually not too long after Brock was born, Mathilde Augustine came to us. She has witches with Seer powers in her ancestry, as you know, Gallad." Reggie looked at Gallad, who nodded. "Actually, Sunny, she might be someone you could talk with if you wanted. Anyway, she came to us and said she had a vision of two more children—a girl, then a boy. And she said their middle names were to be Marie and Dante."

Lilith smiled at her children and added the rest, "She also said they were to mark the beginning of a new era of witch hunters. They were to be key in having the truth of the Blackstone family rediscovered."

"And so they did," Sunny said with a big smile.

And so they did.

EPILOGUE

$\mathcal{B}$rice spent all his free time over the past few weeks studying the Blackstone family journal, and he was surprised at some of the information he found. It took him some time, but with Sunny's help, he was able to learn how the dagger and the journal worked together to unlock more of the family secrets.

"What have you learned new, Brice?" Sunny asked one evening as she joined him by the fire in the great room of his family's home. He turned toward her, his face lit up with a smile, and said, "I found a section that told how a witch hunter extracts the magical essence from a dying witch and absorbs it for their own energy to preserve their life. But then Marie added her own experience, using the power of the dagger, along with Judson's magic, to not only pull the essence from someone who was very alive, but then send it back into their soul without hurting them. She only did it once, and it was to save the life of a young girl who was possessed by a demon who took over her body."

With her eyes wide, Sunny sat on the edge of the seat. "Did it work?"

"Yep, it was awesome!" Brice added, excited about what he had learned. Then his face fell. "It was much like what Dante had told me to do, but he didn't tell me it would kill the person whose magical energy I took."

"But you didn't. And that is what matters," Sunny encouraged, and with her, there was no argument. To change the subject, though, she added, "How are your magic lessons going?"

Brice's face lit up. "It's awesome! It is such an amazing feeling to have magic surge through my veins. But then, it's the weirdest feeling to have your own body wrestle with itself as the hunter tries to attack the magic. It's less and less, though, as I accept more of who I am and learn to control more each day. I think I might be able to get the hang of having the two coexist within me."

"You will," Sunny said with a wink, then got up and moved to the window. After a moment of quiet she asked, "Brice?"

"Hmm?" he looked up from the journal he studied once again.

"Did Dante tell you the vision I had of the two of you together?"

Brice stilled. "He did."

He hadn't brought up the vision with her yet, and truth be told, he hadn't wanted to, for fear of his destiny being entwined with Dante's.

"It wasn't about becoming his successor. It was about exactly what you have already done . . ."

"What's that, Sunny?" he asked quietly as he came up behind her.

"Replacing him in existence by having rediscovered your truth." She turned to him and smiled. Then, unexpectedly, she reached up on her tiptoes, swiped the dark hair from his eyes, and kissed him on the lips.

Brice laughed at the shock of electricity he felt shoot through him at their touch. "Rediscovered indeed."

And he kissed her again, this time with passion. When they came apart breathless and giggling, Brice held Sunny close to his chest with the lights of the town twinkling in the background.

"Are you ready?" he asked, with a suddenly serious expression on his face.

"Ready for what?" she asked, tilting her head, confused.

Brice gently pushed her away while still holding one of her hands so she extended out and away from him, then he tugged her quickly back into his embrace and smoothly transitioned into a gentle sway. She giggled as she clumsily stepped on his foot. But he didn't care. They were dancing.

"This is just how I saw it," she said and laid her head on his chest.

"Sunny, will you go to the Haunting on Main Street event with me for Halloween and then the Cold Moon Ball in December?"

"I will go with you always to every event you want to attend. We belong together, Brice Blackstone."

"Rediscovered indeed," Brice reiterated, then kissed the top of her head as they continued to sway into the night.

~

You might also enjoy Morgan's other stories in the Havenwood Falls universe, about the Blackstone witch hunters:

Reawakened
Dawn of the Witch Hunters
Rise of the Witch Hunters
Redefined

ABOUT THE AUTHOR

Morgan Wylie is an award-winning and *USA Today* bestselling author with several genres published from YA fantasy to adult paranormal romance and other things in between. Morgan published her first novel, *Silent Orchids*, one year after moving across the country with her family on a journey of new discovery. After an amazing three years in Nashville, TN, and the release of two more books, Morgan and her family found their way back to the Northwest, where they now reside. Still working every day with great optimism, Morgan continues to embrace all things: "Mama," wife, teacher, and mediator to the many voices and muses constantly chattering in her head . . . where it gets pretty loud!

You can find her and news on her books at the following:

MorganWylie.net
    MorganWylieBooks on Facebook
    @MWylieBooks on Twitter/Instagram

ACKNOWLEDGMENTS

Writing in Havenwood Falls is such an incredible experience, and I'm honored to be a part of this community. Thank you, Kristie Cook, for allowing me such an opportunity.

Thank you to the following authors for the use of or mention of their characters: Kristie Cook for the use of Saundra Beaumont, Addie Beaumont, Aurelia and Michaela Petran; Kallie Ross for the use of Sheriff Ric Kasun; Liz Ferry for the mention of Celeste Long, Emma Cardin, and Jonathan Burns; R.K. Ryals for the mention of Cade Peters; E.J. Fechenda for the mention of Dalton and Dr. Underwood; Victoria Escobar for the mention of Remy MacKinnon; Amy Richie for the mention of Ava Tate; Amy Hale for the mention of Zoey Mills and Jordan Woods; Katie M. John for the mention of Ellie Lewis; and Cameo Renae for the mention of Weston and Drake Blaekthorn.

Thank you to Kristie Cook and Liz Ferry for your editing and proofreading expertise!

Thank you, David Uhlenkott, for your special assistance and expertise in the world of skateboarding and helping with terms and techniques!

Thank you to my wonderful, patient, and supportive family as I wrote this. I love you!

And last but not least thank you to YOU, the amazing reader that you are!! Thank you.

ASHES OF FATE

APRYL BAKER

HAVENWOOD FALLS HIGH

Ashes of Fate

USA Today Bestselling Author

APRYL BAKER

~ A Havenwood Falls Young Adult Novella ~

BOOKS BY APRYL BAKER

The Ghost Files Series
The Ghost Files
The Ghost Files V2
The Ghost Files V3
The Ghost Files V3.5
The Ghost Files V4.1
The Ghost Files V4.2
The Ghost Files V5
Silas (A Ghost Files Novella)

The Crane Diaries Series
The Crane Diaries: Homecoming
The Crane Diaries: Dirty Blood
The Crane Diaries: Stained
The Crane Diaries: The Red Church
The Crane Diaries: Bayou Secrets

The Bloodlines Legacy Series
The Blackburne Legacy
The Blackwater Legacy
The Blackstone Legacy

The Manwhore Series
Touch Me Not
The Sinner's Touch
The Healing Touch

Forever Your Touch

Kincaid Security & Investigation Series

Kade

Viktor

Mason

Jasper

The DeCadia Series

The DeCadia Code

The Crucible

Destiny's End

The Invasion Series

The Invasion

Fight Back

Stand Your Ground

Hybrid

For my sister Joannie, who has risen from the ashes more than once this year.

CHAPTER 1

"*C*ora!"

Cora Hartwood ignored her best friend's shout, instead focusing on the super cute Dracula sitting beside her. Seth Michaels had been flirting with her for three days and she'd finally worked up the courage to pull him into a semi-quiet corner of the biggest party of the year. Bonfires raged along the beach outside, but she'd never liked fire and chose to stay indoors.

Most everyone was out there, and she and Seth could cuddle and maybe make out a little. At least that was the plan, if Emily would shut up.

"You look hot as a zombie nurse," Seth whispered in Cora's ear, his teeth tugging at her earlobe. She shivered in response, loving the way he made her feel. Cora had made out with a couple guys before, but none of them gave her butterflies in her stomach like Seth did.

"You don't look so bad yourself, Count Dracula." Cora giggled and leaned in closer, snuggling up to Seth.

"Cora Jean Hartwood!"

The sheer desperation in Emily's voice startled her into looking away from Seth, her gaze finding Emily in a few seconds. She looked scared.

Cora pushed up from Seth, who called after her, and went running.

"What is it?" She grasped Emily's arm and pulled her friend around to face her. "Are you okay? Did somebody try something? Just tell me who and I'll . . ."

"No, not me!" Emily's dark brown eyes were wide with so many different emotions, Cora couldn't keep up. "The sheriff's here looking for you."

"Me?" Shock rippled through her. She'd been with some friends earlier but had left before they'd started to egg cars and houses. Surely someone hadn't called and reported her for hanging with them, making the sheriff think she was a part of that nonsense.

"Something happened, Cora, something bad. You need to come with me."

She refused to budge, a knot of fear beginning to twist in her stomach. "Tell me what's wrong."

"I . . . I don't know. Sheriff McCarty wouldn't say. He just said to find you and bring you out front."

"Cora?" Seth came to a stop beside her. "What's going on?"

"I don't know, but I have to go." She didn't even look at him, but followed Emily out of the beach house, her mind sorting through a million different what-ifs. The waves were crashing onto the sand, coming close to the bonfires, which blazed high. The fire held her attention for a brief moment. She hated fire, and right now, it seemed to mock her, to tease her that it was about to rob her of everything precious.

Shivering, she turned away and followed Emily down to where the sheriff's SUV was parked at the very edge of the property. He looked grim.

"Sheriff, this is Cora." Emily grabbed Cora's hand and held tight.

"Miss Hartwood, there's been an accident."

"Accident?" A new kind of fear curled in her stomach, and she got very, very cautious. "What kind of accident?"

"Your parents and brother were involved in a motor vehicle accident this evening. They've all been rushed to the hospital in critical condition."

Motor vehicle accident.

Her mind went blank, and she felt numb. The chill in the air disappeared as well as all the sounds around her. Emily's and the sheriff's faces faded away as those three little words swirled round and round in her head.

"Cora!"

Hands grabbed her as her body sagged. Her family was in an accident while she'd been making out at a party. She was supposed to have gone with them to the pumpkin patch and then to the haunted house in town. But she'd decided to go hang out with her friends instead.

She was supposed to have been in that car.

"Miss Hartwood?"

She blinked, her mind refocusing on the sheriff. "They're not dead?"

"I won't lie. It doesn't look good. We need to get you to the ER if you want to see them."

Cora nodded and took out her phone, texting her grandma. She lived in Florida, but she would find a way to get here. Cora only saw her grandma at Christmas, and they Skyped on birthdays, but despite not being as close as they could be, Hattie should know.

And Cora needed her.

Emily climbed into the back of the SUV with her, but Cora was barely aware of her. She kept thinking about her family. Her little brother had begged her to come with them, but she'd wanted to go to the party where all her friends were. She wanted to hang out with Seth instead of Billy. If she'd just been in the backseat of her parents' car, maybe she could have shielded Billy. Maybe he wouldn't have gotten hurt.

Emily snapped her fingers in front of Cora's face, bringing her out of her haze. "Your phone's ringing."

Cora stared at it. Her grandmother's face was on the screen. Even though she'd texted her a few minutes ago, she couldn't bring herself to answer it. That would mean admitting out loud how bad the situation was.

Emily took the phone from her and answered it, explaining everything to her grandmother. Cora heard her, but it was like she was hearing her from the end of a long tunnel.

Shock. This had to be shock. Her body was in shock.

But she couldn't do anything to help herself.

"Cora, your grandmother said to tell you she'll be on the first flight she can get."

Cora nodded, her fingers twisting each other. Emily pulled her hands apart. "You're going to hurt yourself."

They rode in silence for the rest of the way, and when the sheriff pulled up in front of the ER, Cora's body refused to move. Emily sat with her and eventually coaxed her out, but a fear unlike anything she'd ever known crept up and took a hold of her.

Walking through the ER doors, she all but stopped breathing, holding onto Emily's hand so tightly, the circulation might have been cut off. The girls followed the sheriff to the information desk. The nurse looked over at her, her expression sympathetic and full of pity.

Cora's heart sank.

There would be no reason she'd give her that look unless it was bad. How bad remained to be seen.

They were escorted into the ER itself and into a small waiting area. A few other people were there, but they were told a doctor would be out to see them shortly.

"Wha . . . what happened? Can you tell me?"

"It looks like a hit and run," the sheriff said. "There was a witness to the accident who called 9-1-1. The car in front of the witness was going really fast and swerved into your parents' lane. They hit your family head on. The witness said it looked like your father lost control and spun out, slamming into the guard rail, and flipped, forcing the car over the rail and into the ravine. We have an APB out with the car's description and the partial plate number the witness was able to provide."

Cora nodded. A random act. One swerve and it cost her family so much.

A man wearing scrubs came out a few minutes later. He walked straight to her, his expression kind. "Miss Hartwood?"

"Yes." Cora stood, still clutching Emily's hand like a lifeline.

"I'm Dr. Hall. We've got your parents stable, but they both need surgery. I need you to sign a consent since you're the next of kin."

"My gran is on her way. She's getting the first flight out."

"We don't have time to wait. If we don't operate now, they'll die."

"They'll live if you do?" Cora whispers.

"I can't promise you that. Their injuries are severe, but surgery is their best option."

"And my brother?"

"I'm sorry. He died before he got to the hospital."

"No." Cora didn't recognize the sound that escaped her. It was a half cry, half moan. Her knees weakened, and she sank back down.

"I'm very sorry," the doctor said. "I hate to ask this of you, but we need to go now if we're going to save them."

Why would they ask her to do this? It wasn't fair. She was only seventeen. She shouldn't have to make this decision.

"Miss Hartwood?" the doctor prompted when she didn't answer.

"Okay. Please, just don't let them die. Please."

Papers were handed to her, and she signed them blindly.

"Can I see them before you go into surgery?"

"I'm afraid not. We need to get them into surgery now."

Again, she nodded and watched the doctor walk away.

Emily squeezed her hand. "It's going to be okay, Cora."

"It's not. Billy died. My brother died." Tears started leaking, and once the waterworks began, they wouldn't stop.

Emily hugged her close, whispering things Cora didn't hear.

All she could think about was her brother and her parents as they sat and waited for the doctor to come back.

CHAPTER 2

*C*ora shifted in her seat for the thousandth time. She and
her grandmother had been on the road for three days,
taking turns driving so they'd get to Colorado faster. Not that
Cora cared. Her family was gone in a car accident she should have
been in. It wasn't fair that she lived and they all died.

"We're almost there, I think." Hattie looked at the directions
she had written down. The GPS had stopped working about an
hour ago, much to Cora's disgust.

"I don't know, Gran. I think we're lost."

"We're not lost." Hattie folded up the map and pointed to the
McDonald's building up ahead. "That's where we're supposed to
wait for the bus we'll follow into Havenwood Falls. See the
advertisement for it?"

"The GPS . . ."

"The mountains block the GPS signal."

It sounded perfectly reasonable, but somehow Cora didn't
quite believe that. Even in the mountains there should be areas
where a signal came through, not this wasteland. Even her cell had
no signal.

"I still don't know why we have to move here. Why couldn't
you stay in Charleston or I could have come to Florida?"

"I promised you I'd explain everything once we reached Havenwood Falls."

"Well, we're here, so why not tell me while we wait?" Cora pulled into the parking lot, but she didn't cut the engine. Why did Gran have to move them somewhere cold? She was a beach girl, not a snow bunny.

"Why don't we go to the restroom instead? Once we're settled in, I'll sit you down and explain why we had to run."

"Run?" Cora asked, alarmed. "What are you talking about, Gran?"

"It's complicated, and now is not the time to discuss it."

"Now is the perfect time to discuss it. What did you mean we had to run?"

Gran pursed her lips. "What happened to your family wasn't an accident."

"But the police said . . . there was a drunk driver . . ." What the heck was her gran talking about?

Gran shook her head. "I'll explain when we get inside the boundaries of Havenwood Falls. You're going to have to trust me, Cora. Now, let's go use the restroom and grab something to eat."

Cora stared openmouthed as her gran got out of the car and went into the McDonald's. Her mind buzzed with a thousand questions, but she knew her grandmother well enough to know she wasn't going to budge. Cora got out and locked the car. She did need to go to the bathroom.

Unfortunately, she had no coat. Her clothes were not meant for the mountains of Colorado. So she froze her butt off all the way into the fast-food restaurant. Shivering, she found the bathroom and saw her gran's feet under one of the stalls. She quickly did her business and washed her hands.

"Gran, you okay in there?"

"I'm old. I take longer to pee than you do. It comes out in . . ."

"Not what I want to hear!" she cut Hattie off. *Eww. Just gross.*

Hattie chuckled and slid her purse out from under the stall

door. "Go get us some food. I want two Big Macs. They have that buy-one-get-one-free deal going on right now."

"You're really going to eat two of those things? Do you know how much fat is in just one?"

"I sure do, but at my age, I don't care. And I want a strawberry milkshake."

"Heart attack waiting to happen," Cora muttered, then stopped short, realizing what she'd said. "Gran, maybe you should . . ."

"I'm not going anywhere. Got my ticker checked two weeks ago, and it's in perfect working order. Don't worry about me, sweetheart. The reaper is going to have a fight on his hands should he come knocking at my door. That I promise."

Cora nodded and went out to order the food. She decided to go back to the car after she'd gotten their food because she wasn't sure when the bus was supposed to show up that they'd follow all the way to Havenwood Falls.

Havenwood Falls. She shook her head as she hurried back to the car. It sounded like the title of a romance novel. Her mom used to love to read paranormal romances. The ache in her chest worsened at the thought of her mother, and her breathing sped up. Her hands started to shake, and she all but ran to the safety of the vehicle and the duffel bag on the back seat.

She dug out her anxiety medication and took one. She hated these things, but they helped with the panic attacks she'd been experiencing since the night her family died. Her doctor thought it was due to how much guilt she carried for not being in the car with them. He was probably right, but she didn't know what to do about it. Her gran had mentioned finding someone for her to talk to once they were in Havenwood Falls, but she wasn't sure how she felt about that.

She sat behind the wheel and took deep breaths, trying to calm down. She tried counting while she waited for the medicine to start to work, but it wasn't until her gran came back and started to talk to her that her nerves began to settle.

"Easy, Bug, it's all going to be okay. Everything will be fine. Just take deep breaths."

Bug. Only Gran ever called her that. It was so far from the nickname her parents used, it actually helped to take away some of the panic.

"There's my girl."

"I . . . I'm sorry . . . I . . ."

"Shh, nothing to be sorry about, Bug-a-boo. Swap seats with me, and I'll drive the rest of the way. You took one of your pills?"

Cora nodded and switched seats. The medicine didn't state she couldn't drive, but neither of them were willing to take the chance on another accident.

Hattie opened the bag and handed Cora her chicken nuggets. "I spoke with Greg. He's got both shops packed up, and the boxes are en route to Havenwood Falls. I've already applied for a business license, so we should have the toy shop up and running before Black Friday."

The family toy shop. The Hartwoods had been making toys for over two hundred years. She wasn't sure she wanted anything to do with it now that her family was gone, though.

"The building I'm looking at has enough room for a candy store as well. Your dad said you'd started making candy for the store there, so I thought maybe we could expand on it, have a huge shop. They already have a sweets shop with ice cream and things, but no one makes homemade candies."

"I don't know, Gran, after everything . . ."

"You think about it. It's not like we have to decide right this second. Once we get there and have a look around, we'll talk about it again."

"There wouldn't be time if you want to open by Thanksgiving. It's only three weeks away. I'm not even sure you can be open even with all the stock arriving on time. There's signage and remodeling . . ."

"It'll be open even if I have to work twenty-four hours a day. It'll give me something to do."

The hollowness in her grandmother's voice reminded Cora she wasn't the only one who'd lost family. Hattie lost her son, daughter-in-law, and grandson too. She was in just as much pain as Cora. Getting the toy store together would probably help her to heal. Maybe it could help Cora too.

"We'll get it open, Gran. Let's just hope they have a good construction company that doesn't mind working long days and maybe nights too."

Her grandmother bit into her Big Mac and all but moaned out loud. She reminded Cora more of a teenager than a sixty-year-old woman. Then again, with the streaks of blue hair running through her white locks and the big white sunglasses she had on, she looked more like a teenager than a grandmother.

Cora's own hair was blond with strips of purple and pink running through it. She loved her hair, so who was she to frown on Hattie for being un-grandmotherly?

"We need to get a coat somewhere." Cora dunked a nugget into honey mustard sauce. "I almost froze my butt off going inside."

"It's not that cold." Hattie sat her burger down and took a long pull of her milkshake.

"According to the radio, it's in the low forties. Forties, Gran!"

Hattie grimaced. "Well, maybe it's a little colder than we're used to. I'm sure they have a store there where we can buy some warm clothes and a coat."

"Is that the bus?" Cora pointed to the large bus that had just pulled up.

Hattie looked at her Big Mac longingly. "Yes. Don't you see the Havenwood Falls logo?"

"You'd better eat up then. I doubt they'll be here long."

Hattie wasted no time in consuming her burger. It amazed Cora someone as tiny as her grandmother could eat like she did.

"Feeling better now?" Hattie asked after a few minutes.

"Yeah. I'm tired, though."

"Get some sleep, Bug-a-boo, and when you wake up, we'll be in our new home."

Cora wasn't so sure about calling it home yet, but she was tired and fell asleep before the bus they'd follow pulled out.

CHAPTER 3

*C*ora blinked bleary eyes open when her grandmother shook her awake. It was pitch dark outside, so she must have slept for longer than she intended.

Hattie motioned out the windshield. "Look, you can see the lights of the town."

Dutifully, she looked, and sure enough, the town was laid out before her in a maze of lights. It looked pretty, nestled against the mountains. Snow always looked pretty in pictures, though she herself had very little opportunity to see it up close and personal. She had a feeling she was going to get the opportunity to see more than her fair share in this quaint little mountain town.

They drove through several streets and then turned down another street. Hattie came to a stop at Whisper Falls Inn, an old Victorian mansion. It was just as beautiful as the rest of the town. She and her grandmother got out of the car and hurried inside.

A young woman was behind the front desk and smiled warmly when she saw the two of them approaching. "Welcome to Whisper Falls Inn."

"Yes, I spoke with someone earlier about a late check in. I'm Hattie Hartwood."

"Ah, yes, I heard you were opening a toy shop here in town."

"More like relocating our existing stores to here," Hattie said and shifted from foot to foot. She looked tired. Cora should have driven, even though she'd taken her anxiety meds. Her grandmother was getting on in years, even if she didn't look a day over fifty.

"Well, it will be a welcome addition, I'm sure."

They both turned to see a young woman come striding toward them, another pleasant smile plastered on her face. "I'm Michaela Petran, and I wanted to welcome you to our town. We're all very excited to have you here."

"I wasn't aware everyone knew we were coming," Hattie said dryly.

"Well, Saundra happened to mention it to a few people."

"Saundra?" Cora whispered to her grandmother.

"Saundra Beaumont." Hattie turned toward Cora. "She and I are old friends, and when she heard what happened, she offered us a place to stay here in town. She even found a location for the new store and got the paperwork started for us."

"Handcrafted toys are going to be a big hit with the tourists," Michaela went on. "And she said something about homemade candy too. I have a sweet tooth, so I'm hoping you'll be able to open the store soon."

"My goal is to have it open for Black Friday. I just need to hire a construction crew that's fast and reliable and won't overcharge me."

"I can help you out with that, but that can wait until morning. I'm sure you're both exhausted after such a long drive. I've put you in one of our cottages, if that's okay? That way, you won't be so cramped up in a double room."

"I didn't realize you had cottages."

The woman smiled, her brown hair pulled up and away from her face. It accented her strange but beautiful greenish-gray eyes. "We are a tourist town, after all. We make room for families and for friends coming down to ski. Our cottages are popular, and the ski lodge gets a lot of our overflow. You are in luck that we still have one unoccupied."

"A cottage would be fantastic until the apartment over the shop can be finished." Hattie looked relieved. She apparently hadn't relished the idea of sharing a double room any more than Cora had.

"They come equipped with kitchens, but you're both welcome to eat with us up here as well. Now, if you'll check in, I'll show you how to get to your cabin once you're done."

The woman was way too chipper for eleven o'clock at night.

"Do you think there's anywhere open where we might get a bite to eat this late?" Hattie handed over her ID and debit card to the front desk clerk.

"I'm sure I can find something for you in the kitchen. We had lasagna for dinner, and there's probably leftovers. I can have Reed bring it down to the cottage for you on his way home. He's just about done in the kitchen anyway."

"That would be appreciated, thank you." Hattie signed some paperwork and collected two keys. "Big Macs just don't taste very good cold."

"You two go get settled in, and I'll have your dinner down soon enough."

"Well, she was nice, wasn't she?" Hattie asked as they reloaded their luggage into the car. She glanced down the path to where they both could see the first of the cottages.

"I don't know if I trust someone that chipper this late."

Hattie laughed. "I was thinking the same thing."

The cabin wasn't large, but it was enough, Cora decided when she threw her luggage on the bed. Her bed seemed to be made out of some kind of pine, and the dresser and chest of drawers matched the bed. The two bedside tables were slightly darker, but not by much. The handmade quilt that covered the bed was gorgeous, though. Cora had a thing for quilts, inherited from her mother.

She pushed thoughts of her mother aside. Two panic attacks in one day was more than she could handle. So she opened her closet and started unpacking. Gran said they'd be here a while, as the upstairs apartment over the shop needed renovating, and as determined as her grandmother was to get the store up and running, Cora guessed the construction crew would start on the store first.

Since tomorrow was Friday, they decided she'd register for school tomorrow, but not start until Monday. The school was fine with it, considering her circumstances. That would give her the weekend to get used to the town and calm herself about starting a new school in the middle of the semester.

Her hand brushed against cool metal, and she yanked it back, not wanting to look at the photo she knew was there. It was of her family, all of them at the beach this last summer. Cora's eyes filled with fresh tears, and she brushed them away.

No.

Slamming the lid of her suitcase closed, she ran from the bedroom and all the pain that photo would pull out of her. With that pain would come guilt, and then the panic would creep back in. Her heartbeat was already more than a little fast, and she sat down on the overly comfortable couch and focused on taking long, deep breaths like the doctor had shown her.

It took her several minutes to beat back the panic, but she did it. No small feat either. Her doctor would say she was getting better, but she would say she was just getting better at hiding everything she felt.

She'd been out partying while her family suffered and ultimately died. She'd never forgive herself. That was a fact everyone refused to understand, even her gran.

"Cora?"

She jumped at the sound of Hattie's voice. "Yeah, Gran?"

"You okay?"

"Not really, but it is what it is."

"I know it's hard, Buggy, but we'll get through it. We're starting over in a new town, and we'll make friends and the loss we suffered will ease a little. I won't lie and say it'll go away, because it doesn't. It just eases enough to let us breathe through the worst of it."

"Right now it hurts too much to draw in a breath," Cora whispered, her voice a little broken.

"I know, honey." Gran sat down and hugged her. "I know."

The doorbell rang. "That's probably our dinner. Why don't you go get it, and I'll see if I can find plates and silverware in the kitchen?"

Nodding, Cora wiped at her eyes and went to answer the door. She was starving. She'd eaten her nuggets hours ago, and her stomach growled, reminding her of that fact.

When she opened the door, her breath caught. Not because the guy standing there was overly cute. He *was* cute, but in an average kind of way. She'd dated guys cuter than him. There was something about him that tugged at her, though, like an itch that couldn't be scratched. He stood taller than her by a good foot, his dark brown hair blending into the hoodie he wore. Green eyes, so bright she wasn't even sure the darkness could hide them, stared back at her.

He was carrying a tray laden with covered plates and a bag bearing the inn's logo.

"Where do you want this?"

His voice was deeper than she expected, more like the man's voice he'd grow into. And she liked it.

He cleared his throat when she didn't answer, and she heard her grandmother laugh from behind her.

"Just bring it in and put it on the table, please." Hattie gently pushed her out of the doorway, and Cora felt her face flame up. She seriously didn't just stand there like some dumbstruck teenager, did she?

Well, she *was* a dumbstruck teenager.

So she gave herself an out.

Reed moved past her, and his smell tickled her nose. He

smelled faintly of motor oil and leather. Normally she'd scrunch her nose up, but not this time. It smelled delicious on him.

Her grandmother handed him a ten-dollar bill. "I appreciate you dropping this off to us on your way home . . . Reed, wasn't it?"

"Yes, ma'am." He nodded and took the cash. "Thanks for this too."

"Well, you made me laugh by tongue-tying my granddaughter, so it was well worth it."

His eyes swept over to Cora, and a hint of a smile appeared. "I should get going. Do you ladies need anything else?"

"No, but thank you." Hattie walked him to the door and closed it behind him.

Cora sank down in the first chair and ducked her head. Embarrassed wasn't quite the word for how she was feeling just then.

"Cute little fella, isn't he?"

"That boy is anything but little, Gran."

She wagged her eyebrows at Cora.

"Gross, Gran. Get your head out of the gutter."

"A woman's head should always stay partially in the gutter or she'll have no fun in life."

"Grandma!"

Hattie laughed and sat down on the couch, her white hair on full display. She had it cut in a short, cute style that suited her well. "I have so much to teach you, Bug-a-boo."

Cougar grandmother on the loose. No wonder they only saw her on birthdays and holidays.

The smell of cheese and sauce distracted her from her embarrassment. The lasagna practically bubbled with gooey yumminess. They'd even sent down garlic bread, cold water, and utensils.

Then Cora read the note.

Sorry, all we had left was vegetable lasagna.

She showed it to Gran.

They were both meat lovers.

Gran leaned down and sniffed. "Still smells good. I say we walk on the wild side and ignore the fact it's all veggies."

Cora shrugged and dug in. It tasted good, and her stomach rumbled in agreement. "It's safe."

Hattie sighed and shoved a big heaping bite into her mouth. "This does taste good!"

After a few minutes, Cora decided to broach her grandmother's weird declaration from before.

"Okay, Gran, we're here, we're settled, and we have dinner. It's time to tell me what you meant about us having to run."

Gran took a drink of her water. "I wouldn't say we're settled until all the boxes have been unpacked."

"Gran . . ."

Hattie sighed. "I hoped you'd forgotten about that."

"Not a chance."

"I'd expected to have more time to figure out how to explain things to you."

"Mom always says to just spit it out, even if the truth hurts."

"I wish it were as simple as that." Hattie stood and went down the hall toward her bedroom. Cora stared after her, bewildered.

She was acting strange, even for her grandmother. Her dad always called his mother a free-range chicken. She roamed free and never lived her life with regrets. Flighty was her mother's term for Hattie.

But what if there had been threats made against her and Cora? What if the accident that took her family from her wasn't really an accident? The police might have told her gran something they thought she couldn't handle. After having to make the decisions that night and her family dying . . . she'd been a mess. They may have confided in her grandmother.

Hopefully, she was about to find out.

CHAPTER 4

*W*hen Hattie came back, she was carrying a small wooden box.

"Do you remember when you were a little girl and you snuck into your father's workshop?"

"Yes. I thought he was going to have a heart attack, he yelled so loud." She'd been seven and only curious as to what kind of toy her father was making. They didn't just own a toy store. Her family were toy makers, hand-carved toys being their specialty. She'd picked up a piece of white wood, and her father walked in at the same time. It hadn't been pretty, and he'd kept his workshop locked after that.

"He had good reason." Hattie handed her the box. "Does this look familiar?"

Cora took the small box, no bigger than the palm of her hand. It was carved with delicate yet intricate designs. The wood was smooth and white. It wasn't painted white; that was the natural color of the wood. She tried to find a latch to open it, but there was none. There was no seam at all to indicate where it opened.

"Is it a jewelry box or something?"

"Or something," Hattie muttered. "That box is the reason our family died."

Cora dropped it faster than a hot french fry fresh from the deep fryer. That little box was the reason for the accident?

"What do you mean, Gran?"

"They weren't in a simple accident."

"I knew it!" All of her fears from earlier came rushing back. The police must have told Hattie something they didn't think she could handle. "What did the police say? Did someone make threats?"

"This has nothing to do with the police, Cora, but our family history." Hattie reached down and picked up the box from where it had fallen, cradling it gently.

"I don't understand."

"I know you don't. You were never meant to know any of this, but you are the last of your father's children."

"You're not making sense, Gran. Did the police tell you someone caused the accident on purpose?"

Hattie shook her head. "No, Bug-a-boo. This box told me."

"How can a box tell you?"

"Inside of this box is a fire demon."

What the . . . "Gran, what the hell?"

"Language, young lady." For the first time in a long time, Hattie looked her age. Her body hunched in on itself. "Our family, specifically those with Hartwood blood, have been designing demon traps since before the Roman empire."

"Demon traps?" There was no hiding the derision in Cora's voice. Her gran was off her freaking rocker. Demons? Seriously?

"This is why I wanted more time to explain it to you." Hattie sighed and ran a hand through her pixie-cut hair. "I didn't believe it either when your grandfather told me."

"Grandpa believed in all this nonsense?" Cora whispered.

"The Hartwood men usually only share this secret with the male members of the family. The women are kept out of it."

"That's stupid." Not that Cora believed this nonsense, but she disagreed with that archaic way of thinking. A woman could do anything a man could do. Mostly, anyway.

"Your grandfather agreed. It's why he told me. Did you know you're the first girl born into the Hartwood family since 1742?"

"That can't be right."

"It's true. It's why your grandfather was fighting so hard for your father to tell you about the boxes. He thought it was a sign, you being born under a solstice moon."

"Isn't that witch stuff? Mom and Dad were Christians."

"Not witch stuff, pagan stuff," Hattie clarified. "The practice goes back to the very old world, when Christianity was just beginning to be whispered about. It was the Christians who began to worship differently and then branded everyone else pagans. Did you know that?"

Cora shook her head, confused. What did this have to do with anything?

"Our family worshiped the old gods for a very long time before we converted to Christianity, and we learned how to create the boxes to trap demons and other harmful spirits from those days. I just wanted you to understand how we learned to do this, or rather how the Hartwoods learned to do it."

"Gran, I . . . why are you saying all this? Losing Mom and Dad and Billy . . . it hurt. I hurt all the time. Why would you make it worse by telling me some kind of scary fairy tale?"

Tears shimmered in Hattie's eyes. "I'm telling you because you need to know, Cora. You need to be on constant alert for the woman who caused the accident."

"How do you know it wasn't an accident? Dad lost control of the car and flipped it, going over the hill. It's awful, but there's nothing nefarious going on."

Cora's hands started to shake as she talked about that night. She could feel the panic starting to claw its way up her throat as she imagined them spinning out of control and falling down the ravine when the car went off the road. What did they feel? Were they in pain? Did her mom scream and try to reach her brother? Did her dad know it was useless?

"Cora!" Her gran snapped her fingers in front of Cora's face, bringing her out of her thoughts, but the panic remained. Hattie got up and came back with one of her anxiety pills. She took it gratefully and allowed her grandmother to help her with the water bottle. Her hands were shaking that badly.

"I'm going to find you a therapist first thing tomorrow morning. Saundra should know someone." Hattie proceeded to rub Cora's back until some of the panic subsided. "There, you're feeling better already."

"I'm sorry," Cora said miserably. "I don't know why this keeps happening."

"Because you've suffered a traumatic loss, sweetheart. Your mind and your body have to heal from that. None of this is your fault."

"You need to stop with all this nonsense, Gran. It's not good for me."

"I wish I could, but I can't. I had to get us somewhere safe, somewhere we couldn't be found."

"Gran . . ." Cora took a shaky breath.

"No, you have to listen to me, Cora Jean. I received a phone call from the woman whose lover is trapped in that box. She wants him back and said if I didn't let him out, she'd do to you what she did to the others."

"What?" *No. No. No.* This couldn't be happening.

"I can't open that box, Cora. I'm not a Hartwood by birth. Only a Hartwood can open it. It's what makes our traps so useful. They're immune to magic. Once a spirit or demon is trapped in them, they're there for life unless a Hartwood lets them out."

"You're serious." For the first time since this conversation began, she actually looked at her grandmother. The woman was as serious as a heart attack. Her eyes, which usually always laughed, were somber and full of nothing but honesty.

"I am. As soon as the call ended, I called an old friend of mine, Saundra Beaumont. She's the head of the Luna Coven here in

Havenwood Falls. It's because of her we have a safe place. Havenwood Falls has protections in place that will hide us. If the witch follows us, she'll trigger an alarm that will set a manhunt in motion for her. She can't get to you here."

"Coven . . ." Cora whispered, her mind reeling.

"It's a lot to take in, Buggy, I know, but I'm telling you the truth."

"Then why not let me try to open the box? Give her what she wants?"

"Because your father told me the creature in that box is one of the most dangerous demons he's ever come across. He devours whole families in fire. Letting him go free would be condemning who knows how many innocents. No. Your father died to protect people. I won't let that be in vain."

"I'm not saying I believe you, Gran, but I don't want anyone else to get hurt either." The anxiety medicine was finally starting to really work, and a calmness came over her. She relished the feeling, because she hadn't been truly calm without meds since that night.

"I have all your grandfather's journals. He thought one day you might need to know how to build the traps, and he knew your father would never tell you."

"So Grampa was a forward-thinking man of the times?"

Hattie laughed. "Your grandfather truly believed in women's rights. He thought we deserved the same opportunities as men and did a little lobbying in his day for equal pay. And when it comes to the family secret, he firmly believed you should be told and taught how to make the traps. Your birth was a sign to him."

Cora wasn't sure what to think. Her grandmother wouldn't lie to her, of that she was sure. She was a jokester, but not about something as serious as the death of her only son. How she was supposed to believe all this, now that was another story altogether. With the anxiety meds in her system, she wasn't freaking out, though, and it allowed her to see how serious her grandmother was. She believed every word she was saying, and Cora had to decide if she should believe it too.

But how could she not? If what her grandmother said was true, then every single thing she'd ever believed was gone. If demons and ghosts were real, what else was real? She ate while she thought, letting the warm delicious gooey cheese help to soothe her. Food had always been her place of comfort.

And for the super high metabolism she'd always had, she was grateful. She'd hate to give up her favorite things when stressing.

"Gran, did you ever see one of the things Grampa trapped in those boxes?"

"I did, Cora. That's why I believe what I'm telling you. I witnessed it firsthand."

Well, how was she supposed to argue with that?

"You said we'd be safe here, that there were protections in place? What's to stop this witch from just coming back?"

Hattie smiled. "There's a memory spell in place. Once you enter Havenwood Falls and then leave, you lose all memory of the Falls and the people here."

"So if I go away to college, I'll forget you?" Alarm splintered her calm, and she sat her plate down for fear of dropping it. "You're all I have, Gran. I don't want to lose my memories of you."

And it sounded even to her like she was beginning to believe the nonsense.

"You won't completely forget me, only our time here in Havenwood Falls. You can still call me and send me emails and texts. Don't panic, Buggy. There are online classes if you don't want to go away, and even if you do leave, when it's finally safe for you to leave, I'll always pull you back. You're not going to lose me, Cora."

"You can't promise that, Gran. No one can."

"You're right." Hattie got up and came to sit beside her, pulling her into a hug. "Our days on this earth aren't guaranteed, but what I will promise is that I'll be here fighting with the Grim Reaper for every single day, for you. I'm not going anywhere for a good long time."

"You swear?"

"I pinkie swear." She hooked her pinkie with Cora's and winked. "Now, let's finish our dinner and get some sleep. Tomorrow is going to be a long day."

Cora nodded and did as she was bid. Her mind was in shock, and when she went to bed, for once she fell into a dreamless sleep.

CHAPTER 5

*M*orning brought with it a whole world of new anxieties for Cora. Not only was she dealing with her guilt about the accident, but now she added a new fear to the mix. Someone was trying to kill her over a demon trapped in a box only she could open.

She wasn't sure she quite believed it, but she knew her gran wasn't lying. Hattie might be a flake and quirky, but she loved Cora with everything she had. Cora could feel it every time she was in the same room with Hattie.

She took a shower and then rummaged around in the kitchen for coffee. There was a coffee maker, but no coffee. She really needed caffeine this morning.

"Gran!"

"What?" came her grandmother's answering shout.

"Is there a place to get coffee around here?"

"I'm sure there is." Gran stuck her head out of her bedroom, the wet strands of hair sticking to her skin. "Why don't you take the car and look for some?"

"Thanks. I need me some java."

"You and me both. Just be careful."

Careful was something she'd be from now on. Driving gave her hives, but she knew it was necessary, and so she faced that fear every time she got behind the wheel. She needed to get from point A to point B, and driving was the fastest way.

Once she was on her way, she looked around at the square. Several shops stood out to her, specifically Coffee Haven. Truthfully, she could have walked, it was so close, but she was freezing. For a beach girl, the weather here was not a check in the pro column. It was too cold to walk.

For her at least. People were out everywhere in light jackets as they strolled through the square and along Main Street. Everyone seemed happy and at ease, the way she was just a few weeks ago. Shaking her head before she slipped back into that dark place, she parked and hurried into the cafe.

The place was light and airy with all sorts of artwork on the walls. Cora fell in love with it, and all dark thoughts of no Starbucks in town went right out of her head as the scents of fresh coffee and pastries invaded her nostrils. *Starbucks who?*

She got in line and studied the menu as she shuffled forward. They had everything she loved and then things she'd never heard of. This was not a morning to be adventurous, so she ordered a caramel latte and a large coffee with hazelnut syrup for her gran. She also bought two large pastries. Breakfast of champions.

Thanking the woman at the counter, she turned and ran right into someone, spilling her coffee all over them.

"Oh, my gosh, I'm so sorry!"

She looked right up into a pair of green eyes, the same eyes she'd looked into last night. While they weren't amused, they weren't angry either.

He shook his head and looked down at his jacket, now covered in coffee stains.

"Reed, are you okay?" A girl about their age rushed over to him and gave Cora the side eye that said *who are you and get the f out right now.*

"I'm fine, Josie." His voice was just as deep as it was last night, and it still made her shiver. He wasn't built, but he wasn't small either. Nice and normal, Emily would call him, but sometimes nice and normal was better than built like a linebacker. At least it was for Reed.

"You need to watch where you're going." Josie glared at Cora from where she was hanging onto Reed's arm. Girlfriend?

"I'm sorry. I turned around and wasn't expecting anyone to be right there." He had been awfully close.

"She's right. I saw her turning and should have stepped back. This is my fault, not hers."

Josie made this clucking noise, but the back-off signs shooting like stars out of her eyes said she didn't think it was all his fault.

"Let me rebuy your coffees for you." Reed gently disentangled himself from Josie and turned those very serious eyes of his right on Cora. She felt like squirming under their direct stare.

"Oh, no, please. I dumped it all over you. The least you can let me do is buy yours for you."

He smiled and dimples appeared. Oh dear God, the boy had dimples!

"Sure. Cora, right?"

She nodded, suddenly tongue-tied.

"I'm Reed, but you know that, and this is my friend Josie."

It wasn't lost on me or Josie that he introduced her as his "friend."

"Hi. It's nice to meet you both." Not. She'd rather Josie walk away. She wasn't up for all that anger this morning. She was finally starting to feel less like a zombie, and she wanted to stay Zen. Waiting on her morning dose of caffeine was starting to eat into her Zen-ness. "What kind of coffee did you want?"

"Just a large regular coffee."

Cora nodded and placed her order again. Thankfully, the pastries survived.

"So, are you heading over to school?" Reed asked as they moved aside to wait for the order.

"No. My Gran and I are going over later today so I can register, but I'm not starting until next week."

"Lucky," Reed drawled, his dimples coming back out to play.

Sweet baby Jesus, please don't let me say something stupid right now or get tongue-tied.

"You're not a tourist?" Josie looked a little green around the edges.

Cora shook her head. "Not a tourist. My gran and I are moving in."

"You're the one opening the new toy store, right?"

"Yeah," Cora answered Reed. "It's been in my family for over two hundred years. We do a lot of handcrafted toys as well as the mainstream ones."

"Like those lame wooden toys that are ancient?" Josie's tone was as derisive as the look on her face.

"My dad took a lot of pride in his work, and those lame wooden toys are the ones most parents want their kids to have when they're young because they're not a hazard to them like all that plastic junk. People contacted my dad daily to commission toys, one-of-a-kind toys that you'll not find in any department store. So keep your snotty little attitude to yourself, especially when you don't know what you're talking about."

Josie's eyes went wide and before she could say anything, the girl behind the counter told them their drinks were ready. Cora took hers, gave Reed a nod, and hurried out the door, anger burning in every fiber of her being. That nasty girl had better learn to keep her mouth shut.

Tears pricked Cora's eyes as she got into the car. She'd overreacted, she knew, but the pain of losing her father was so fresh, anger was easier to deal with and didn't bring on the panic attacks.

The knock on the car window startled her, and she did this meow-like scream. She let out a shaky breath when she saw it was Reed. Rolling down the window, she arched a brow.

"Hey, I'm sorry about Josie."

"Not your fault she's a grade A bi—"

"She is," Reed cut her off. "She's also a good friend who wants to be more than friends, but I've told her again and again I don't want that. She can get possessive, and that's what that was in there. I told her to leave you alone."

"I can defend myself," Cora said, feeling a little raw. Her emotions were running high, and if she didn't get away from everything, she might have another panic attack. She hadn't even brought her meds, because she was just going a short distance from the cottage.

"I know you can." Reed gave her a little smile. "I have to work tonight, but I'm free tomorrow. Why don't you let me show you around town?"

"I . . . I don't know. We just got here and . . ." She was rambling. Bad habit of hers when she got super nervous. "I'm dealing with some stuff . . ."

"It's cool," Reed said. "I'll catch you at school or maybe I'll see you up at the inn." He gave her one last smile and turned and walked away.

Cora let out a breath she didn't realize she'd been holding and let her head drop to the steering wheel. She was such a dork.

Not that spending a whole day with Reed would have been a hardship, but with her anxiety like it was, she'd been afraid of freaking out. And it didn't seem right she should be out there having fun when her family had been buried just a few weeks ago.

Sighing, she started the car and headed back to the cottage. At least within those four walls she didn't have to deal with anything but missing her family.

CHAPTER 6

*R*egistering for school hadn't taken nearly as long as Cora thought it would, but then again, she'd never moved before. Her family had been in the same house since she was three. Her grandmother filled out all the paperwork while she sat and did a whole lot of nothing.

The thought of starting a new school in the middle of the semester was harrowing. Everyone already had their own little cliques, and finding one where she'd fit in was going to be next to impossible. She'd seen it happen at her own school. Cora liked to think she'd never been the mean girl to a new student. She always tried to say hello and make people feel welcome, but who knew if there was someone like that at Havenwood Falls High?

She pushed those thoughts aside as they pulled up to the building that would house the new toy store. It didn't look too bad, on the outside at least. It could use a coat of paint, but even that wasn't bad. Her grandmother said it was a double-wide building, which could house both the toy store and her sugar shop if she wanted to do it. She loved making candy of all kinds, but since her family died, she hadn't been in the mood.

"What about the workshop?" She pulled the sides of her brand new coat together as she waited for Hattie to unlock the building.

They'd just come from the agent's office and signed the paperwork for the shop. The key looked to be sticking in the lock when her gran tried it.

"The basement?" Hattie gave up and handed the key to Cora. "Here, you try."

Cora stuck the key in the lock and jiggled it several times until it finally turned. "We need to call a locksmith and get the locks changed anyway. Do you know if they have a security company in town?"

"I'm sure they do. I'm having lunch with Saundra in a little bit, and I'll ask her then. Do you want to come, Buggy?"

"No, I think I'll stay here and clean up a little, then take all our shopping bags back to the cottage." She pushed the door open and gasped. The windows were covered so you couldn't see inside, and now she understood why. The place was covered in dirt and abandoned furniture. "No wonder it's so cheap. It's going to cost thousands just for garbage removal."

Hattie sighed. "This is not what I was hoping for. God knows what it looks like upstairs."

Both women grimaced and picked their way through the garbage to a door toward the back. Two empty rooms and a staircase lay hidden behind it. Both rooms were just as dirty as the front room, and Cora took the stairs first. They looked shaky, and she'd rather break a leg herself than let her grandmother be injured. Who knew how well she'd heal at her age?

There was another door at the top of the stairs, but she didn't need to worry about a lock. The door was hanging off its hinges. It took her minute to get it pushed aside so they could enter. The room was small and closed off, the carpet ruined and wallpaper peeling. The room overlooked the back parking lot, hidden from the square. The window was pushed up, and she saw dark spots underneath it. Who knew how long rain and snow had been getting in?

"I think they're gonna have to start with this floor first, Gran. There's water damage."

"Hell's bells," her grandmother muttered, and Cora suppressed a grin. Her gran was no stranger to four-letter words, but she tried to tone it down around her grandkids. Not that it worked out well, but she did try.

"We may be at the inn longer than expected. Maybe we should see if the apartment complex leases by the month." Hattie started to explore and moved through the doorway. "Kitchen's in here. You don't want to look at it."

Cora laughed and moved off down the small hallway. The first two doors were bedrooms, and the last door was a fairly spacious bathroom. It stank, and as soon as her eyes landed on the toilet, she covered her nose and backed out.

"Gran, don't go in the bathroom."

"Why?"

"Uh, it's painted brown."

"Why would anyone paint a wall brown for any reason?" Hattie curled her nose and did just what Cora told her not to. She let out a squeal and ran, nearly knocking Cora over in the process.

"I told you not to go in there."

"You should have said someone smeared crap on the walls."

"I did. I said they painted the walls brown. It was a nicer way of saying it."

Hattie glared. "There is no nice way of saying that!" She pointed toward the offending room.

Cora shrugged, suppressing a smile. Her grandmother was the only person who'd been able to make her smile since that awful night at the hospital, and for that she was grateful. Her mom always said laughter made everything better, and Cora had to admit, when she laughed, some of the ache inside her eased up just a little.

"Why don't you take the car to lunch, then swing by here and pick me up afterward?" Cora asked. "We'll find the grocery store and stock up on a few things."

"Sounds like a plan, but I'm not sure you'll be able to do much here without cleaning supplies."

"True. I hadn't thought about that." She shrugged.

"I think I'll walk around and get the lay of the land. I can even walk back to the inn from here. The exercise will do me good."

"Are you sure?" Her grandmother hated leaving her alone. She'd seen firsthand just how broken Cora was, and leaving her to wallow in grief by herself wasn't high on Hattie's to-do list.

"Yeah, I'll be fine. I might even swing back by the coffee place and get some more of those blueberry scones you oohed and ahhed over this morning."

"You know I can never say no to sugar." Her grandmother winked. "Of any kind."

"Gross, Gran!"

Hattie laughed. She loved shocking her granddaughter.

"We'll get you feeling up to enjoying some sugar of your own, maybe in the form of that little hottie who showed up at our doorstep last night." Hattie wagged her eyebrows suggestively.

"Gran!" Cora gasped, pretending to be outraged. Truthfully, she was rolling inside with laughter.

"What? Someone has to get you back in the saddle. Besides, I hear this town is known for its festivals. Did you not notice all the harvest-themed decorations that are up everywhere? There are even some shops that already have Christmas lights up. We'll get you a date in no time . . ."

"Gran, I'm not up to festivals and all that other stuff just yet. I don't even know if I want to do Thanksgiving this year." Just like that, all her happiness got sucked away.

It wasn't fair that she got to go on living while her family were all cold and buried beneath the dirt.

Hattie came over and hugged her tight. "I'm sorry, Buggy. I'm just trying to take your mind off things."

"I know, and I appreciate it, but doing all that and pretending to be happy?" Cora shook her head. "It feels like I can't breathe most days, Gran. Going out and having fun at a festival is so far from what I'm up for, it's not even funny."

"It's okay, baby girl. We'll take this as slow as you need to, and if you don't want to do Thanksgiving, that's fine with me. Less for me to have to do while trying to get the store ready to open."

"Uh, Gran, I don't think this place is going to be ready by Black Friday, especially if they have to replace sub-flooring up here, and I hate to ask what the electrical and plumbing looks like."

"When did you get to be so construction-y?"

"When I started watching HGTV while I did my homework."

"Then maybe you should supervise repairs, and we'll save some money."

Cora scrunched up her nose. "I'm not that good, Gran. Besides, if I did that, then you wouldn't get to ogle all the guys coming in and out on work crews."

"See, you're starting to get to know your grandmother all too well. You're even looking out for my fantasy daydream material."

"Ewwwww."

Hattie laughed and hugged Cora. "You know I love you, don't you?"

"I do, Gran, and I love you."

"Well, now that we've got all the mushy stuff out of the way, let's go back downstairs and try to start making plans for the store until it's time for me to meet Saundra."

Cora nodded and followed her grandmother back downstairs.

CHAPTER 7

Cora stepped outside and zipped up her new fur-lined coat. The light pink color matched her hair perfectly. New boots kept her feet warm as she walked down the path leading to Main Street. She'd changed her mind about walking around town earlier and asked her gran to take her back to the cottage before her lunch with Saundra. She'd warned Cora she wanted to meet with the contractors after lunch and would be gone a while. Cora found herself alone with her thoughts far longer than she'd expected. Not a good place for her to be.

So she decided to take the walk she'd put off earlier and get to know her new town. This morning had introduced her to the new store, and her curiosity got the best of her as the day wore on. She wanted to do a little exploring before the sun went down.

Hattie assured her they were safe here, that the person responsible for her family's death couldn't reach her here. Cora wasn't so sure. If everything her grandmother said was true, then she wasn't going to bet on her safety behind some kind of magical ward. She'd taken the small pocket knife her father gave her on her tenth birthday and slipped it into her jacket pocket just in case. Normally she used it for carving, but it would work as a weapon too.

279

She would give her gran one thing—Havenwood Falls was breathtaking with the Colorado mountains as a backdrop. The town was nestled right up against a mountain range, giving it an almost storybook quality. She strolled along Main Street, looking at the shops, then wandered to the fountain in the middle of the square.

"Hey."

Cora couldn't help the scream that escaped her at the sound of that voice. She turned to see Reed standing there, wearing jeans and a light jacket.

He held up his hands. "Easy. It's just me, your friendly neighborhood boy next door."

She let out a shaky sigh that turned into something resembling a laugh. "Sorry. I . . . I'm a little jumpy."

"You okay?"

She nodded. "New place, you know?"

He studied her, and she could tell he didn't believe her, but he didn't push either.

"I saw you standing here on my way to work and thought I'd say hi. You looked a little lonely."

She didn't quite know what to say to that. The truth was she *had* felt lonely. She needed a better poker face.

"My gran is out, and I guess I got a case of cabin fever."

He nodded. "Come on up to the inn, and I'll see if I can filch you some sweets. Michaela makes the best desserts this side of the mountain. Since I'm working in the kitchen today, I should be able to swipe you some."

"I do have a sweet tooth."

He grinned. "I guessed that this morning, and all that pink and purple hair of yours is another clue."

"Is that so?" Cora asked as she fell into step beside him.

He nodded wisely. "Yup. My mom says anyone who dyes their hair to look like candy has a definite weak spot for the sweet stuff."

"Candy?" She self-consciously stroked her hair.

"I'm not dissing your hair. It's cute."

"Yeah?" A warm feeling seeped into her limbs, and she felt a light flush heat her cheeks.

"Yeah. Did you get registered at school okay?"

"It was easier than I thought it would be."

They turned the corner, heading for the inn. "About earlier, I wasn't hitting on you or anything. I was just offering to show you around, maybe get your mind off everything."

Cora went still and turned to look at him. "What do you mean?"

He flushed. "It's just . . . we all know what happened, why you're here. Small town and all that. I was trying to help."

Everyone knew she'd lost her family? It's not like it was a secret or anything, but the thought of everyone knowing . . .

"Not everyone. I know because I work at the inn, and there are gossipmongers in the kitchen. Josie didn't know. If she had, she wouldn't have been so . . ."

"Territorial?"

He shrugged. "I've told her all she and I will ever be is friends. If she doesn't get it through her head, she and I are going to have to stop hanging out for a while. I don't want to hurt her."

Reed gestured toward the inn, and Cora started walking again. She wasn't sure she liked everyone knowing her business, but it made sense they'd know. It really was a small town.

"I hate walking into a room and seeing that pitying look on people's faces." She stopped on the porch and stared out at the town square. "It's part of why I agreed to come here so quickly. No one would know unless I told them. I wouldn't see that look anymore."

"I'm sorry." Reed took her hand and squeezed it. "I was just trying to help."

Cora nodded. She believed him.

"Come on, let's get you all sugared up."

She really didn't want to go inside now, but she put one foot in front of the other and followed him. Reed was just being nice, even if he had made her feel self-conscious. He didn't deserve her anger. As her daddy always said, *suck it up, buttercup, and get it done.*

The inn was bustling today with people downstairs sipping coffee and reading what she assumed were the remnants of this morning's newspaper. The staff seemed to be just there out of the corner of your eye, ready to help before you even realized you needed help.

Her mom would have loved this place. It was so comfortable. As she gazed around, she decided that was the right term for the front area. It was designed so guests would feel more at home.

"It seems busy," Cora noted.

"It's our busy time of the year. The ski slopes are opening, so we get an influx of tourists. It's why I have a job here. I help out in the kitchen when they need me, and I do some maintenance work too."

"Jack of all trades, huh?"

He nodded and put his finger to his lips before hustling her toward the back of the inn, where she assumed the kitchen was. Sure enough, the scent of what she thought was roast chicken tickled her nose. Reed had her wait outside, and she peeked in when he went through the door.

A small kitchen greeted her. There were a few people doing prep work. It looked clean too. That was always a plus. She'd waitressed at a restaurant in Charleston that didn't put too much effort into cleaning. She lasted about a week. She started working at her family's toy shop after that fiasco.

She saw one of the waitstaff coming toward the door and moved out of the way. It would be just her luck to get a black eye or busted nose right before she started a new school due to her own carelessness.

Reed came out a few minutes later, carrying a plate with a huge piece of strawberry shortcake piled high with whipped cream. Her taste buds started to tingle right as her stomach growled.

"Somebody's hungry." Reed handed her the plate and the fork he'd filched.

"I haven't eaten since breakfast."

"In that case, maybe we should wait on the cake and let you eat something first."

He reached for it, and she fake stabbed at him with the fork. "Don't you dare. I'm starved. Trust me, I eat dessert before dinner all the time."

"Come on, Shortcake. Let's get you settled while I clock in."

She scrunched her nose up at the nickname, which only caused Reed to smirk. He laughed under his breath and led her to a quiet corner in the parlor. Several people glanced her way, but soon turned their attention back to whatever they were doing.

Reed told her he'd be back to check on her. Once he disappeared, she dived into the heavenly dessert. Strawberry shortcake was her favorite . . . outside of the raspberry chocolate deluxe her gran made for her every time she came to visit.

Cora finished her cake and set the plate on the small table beside the armchair she was sitting in. Her gaze wandered back to the people around her. She couldn't help but wonder if any of them were supernatural. Ever since her gran told her about the box, her mind wandered back to all those paranormal romances her mother loved, where the super sexy alpha swooped in and saved the day.

She could use someone to save the day. After everything that had happened, the thought of even more coming at her and her grandmother was debilitating. Cora had been outside feeling alone and scared. She'd give almost anything to have those feelings go away. She didn't want to feel like a victim. Her parents had taught her to never be a victim, to be a survivor, but that's exactly what she felt like right now. Someone who had no control over anything that happened to her. Someone who didn't know how to survive in her new reality.

"Hey."

Reed startled her again. Man, he moved super stealthily. Maybe he was a supernatural creature?

He squatted in front of her, bringing him to eye level with her. His green eyes were bright and open. "You doing okay?"

"Yeah, just people-watching. Thanks for bringing me here. I needed to be around people."

"That's what we do here in Havenwood Falls." He flashed her a smile. "We take care of each other, and you're part of our community now. Plus, anyone with hair like yours shouldn't be sad all the time. If I can help you to feel better, I will."

That was the nicest thing anyone had said to her in a long, long time. It caused the butterflies to flutter to life in her stomach again, and her mouth got all dry. Nervous. He made her nervous, but a good nervous. The kind of nervous her mom said she'd feel one day when she met the right person.

"I, uh . . ."

He winked. "If you're up for seeing the town, my offer still stands. I'll show you around tomorrow. It could be fun, and I know fun's probably the last thing you're up for, but I promise it's the only thing that's going to help you heal."

"You sound like you know something about that."

"I do. My brother died a few years ago. Took me a while to get myself out of a dark hole. Still hurts every day, but some days are easier than others. Like today. All that rainbow hair of yours distracted me from a little pain."

Cora didn't know what to say. Again.

"Don't answer me now." He took her hand and wrote a number in her palm. "Call me tomorrow if you want a tour guide."

She looked at the number in her hand. People didn't do that anymore. They traded numbers through their cells. It was old school, but it was charming.

"Thank you."

He tweaked her nose. "I have to get to the kitchen, but stick around for dinner if you want. Our roast chicken is pretty famous."

"I made plans with Gran already."

His half smile curled her toes.

"Then I'll see you tomorrow."

"I didn't say I was gonna call."

"You will." He jumped up and leaned down to kiss the top of her head. "You will, Shortcake."

Then he strolled off and left her staring after him, confused and guilty for feeling the butterflies.

Who the heck was he?

CHAPTER 8

"Why are we here at six in the morning, Gran?"

Cora yawned and stared at the empty streets of the town square. The heavy clouds overhead hinted at bad weather. She pulled her coat tighter around her and tugged the key out of her grandmother's hands. The locksmith needed to get here today.

"Because we agreed to meet the contractor at six-thirty. If we agree on his bid, he can start work by eight."

"You mean *you* agreed to meet him here. I still don't know why you dragged me out of a perfectly comfortable, *warm* bed."

The key turned, and Cora opened the door. "That's why I dragged you out here. I'd be standing here in the cold until he arrived because that cursed key hates me."

"Did you contact the locksmith yesterday?"

"No, I forgot. Saundra and I talked for a long time yesterday, and it slipped my mind. I did, however, remember to have them turn on the electricity." Hattie flipped the light switch, and one single bulb in the light fixture flickered to life.

"Uh-huh," Cora muttered and walked over to where she'd seen a thermostat yesterday. She set it to heat, and then a loud clanging noise started up. That nasty heat smell filtered through the vents. "At least we can stay warm."

A louder noise followed that statement, and then the noise from the heat pump died.

"You had to say it, didn't you?" Hattie shook her head.

There was a knock on the open door behind them, and a man stepped in carrying a clipboard, a toolbelt wrapped around his waist. He was an older man, maybe a little older than her father had been, but he was quite fit in his jean jacket, red flannel shirt, and well-worn jeans. His hair was a light brown, but a few strands of silver were starting to show at his temples. She couldn't help but notice his right earlobe was missing, too. How in the world—she looked away to keep from staring. He moved with a grace Cora would never have. If this man wasn't some kind of supernatural creature, then she might as well stop guessing.

"Mrs. Hartwood?"

"Yes, I'm Hattie, and this is my granddaughter, Cora. You're Mike McCabe?"

"Yes, ma'am. Everyone calls me Big Mike, though." He shook her hand. "Owner of McCabe & Sons Construction. Saundra Beaumont said you had an urgent job?"

"We do. We want to have the shop up and running by Black Friday. The apartment upstairs needs to be redone too."

"The toy shop?"

"How did you know we were opening a toy shop?" Cora asked.

His blue eyes cut to her, and she glanced away. There was something there in his eyes that was very commanding, something that made her feel the need to respect him. His eyes were stern, like her grandfather's used to be. Maybe that's why she felt the need to respect him.

"It's a small town. Everyone knows everything."

Cora sighed.

"It's not a bad thing. It means help is always just a shout away, should you need it."

That brought her eyes back up to his. Did he know about the threats to her?

She had a feeling he did.

"If you give me a few minutes, I'll walk the property and give you a list of what I think you're going to need."

"Will it be a problem to add in a workshop downstairs and make sure the outside resembles the old shop? The design has been in our family for hundreds of years."

"It won't be a problem. We're big on tradition here. If we need to, there's a very good architect in town who can help us create what you're looking for. You have pictures?"

"We have a website," Cora told him. "It has pictures of the shop. Also, we want one section of the main floor to house a candy shop and a kitchen somewhere as well."

He frowned. "We have a sweet shop . . ."

"We're not looking to take away any tourist or local business from existing shops in town," Hattie hurried to assure him. "Cora makes homemade candy like fudge and caramels and hand-spun lollipops. We'd probably bring in candy for a section for kids to build their own bags of candy too."

Mike nodded, his eyes giving nothing away in his weathered face. He looked like someone who spent a lot of time outside, but then again, he was in construction. Made sense for him to be so tan and rugged.

"This is going to take me a while to walk through, and I need to contact that architect I told you about. I can have him here in about an hour to go over everything you want to do. Why don't you two go grab breakfast, and I'll text you when we're ready to talk about the job?"

"That sounds good." Hattie nodded. "Where's the best place to get breakfast?"

"Let's just walk to Coffee Haven. That's where I got the scones from yesterday."

"You know I can't turn down pastries."

The two of them wandered over to the coffee shop and ordered pastries and coffees. Once they were seated, Hattie leaned down and just inhaled the scent of her warm scone. She bypassed her coffee for a huge bite of the blueberry sweet.

"So, Gran, do you think we can get the store open by Black Friday?" Cora sipped her coffee, relishing the taste. She loved coffee more than she did most food, outside of sweets. "I know we talked about this already, but is it even worth it? I know it's a touristy town, but most people are home for Thanksgiving, aren't they? Our online sale should be more than enough."

"There are lots of families here in Havenwood Falls that shop for their kids just the same as everyone else. With a toy store right here in town, we should be able to do very well, because they won't have to travel to the big box stores and deal with the crowds. This is also the beginning of the ski season, and there should be lots of tourists in town, or so I've been told. I take it you've decided to do the candy store?"

"I thought about what you said, about needing something to take your mind off everything, and I guess I need something too."

"That's good, honey. That's very good." Hattie smiled at her. "I did find a therapist right here in town I think you should see. It'll be good for you."

"I don't know, Gran . . ." What if people in her new school found out she was seeing a shrink? Not only would she be the new girl who lost her entire family, but one who needed a shrink too.

"This is something I'm going to put my foot down on, Cora. You need to talk to someone."

Gran hardly ever called her anything but Bug or Bug-a-boo. She was serious when she used her name.

"Fine."

"Good girl. Do you know what you want the candy section of the store to look like?"

"Have you ever seen Sweet Pete's? It was featured on that show *The Profit*. He has all these bright colors, and I was thinking that maybe we could update the store itself with some brighter colors to match the candy store."

"I guess maybe we should update it, since we're starting over from scratch. We haven't had a redesign since the seventies."

"Trust me, I know."

Hattie laughed. "If we do the redesign, we might not be open for Black Friday."

"It doesn't matter to me. We can advertise a big Black Friday sale online."

"When did you get so business savvy?"

"I've been working in the store since I was little in one way or another, Gran. Daddy taught me how to do the books and the day-to-day because I really liked it. I learned the online business and how to market from Mom. She was the techie person. She showed me everything about it, from the back office to how to create and send out our newsletter full of sales."

"I had no idea you were so involved with the store. I just assumed your father would have turned the business over to your brother, all things considered. It's how it's done in our family."

"That's archaic and not at all fair." Cora didn't like the thought of getting shut out of the business one day by her father. He seemed so happy she loved working there. She just assumed she and her brother would inherit the store together once her father decided to retire or he passed.

"No, Buggy, it's not fair. But it's just us now, and we have the chance to change all that."

A sliver of pain knifed across her chest. She knew she wasn't alone. She had her Gran, but she wanted her mommy and daddy and her little brother back. That was what wasn't fair. She'd give anything to have them back.

"Bug, you okay?"

"Yeah, I'm fine. Just tired. Someone woke me up before the crack of dawn."

Maybe going to see this therapist would help. She hated talking to her gran about how sad she was. It only upset the woman and there was nothing she could do to help Cora that she wasn't already doing.

Gran finished her pastry. "I'm going to be at the store most of the day. Do you have any plans or do you want to come hang out with your super cool and hip grandma?"

Super cool she might be, but she could be super weird too and very cougarish when it came to men. She flirted more than Cora.

"Well, I uh . . ."

"You uh what?" Gran's eyes sharpened, and Cora felt like squirming.

"Reed asked me again if I wanted him to show me around town today."

"The hottie from the inn?"

"Gran, that sounds so wrong coming out of your mouth."

"I may be old, but I'm not dead. Are you going?"

"I don't know. What if I'm out and I have a panic attack?" That fear had bothered her all night. Her panic attacks were severe when they happened. No one wanted a guy to see them all messed up like that. She'd never be able to look at Reed again.

"But what if you don't?"

"I don't know," Cora said miserably and nursed her coffee.

"You'll never know if you don't try," Hattie coaxed.

"Did you know the town knew about everything?" Cora deflected the question.

"It's a small town, Bug. Everybody knows everyone else's business."

"I don't like it."

"Well, you might learn to like it."

"Learn to like everyone knowing every single thing I do? Not a chance. What if I go to school on Monday and everyone stares? How do I not have a panic attack if that happens?"

Cora felt herself start to sink into the darkness that pulled her panic front and center. She took deep breaths to steady herself and fight it off. Closing her eyes, she breathed in and out. Stress was a big factor in setting her off.

Her grandmother stroked the short locks of her hair. "Just breathe, Bug. Breathe through it."

It took her a few minutes, and thankfully no one but the staff saw, but she knew it would get around. She hated that she had these stupid attacks. Hated it.

"Let's go, sweetheart. I'll get you home, and you can go back to bed. Maybe a nap will do you some good."

She didn't mention Reed again, and neither did Cora. An outing was out of the question. As much as she wanted to go, she couldn't.

CHAPTER 9

*C*ora spent the rest of the weekend holed up in the cottage, binging on Netflix and pizza. She hid from Reed, from the prying eyes of the town, and from her Gran, who seemed to grow more worried about her by the day.

She was depressed and anxious. Riddled with guilt and anger. Half the time she felt so lost, she wondered what it would be like to just go to sleep and never wake up. She knew all this negativity wasn't good for her, and she hoped this shrink would be able to help. Thinking about herself dying scared her, but those thoughts wouldn't go away.

As much as she loved her grandmother, she missed her family. She kept thinking her mom was going to come waltzing through the door carrying grocery bags, or that her dad was going to yell for her to help him with something. Or that her little brother was going to flop down and demand she play *Black Ops* with him.

She missed them so much.

Being here without them was the hardest thing she'd faced in her seventeen years.

And she wasn't sure how much more pain she could go through.

Which was why she found herself staring at her closet,

debating whether she should try to convince her gran that she'd be better served by homeschooling. The thought of all those prying eyes staring at her, judging her . . . it freaked her out.

She didn't know anyone.

Except for Reed. Whom she'd totally blown off. He'd probably not even speak to her.

There was a knock on her door, and her gran opened it, holding a cup of coffee, which Cora took gratefully.

"Nervous?"

"Do I have to go? Can't we just like homeschool me or something? I could help at the store full time."

"Store's not even open yet, and you need to go to school. Socialize, flirt, take down some mean girls. You need normal right now, Cora, more than you need to hide in your room all day."

"Fine."

She pulled out her favorite jeans and a light blue sweater she'd pull over a tank. Her new boots completed the outfit. At least she'd be warm.

It took her longer than usual to get ready because she fussed with her hair and makeup. Her mom always said makeup was a shield from the world. No matter what you might be feeling, put on your best face. It made dealing with everything easier. You might not have confidence, but you could fake it with good makeup.

She needed all the help she could get.

Her grandmother dropped her off at the high school a few minutes before classes started. She'd gotten her locker assignment when she registered, but she didn't bother with that. She had nothing to put in there. Her ID and some cash were tucked away in her book bag.

The school was just as quaint as the town with its three-story red brick structure. Any other time, she'd be enthralled with the architecture, but she was too nervous. She dug out her schedule and looked around, feeling overwhelmed.

It was a weird schedule. In Charleston, they'd had the same

classes every day, but here class schedules changed depending on the day of the week. Not that she minded; it was just a lot when she was new.

"Hey!"

Cora jumped at the sound of the bright voice. She turned to see a girl standing behind her, her blond hair shining in the early morning sunshine. Bright blue eyes stared back at her.

"You look a little lost."

"I guess I am. I'm new, and I have no idea of where I'm going."

"I'm Celeste Long."

"Cora Hartwood."

"Well, Cora Hartwood, let me see your schedule, and I'll help you find your class."

"Thanks." Cora handed it to her, and she looked it over.

"Oh, we have biology together!"

"It'll be nice to at least walk in and know one person."

"Yeah, being new has to feel weird, huh?"

"Weird isn't the word for it."

"I bet. Looks like you have Spanish with Mr. Fernandez. I can show you where it is."

"Thanks. I appreciate it."

"I love your hair."

"I wasn't sure how it would go over here. I'm from South Carolina, and lots of people have strange hair colors."

"You'll fit right in," Celeste assured her. "We have just as many people here with all shades of hair."

Cora followed her into the school, and they chatted about hair as Celeste led her to the right classroom. She then gave her directions to all her other classes through lunch.

"I'll see you in biology and good luck!"

I'm going to need it, Cora thought, as she watched Celeste walk off toward her own class.

The morning passed fairly quickly, and while people did stare, there were no whispers or fingers pointing. Several people talked to her, and she hoped a few of them would turn into friends, including Celeste, who reminded her of her own best friend, Emily. She was confident and not afraid to say what she wanted.

It was in the last period of the day that she saw Reed. He came into the room, his gaze sweeping over everyone and settling on her. That charming smile of his appeared, and he strode over, taking the seat right beside her.

"Hey, Shortcake." His deep voice sent a thrill of shivers cascading over her skin. "How'd your first day go?"

"Not as bad as I thought it would, honestly."

"Awesome. I looked for you at lunch, but I got snagged by some friends before I found you."

"That's okay. I had lunch with Celeste Long and some of her friends. They liked my hair too."

"Celeste is a cool girl." He pulled his book out of his backpack, along with a notebook. "You want a ride home or did you drive?"

"Uh . . . Gran dropped me off." He was actually talking to her. She thought for sure he'd be mad about her not calling.

"Cool, I'll take you home. Hope you don't mind if we grab some pizza first. I'm starved."

The thought of pizza caused her stomach to turn. She'd binged pizza all week.

He quirked a brow at her expression.

"Let's just say pizza is not my first choice right now."

"You got something against pizza?"

She shook her head. "It's what I ate all weekend while I binged *Stranger Things* and *House on Haunted Hill*."

"So that's what you were up to."

"I . . ."

She was saved from having to answer when the teacher called them all to attention. But through the entire class, she barely paid any attention to the lecture going on.

Instead, she focused on Reed sitting right beside her and his offer of a ride and food.

And the butterflies that refused to calm down in her stomach.

CHAPTER 10

*R*eed drove a red Chevy Blazer. It made sense, considering they were in Colorado. Cora threw her book bag in the back seat and climbed into the SUV. It was a newer model, and it was clean inside. Most guys she knew took care of their vehicles religiously.

Reed got in, buckled his seat belt, and turned on the heat. It only took a moment for warm heat to begin to blow out of the vents, and Cora held her hands up. Colorado was cold. Even bundled up in her coat and boots, she was freezing.

"You'll get used to the cold." Reed adjusted the vents so they were all pointing directly at her.

"I don't know about that. I lived in Charleston, South Carolina. We got the occasional snow flurry and the temperature could dip down pretty low sometimes, but it was never this cold this early."

"We're expecting snow tonight." His eyes twinkled when he said that.

"Snow?"

"You did just say you got snow in South Carolina, didn't you?"

"Very rarely, and when we did, it shut the whole city down."

Reed laughed. "Not here. We're used to it. Don't worry, though. If it snows tonight, I'll come pick you up so your grandmother doesn't have to get out on the slick roads."

"Why are you being so nice to me?"

"Do you always question people's motives when they're nice to you?" He backed out of his parking spot and then drove out of the school lot and onto the street.

"You barely know me, so I just . . . I don't understand."

"You looked like you needed a friend, so I'm offering myself up as a friend."

A myriad of emotions assaulted Cora, and she pushed them down enough to talk. "Thank you, Reed."

"No worries, Shortcake. Not everyone in this town has an agenda."

"What do you mean?"

He licked his lips and glanced at her. "Why did you guys move here?"

"My gran has a friend here, Saundra something or other, and she talked my gran into it."

"Saundra Beaumont?"

"I think so." She frowned, trying to remember. "Anyway, she offered and here we are."

Reed was quiet while they drove basically across the street and pulled into the parking lot of Burger Bar. It was already packed, considering Reed had to drive around twice before he found a parking spot. It looked like the students had fled the school and flooded here.

"Is this a drive-in restaurant?" Cora asked, excited. She'd seen this kind of place on TV, and she knew Sonic of course, but this had a more authentic feel than Sonic. A lot of people had gathered outside around the stalls, and waitresses on roller skates delivered food to the occupants. She saw a guy leaning against a car filch a fry from the basket and the girl in the driver's seat mock stab him with a pencil. It was the coolest thing ever.

"Do you want to order out here and eat in the car?"

Cora was tempted, but it was too cold. "Maybe when it's warmer."

"Come on, Shortcake, let's get you and me both fed."

"Do they have milkshakes?"

"Best in town."

The inside was very retro with a black-and-white checkered floor. Booths and metal tables took up most of the floor, but there was a large counter with stools as well. Reed led her over to one of the booths in front of a large window so she could see outside.

"I love this place!"

Reed just smiled at her obvious excitement. He handed her a menu that was tucked behind the napkin dispenser.

She'd barely opened it when the waitress came by. Reed ordered a double bacon cheeseburger, fries, and a Mountain Dew. Cora decided to get a regular cheeseburger, tots, and a strawberry milkshake.

Reed chuckled.

"What?"

"Strawberry milkshake?"

"I like strawberries."

"Maybe I should call you Strawberry Shortcake then."

"Don't you dare. I'm still not sure I like the nickname Shortcake."

"You like it."

"How do you know?"

He only smiled.

"I'm sorry I didn't call you on Saturday. I wasn't up to going out."

"That's cool." He leaned back and threw his legs up beside her on the seat. "I ended up taking an extra shift on Saturday anyway. Xandru needed help fixing some plumbing. I would have called, but I didn't have your number."

Well, at least now she didn't feel so bad about not calling. He had to work anyway.

Reed cleared his throat. "That was a direct hint there, Shortcake."

"What?" She glanced up to see him shaking his head, smiling.

"Your phone number, Cora. That was me asking for your number."

"Oh." She got a little flabbergasted, those same deer in the headlights feelings she'd gotten the first time she met him rushing back.

He fished his phone out of his pocket and tossed it to her.

"What if I don't want to give you my number?"

"You do."

"Are you always this confident in your own charm?"

"Yup."

She laughed, picked up the phone, and added her number to his contacts.

"See?" he teased when he took the phone back. "You wanted to give me the number."

Cora was completely charmed, and for the first time in weeks, she didn't feel guilty for being a little happy. It had more to do with the boy sitting across from her than her healing. He put her at ease even as he made her tongue-tied. It was weird, but her life was so out of control, she'd take weird and be glad of it.

"So how ya been, Shortcake?" He tilted his head, and the sun picked out lighter colors in his dark brown hair. "You doing okay?"

"Didn't we do this already?"

"Nope, we talked about school. I meant how are you doing after everything and moving to a new town. You handling things okay?"

"Can I ask you something?"

He nodded. "Sure."

"Did you . . . did you feel guilty after your brother died?"

He sucked in a breath, and a shadow passed through his eyes.

"Every day. Still do some days. It doesn't feel right, me being here without him."

"I was supposed to be in the car, but I blew them off to go to a party. I keep thinking that if I'd been there, maybe I could have done something to save my brother, shielded him or something."

The waitress came back with their food before Reed could answer, but she could see how serious his eyes had become.

Cora took a long pull on the straw of her milkshake to avoid looking at Reed. She wasn't sure why she'd told him that. She barely knew him, for Pete's sake. No, that was a lie. She'd told him because he'd lost a brother, and Reed was her age. Not some therapist who didn't understand how her teenage brain was processing the grief of losing her entire family. Reed did, though.

"Shortcake, look at me."

Cora looked up. His expression was full of empathy.

"I can't tell you that you being in that car would have made a difference or that you might have died too. Nobody knows that, but what I do know is that you're here now and you can only control the situation in front of you. My mom says everything happens for a reason. What that reason might be is for you to discover. I'm not going to tell you how to feel, but I will tell you the same thing my mom said to me. Would your brother be happy knowing how you're torturing yourself? Would your parents? Or would they want you to try to find some kind of happiness where you can get it?"

"You're a real Dr. Phil, huh?"

He snorted. "Please. He's got nothing on all this." Reed swept his hand around himself. "Seriously, though, the guilt is a part of grieving. Just don't let it suck you down so far you can't come back."

"It's hard some days. So hard."

"Tell you what, Shortcake, when you get to that dark place, you call me. Day or night, even if you think I'm at work, in class, or asleep. You call, and we'll talk for as long as you need to."

"You barely know me."

"I have a feeling about you, Cora Hartwood. Now eat your food before it gets cold."

Cora dutifully tossed a tot in her mouth, feeling more at ease than she had since right before the sheriff showed up at the Halloween party.

They chatted about movies and music until they'd finished their food, and then Reed drove her home, promising to pick her up in the morning if it snowed.

CHAPTER 11

*J*t had been a week since Cora started school. Reed came and picked her up every day, since it had snowed for three days straight, and brought her home.

It was Saturday, and she rolled out of bed at ten a.m. because it was Saturday and she refused to get up until a decent hour. She ran to the bathroom and took a quick shower.

Her wardrobe was sorely lacking, though, so she put her pajamas back on. She found her grandmother in the kitchen looking at something on her laptop.

"Gran?"

Hattie jumped about half a foot when Cora spoke and slammed the laptop shut. Instant suspicion. That's what that little action inspired.

"What were you looking at?"

"Nothing." Hattie ran a hand through her short hair.

"Grandma, don't lie to me, please. I'm not six anymore."

Hattie let out a long sigh. "I don't want to worry you."

"Gran, not telling me is going to make me worry more. What were you looking at?"

Hattie reluctantly opened the laptop and turned it so Cora could see.

"I was going through emails and found this. It's from the woman who . . . who took them from us."

Cora blinked several times, her panic starting to rise. She took several deep breaths. "What does it say?" She couldn't bring herself to look.

"It's another threat. She wants the box opened."

"And if we don't?"

"Then she'll take you from me too."

"But she can't find us here, can she?" Cora felt the panic crawling up her spine, wrapping around her throat.

"I don't think so. I'm going to speak with Saundra this morning about it. Do you want anything from the Broastful Brew?"

"What's that?" Her voice sounded distant.

"Another coffee shop." Hattie got up and hugged her tight. "It's okay, Bug-a-boo. No one's going to hurt you. I promise."

"You're sure she can't find us here?"

"If she manages to get into Havenwood Falls, they'll know immediately. Like I told you before, there are protections in place. Do you need your pills?"

Cora nodded, hating that she did.

Hattie sat her down at the table and closed the laptop before going into Cora's room to bring her back her medicine. She swallowed the tablet and sat there, taking deep breaths. Her gran sat with her until the medicine started to work and she began to calm down.

"I'm sorry, Gran. I hate that this happens to me."

"Don't be sorry, Buggy. Your first appointment with the therapist is on Monday. I think that's going to help more than anything. You need to talk to someone about how you're feeling."

Cora wasn't looking forward to it. She didn't want to discuss her feelings. She didn't want to admit the things she thought about. Reed was helping. He never asked her to talk about her feelings, but just his being there seemed to make her feel calmer, more at peace.

"Maybe I should cancel my breakfast with Saundra."

"No, don't do that, Gran. I'll be fine. I'm already feeling better."

"I don't know . . ."

"Go. Your friend might be able to help with that woman."

"Are you sure?"

"Yes. I'm not going to do anything but laze on the couch and watch Netflix all day anyway."

Her gran didn't look convinced, but she did finally leave. Cora was slightly worried because it was snowing and the roads were still a little icy, but her grandmother handled it like a pro, as she proved when they went to the grocery store. Still, given she'd lost her family to a car crash, she worried.

After getting herself a bowl of cereal, she plopped down on the couch and turned on Netflix. She had her laptop hooked to the TV and a Beats speaker hooked to the laptop. She settled on *The Santa Clarita Diet*. It looked funny.

A knock at the door interrupted her halfway through the first episode. Thoughts of the email her gran had received were front and center, so she approached the door warily. She peeked out the window and saw Reed standing on the porch. What was he doing here?

She opened the door and then slammed it in his face, realizing she hadn't even brushed or dried her hair yet. Oh God, he'd seen her in her rattiest pajamas too.

He knocked again.

"What?"

"It's rude to slam a door in your friend's face," he said though the door. He didn't sound mad, though. More like amused.

"I, uh . . ."

"Open the door, Shortcake. I don't care what you're wearing."

She closed her eyes, embarrassed. Why did this sort of thing always happen to her?

Shaking her head, she opened the door. No point in trying to run back to her room and change. He'd already seen her.

His green eyes were laughing even if he'd schooled his expression. "You got plans today?" he asked.

"Uh . . . just Netflix. I'm not up to going out."

He nodded. "Thought you might say that, so I brought the day to you." He turned and pointed to where his SUV was parked. A girl and a guy stood there. He motioned for them to come over.

"What are you up to?"

"You are going to experience your first real snow the right way."

"I'm a beach girl, Reed. Snow and I don't mix."

"You say that now." His eyes twinkled with mischief. "But before the day is up, you are going to be a snow girl."

Cora highly doubted that.

"Cora, this is my twin sister Molly and my best friend, Henry Cole. Guys, this is Shortcake."

"So you're the one who's been stealing all my brother's time." The girl had the same laughing green eyes and dark brown hair as Reed. She was shorter than Reed, but taller than Cora.

"Don't we have a few classes together?" Cora asked to keep from answering that question.

"You're in all of my morning classes." Molly swept past her and into the cottage. "Ohhh, you're watching *The Santa Clarita Diet*. Shame they canceled it. It was funny."

Cora moved aside so Reed and Henry could come in. Henry's super short blond hair was styled and showed off his blue eyes. He looked around curiously, and Cora once again became conscious of how many boxes were strewn around. The moving van had arrived a few days ago, and while most everything was put into storage, several boxes made it inside. Her bedroom was littered with them too.

"I always wondered what these cottages looked like on the inside." Henry moved around the boxes like they weren't even there. "Cozy."

Cramped was more like it. Not that there wasn't enough room for her and her gran; the boxes just made it feel like that. She made a note to unpack as many as she could and push the rest into a corner.

Molly flopped down onto the couch and hit play on the laptop. "Well, don't just stand there. We got movies to watch."

"I'll just go get dressed."

"And comb your hair?" Reed asked, a smile playing with his lips.

She died a little inside. He'd caught her looking her worst.

He laughed at her expression. "Go on, Shortcake. Put on warm clothes. We're not going to be inside all day."

That gave her pause. She wasn't sure going outside was such a good idea, especially after the email her gran got. Instead of letting them see her panic start to rise again, she fled to her bedroom.

She'd stood him up last week, and he came to her this weekend. If she wasn't so worried, she'd be grinning like a fool, but she was scared. What if that crazy lady found her way here? What if she decided to stop waiting and just kidnap Cora? She was freaking out.

Twenty minutes later, she was still standing in the middle of her room, the what-if's going round and round in her head. If it wasn't for the anxiety medication she'd taken right before they'd arrived, she'd be a mess right now. Small blessing, that, but she'd take it.

She did the squeak scream she laughed at other girls for doing when someone knocked on her door.

"You okay in there, Shortcake?"

No, no she wasn't.

"Cora?" Reed knocked again when she didn't answer him.

"I . . ." She cleared her throat. "I'll be out in just a minute."

"Thought maybe you went back to bed on us."

"No." She forced a laugh. "Just trying to find clean clothes."

Cora yanked on a pair of jeans and pulled on a short-sleeved shirt. She found her SCU sweatshirt and added it before quickly blow-drying her hair. Venturing back out into the main room was easier with a semblance of normalcy now that her wet hair wasn't all over the place.

She really wished she hadn't when she saw Molly holding the small wooden box that held a trapped demon like it was the holy grail.

Three pairs of curious eyes nailed her to where she stood. Her grandmother's warning that this town was full of supernatural creatures, some of them probably not as friendly, came roaring back.

She'd wondered all week if Reed was one of those creatures.

Molly knew what that trap was. Cora knew it as well as she knew she herself was terrified of spiders.

And that wasn't good.

She slammed her bedroom shut again.

CHAPTER 12

"Cora, open the door." Reed's calm voice drifted to her from the other side.

What if they were working with the crazy lady?

But Reed had been so nice . . .

Of course he had. He'd been trying to get on her good side so she wouldn't suspect he was up to no good.

That's stupid, though, she told herself. She was overreacting because of that email.

"I'm good here. Why don't you guys go home? I don't feel so well."

"You're good, but you don't feel well?"

"Pretty much."

Reed said something to the others, and then she heard footsteps and the front door opening and closing.

"Okay, Shortcake, it's just you and me."

That didn't make her feel any better.

"I'm not leaving until you come out here and talk to me."

Cora closed her eyes and bowed her head. She heard the stubborn tone in his voice. He wouldn't leave until she talked to him. Getting what little courage she had left together, she straightened her spine and opened the door.

Reed was leaning against the wall right beside the door, and when she stepped out, it brought her so close, she could feel the heat radiating off him. And despite her trepidation, those danged butterflies came back.

"What's going on?" Reed asked, concerned.

Cora moved farther into the living room, her eyes looking for the box. She found it sitting on the mantel where her grandmother had put it. At least they hadn't taken it.

She turned to face him with all the bravado she could muster. "You tell me."

He studied her in that intense way of his, giving nothing away. "Why did you and your grandmother come here, Cora? Specifically here to Havenwood Falls, and don't tell me the same BS you did before. Tell me the truth."

"What makes you think it was BS?"

"The demon trap on your mantel."

Cora sucked in a breath. She was right. He did know exactly what it was. She started to slowly back away from him, and he frowned.

"Shortcake?"

"Stay where you are." She started looking for her phone, but then remembered it was charging beside her bed. Reed stood between her and her bedroom.

"Do you think I'm going to hurt you?" He sounded bewildered.

"You know what that thing is, don't you?" She asked to make sure she'd heard him right.

He nodded. "Almost anyone who deals in any kind of magic would understand what it is."

"What are you? A witch or something?"

"No. I'm as human as you can get."

"Then how . . ."

"My family deals in alchemy. We combine magic and science together to create things and find unorthodox solutions. Alchemy created that box, or don't you know that?"

She shook her head.

"How can you not know?"

"Because I'd never seen that thing until my gran showed it to me our first night here."

"Did she tell you about Havenwood Falls' secret before or after she showed you the box?"

Cora didn't know what to do. Should she trust him and confide in Reed? Just a minute ago she was thinking he was in cahoots with the crazy lady.

"I don't know what to do, who to trust."

"Have I done or said anything but be your friend?"

"No, but what if you're working with her?"

"Her?"

Cora let out a frustrated sound and sat down. If he attacked, he attacked. She was too tired for this.

He approached her like one would a wild animal—slow and with his hands held out to show her he meant no harm. He sat down in front of her on the coffee table.

"I'm not going to hurt you, Cora. I promise."

Her shoulders slumped. She was so tired, and her heart ached. She needed to trust someone, and Reed had been kind. He was right. He'd done nothing but be her friend. She couldn't let her own fears and anxieties rule her every thought and action.

"Can I trust you?"

His eyes turned solemn. "You can."

She searched his eyes, and she found nothing but truth there. And deep down she did trust him, even if she'd had a freak-out moment. Something about him sparked a deep-seated trust inside of her.

So she blurted out her truth.

"My family didn't die by accident. They were murdered."

Reed's eyes widened.

"I didn't know until we came here. Gran was in such a rush after the funeral to get us packed up and on the road. I thought it was just to get me away from all the memories. My anxiety attacks were so bad that first week."

"Anxiety attacks?" Reed took her hand and gently rubbed his thumb back and forth over the back of it. It soothed her more than almost anything else. Lulled her even. Or at least that's what she told herself.

"I was supposed to be in that car, but I blew them off to go to a party."

"And you've been blaming yourself." Reed nodded. "The what-if game will screw with your head, Shortcake."

"Every time I think of them too long, I start to panic. Gran took me to my family doctor, and she prescribed me anxiety meds. They work. I took one earlier when we got the email, or I'd be having one right now."

"I'm sorry, Cora. We have a good therapist here in town. I had to talk to her after my brother died. It helped me a lot."

"Gran has an appointment set up for me, but I don't know if I want to go or not. The thought of talking about my feelings with a stranger is weird."

"I get it, but I still think you should go. She helped me, and I think she can help you too, if you let her."

Time to change the subject. "Back to why we left. I thought it was because of my panic attacks. I couldn't even walk into my brother's room without breaking down. Gran told me about Havenwood Falls and that we were moving here instead of her home in Florida. I didn't even question it when she said we both needed a new start. It wasn't until we were almost here that she said we were running."

"Running?"

"She wouldn't explain anything until we got here. Then she told me my family makes demon traps. That my father had trapped a particularly nasty fire demon in that box on the mantel, the boyfriend of a witch. She caused the accident that took my family and then she threatened my life. That's why Gran came here. She said the town has protections that we can't get anywhere else."

"She's right. There's a spell around this town that will alert the people who need to know when another supernatural enters it. There are rules. They have to register when they come in, and if they don't, then they're dealt with. You're safer here than anywhere else."

"I thought so, but Gran got an email this morning demanding I open the box and free him or she's going to kill me. It's why I had to take my meds. I had a panic attack."

"Do any of the people in charge here know about these threats?" Reed asked, keeping up his gentle massage on her hand.

"Gran has been talking to her friend Saundra."

"Saundra will get to the bottom of it."

"I don't know. At first I didn't believe any of it, but my gran wouldn't lie to me. It's just so surreal."

"If your dad made demon traps, how is it you didn't know?"

"Because apparently the men in my family are still living in the dark ages. Only the male members of the family were ever told anything about this. My gran only knows because Grampa was a man of the times and supported women's rights."

"All the women in my family are part of our alchemy heritage. It blows my mind it was kept from you."

"I wish it still was, honestly. I liked my average life full of nothing but friends and parties and living blissfully in ignorance of the supernatural world."

"It's rough, having everything you thought you knew ripped away from you right after everything that happened. It takes some getting used to, but the supernaturals here are just like us humans in the respect that they're still people. They have feelings, and some of my good friends are supernatural. Don't judge them based on something you've read or seen on TV."

"Maybe you're right."

"I am right." He winked. "You need to stop worrying so much. If Saundra knows, then those who need to be on the lookout are."

"I guess." She'd worry no matter what.

"Now, go grab your coat. We've got stuff to do."

"I don't know . . . What if . . ."

"What did I just say about what-ifs?"

"They'll drive you crazy."

"Exactly, Shortcake. Get your coat. I'm going to show you the magic of snow."

"Uh, no. I'm perfectly content to admire it from here."

He laughed. "Come on. It'll be fun. I promise."

"You make a lot of promises, Reed Spencer."

"And I always keep them. Coat."

Begrudgingly, she got up and pulled on her boots and her coat. If he so much as threw a snowball at her . . .

CHAPTER 13

"*D*uck!"

Cora dived for the ground beside Molly as a volley of snowballs whizzed over her head. Henry and Molly hadn't left as she thought. They'd just walked to the square to get coffee before coming back.

"Henry is lethal with a snowball," Molly whispered as she and Cora huddled behind their makeshift fort.

Considering he'd nailed her twice in the space of twenty seconds, Cora agreed. Reed's aim was good, but Henry's was professional-sports-worthy.

"I have a plan," Molly went on as she started shaping snowballs.

"Good, because I don't," Cora muttered. "Take me to the beach and I can win a sandcastle competition without trying, but anything that involves snow flying at my face and I'm worthless."

Molly laughed. "Just keep making these things and leave the rest to me." Her green eyes danced with mischief. "Henry is going down."

"He likes you, you know."

"What? No, he doesn't."

"He does." Cora smiled slyly as she formed snowballs. Reed

315

had been right when he said this would help to relax her a little. She'd all but forgotten her worries from earlier, at least for a little while. "I've seen him watching you when he thinks no one else is looking."

"You mean the way my brother watches you?" Molly shot her a cheeky grin.

"We're friends."

"Uh huh. I give you another week before he kisses you."

A little thrill went through her at the thought of Reed's lips on hers, but she shoved it down. She had other things to worry about.

"Nice try changing the subject, but you like Henry as much as he likes you. Is Reed the problem?"

Molly huffed. "I do like him, but I don't think he likes me. Besides that, you're right about Reed. I don't know what he'd think if I went out with his best friend since before kindergarten."

"He'd get over it."

Molly snorted. "He once held a grudge against me for over a year because I broke his Transformers toy when we were little."

Molly raised up enough to peek out over the wall of snow that barely counted as a wall. A dozen snowballs came hurtling toward her, and she all but fell back down.

"You really have a plan to get by that?"

"I do." Molly surveyed their haul of snowballs. "Get ready."

Cora grabbed as many as she could hold and waited.

"Here, Fluffy, Fluffy, Fluffy."

Fluffy?

There was an immediate reaction from across the way. The boys started shouting.

And Molly stood and started slinging snowballs at them. Cora did the same, unsure of why a cat would terrify the boys, but she threw the snowballs as best she could. When Molly shouted for them to make a run for it, she took off running for the front door of the cottage, dodging around the snowmen they'd built before the epic snowball fight.

Just as they slammed the door, they heard the thudding of countless snowballs hit the wood.

"We win!" Molly sang through the door.

"You ran!" Henry shouted. "That means you forfeit."

"Nope. We hit you guys with the most snowballs."

"You cheated!"

"I used a weakness to my advantage, so suck it up boys and go get us some pizza."

There was some grumbling, but they left to do as Molly bid.

"Why are they so afraid of a cat?"

"Because it's not a cat." Molly laughed so hard she bent over.

"What is it then?"

"A skunk who sprays Henry every time she sees him. She's a pet of a little old lady who lives near here, and the skunk roams free most days."

A skunk? Cora laughed, picturing the two boys climbing up onto anything they could to escape the stinky little black-and-white creature.

Peeling off her gloves and coat, she turned the heat up a little to thaw them out. If she could have started a fire, she would have, but she was not outdoorsy at all and she lumped wood-burning fireplaces in with outdoor activities.

"You want something to drink? We have water and Mountain Dew."

"Nectar of the gods, Mountain Dew."

Cora grabbed them each a can of pop and then came back over to the couch, her eyes going to the now-empty mantel. She'd put the demon trap in her gran's room. Out of sight, out of mind. Didn't really work that way, but it helped her pretend it didn't exist. At least for right now.

"So, what do you think of our little town?"

"It's beautiful."

"But?" Molly prompted.

"I miss the city. Charleston wasn't huge, but I could find any restaurant or big box retailer I liked within five minutes of where I lived. And it wasn't as quiet as it is here. I think the quiet is what takes so much getting used to."

"I've never lived anywhere but here." Molly's expression turned disgruntled. "We drive in to some of the bigger cities near here that have the big box retailers, and we've gone to Walt Disney World and a few other places for vacation, but we can't be gone more than a month from home and that bites."

"The memory spell."

Molly nodded. "Yeah. I can't even go away to school, because I'll forget everyone. I love my home. I love Havenwood Falls, but sometimes . . ."

"Sometimes it feels restrictive and unnecessarily harsh?"

"Exactly. I want to travel. I want to see New York City and go to Europe and do a lot of things, but I can't if it'll take longer than the allotted twenty-eight days."

"Can't they make an exception or something?"

"No. The rules are there for a reason, and they keep us all safe."

"The thought of losing my gran after losing everyone else is . . . it scares me. I guess if Gran puts down roots here, then so will I."

"I'm sorry about your family. I didn't want to mention it before because, well, Reed thought you needed distracting from it. The goal was to make you laugh today."

A soft smile graced Cora's lips. "He's a really good guy."

"Yeah, he is, and he really likes you, so don't make me pull my B-switch out if you hurt him. I like you, and I'd hate to do that, but I would."

"Reed has been nothing but nice to me even when he gets a little cocky, so if I ever hurt him, you have my permission to flip that switch."

"I knew I liked you for a reason." Molly grinned. "So, you really think Henry likes me? He usually treats me like the little sister he never had."

"Girl, please. That boy can't keep his eyes to himself."

"He did just break up with his girlfriend." Her voice turned thoughtful. "Maybe I'll corner him and make a move. If I wait for him to do it, I'll be eighty with ten snotty grandkids."

"You should. No one says you have to wait for him to man up."

"Right? Reed can just get over it if he has an issue. Or maybe you can distract him for me." She wiggled her eyebrows suggestively.

"I'm not in the right place for a boyfriend right now. I'm still dealing with stuff."

"That's cool, but Reed's patient. He'll wait until you are ready because he really likes you."

"He's just being a good friend."

"Please. You are all he's talked about since he met you. Reed has never acted like this about any girl. It's why I demanded to meet you. I could have introduced myself, but he swore me off. He didn't want to freak you out, all things considered."

"Really? He talks about me?"

"If I heard your name one more time, I might have resorted to supergluing his mouth shut."

Cora's stomach got all fluttery, and a warm glow started to burn away some of the unbearable pain she'd been in for weeks. Not so much that it took the pain away, but it dulled just a little.

"I'm notorious for spoiling movies, so let's find something else to watch until the guys get back with the pizza." Molly leaned back and took ownership of the remote control and Cora's laptop. "What are you in the mood for?"

"Something the guys will groan about having to watch."

"I like the way you think." Molly grinned and started looking through Netflix.

Cora sat back and let her pick out the movie, content and a little better than she had been since her family died.

And that was all because of Reed Spencer.

CHAPTER 14

"Gran, have you seen the box with all my books in it?"

Hattie looked up from the TV. She'd become addicted to *iZombie*. "It's in your room. I saw it yesterday."

Cora was in the mood to read, and her favorite series was *Chronicles of Nick* by Sherrilyn Kenyon. She owned every single copy in hardback. The urge to get lost in that world tonight was strong, so she'd gone to look for her book box.

Going back into her room, Cora rummaged in the boxes she'd piled up in the corner. After everyone had left, she spent the rest of the afternoon cleaning the boxes up.

Of course the box she wanted was on the very bottom. Sighing, she moved them until she'd unearthed the box and dragged it over to her bed. Books were heavy, so she didn't even try to lift it up. The foot of her bed would be its new home until they moved into the apartment over the store.

Eyeballing the mess she'd made, Cora decided to worry about it tomorrow. Instead, she pulled the packing tape away and started piling books out, looking for the series. Her hand closed around a small white box with a red ribbon around it. Her name was written on the gift tag in her mother's handwriting.

She sat down on the floor and held the package like it was the most precious thing in the world, and in a way, it was. At least to her. How had it gotten into her books? She didn't remember putting it in there, but she wasn't the only person who'd packed her room up. Emily had come over to help. Maybe she'd put it in there, thinking Cora would find it later when she was ready for it.

This was the last thing her mother had ever gotten her.

She set the box gently on the floor and stared at it. It must have been a Christmas present. She traced the outline of the red ribbon almost reverently. Could she open it without a panic attack rising up?

Her hand started to shake when she pulled the ribbon and slid it off. Slow deep breaths, she reminded herself. It took her a minute, but the shaking stopped, and she was able to lift the lid of the box.

A dark black velvet jewelry box lay nestled amongst the white tissue paper. She picked it up and opened it, a gasp falling from her lips.

Inside she found a necklace with a crescent moon and star design. She used to read to the man in the moon when she was little, telling her mom that even the man in the moon needed a bedtime story. Her mom must have seen this and remembered it.

It was sterling silver because she was allergic to gold. Little diamonds were scattered throughout the interlocking pieces of the moon and star, making it sparkle in the light. It was such a thoughtful gift.

Cora lifted it out of the box and latched it around her neck. Tears trickled down her cheeks, falling unabashedly. This would be a gift she cherished—

Pain lanced her skin all at once, and she screamed. The place where the pendant lay against her skin felt like it was on fire. She tried to pull it away, but it was stuck, and she screamed again, calling for her grandmother.

Hattie ran into the room. "What's wrong?"

"It's burning, get it off, get it off, get it off!" Cora tried to pry the pendant from her skin, but it wouldn't budge.

Hattie rushed to her and tried to pry the necklace off Cora's skin, but nothing moved it. "It won't come off. Where did you get this?"

Cora pointed to the box. "It was in with the books. I thought Emily found it and put it in there."

Hattie picked up the box. "This is your mother's handwriting."

The pain increased, and she jumped up, running to the bathroom. She turned on the cold water and scooped some in her hands, then poured it over the necklace. The burn didn't waver.

"Gran, do something!" She was crying in earnest now. It really hurt.

Hattie ran out of the room and came back with her phone pressed to her ear, explaining to whoever was on the other side what was going on. She hung up a moment later.

"Saundra is on her way over. She may be able to help."

Cora tried the water again, but there was no relief to be had. She kept pulling at the pendant and then grabbed the chain and yanked hard. All that accomplished was breaking the chain. The pendant remained glued to her skin.

The burn started to spread, and she cried out as it lanced across her chest and toward her arms.

"Get in the shower, Cora." Her gran turned the cold water on, and Cora stepped into the tub, letting the ice-cold water flow over her. It didn't lessen the burn slowly spreading across her body.

"It's not helping." Cora turned her face up, letting the water hit her chest where the pendant lay. She bent over, unable to breathe because of the pain.

"I'll get the box. Open it and let him out."

Everything in her rebelled against that. She knew what it took to open the box. She'd read it in her family's journals.

"If we do that, he'll just kill us both and then go out and do God knows what to the people here in town. That's not an option, Gran."

She would never let that thing go out and kill people. Never.

Trapping that thing cost her father his life, and she would not let him have died in vain. Him, her mother, or her brother. Their lives should mean something.

Even if it meant her death, she'd keep him locked in that box.

The irony suddenly occurred to her. The demon was trapped in a white box, and her death came in the form of a white box.

Someone started pounding on the door, and her gran ran to get it. She came back followed by several women, most of whom waited just outside the bathroom door. The one directly behind Gran seemed to be in charge. Her silver hair was piled up in a twist, and her lighter jacket contrasted with the black skirt she had on. Very businesslike. She had this air about her, a sense of power and confidence. This must be Saundra Beaumont.

"Let me see."

Saundra came forward, and Cora turned to let her see the pendant, the cold water from the shower head spraying her back. Saundra held out her hand, and an intense look of concentration overtook her expression.

When she stepped back, her concern was more than apparent.

"Tell me everything that happened." Her tone wasn't overly kind, but her concern shone through, which worried Cora.

"I found it in my box of books. The box had my mom's handwriting on it. I put it on thinking it was a gift from her. It started to burn the minute it touched my skin."

"Is the cold water helping?"

Cora shook her head.

"Then there's no reason to freeze to death," Saundra said. "Hattie, get her some warm clothes while we discuss this. Your granddaughter put on a cursed object. We need to work fast before it does what it was meant to do."

"What was it meant to do?" Cora asked, stepping out of the shower.

"Kill you."

Fear rushed to the surface, but behind that fear was the

thought that this thing could do exactly what she'd thought about doing for weeks. She could die. She could be with her family again. Her pain would stop. The guilt of living when they were gone would go away.

But then she looked at her grandmother.

Hattie was the reason she hadn't killed herself. It wasn't just Cora who lost everyone. Hattie had too, and killing herself would leave her gran all alone. She couldn't do that to her.

She would fight this to the bitter end.

CHAPTER 15

 ora changed into a pair of flannel pajamas, and her gran toweled her hair dry. She couldn't do it herself. Moving hurt. It caused the burn to worsen. Walking into the living room was a chore. The more she moved, the more the pain spread.

Saundra and the other women were huddled together when she walked in. They looked more than troubled.

"This is a strong curse, one we can't break."

Well, she certainly got right down to business.

"But we are not going to give up hope. The fact that you're not dead yet means the witch is hoping the pain she's causing is enough to make you release her lover from his prison."

"I won't do that."

Saundra nodded, a little hint of respect entering her gaze. "We are going to take the chain and see if we can use it to locate the witch. I've seen a version of this curse before, and the caster is the only one who can break it. We do have an alternate option I've got people researching now, but I'm not sure it'll work."

"So I just sit here in pain until she decides to kill me or you find a workaround?"

"Unfortunately, yes."

Great. Just freaking great. Cora took several shallow breaths when a band of pain wrapped around her chest.

"She's thought this through, going so far as to plant it before the moving van left your driveway."

"Is there any way we can trick her into thinking I'll let him out?"

"No." Saundra shook her head. "I wouldn't fall for it, and I'm not about to underestimate a woman whose sole purpose is to free the man she loves. Unless your situation becomes critical, we wait for her to contact you. She won't wait long, because that curse is fast acting, and she'll want you to free her lover before you burn up."

"Burn up?"

"The curse is designed to act like fire, burning you up from the inside out until you burst into flame."

She swallowed. Dying in a car crash was completely different than burning alive.

"We're not going to let you die, Cora," Saundra reassured her. "You have to hang in there until we can find a way to fix this."

"Is there anything you can do to dull the pain?" Hattie asked, wringing her hands, looking every bit her age in that moment. Gone was the flippant cool flighty grandma and there stood a woman who had aged in minutes.

"No. I'm sorry, Hattie."

"What can I do for her?"

"Trust that I'll fix this. We are going to work through the night, and I'll be back as soon as I have a solution. Before I leave, check to see if she emailed again."

Hattie opened her laptop and logged into her email. Her face blanched.

"She says we have two hours to release him or Cora dies. The email came through half an hour ago."

Saundra muttered something Cora couldn't hear, but she was too focused on the fact that she had an hour and a half left to live.

"I have an idea, but it's going to take time to gather the things we need. In the meantime, I think you should come with me, Hattie."

"No, I'm not leaving her here alone."

"Hattie, if I don't get back in time, then . . ." Saundra broke off and looked at Cora regretfully.

"She's right, Gran. You need to go with her." Cora understood what Saundra didn't say. If she wasn't able to fix this, then she'd burst into flames, and it could cost her grandmother her life. She wasn't about to let that happen. "I need you to be safe."

Hattie shook her head, that stubborn glint coming into her eyes.

"Please, Gran. Go with Mrs. Beaumont. If you died because of me, my soul would always be haunted. Don't make me blame myself for your death too. Please, Gran."

Her grandmother's shoulders slumped, and Cora knew she'd won. Hattie understood what all the blame Cora lived with did to her, and she wouldn't add to that pain if she could help it.

"I'm not going far. Just to the main house of the inn."

Cora smiled, biting back another scream that was welling up in her throat. The pain was starting to become unbearable. "Take the box with you, Gran, just in case."

"We'll lock it away where no one will be able to get to it." Saundra nodded to her and waited for her gran to fetch the box. "I'll be back as quickly as I can."

Cora gave her grandmother a quick hug and tried to smile. She was pretty sure it came out more of a grimace.

"I love you, Buggy."

"I love you too, Gran."

She watched them leave, and only then did she let the barest of whimpers out. She hurt more than she'd ever physically hurt in her life. And sitting here alone with nothing to do but watch the clock was torture.

The minutes ticked by as she tried to not think about anything. A half an hour came and went. Then another half an hour.

She tried again to pull the pendant from her skin, which was so hot it was starting to blister. It wouldn't budge.

Cora couldn't help but to think that maybe she deserved this for blowing off her family that night. For not being there for her little brother. It would be simple to just let go and not fight this. It would ease her guilt.

Those thoughts were not good, and she needed to shut them down. Her grandmother deserved to not lose everyone, but sitting here watching the minutes tick by wasn't helpful. She needed something to distract her from her deepest thoughts.

So she forced herself to get up and go find her phone.

Each step was excruciating. The pain radiated down her arms, her back, her stomach. By the time she returned to the couch, she had to just sit there for a few minutes and let the pain subside—either that or she got used to it.

She called Reed.

"Shortcake?"

"Hey," she whispered. "That offer to talk anytime still open?"

"Are you okay?"

"No, Reed, I'm not."

"What's wrong? Do I need to come over there? I'm at work, but I'm sure I can get off . . ."

"No. It's too dangerous to come here."

"Dangerous? What's going on?"

She told him everything from the necklace to her dark thoughts and why she was trying not to think like that.

"I'm coming down."

"No, Reed. I don't want you to get hurt."

"I won't come inside, but I'll be right in front of the cottage so you can see me, okay? You're not alone, Cora. You'll never be alone as long as I'm around."

That was the sweetest thing anyone had ever said to her.

Cora's leg shook as she pushed up off the couch. The pain had spread through all her limbs. She was so hot she had no doubt her blood was boiling. She focused on putting one foot in front of the other until she reached the window.

"You still with me, Shortcake?"

"Yes." She gripped the curtains and looked out, surprised to see a large number of people gathered outside. "There's people here, Reed."

"It's probably Saundra and members of her coven. You said they were trying to help."

She hoped they'd found a way to stop this for her grandmother's sake.

"I'm here, right outside. Can you see me?"

Cora searched the crowd and found him pushing through so he stood in front of the coven, facing her. Just seeing him wilted away some of her fear and dark thoughts about dying. Reed rooted her in the here and now. She didn't understand that until this moment.

"I see you."

"Hang on, okay? Don't give up yet. I just found you, Cora. I don't want to lose you."

"I'm trying."

A whoosh interrupted her and she turned her head to see the curtain erupt into flames where she was clutching it. The phone in her hand sizzled and started to melt. She dropped it and looked out the window, seeking Reed, horrified.

A fresh burst of pain scorched her skin, and she screamed, unable to stop herself. Flames erupted and licked her skin, racing to cover every inch of her, and she stumbled backward, the fire around her spreading as she was consumed in flame, the pain unbearable.

She glanced toward the window as she fell to her knees, but she couldn't see outside. She was alone, but she wasn't. Reed was there, and his presence gave her strength.

But even that wasn't enough to conquer a house on fire, and when one final blast of pain ripped through her, she fell backwards, her vision going dark as the fire from within and without consumed her.

CHAPTER 16

*T*he sound of whispers reached her first.

She tried to open her eyes, but they refused.

Her body ached. Her skin tingled.

She was fuzzy.

What happened?

She searched her memory, and when those memories came back, so did the fear and the feel of the pain as the fire consumed her. It would be a memory forever etched into her skin.

Was she dead?

Maybe that was why she couldn't open her eyes and only heard whispers. Was she in the realm of the dead?

She thought she'd feel relief in death, like some weight would be lifted off her, but in truth, all she felt was regret.

Her gran was all alone now, and Reed . . .

She'd never be able to see where things would have gone with Reed. Cora suspected her mother's advice on *the one* had been right. Reed was her one. And now that chance was gone.

She thought death would be more than this, more than shadows and whispers. Weren't your loved ones supposed to greet you? Where were her parents? Her brother?

Soft, gentle fingers stroked her cheek, and she calmed, recognizing her grandmother's touch.

But that made no sense.

Her grandmother wasn't dead. She'd gone to the inn. She should have been safe from the fire.

"Shh, Buggy, you're safe."

Gran? She wasn't dead? But how was that even possible? She'd burned to death. There was no denying that simple fact.

"Open your eyes for me."

She tried again, but still no luck.

She really wasn't dead?

"Give her time, Hattie. She suffered through a horrible ordeal."

"What if you're wrong and she doesn't wake up?"

There was true fear in her grandmother's voice.

"She will."

Reed? Reed was here?

"He's right, Hattie. His sacrifice ensured she'll wake up. Let's go get a cup of coffee. Reed, you'll wait with her?"

"Yes, ma'am."

"You'll call me if she wakes up?"

"Of course." His deep voice sent a shiver through her. It seemed to affect her more now than it had before.

She heard the shuffle of feet and then nothing.

Movement to her right caught her ear's attention. She heard the scrape of a chair being dragged and then she felt him settle beside her.

"Shortcake, you need to wake up. You're scaring us all. It's been two days." He took her hand, and his thumb started rubbing back and forth across it like he had the day she told him the truth about the demon trap. It calmed her even more.

She tried to open her eyes again and managed a small slit. She could see his outline, but after a moment, she let them fall shut again. It was hard, waking up.

"When I thought I lost you, it was like I couldn't breathe. Everything in me died a little."

She understood that feeling all too well. She lived it after her family died.

"I'm still going to be your friend first, Cora, but after watching you burn up in that fire, I'm going to be more when you're ready. I'm not going to lose you again."

What did he mean, she burned up? How was she here?

"Cora?" he whispered, leaning closer. "Can you hear me? Squeeze my hand if you can."

She tried, but she wasn't sure if it worked.

"Come on, sweetheart, you can do it. Squeeze my hand."

She concentrated on the feel of his fingers wrapped around hers and tried with every ounce of strength she could muster to do what he asked.

"That's it. Open your eyes for me, Shortcake."

Cora fought hard and managed to open her eyes. Everything was blurry at first, but soon her vision cleared and she was able to see. Reed had moved from the chair to the bed, and she could see him in the stark light of the florescent lights. Her eyes were a little sensitive, but it was nothing she couldn't handle.

"There you are." He smiled, and his dimples came out of hiding. She loved those dimples.

Cora tried to speak, but nothing came out.

"Don't try to talk. Your body has to acclimate itself. It'll take a few minutes before your speech comes back."

What was he talking about?

"I know this is confusing, but I'll clear everything up. I promise."

He was always making promises to her and he had yet to break one. She'd only known him for two weeks, and yet she trusted him to keep his word, to be there.

"Are you thirsty?"

She managed a nod, and he got up to get a bottle of water. She looked around and saw that she was in a hospital room, connected to an IV machine. The tickle of the plastic oxygen cable rubbed along her nose.

He came back with an opened bottle of water and helped her drink a few sips. "Sorry it's warm."

When the water hit her tongue, her senses woke up, and her mouth felt jammed full of cottontails. She coughed, and Reed made a distressed noise. He went to set the water down, and she shook her head. She needed more water.

He frowned but let her drink more. When she tried to guzzle the water, he took it away. "Careful, you'll get sick. You've been out for two days."

"I . . ." She coughed again, her vocal chords loosening up. "Wha . . . whaaa . . ."

"What happened?" Reed asked, helping her lay back down and setting the water aside.

She nodded.

"The Luna Coven couldn't stop the curse, so they changed it."

Changed it?

"The fire was meant to destroy, but fire is cleansing too. It's a form of rebirth, so they twisted the curse so that you would be rebirthed from the flames consuming you."

That made no sense.

Reed chuckled. "I'm terrible at explaining. There is one creature that is reborn from the ashes of a fire and that's a phoenix. So they changed the curse to create a phoenix from your ashes. But there had to be a sacrifice for the spell to work. In order to bring you back, you had to have an anchor here in the world of the living, someone who keeps your ashes from floating away in the wind. Your grandmother wanted to do it, but Mrs. Beaumont didn't think she was strong enough because of her age. So I volunteered."

Her eyes widened. He volunteered?

"It means that every time you die, I age a whole day. As long as you're young, so am I. Not too much of a tradeoff. Think of me as your new protector. I'll always be here watching out for you. Told you I keep my promises."

"I . . ." Cora cleared her throat. "I . . ."

"Shh, no talking. Just listen, okay?" When Cora nodded, he continued. "The threat to you isn't gone. That's part of why they didn't want your grandmother to anchor you. Each time you die, it steals a day of your anchor's life. Given her age, it might do more than steal a day of life. Until the witch is found and dealt with, you're still a target. A little harder to hurt now, but still a target."

No.

"You're safe here in Havenwood Falls."

She snorted at that. The crazy witch lady still managed to get to her despite all their protections.

"I know you probably don't believe it, but it's true. No one knew the depths the witch would resort to. She used something she found in your things, something that would mean more to you than your fears. That won't happen again. *I* won't let it happen."

Cora believed he'd do everything in his power to make sure that never happened again, but until the witch was found and dealt with as he'd said, she wasn't safe.

She might never be safe again.

"There are a few things that are going to change, though. You need to register with the Court of the Sun and the Moon because you're no longer quite human. You're a supernatural creature, a phoenix."

She wasn't human anymore. Cora didn't quite know how to feel about that.

"Because you're not a natural born phoenix, they're not sure what you can and can't do. Or if you'll be able to control any abilities you gain. And that puts the students at Havenwood Falls High in danger."

She didn't want to hurt anyone.

"What that means is that you'll probably move to the private school where you don't have to hide your supernatural abilities and you'll learn to use and control them. But that's only if you manifest any sort of ability. Until that happens, they may let you stay at school with me and Molly."

Cora blinked. He threw so many things at her so fast, she didn't know what to think.

"It's a lot, I know, but you have time to deal with it. You're alive, Shortcake. That's what matters. We will handle everything one day at a time. You and me, your gran and the coven. You're not alone. Never ever again will you be alone. One more promise I kept.

"I better call your gran. She's been worried about you."

Cora nodded and smiled. He was right. She wasn't alone, and she would deal with this one day at a time.

For now she would just be grateful to be alive even if that dark voice in the back of her mind said she cheated death again.

But that was a problem for another day.

She'd enjoy today and deal with the rest tomorrow.

CHAPTER 17

*C*ora Jean,

  My time is almost up, and I've worried over this since the day you were born. I know you father will raise you in the ways of Christianity, as all the women in our family are. He will not tell you about our darker history. It is the Hartwood way. Our women are kept out of the family business and their souls remain pure.

  But I think it is your destiny to carry on the family business. I've watched you grow up, seen your affinity with the elements that are necessary to do the work we do. I know I'm not making sense, but I'll get to that soon enough.

  You're special, baby girl. I've known it since the day you were born under the solstice moon. You are the first girl born into our family in over four hundred years—did you know that? The magic of our ways lies within you. Your father disagrees, but an old man knows what he knows. And I'll be damned if I let your father dictate to me what I know to be right.

  Our family is different, our origin going back to before the Roman Empire. Hattie has promised to explain anything that you might be confused about after you read this letter and my journals. I kept nothing from her, as I knew one day she would be here when I wasn't.

I wish I could be the one to help you through this, but cancer has robbed us both of that experience.

But I digress. Our family learned of the other world that lives around us, a world full of magic and dark creatures. There are truly evil creatures in the world, and our family was tasked with containing them. We learned how to use rituals, magic, and science to craft a cage of sorts for malevolent beings in spirit form. These could be anything from ghosts that have gone bad to demons that move among us through a host body. Not all demons require a host, but for the ones that do, our family knows how to keep them from hurting others. My journals detail the process for you.

I know you must be thinking your Grandpa was off his rocker. That's what your father said to me when I sat him down and explained it all. I had to show him what the traps did before he believed me. Once he understood, he took up the mantle of our cause. Learning of the horrible things that are in this world is one thing, but being able to prevent an innocent from being harmed . . . well, that's the most important part of what we do. It's a great responsibility that has been thrust upon our shoulders and one I hope you decide to carry alongside your brother. We can prevent harm, we can save people, and that is the greatest reward there is.

I have outlined in the journals the process for making the traps. They have to be made from the wood of a specific tree, a tree we have cultivated on our land in Ireland. The forest is hidden from the naked eye and tended to by our allies. Your father planted a few in the States as well and harvested wood from time to time. It is an ancient, sacred tree and has to be protected. Your grandmother has all the information you need on the property in Ireland in case your father tries to deny you access.

I wish our family didn't try to keep the women away from this. In the old days, women were seen as the weaker of the sexes, more susceptible to temptation and therefore susceptible to being manipulated by the spirits we trapped. We don't do the trapping ourselves so much anymore, but when we do, it is a hard task, one that

*can leave scars on your soul. I understand wanting to keep you safe,
but I think you are strong enough to do what needs to be done.*

*You are special, baby girl, and it is my hope that you carry on our
family tradition. It is also my hope that you bring the traditions of the
old world back into this, strengthening what we've lost.*

*I love you, Cora Jean, and even though I am not there with you, I
am in spirit.*

With all my love,
Grandpa

~

Cora looked up from the letter her grandmother had handed her
to three large journals on the foot of the hospital bed. Her
grandfather had laid out his plans for her, and it seemed that no
matter what she might want, fate had chosen a different path for
her than she'd planned.

"I don't know what to say to any of this."

"You don't have to say anything, Buggy. Take some time and
read through the journals. Look over the process of making the
traps. Learn the spells and the science of it. Ask me your questions
as you come to them. Then, if you decide you don't want to
continue to make the traps, we'll put all this away and never think
of it again."

Hattie sipped her coffee and nibbled on one of those scones
she had recently been obsessed with. Just a few days before the fire,
Cora had teased her she was going to break out in a blueberry pox,
she ate so much of them.

"I do have a question for you, Gran, one that has been
bothering me since the fire."

Hattie leaned back and set her coffee down. "What question?"

"Well, you said I was the only person who could open that box
because it had to have Hartwood blood. Why would the witch kill
me if I was the last Hartwood? She'd never get her boyfriend back
with me dead."

"You are not the only Hartwood left, Buggy. You're forgetting your uncle, your grandfather's brother. Your great-grandfather chose your grandpa as his successor and while George never knew of the traps, his blood, and that of his sons, would still open the trap. That was the witch's last resort since we were the ones that had the box."

Cora didn't really know her great-uncle, since they lived in England. She'd only met that side of the family once, when she was little and they came to the States for a family reunion. It made sense, though, that they could open the traps and why the witch was willing to kill her. It would be another message to her uncle's family that the woman would kill anyone to get what she wanted.

"Are you and Saundra sure I'm safe here, Gran? What if the witch realizes that I'm not dead?"

"The coven is working to identify the witch. It's why they didn't immediately move the trap into a place the witch couldn't reach. They wanted to lure her here to you. Your father left very little by way of notes. We know who the demon is and they're hoping they can use that as a starting point to find the woman. In the meantime, they've decided to work a new spell into your Registry tattoo to hide you from her. No matter how many location spells she casts or who she sends to track you down, it won't work. She could pass you on the street and never realize it was you. They've also moved the trap to a place that it can't be found either."

"What do you mean, Registry tattoo?"

"Every supernatural being here in the town has to register with the Court of the Sun and the Moon, the supernatural leaders of the town. The Registry is the town's way of keeping track of everyone. All not-quite-human residents require a tattoo. Visitors are granted a temporary one. It's part of the town laws."

She remembered Reed saying something about some kind of registration, but the only thing she'd really focused on was the fact that she wasn't human anymore. She was still trying to wrap her head around it.

A tattoo, though? That she could get behind. Cora had always wanted a tattoo, and now she was being given permission to get one.

"What design?"

"Addie will be here later to ink you, so you can talk to her about what you want."

"Who's Addie?"

"She does all the town's tattoos for the Court. Now, do you have a design in mind?"

She loved the crescent moon, but that cursed necklace ruined it for her. She did have an idea, though.

"Why not a phoenix rising? This whole thing started with fire and ended with fire, but I'm going to look at it as a second chance instead of the nightmare it was. Reed said fire can mean rebirth too, so that's what I'm going with. It's a second chance for me."

"That sounds like a wonderful idea, Buggy."

"Gran, do you think it's okay to be happy even though they're gone?"

"Honey, your parents and your brother loved you. They'd want you to stop torturing yourself and be happy. It's not wrong. You can be sad and even angry because they're gone, but you can be happy to be alive too."

Cora nodded. "Think we can reschedule the therapist session? I want to be happy, Gran. Reed helps, but I do need to talk to someone. Someone who can help me to deal with their deaths, but also who can help me deal with all of this being thrust upon me. I mean, I was human one second and a fire girl the next."

"Fire girl?"

"I may have gone to the bathroom and noticed smoke coming out of the tips of my fingers last night."

Hattie frowned. "I . . ."

"I'm joking, Gran. I have no idea if I'm a fire bug or not. I don't feel any different. I don't think I've got any special powers."

"Saundra thinks once your body finishes acclimating, you might start manifesting."

"We'll worry about that when the time comes. But back to this tattoo business. You said I'd be safe from her and anyone she might send? How does that work?"

"It's a spell they crafted, like a memory spell. Anyone wishing to find you that is not a town resident will walk right past you. Only the town will know who you are."

"Huh. Witches can do that?"

"A single witch, no, but a coven of witches working together—you'd be amazed at what they can do."

"So I'm really safe?" Cora thought back to the night of the fire and how scared she'd been. She'd thought she was done for, but now that she'd been given a second chance, she wanted it. Her biggest fear was the witch realizing she wasn't dead and coming back for her. Maybe hurting Gran or Reed.

But if her gran was right and this tattoo thing worked, then she was safe. They were all safe.

"Gran, I don't want to make demon traps. At least not right now. Maybe once I'm done with college. Reed said there was a new college right here in town. I was thinking I could maybe go there or do online classes. I want to make candy and watch all the little kids' faces light up when they see me making it. I want to do so much."

Her gran picked up the journals from the hospital bed and put them back into the massive purse she was sporting. "These will always be here if and when you're ready. You be you, Cora, not who everyone else wants you to be, and life will lead you to the path you're meant to be on. It always does."

That much was true. Life would always push you to where you needed to be. Sometimes those pushes were so painful, they were debilitating, such as losing her family, but it brought her here and it brought her Reed.

Maybe one day she would make traps, but right now she wanted to be seventeen. She wanted to graduate high school and then college. She wanted to learn what it meant to be a phoenix, if anything. She needed to do all that before she thought about anything else.

And she had a feeling Havenwood Falls would help her with it and so much more.

For the first time since she lost her family, a sort of peace settled over her.

She was home.

We hope you enjoyed this story in the Havenwood Falls High series of novellas featuring a variety of supernatural creatures. The series is a collaborative effort by multiple authors.

Stay up to date at www.HavenwoodFalls.com

ABOUT THE AUTHOR

Apryl Baker is a USA Today bestselling author. She lives in a small town in West Virginia where she writes when she's not playing with her nieces and nephews.

ACKNOWLEDGMENTS

First I want to thank Kristie Cook for allowing me to create a story in her wonderful Havenwood Falls world. I fell in love with the world a few years ago when I first stumbled across the books through a friend of mine who raved about them. I was very honored to be asked to write a new Havenwood Falls High novella. She gave me a chance and I hope you all love Cora and Reed's story. Thank you, Kristie.

A huge thank you to Kay Steele for reading and giving me advice when I needed it. She is one of the few people who reads my work before the editor gets it, and her feedback is invaluable. She'll tell it to you like it is, even if it's not what you want to hear. And that is gold to an author. Thank you, Kay.

Also, I'd like to thank the readers of the Havenwood Falls series. Without you guys, there would be no reason to write more books. You keep us all working to create new characters and building on the lore of the town. You make what we do fun. So thank you all for reading.

And a big thank you to my readers. You guys never fail to show up and read my silly nonsense. You give me strength and courage even when writing has become so hard for me. Some of you who are new readers may not know that I am losing my eyesight slowly and writing has become difficult. On days when my eyes are so blurry I can barely see, I remember all the kind words and how much you all love my characters, and it keeps me out of a dark place myself. So thank you so much for everything.

And last but not least, thank you to my family. You put up with me when I'm working, and that's not easy. You make sure I'm fed so I don't go days without eating when I get lost in a story. I appreciate all you do for me and I love you.